PRAISE FOR

While We Were Dating

"Jasmine Guillory is the undisputed queen of the modern-day romance, and this novel . . . is yet another jewel in her crown."
—*Vogue*

"This romance will sizzle off the page, and leave you excited for whatever Guillory writes next." —*Real Simple*

"Jasmine Guillory has long since established her reign as the romance queen . . . *While We Were Dating* is as good as you've come to expect from the author—stuffed with glamour and wit . . . it's juicy yet meaningful, like every Guillory classic." —*Elle*

"Romance author Jasmine Guillory spins another dazzling love story." —*Time*

"The novel introduces thoughtful commentary on mental health, racism, and body image issues in Hollywood, while still tying together all the components readers want from a dreamy celebrity romance." —*USA Today*

"An Instagram-flavored remix of *Notting Hill*. Glamorous and sexy? Sounds like the perfect beach read." —*Harper's Bazaar*

"Love yourself and pick up this witty, glitzy novel." —Vulture

"A delectable tale." —GoodMorningAmerica.com

"The best-selling romance novelist does it again, this time with a delicious tale of an advertising executive and the movie star he casts in his new campaign." —*Entertainment Weekly*

"Steamy and swoon-worthy." —PopSugar

TITLES BY JASMINE GUILLORY

DRUNK on LOVE

JASMINE GUILLORY

Berkley Romance
New York

Berkley Romance
Published by Berkley
An imprint of Penguin Random House LLC
penguinrandomhouse.com

Copyright © 2022 by Jasmine Guillory
Readers Guide copyright © 2022 by Penguin Random House LLC

ISBN: 9780593100882

The Library of Congress has cataloged the Berkley hardcover edition of this book as follows:

Library of Congress Cataloging-in-Publication Data

Names: Guillory, Jasmine, author.
Title: Drunk on love / Jasmine Guillory.
Description: New York: Berkley, [2022]
Identifiers: LCCN 2022011330 (print) | LCCN 2022011331 (ebook) |
ISBN 9780593100875 (hardcover) | ISBN 9780593100899 (ebook)
Subjects: LCGFT: Novels.
Classification: LCC PS3607.U48553 D78 2022 (print) |
LCC PS3607.U48553 (ebook) | DDC 813/.6—dc23
LC record available at https://lccn.loc.gov/2022011330
LC ebook record available at https://lccn.loc.gov/2022011331

First Edition: September 2022

Printed in the United States of America
1st Printing

Book design by Daniel Brount

To Kimberly Chin.
For your friendship, support,
and the many glasses of wine.

One

MARGOT NOBLE BIT HER lip so she wouldn't scream.

"I know that Uncle Stan never had parties here," she said to her brother, as calmly as she could. "But I'm suggesting that we do something different this year. Shake it up a little. It's the twenty-fifth anniversary of Noble Family Vineyards, and I think it's worthy of celebration. A party for our wine club members and other guests seems like a perfect way to do it."

By the look on Elliot's face it was like she'd suggested turning the vineyard into a corn maze.

"This sounds like a huge amount of hassle, Margot," Elliot said. "You want to have this party here? Why would we do something like that?"

She'd known Elliot would hate this idea.

"First, like I said, it's the anniversary—I know we've never really celebrated it, but it seems like a great year to do it. Second, a number of our wine club members and other visitors to the winery have asked why we don't have parties here, especially since we have such a great space, so I think people would be excited to come. Third, it's excellent marketing for us and our wines—it'll sell wine, give us some great publicity, get people here who haven't been to the tasting room before, and keep them coming back. And it'll add members to our wine club." She hoped. "And fourth, it might earn us some money—we'll charge a fee for the party, and parties like this tend to sell a bunch of wine anyway, so it'll be a win-win."

Elliot's face closed up. She knew what he was thinking. She kept using "we" and "our," like the first person plural encompassed her, too. But she knew he thought of the winery as his, and his alone. He'd been the one who had worked here for ten years, not her. Well, they'd owned the winery together since their uncle had died and left it to the two of them, almost three years ago. It felt like Elliot would never get used to that.

"Stan didn't want to have parties," Elliot said. "He didn't want us to become one of those wineries where people would go just to get drunk and make scenes. That's not who Noble is."

Margot made herself take a deep breath.

"It's not going to be that kind of party," she said. "Just a time for people to come, see what we've done here, taste the wines, bring their friends along, celebrate with us. It will give us a publicity boost, it'll sell some wine, it'll drive more visits to the winery, all good things."

Do you remember what a shaky financial situation this place was in when I came on board? she wanted to—but did not—say. *Do you see how much better we're doing now, with all of the changes I've instituted? Can you, just once, not argue with me about my ideas? Maybe even trust me?*

Instead she took another deep breath. "Plus, it's a great opportunity to do some of that landscaping I've been wanting to do."

They had a lot of outdoor space at the winery, but it was kind of bare. The lawn between the winery building and the barn needed work, and she wanted to add more flowers, herbs, and greenery to the grounds. Maybe even a little garden. She'd mentioned all of this to Elliot before, but he'd mostly ignored her.

"Seems like you've made up your mind to do this, whether I like it or not," he said. "When will this party be?"

She wasn't going to let herself react to that.

"I wanted to talk to you about it before I decided that." Well, she also wanted to talk to other people in the area first, see when other wineries had scheduled their parties, check to see when she could get the landscaping done, and catering, and all of those details that Elliot wouldn't care about.

"Okay," he said. "Thanks for letting me know."

That sounded irritable, but she wouldn't take the bait. She looked down at her notepad.

"That's it on my agenda. Anything else we need to go over?"

She'd pulled her brother into an impromptu Sunday-night meeting to go over winery business. She'd been out of town for the past week, and Elliot had been in charge of the winery, so they needed to catch each other up. She already knew a lot of what had been going on at the winery in her absence; she handled all of the social media, so she'd seen all of the posts and tags over the past week, all of them good, thankfully. She'd been down in San Francisco and the East Bay, visiting restaurants and wine stores. Some of her visits had been to sell them on the Noble Family Vineyards wines; some had been to schmooze with people at the places that already sold their wines, so they'd sell more of them. Her trip had been very successful—not that Elliot had congratulated her on that.

She shook her head at herself. That was unfair. Elliot just didn't think about things like that. That's what she was here for. She took care of the business side of things; he handled the wine side.

He stood up.

"I don't have anything." He stopped, right when he got to her office door. "Oh, wait. I hired someone on Friday. For the tasting room job. I told him to come in tomorrow at ten. William something. Isn't the other new person starting tomorrow, too?"

Margot stared at her brother.

"You hired someone? Without me here?"

He had the grace to at least look ashamed.

"I know, I'm sorry. But he came by on Friday and I interviewed him on the spot. I liked him a lot, and I think you will, too."

Margot knew she shouldn't have left her brother in charge at the winery for a whole week.

"You keep saying we're short-staffed," Elliot said, "and I know you wanted to get someone in before summer. And I need plenty of time to train staff on our wines, so when I found a good person, I thought we should hire him right away."

Margot took a deep breath. Just as she'd told herself she'd been unfair to Elliot, this happened.

"I wish you'd waited," she said. "I'm the one who works closely with the tasting room staff, not you. We aren't in that much of a rush."

They were short-staffed and they did need to get someone hired and trained up quickly. But the wrong person would make her life more difficult, not his.

Elliot let out a huff.

"I have his résumé somewhere," Elliot said. "I can call him, tell him it's not final, that he has to interview with you tomorrow."

Margot sighed. That would just make them look unprofessional.

"No, that's okay. I'll deal with it."

Elliot nodded on his way out the door. He'd probably known she would say that.

"Okay. See you tomorrow."

Margot looked around at her office after her brother walked out. She had mail to open and file, messages to listen to, and all sorts of notes from the past few days that she needed to put into a spreadsheet. She'd planned to do all of that tonight. But her irritation was high, like it often was after dealing with her brother. She needed to get out of here, vent, see a friendly face. She'd deal with all of this in the morning.

She drove home, to her little house in Napa, and fumed the whole way. She'd known—of course she'd known—that her brother wouldn't be excited about having a party (for the public!) at the winery. But somehow, she'd still hoped that he'd tell her it was a good idea, that it would be good for the winery; compliment her on her initiative; say something about how proud he was that they'd brought this winery back from the brink together. Of course he hadn't.

Noble Family Vineyards had been tiny for the first fifteen or so years; a winery that barely anyone had ever heard of, except for a few connoisseurs. Uncle Stan had bought more land and increased production about ten years before, soon after he'd hired Elliot as his assistant. She'd spent the past three years trying to make his—and Elliot's—hard work succeed. And now they were almost there. That's why she'd wanted to have a party in the first place.

All she could do now was to make this party as great as possible. She parked in her driveway and, without even going inside her house, walked the few blocks to the Barrel.

"Hey," she said when she sat down at the bar.

"Hey yourself," her friend Sydney said from behind the bar. "Welcome back. I thought you'd be working late tonight." Sydney owned the restaurant and was often either at the bar or at the front door on a busy night.

"I should still be working, but I had to leave the winery so I didn't yell at my brother, and I thought I'd come yell here instead."

Sydney grinned. She knew all about Margot's brother.

"What did he do this time?" Sydney picked up a glass, poured some wine into it, and set it down in front of Margot.

Margot hadn't purposely rented a house within walking distance of the Barrel, but it was definitely an advantage. Especially since Sydney rarely let her pay for her drinks.

"He hired someone for the tasting room while I was gone. And you know my brother has a one-track mind when it comes to hiring—all he cares about is whether they can talk intelligently about wine in the way he wants them to. Yes, of course, people have to be passionate about wine and be able to represent our winery correctly. I care about that, too! But the tasting room jobs are customer service at their core; it's also important for tasting room staff to be engaging, not to bore people about wine, not to be condescending. But Elliot doesn't care about any of that. He didn't want me to expand our tasting room in the first place, even though it's been successful! And do you know who's going to have to deal with the fallout if this William or whoever Elliot hired sucks?"

Sydney pushed a jar of breadsticks in front of her.

"You?" she asked.

"Me!" Margot said. She took a sip of wine and picked up a breadstick. "I need people who can sell wine, not just talk about it! Make people want to stay longer, join our wine club, all of that! What good will it do us if we have to get rid of whoever this is in the midst of the busy season, or if they quit and leave us in the lurch, or . . ."

Margot stopped herself, and looked at Sydney. Then they both burst out laughing.

"I'm doing it again, aren't I?" Margot said.

Sydney nodded.

"You're absolutely doing it again. I wasn't going to say it, though."

Not two weeks before, Margot had been sitting right here at the bar, and had told Sydney she was going to work on not letting the little things get to her, especially the little things about working with her brother. And now here she was, doing it again.

"You could have said it." She waved a breadstick at Sydney. "You're probably the only person who could, actually. Okay, you're right—no more work talk out of me tonight. Tomorrow, I'll tell you about my trip and what a success it was, but tonight, I'm just going to sit at the bar and keep you company and eat all of the snacks that chef of yours wants to send over to me."

Just then, a plate of arancini landed in front of Margot, and she grinned, first at the waiter, then at Sydney.

"See? A sign."

Sydney laughed.

"A sign indeed. And yes, definitely, no talking about work, but did anyone tell you about the local drama over the weekend while you were gone?"

Margot's eyes widened as she picked up one of the cheese-filled fritters.

"No. This sounds juicy. Tell me."

"Well . . ." Sydney looked over Margot's shoulder. Margot saw her friend's professional smile flash on.

"Welcome to the Barrel. Would you like to sit at the bar?"

She left Margot to go serve the couple who had just walked in, but that didn't bother Margot. That's what they did, these nights that she came in when Syd was behind the bar. They had snatches of gossip and catching up and laughter, whenever Sydney could spare time from serving people and putting out fires elsewhere in the restaurant.

Margot pulled her phone out as she sipped her wine and snacked. She should deal with some of these emails that had come in over the weekend, and get responses ready to go out on Monday morning. This was especially important since she'd have to spend her Monday—and much of the upcoming week—training two new staff members. If only her brother had checked with her schedule and . . . no. No, she wasn't going to do that now, remember?

This was fine. It would be fine. She would just deal with these emails tonight and then this new person tomorrow and she would figure it all out. She hoped.

Sydney came back to take the drink order from someone who had just sat down next to Margot, and then poured more wine in Margot's glass.

"You know what you need?" Sydney said. "You need a vacation."

"I was just out of town for a week."

Sydney shook her head.

"That wasn't a vacation, you were working the whole time.

You need a real *sit on the beach, go out to dinner without it being a work dinner, wander around a city for fun, no checking your work emails at seven p.m. on Sunday night* kind of vacation."

"That sounds incredible," Margot said. "But I don't have time—or the mental energy—to actually plan a vacation. I just want to *be* on vacation, without having to deal with any of the decisions that go into that. What I need is someone else to plan it for me."

"You would never let anyone else plan a vacation for you," Sydney said. "Well, other than me, and I don't have time for that, either."

Margot thought about that.

"Maybe if they knew me well enough? If I trusted them enough?"

They looked at each other and laughed.

"Right," Sydney said. "Never mind."

Someone called Sydney's name at the door, and she came out from behind the bar. Margot slid her phone into her jacket pocket and went to the bathroom. When she came out of the stall, she looked at herself in the mirror. Well, even though she was exhausted, at least her hair looked good today. That's probably why she'd managed to keep her cool with her brother—she had special powers on good-hair days, she was almost positive. She touched up her lipstick and walked out of the bathroom.

On the way back to the bar, she poked her head into the kitchen to say hi to Charlie, the chef at the Barrel.

"Loved the arancini, Charlie," Margot said.

"Thanks, Margot. And welcome back," Charlie said.

Sydney stopped Margot outside of the kitchen.

"How much do you love me?" she asked.

Margot looked at her sideways. This meant either something very good or very bad.

"Very much. Why are you asking me this, here, right now?"

Sydney grinned at her. That grin meant it was very bad.

"Oh no. Don't do this to me again," Margot said.

Sydney's grin got bigger.

"Oh yes. You didn't even glance at him when he sat down, but that guy sitting next to you is adorable. And because you love me, you'll take advantage of this."

Sydney had been trying this for months now. Margot never took the bait.

"Are you going to just keep this up until I give in someday?"

She looked over at the bar and saw the guy Sydney was talking about. He was adorable, Sydney was right. Black, warm brown skin, a slightly scruffy beard, kind of dorky looking, but in a good way. However.

"Oh good Lord, my answer is definitely no. What is he, like twenty-six? Twenty-seven? Way too young for me! I'll be thirty-five in a few months, Syd!"

Sydney rolled her eyes.

"Who cares how old he is? I'm just telling you to talk to the man, not have babies with him. You need some stress relief! Come on, it'll be fun. If you do it, I'll give you free wine."

Margot laughed.

"You always give me free wine."

"Okay, fine, I'll give you free food," Sydney said.

Margot just looked at her.

"Fine, fine," Sydney said. "If you say hi to him—just hi, that's all you have to do—I'll let you pay for your wine."

Oh wow. Sydney had never tried that one before.

Margot shook her head and walked back to her seat.

"Nice try," she said over her shoulder.

As Margot shimmied up onto her barstool, she glanced at the

guy next to her. He stared down at the menu with a small frown on his face. He let out a sigh and looked up at the bar; she could tell his mind wasn't on the menu.

There was no reason for her to wonder where this man's mind actually was, or what was bothering him, or why he was here at the Barrel tonight. He was far too young for her.

He pulled off his hoodie, seemingly for no other reason than to show off his biceps, right there next to Margot. But hey, they were very good biceps; if he wanted to show them off, Margot wouldn't stop him.

Sydney caught her eye and grinned. She'd definitely seen Margot checking this guy out. Margot couldn't help but grin back. Okay, fine, after the day she'd had, it was a nice break to ogle the guy sitting on the barstool next to her—she'd admit it.

Might as well make Sydney's day. Plus, maybe if she did it, just this once, Sydney would get off her back.

"Hi," she said as she picked up her wineglass. "I'm Margot."

He turned to her, with a quick smile.

"Hi, Margot. I'm Luke."

"HI, LUKE," THE WOMAN sitting next to him said.

He'd noticed her right when he'd walked into the restaurant: She'd laughed at something the bartender had said, and her laugh had carried all the way to the front door. It was a deep, throaty, warm laugh, and it had made him look at her right away, and had made him particularly pleased that the seat next to her was empty. He'd eavesdropped a little on her conversation with the bartender after he'd sat down, but after she'd left to go to the bathroom, he'd gone back to staring down at the menu and wondering if he'd made the biggest mistake of his life.

It was a relief to turn to her, to have someone else to talk to, to get out of his own head, if only for a few minutes.

"Are you new in town, or just visiting?" Margot asked him.

He tried to figure out how to answer that.

"Neither," he said. "I grew up here, and I just moved back, but only for a little while. Three months, max. Probably less." That was probably way more information than she'd wanted. "But how could you tell? That I'm not a local, I mean."

"Oh." She swirled the wine in her glass and grinned at him. "Your clothes."

He frowned at her and looked down at himself.

"What's wrong with my clothes?"

She laughed that throaty laugh again.

"Nothing is wrong with your clothes. They're just tourist clothes." She looked him up and down. "Your jeans are too clean—and expensive, your shoes are way too expensive, your T-shirt is perfectly fine but probably too new. And if I was a betting woman, I'd bet that hoodie over the back of your seat has the name of a tech company on it."

Damn. She'd pegged him well. He silently picked up his hoodie and turned it around so she could see the logo of his former company.

This time, they both laughed.

"I'm so used to wearing this that I forgot what was on it," he said. "I quit this job, a few weeks ago."

Why had he even told her that? He knew what she'd say. *Why would you do something like that? It was so prestigious! You were making so much money! And you didn't have a new job waiting for you? Never quit a job without another job!* He'd said it all to himself, and it all made him feel like shit. He didn't want to hear it from this attractive woman drinking wine next to him. He didn't want to talk about that job, and whether he should have quit, and whether it meant he'd failed, and what the hell he was going to do now.

"You obviously need a new favorite hoodie," she said, instead of asking him any of the questions he was dreading. He looked up at her and smiled.

"I think you're right," he said. "But wait, does all of that mean you thought I was a tourist? As someone who grew up here, I'm appalled."

She grinned at that.

"Actually, no, I didn't quite think you were a tourist, because tourists are usually gone by this time Sunday night, at least at this time of year. And second, even if they are still here, tourists are rarely up in the valley by themselves. A single man? Sitting at the bar at the Barrel on a Sunday night? I was sure there was a story there."

She was definitely right about that.

"Are you the Napa Valley answer to Sherlock Holmes?" he asked her. "I'm scared of what else you've managed to figure out about me."

She grinned over her wineglass at him.

"No need to be afraid. I'm just observant, that's all."

He glanced down at the menu again.

"Okay, so I'm presuming that you are a local, which hopefully means you can tell me what on this menu I should order. I've had a long day and I'm starving."

He'd finished moving into his new apartment, after two days of helping his best friend Avery move into her new, post-breakup apartment. He'd planned to just get pizza for dinner, but instead he'd obeyed his sudden impulse to go to the place right down the street. He was glad he had.

"I am a local," she said. "And I've had almost everything on this menu. Any food restrictions?"

Margot leaned a little closer to him and looked at his menu. God, she smelled good. And did she realize that the way she was sitting gave him a fantastic view of her cleavage in that snug dress she had on? He had no idea if she was doing that on purpose or not, but no matter what, he appreciated it. He forced himself not to stare.

"Shellfish allergy, that's all. Not like, one that would kill me, but it's generally unpleasant."

She looked up at him. She was still leaning in toward him, so he did the same.

"So not the shrimp cocktail, but the rest of the appetizers should work, and I love them all. The deviled eggs with bacon on them are amazing. If you're hungry, the burger here is excellent, as are the fries. The roast chicken is great, but it takes a while."

He looked around for the bartender, who came right over to him.

"Hi," he said. "Can I get the cheeseburger, medium rare, with the fries? And the deviled eggs and charcuterie plate to start?"

The bartender nodded at him, a smile in her eyes.

"Anything else to drink?"

He looked down at his whiskey, which was halfway gone.

"Not yet, but I'll definitely want another."

She looked over at Margot.

"Anything for you?" the bartender asked.

Margot grinned at her.

"I will also have the burger and fries, please. Thank you."

When the bartender walked away, Margot looked at Luke and shrugged.

"I hadn't intended on having the burger tonight, but I knew once you'd ordered it there was no way I could sit here next to you without wanting one of my own."

Why was he suddenly so pleased that she intended to sit here and have dinner with him? That's not what he'd come out for tonight; he'd just wanted to sit somewhere and drink a little too much and eat something halfway decent. But now he was suddenly having dinner with Margot, and he was very glad about it. Flirting with a strange woman at a bar who didn't ask anything of him—and who looked just as good for the soul as the whiskey in front of him—was exactly what he needed right now.

"So, Margot," he said as he picked up his drink, "what do you do?"

She lifted her hand in the air and swatted his question away.

"Oh no, please, let's not talk about work. It's Sunday night, no one should talk about work on a Sunday night, don't you agree?"

A strange woman at a bar who not only didn't quiz him about why he'd quit his job, but didn't want to have the normal bar conversations. Even better.

"I agree, absolutely," he said. "Okay, then, tell me something more interesting." He stopped and thought. "When's the best time you ever had to get a tow truck?"

She laughed loudly this time. Her laugh was less throaty, more explosive. He was glad that he'd made her laugh like that.

"That's a much better question," she said. "And I have a good story about that, actually."

His appetizers landed in front of him, and he smiled at the server.

"Thanks," he said. He pushed the plates over so they were in between the two of them. "Please. Feel free."

She reached down and picked up a piece of prosciutto.

"If you insist," she said.

"I also insist that you tell me your story," he said.

She took a sip of wine and grinned at him.

"Well," she said. "I was in graduate school, and two friends of mine and I were in a rented pickup truck, driving through Death Valley."

He looked up from the charcuterie plate to her.

"Oh, this is going to be good," he said.

Her grin got wider.

"It absolutely is."

He listened to her story and tried to figure out more about her. If she hadn't said she was a local, he wouldn't have pegged her as being from here. Partly, yes, because she was Black—when he'd gone to high school here, he'd been one of the only Black people in his class. But also, just in the same way she'd been able to tell he wasn't local from his clothes, he wouldn't have guessed that she was local because of hers. She looked too . . . stylish to live and work in the valley. Not that people around here dressed badly—it was just that they dressed for work, and work was at wineries or on farms or at hotels or spas, and each of those jobs had their own kind of uniform, official or unofficial.

None of those uniforms were the snug, sleeveless black dress Margot wore—a dress that showed all of her curves—or the armful of bracelets that jangled every time she gestured, which was frequently, nor the leather jacket slung over the back of her barstool.

But more than the clothes, it was the attitude. Margot walked, talked, even sat, like she was in charge. Like she commanded all of those around her to do her bidding, and they did it, no questions asked.

He was already very glad she'd introduced herself to him.

"And that's when we decided to stand by the side of the road and see if we could hitchhike back to town," she said.

He laughed out loud.

"What? Hitchhike? Forgive me if I'm wrong on this one—we only met ten minutes ago, but you don't strike me as much of a hitchhiker," he said.

She laughed, too.

"You're correct about that—it's the only time I've done it."

He turned his whole body to face her, to make it easier to watch her.

"So you were successful, then?"

She opened her eyes wide and gave him a sly smile.

"We were indeed. You see . . ." She leaned in closer to him and lowered her voice. That, of course, made him lean in closer to her. "We made my friend Julian be the one to flag down a car. He was the only white guy of the three of us, you see."

Luke burst out laughing, and she joined him. She seemed very amused with herself, and—he thought—with him, for appreciating her story. He liked the way her eyes shined at him.

She'd given him another bit of information, he realized—she'd said this had been when she was in graduate school. Business school, it must have been. She must be an executive, somewhere here in Napa; high up at a hotel, or a big wine conglomerate, or something like that. She probably wasn't from here at all, but had come here for this job, and despite all of what she'd said to him about the way people dressed in Napa Valley, she still dressed however she wanted to.

He liked that about her.

Especially since he really liked the way she looked in that dress.

"Okay, but where does the tow truck come in?" he asked her.

She picked up her glass of wine. The light reflected off the red liquid and onto her face.

"I was getting to that," she said. "We had to get our truck unstuck, didn't we? When we got to town, we called for a tow truck." She grinned again, that slow, wide grin that made him smile back at her, even though he didn't know the joke. "And when *that* tow truck got stuck, we had to call a second, more powerful tow truck that could get both our rental truck and the original tow truck out." She shook her head. "I have absolutely no memory of how much all of that cost us but I'm certain it was very expensive."

Luke moved to the side to allow the server to clear their plates. He hadn't even realized they'd finished the charcuterie plate while they'd been talking.

"What did you do once you got your truck back?" he asked.

She laughed.

"We did the only thing we could do, after sunset, in a hotel in a tiny town in Death Valley. We got very drunk."

Speaking of. That had been his general intention when he'd walked into this bar, which was why he'd ordered whiskey instead of beer. That's why he'd come here, after this week, before the week to come. But Margot had done a good job of distracting him from all of that.

"Sometimes—not all the time, but sometimes," he said, "that is the best course of action."

She looked at him, and smiled slowly.

"Indeed," she said.

TWO

THREE HOURS LATER, MARGOT got up from the bar and slid her leather jacket on. Despite what she'd said to Luke, she hadn't gotten drunk, but then, neither had he. They'd been too busy talking to drink that much.

They'd talked about so much over the last few hours. About his best tow truck adventure, which included an accident and rescue by the side of Highway 101; how they both felt about cheeseburger toppings—they agreed that the trend of far too many toppings was just a way to mask a bad burger, but vehemently disagreed on fried eggs on them (she was pro, he was con), and tomatoes (vice versa); and books they'd read recently—she'd raved to him about a mystery novel, he'd raved to her about a celebrity memoir (she'd been skeptical, but he'd convinced her to read it).

Sydney raised her eyebrows as both Margot and Luke got up, but Margot shook her head. She didn't think anything was actually going to happen between her and this adorable, far-too-young-for-her man she'd been talking to all night. Sure, he'd listened very closely to her at the bar, asked her lots of questions, and hadn't then immediately jumped in to tell his own stories. But while they'd sat closely together for the past few hours, he hadn't done any of the moves that made her know a guy would try to get her to go home with him that night: no "accidental" brushes of her arms or back, no hand on her thigh, no staring at her cleavage.

And yeah, she could have made some "accidental" touches of her own, of course, just to see what would happen. But it had been a long, stressful day, and she didn't want to deal with the ego blow that she'd get if she made a move on this guy and he told her no, he wasn't interested, he had a girlfriend, whatever. Better to just leave the bar smiling. Maybe it was enough to have a few hours of good, old-fashioned flirting with a guy who seemed charmed by her, whether he actually was or not.

She let out a small sigh as they approached the door. She was sad that the night was ending. Even aside from how fun it had been to flirt with Luke, it had been one of her best actual conversations with someone in a while. They hadn't talked about work—as a matter of fact, they hadn't talked about wine at all. She couldn't remember the last time she'd had a conversation with *anyone* that didn't touch on wine. She didn't even know what wine Sydney had poured for her—a Cab, obviously local, but that was all she'd recognized. God, that felt great. It wasn't that she didn't love her job—she did love her job—but it was all-consuming sometimes. Most of the time.

As they stepped out of the Barrel, they walked into a crowd of slightly rowdy tourists, complaining about Napa's early last call. One guy got in Margot's way, and she almost stumbled as she pushed past him. Luke put a hand on her back to steady her and then stepped in front of her. Margot didn't even see how it happened, but the path in front of her cleared, and she followed him until they were around the corner from the Barrel. The tourists were now halfway down the street, still complaining.

"Thanks for that," she said.

He shook his head and smiled at her.

"It was nothing."

Okay, that was obviously her cue to say good night and walk home. Just as she opened her mouth to do that, Luke looked up at the sky.

"Up here in Napa, you see so many more stars than you do down in the city," he said. "I always forget that."

"You do," she said. She looked up, too. "I miss a lot about living in a bigger city, but this is one of the things I love about living up here."

They were silent for a moment as they stood close together, both staring up into the clear night sky, bright with stars.

"Can I ask you a question?" he asked. She was still looking up, but she could tell, without even looking, that he'd moved closer to her. She looked at him. She liked that look in his eyes.

"Sure," she said.

He took another step closer to her. It would be too close, if this were someone else, if this were a different night, if she hadn't just spent two and a half hours wanting this, even as she'd pretended to herself that she hadn't.

He leaned down, his lips close to her ear.

"Can I kiss you?" he asked. His voice was low, warm, clear. He asked the question politely, but there was a rough edge to his voice. She liked both of those things, too.

His lips were so close to her ear that he could have kissed her there easily, without even moving. But he stopped, a hairbreadth away from her, and waited for her answer.

She turned toward him so they were face-to-face, eye to eye.

"Absolutely," she said.

His lips were on hers immediately. His lips were soft, firm, demanding. He kissed her like his whole day had been leading up to this, like he'd been thinking about how to do it since she'd sat down next to him, like all he wanted in the world was to keep kissing her. He kissed her exactly how she wanted it.

They moved together, slowly backward, kissing the whole time, until she was pressed up against the side of the building. His hand stayed right where it was, at her waist, and she realized how much she wanted it to roam around her body. She wanted more than just this kiss. She wanted it all.

That's when she forced herself to pull away.

"We can't do this here," she said. "Too many people know me around here."

He dropped his hand and took a step back. She was gratified to see how fast he was breathing.

"Okay," he said. "Sorry. I got carried away." Then he smiled slowly. "Wait. Did you say *here*?"

She nodded.

"I thought you were an unusually good listener." She stayed close to him. "You said you lived around here—how close? I'm four blocks that way." She gestured down the street.

He put his hand on her back and turned her in the opposite direction.

"I'm two blocks this way."

They didn't talk as they walked those two blocks. What was there to say? They'd made all of the necessary small talk—and more—at the bar. They weren't going back to his place for more conversation—they both knew that.

They kept their distance from each other—he dropped his hand from the small of her back, they were arm's-length apart on the sidewalk, and anyone looking at them from a distance might think they weren't even together.

But the air between them almost crackled. She was so aware of him—of the way he walked, long limbed, relaxed, but with purpose; of the way he glanced over at her every so often, a smile on his lips. Not that same smile from inside the bar, the friendly, interested one, but a smile of anticipation, one she could feel on her own face.

And God, she was aware of his body. At the bar, they'd been too deep in conversation for her to get a chance to look at him more than shoulders up. But after that kiss, after the way he'd touched her, after the way she'd touched him, she couldn't stop looking at him—at his broad shoulders, long legs, firm chest. When they were at the bar, she'd noticed a little hair peeking out from under his shirt.

She wanted to see more.

"I'm this way," he finally said. Thank God she'd asked him where he lived—she didn't think she could have made it the four blocks to her place if these two blocks had felt so endless.

She followed him into a newish apartment building, and down the hall. Oh good, he was on the first floor. An elevator would have been too much for her.

He unlocked his door and she followed him inside. And then, before she could take another step, his arms trapped her against the door.

He smiled down at her. His eyes roamed over her body, and she felt herself flush under his gaze. She was glad he hadn't looked at her like this at the bar. She wouldn't have liked it then. She liked it now.

"Hi," he said.

"Hi," she said. Despite how fast they'd walked here, she was in no rush now, and she could tell he wasn't, either. They'd both hurried to be here, to be alone together. They'd both known that once they'd made the decision to do this, they needed to get here as fast as possible. But now that they were here, they could slow down.

"I like this jacket." He traced a finger down her zipper, and moved it slowly up and down.

"Thank you." She watched his face as he stared down at her. "I like it, too."

He put his hand on her waist, and she couldn't prevent her sharp, inward breath at the touch of his fingers, their warmth through her thin dress. He smiled when she did that, and she smiled, too. She needed this tonight. Right now.

His hand crept slowly, so slowly, up her body, until his thumb circled her nipple. She sighed and closed her eyes and let her head rest back against the door.

"I also like this dress," he said in her ear. "I like the way you look in it. Even though it was all I could do at the bar to not stare at you in it."

She opened her eyes to see the look on his face.

"You can stare all you want now," she said.

He moved his hand up again to her chin, her cheek, her hair.

"Oh, I intend to," he said. "In just a moment."

And then, finally, he bent down to kiss her. She slid her arms around his waist and pulled him close as their lips danced together. It was everything it had been outside the bar, but more, because they were alone, because they were both sure of each other, because now they both knew where this kiss was going.

They kept kissing as they explored each other. He pushed her jacket off her shoulders, she tugged his shirt up and put her hands against his bare skin, he moved his fingers back down to her breast and rubbed her hard nipples until she cried out.

They pulled back and looked at each other, both breathing hard, both smiling. He rested his forehead against hers, then pressed his lips against her cheek.

"I've got to get this dress off of you," he said. He took a step back and reached for her hand. "Maybe we could even get all the way into my apartment."

She put her hand in his.

"What an idea." She kicked her shoes off and left them by the door with her—now *very* lucky—leather jacket, and followed him through the apartment. His tiny hallway opened up into a small kitchen and spacious living room, both minimally furnished. He pushed open the bedroom door and gave her a self-deprecating grin.

"I did tell you I just moved in," he said.

She glanced around the big bedroom, with boxes stacked all against one wall. There was a bed, thank God, a real one, with a headboard and sheets and everything, or she might have had to call this off.

Okay, she wouldn't have—obviously she wouldn't have—but she was still grateful.

"I meant to finish unpacking today," he said.

He looked sweetly apologetic. She smiled at him.

"You got the most important thing taken care of," she said, gesturing to the bed.

He grinned at her.

"If I hadn't, would this be it for me for tonight?"

He'd read her mind. She grinned back at him.

"Depends how comfortable that couch out in the living room is," she said.

He laughed out loud and took a step toward her.

"Luckily, we won't have to test that." His hands moved slowly up the sides of her arms to her shoulders. "Or, rather, luckily for me, I won't have to undergo that test."

She laughed softly as he bent to kiss the side of her neck. She was pretty sure it was lucky for her, too.

LUKE HADN'T PLANNED THIS. He'd had a stressful few days, and he knew this upcoming week would likely be just as stressful. He'd enjoyed the distraction of talking to Margot at the bar, and yes, he'd thought more than once as she'd gestured or laughed that he'd really like to see what this expressive, engaging woman was like in bed. And he'd *definitely* thought that he wanted to see her out of that dress that skimmed her body so well and that made the hard points of her nipples all too evident to him as he sat there next to her and tried not to look at them.

But he hadn't expected that a woman like this would come home with him. She'd seemed amused by him at the bar, sure, but he didn't think she was actually interested in him. He'd planned to just say good night to Margot at the door and walk home. Alone.

But then that crowd of people had tried to push past her at the door, like the entitled tourists that he could tell they were, and had made her stumble. So he'd had to shoulder his way through that crowd, to guide her through them. Though he'd noticed that she'd managed to put one of her elbows neatly in that one guy's stomach, hard enough to make him trip into the guy next to him.

And once he'd touched her, he hadn't wanted to let go. So he'd delayed saying goodbye at the door, by saying something trite but true about the night sky. And when he'd seen her face, all soft and open and full of wonder as she'd looked up at the sky, he'd had to just see if he could kiss her.

And now she was here, and all he could think about was Margot, right in front of him.

He pushed the strap of her dress to the side and kissed her shoulder. She let out a soft, gentle sigh, and her eyes fluttered shut. He trailed his fingers up her arm, and pressed kisses along her shoulder, her collarbone on one side, then the other. As he kissed her, she moved her hands from his hips and slipped them under his shirt. He liked the way she explored his body—eager, confident, almost demanding. He felt pretty demanding right now, too.

She moved back, and tugged at his shirt.

"This is in the way," she said.

"I absolutely agree," he said.

He pulled it off and tossed it into the corner.

"Now, that's better," he said.

Her eyes sparkled as she looked at him.

"I absolutely agree," she said. They grinned at each other.

He ran his hands up her body and stopped at those nipples that had so tormented him in the bar. He very gently pinched them both, and she laughed again, that throaty laugh that he felt all the way to his cock.

"Was that meant to be a request?" she asked him, that laughter in her eyes.

He shook his head, his hands still on her breasts.

"Oh no," he said. "I've just been wanting to do that for hours." He bent his head down to hers. "When I have a request, I'll make that very clear."

She moved her hands into his hair and looked at him with eyes full of need.

"Kiss me."

He didn't hesitate. He kissed her, again and again, as her hands roamed around his body, as his hands pulled her flush against him. He slowly backed her up as they kissed, until finally her legs bumped up against the bed.

"I thought," he said, breaking the kiss, "that we might be more comfortable if we didn't have to worry about standing up."

Margot sat down on the side of the bed and swung her legs over to join the rest of her body. She reclined on the pillows he'd bought just the day before, and looked up at him with half-lidded eyes.

"It's really amazing how much we agree on this evening," she said. "I'm excited to see if this continues."

He sat down at the foot of the bed and put his hands on her ankles.

"So am I," he said. He crawled up her body, pushing her dress up with him. His hands moved up her ankles, her calves, and up the insides of her thighs. He watched her face as he went, and saw her amusement turn to desire in seconds. He hooked his thumbs under the thin material at her hips, and looked up at her, his eyebrows raised. She nodded, and watched him as he pulled her underwear down her body and tossed it onto the floor.

He pushed her dress up again, farther this time. When he got to her torso, she lifted her arms up so he could pull the dress off her body. He bent down to kiss her, but as soon as he did, she rolled them both over so he was beneath her.

"My turn now," she said. She moved down his body and reached for his belt, a gleam in her eyes.

She smiled as she felt the hard length of him through his jeans. If he hadn't already been hard after the last thirty minutes, her hands at his zipper would have done it right away. That look of wicked anticipation in her eyes made him want to pull her down to him immediately, rip that very sexy black bra off her, and slide inside of her. He reached for her, but she pushed his hands away, a laugh in her eyes.

"I said it was my turn now." She unbuckled his belt and stroked her thumb up and down his zipper.

"I know," he said. "I'm sorry. Patience is not one of my virtues."

She finally slid his zipper down. He lifted his hips so she could pull his jeans and boxers off.

"Mmm," she said. "You might want to work on that. However, I am now very aware of one of your virtues." She wrapped her hand around his cock.

She wasn't shy at all. He liked that about her. So far, actually, in their three hours or so of acquaintance, he was pretty sure he liked everything about her.

Especially the way she touched him. So forceful, yet soft. He wanted to close his eyes, let himself enjoy this feeling. But he couldn't stop looking at her.

She put her hand on his chest.

"What do you want?" she asked as she moved up his body.

He pulled her close and let his fingers slide into her hair.

"Good question," he said. He pushed her bra down and rubbed her hard brown nipple. "I want to finally take this fucking bra off of you, like I've been wanting to do for the past two hours. And then I want to suck on these incredible breasts of yours until I drive you wild, and then I want to slide my fingers into your wet pussy and find out how you like to be touched there, and then I want to fuck you until neither one of us has the energy or ability to ask another question. How does that sound?"

He could feel a shudder go through her body as he spoke. Still, though, he didn't move as he waited for her answer.

"That sounds like exactly what I want," she said.

He unhooked her bra in one smooth motion and threw it on the floor.

"Oh, thank God," he said. And then neither of them said anything for a very long time.

Three 🍷

MARGOT WOKE UP AND blinked for a few seconds. It was still very early; she could tell from the dim light coming through the window. Scenes from the night before—and the early morning—ran through her brain. The first time—slow, at the start, and then hard and fast and very satisfying. And then, after they'd both recovered and she'd gotten up to go to the bathroom, she'd gotten back in bed and kissed him, in what she'd meant as a thanks-for-the-orgasm kiss, or maybe even an it's-time-for-me-to-go kiss, depending on how he reacted. But the kiss escalated, and he slid down her body and gave her another great orgasm . . . and then a third. And then, they'd fallen asleep, but sometime in the middle of the night had both woken back up, and . . . damn, it had been an excellent night.

She opened her eyes all the way and saw Luke smiling at her. He looked very disheveled, very relaxed, and very attractive. He looked like he'd spent all night having a whole lot of sex. She smiled back at him.

"I thought I'd dreamed you," he said.

She laughed out loud.

"I'm at least five years too old for that line to work on me," she said, "but that's adorable that you tried it."

He grinned sheepishly at her.

"Thank you. I think," he said.

He lifted himself up on one elbow and looked at her. She forced herself not to move, turn over, or cover her body with a sheet. She was nervous for him to really look at her in the daylight, now that it was morning and she was no longer drunk on his kisses and his touch and his gaze. She liked her body fine, most of the time, but now she was in bed with a guy who was probably used to perky boobs and small waists and no stretch marks. But she didn't let herself flinch, and instead smiled up at him. That ship had already sailed, hadn't it?

He gazed down at her and then moved his hand up to her breast.

"Mmm, I feel lucky to be here right now," he said.

Good God, she liked the way he did that.

"Oh, you should feel very lucky," she said.

He laughed, and bent down to kiss her.

Afterward, when she could breathe again, she suddenly remembered something.

"Yesterday was Sunday," she said when he got back in bed from going to the bathroom. "That means today is Monday. What time is it?" Her phone was in her jacket pocket, which was wherever she'd abandoned it after he'd pushed it off her.

He pulled himself out of bed again and found his jeans on the floor.

"Seven thirty," he said.

She sighed in relief. This had been fantastic, but if this interlude had caused her to be late to work this morning, she'd be pissed at herself.

"Oh good," she said. "I have plenty of time." She swung her legs out of the bed and looked around for her bra. He picked it up from the foot of the bed and handed it to her, and she put it on, then pulled her dress back on.

"Didn't you just say you had plenty of time?" he asked her. "Why are you rushing to get dressed?"

She grabbed her underwear from the bed.

"I meant I have plenty of time if I leave now. I still have to walk home, and once I get back, I have to get ready for work."

He shook his head and pulled his jeans on.

"No, you don't," he said. "I'll drive you."

She hadn't expected him to offer that—he knew she lived nearby. Or maybe he didn't remember?

"I can walk," she said. "I'm only six blocks away."

He grabbed his shirt off the floor and put it on.

"I know," he said. "But my car's right downstairs. I can drive you, it's no problem. If too many people around here know you for you to kiss me outside a bar after dark, how much worse will it be for you to do the walk of shame at seven thirty a.m. on a Monday morning?"

She laughed. She hadn't heard that phrase in a long time. And the man had a point.

He stopped, midway through buckling his belt.

"Unless you don't want me to drive you?"

He was far more thoughtful than she would have assumed at first glance. Both offering to drive her, and then pulling back when she'd hesitated, showed a lot more perception than she would have given him credit for.

"Thank you," she said. "I'd love a ride home."

He nodded.

"Great. I'll be ready in a second."

It was kind of funny, how polite and almost formal they were with each other, after last night . . . and this morning. Both of them making carefully worded requests and acceptances that made them sound like the strangers to each other they really were, even when they did make reference to the reason she was here right now, and not in her house, six blocks away. It made sense, after all. They barely knew each other. She didn't even know his last name. They'd spent, what, three hours talking before they'd tumbled into bed together?

She grinned to herself. It had turned out pretty well, though.

She retrieved her jacket and bag from the front hallway and then went into the bathroom to wash her face and do something to her hair so it didn't look like she'd been having sex all night. She found a few bobby pins in the crevices of her bag and managed to twist her hair up into a more or less presentable topknot.

When she came out of the bathroom, Luke looked at her with just a hint of that admiration from the night before.

"Ready?" he asked.

She nodded, and slid her feet into the shoes she'd kicked off by the door.

His car was right downstairs, parked in a prime spot outside of his building. She grinned when she saw it.

"What are you smiling about?" he asked her.

She shook her head.

"Oh, just that if I'd seen this car last night, I wouldn't have needed to look at your clothes to know you were new in town."

He opened the passenger-side door for her.

"People don't have cars like this in Napa? I know that's not true."

She pursed her lips as she got in, and waited for him to join her before she answered.

"Sure, *people* do. Mostly tourists do, though. Some weekend people, absolutely. And some of the major Valley players, but then, I know who all of those people are. But not a lot of people who really live around here, if you know what I mean."

She gestured to the apartment buildings around them.

"Yeah," he said. "I know what you mean." He turned to her. "Which way?"

"Two blocks this way," she pointed. "And then left on Washington Street."

She was glad, as they drove the short distance, that she wasn't walking home right now. There were a lot of people out and about in downtown Napa at this time of morning—runners, restaurant workers setting up for breakfast or coffee service, people chatting while they waited in line for coffee or pastries. She very possibly may have seen someone she knew. She was glad Luke had spared her that.

"I'm here," she said as he pulled onto her street. "That little blue house."

He stopped in front of her house, and smiled at her. His smile had some of that heat from the night before in it.

"Margot. It was a pleasure." Laughter jumped into his eyes. "Actually—quite a few pleasures."

She grinned back at him.

"Likewise."

He leaned in to kiss her, and it felt natural for her to meet his lips with hers. At first she thought it was going to be a simple, chaste goodbye kiss, but then her tongue slid into his mouth, and his fingers tangled in her hair, and the kiss became a lot more. Finally, she pulled away.

"I should, um, go," she said.

He kissed her softly again.

"Maybe we could . . . see each other again sometime?"

This guy was so nice he even wanted to pretend it wasn't a one-night stand.

"Yeah, maybe," she said.

He pulled open the console between the two front seats and grabbed a scrap of paper and a pen.

"What's your number?" he asked.

Oh, he was serious? She hadn't expected that. He looked at her for a second, and his smile faded.

"Why don't I give you mine?" he said.

He scrawled a number on the paper and handed it to her, and she tucked the paper with his number on it into her wallet.

"Thanks," she said. "And thanks for the ride home."

She opened the car door and turned to him.

"Bye, Luke. Have a good week."

He grinned at her.

"You, too, Margot. It started off well, at least."

She laughed the whole way up to her door.

Once she got inside, she immediately pulled her phone out of her bag. Okay, thank goodness, there were no emergency text messages from her brother this morning. Not like that happened often—it had happened only four times since she'd started this job—but it would be just like him for the fifth to happen when she'd woken up in some stranger's bed.

Some twentysomething stranger's bed.

She laughed out loud, stripped her clothes off, and got in the shower.

When she got out of the shower, she pulled her Monday dress off its hanger. Because she hated both early mornings and making decisions when she was tired, she'd long ago simplified certain things about her life. Hence, her Monday dress: It was a simple black wrap dress with short sleeves, and she wore it every single Monday. She could add accessories, dress it up or down, wear a heavy cardigan over it in the winter, etc., and she was almost positive no one had ever noticed that she wore it every Monday. That was the great thing about living in a temperate climate—she could wear the same dress all year and be just fine.

She turned on her coffee maker while she put on moisturizer, attempted to make her hair look like it was in purposeful beachy waves instead of like she'd just been fucked senseless, and swiped on some mascara. She tucked her favorite red lipstick in her bag, filled up her travel thermos with coffee, and then got in the car for the drive up to the winery.

She unlocked the front door of the winery when she arrived, but she knew Elliot was already there. He was probably just in the barn out back, where all of the winemaking happened. He always got here before her, though she often left after him. Early on, she'd tried to prove herself and get to the winery before him, just so he'd know she really meant it, that this wasn't just a lark for her, that she was really dedicated. She'd tried for a whole week, and by the time she'd arrived one morning, triumphant, at six a.m., and saw his truck already in the parking lot, she knew it was time to give up.

She walked into her office and spent time before her nine-thirty call doing some of the organizing of her desk and her emails that she'd meant to do the night before—before she'd driven off, furious, to the Barrel. She grinned to herself. For once, she was glad she'd left some work unfinished.

The whole time she worked, she could feel that hum in her

body. She was sore, almost everywhere; she was pretty sure she was developing a significant hickey on her right collarbone; she was exhausted from lack of sleep. And she felt fucking fantastic.

Since she'd moved to Napa, she'd kept her head down, worked hard at the winery and at becoming a part of this community, to prove to her brother and everyone else that she was committed to this job, to this life. She had occasionally let men next to her at bars strike up conversations with her, but they'd always been either obnoxious or boring. Luke had been neither.

She glanced over at her bag, hanging on the back of her office door. His number was still there, tucked inside of her wallet. Would she call him? Luke, of no last name. Hell, that might not even be his real first name. She hadn't expected him to give her his number, just like she hadn't expected him to drive her home. The man certainly had been polite, that was for sure. Her grin grew wider. Polite, and excellent in bed. She liked that combination.

Did he actually want to see her again? Or had he just given her his number because he was polite, and so it wouldn't so obviously be a one-night stand? Was he hoping she didn't text him, so he wouldn't have to either ghost her or reluctantly go out with her again? Had he even given her a real number? It was weird that he'd written it down for her, right, and not just put it in her phone?

She shook her head. No, it was better not to find out. She didn't want to spoil the memory of last night. And this morning. They'd been close to perfect. Why mess with perfection?

She swiped on lipstick and reached for her phone. This was just a phone call, not video, but she liked to put lipstick on before important calls to give herself a little boost. She dialed the number of the head of the restaurant group she'd been wooing . . . though, she was pretty sure he thought he was wooing her, which was just how she liked it. In her love life, she'd never been a fan of playing hard to get with men, but in business it was a strategy that hadn't failed her yet. It was especially key in the wine business, where part of the allure was to seem exclusive—Elliot hated it when she said this; he liked it to be all pure and about the wine, but that's why he was the winemaker and she was in charge of the business side.

Midway through the call she folded her hands together.

"Oh, thank you, Jeff," she said in a cool tone, even though she wanted to jump up and down. She was very glad this call wasn't a video call—her face might have betrayed her. "We have pretty limited quantities, so I don't want to overpromise, but I think we can make this happen."

Even she was impressed with herself for this one.

"I'll take what you can give me," Jeff said. "I'll get the new wine lists ready now."

She tried not to let herself smile, just in case it showed in her voice.

"Excellent," she said. "I'll email you the details." She glanced at the clock on her wall. Oh God, it was after ten already?

"Jeff, I have to run, I have another call in a few minutes. But I'll be in touch."

"Thanks, Margot. And . . ."

For a busy executive, it took forever to get this guy off the phone. But finally, a few minutes after ten, she managed it.

That call couldn't possibly have gone better. Of course she knew how much wine they had to sell him, but you couldn't promise people like this everything all at once.

She'd actually wanted to get off the phone before ten so she could greet the new people starting in the tasting room today. She hadn't heard anything at the door—maybe they hadn't arrived yet. She stood up to go out into the tasting room to check. Just then, her office door swung open all the way.

"Oh good, there you are," her brother said. "I heard you on the phone, so I let our new staff in. You already know Marisol, but I'd like to introduce you to Luke. Luke Williams, my sister and the CEO of Noble Family Vineyards, Margot Noble."

Margot could only stare. Standing next to her brother in her office doorway, in a white button-down shirt and jeans, was Luke. Her Luke. The Luke whose bed she'd woken up in that morning. Wearing—she was pretty sure—the same jeans she'd pulled off him last night.

How the hell did she get herself into this?

———

LUKE WAS PRETTY SURE that the stunned look on Margot's face exactly echoed the look on his own face.

He'd slept with his new boss? Seriously? After everything that had happened with his old job, this was supposed to be his nonstressful new job, the one just for fun, to give himself something to do. And now he'd done this? He had the wild impulse to laugh out loud, which he barely overcame.

Margot recovered before he did. A bland, businesslike smile descended over her face, and she walked around her desk to them.

"Hi, Marisol. Hi, Luke." She held out her hand first to Marisol, and then turned to him. "Nice to meet you. Welcome to Noble Family Vineyards."

Not by the slightest look or wink or curve of a smile did she intimate that they'd already met. Or that they'd had sex less than three hours ago.

Luke tried to put that out of his mind.

"Hi, Margot," he said. "Nice to meet you, too. Excited to be here."

She looked at her brother, the serious, thoughtful guy Luke had interviewed with, on an impulse, the Friday before. Why hadn't Luke looked on the winery website more? Why didn't he know that the other half of the Noble Family was the sister named Margot?

"Shall we give them a tour?" Margot asked her brother.

Luke tried not to look at her. Especially not at that V at her neckline, at the valley between her breasts that he'd dragged his tongue through last night. Good God. This could not be happening.

He'd driven away from her place this morning with no idea if he'd ever see her again. He hadn't really been able to read her. She hadn't given him her number, but he'd hoped she'd text him. He liked her, he'd liked talking to her, he'd liked that she was a person in Napa Valley who was neither related to him nor had known him since he was a teenager, but whom he'd met on his own.

And he'd really liked having sex with her. He'd definitely wanted to do that again.

"Great idea," Elliot said. Luke looked at him. What was a great idea? He couldn't remember now.

Elliot turned and walked down the hall, and Marisol and Margot both followed him. Right, a tour. Luke walked fast to catch up with them.

"Back here are the offices," Margot said. "Mine, where I usually am during the day, if I'm not out in the tasting room or at a meeting."

"Which is often," her brother cut in.

"Elliot's office, where he almost never is," Margot continued, with a sideways smile at her brother. "He's usually either down in the barn or out in the vineyard—just FYI, if someone makes a big to-do about wanting to meet the winemaker."

Elliot made a face, and Margot laughed. There was clearly some backstory there.

Margot turned back to Marisol and Luke.

"Actually, if that does happen, come find me. I have to prep Elliot for stuff like that."

Luke tried to catch her eye, but failed. She was so smooth and businesslike right now. But in the way that she'd joked with her brother, he'd seen the funny, alluring woman he'd kissed outside the bar last night, who had gone back to his apartment with him after very little consideration, who had woken up this morning, her hair all tousled and makeup smeared, and had made fun of him for using a line on her and then had rolled over and fucked him again.

Shit. He had to stop thinking about that. At least, for the moment.

"The tasting room is in here, but I'm sure you both already know that," Margot said as she walked through the door to the tasting room. "This is where you'll both spend most of your time; Taylor, our tasting room manager, and I will train you on all of that. We have other tasting room staff, and you'll meet them as your shifts align."

Luke nodded as she and Elliot showed them around the spacious, well-organized room. The winery had obviously been a family home at one point. Those offices in the back must have been bedrooms, and the tasting room seemed like it was a few rooms that had been knocked together and renovated to feel like a library, just with lots of wine in it. There was a bar by the back wall, with stools in front of it, and the rest of the room was full of clusters of easy chairs and love seats and coffee tables. It was a great room; he'd liked it immediately when he'd walked in on Friday.

"We have different levels of tasting," Margot said. "Some people just want to drop in to taste a few wines, maybe buy some, and get a discount if they do—those people sit at the bar. Then, there are the people who want to hang out longer—often members of our wine club. We craft a more extensive—and more expensive—tasting for them, and we seat them at the tables or on the couches. And then the top level is for people who want to get a tour of the winery, see where we make the wine, and get to taste some of our library wines." She grinned at them. "Don't worry, we'll give you lots of training on our wines before you do one of those; the people who take the tour ask lots of questions."

Margot started to turn away, but Luke stopped her.

"What kinds of questions do they ask?" He'd applied for this winery job just to have something to do all day for the next month or however long he'd be up here. His best friend Avery had told him to take a real break after quitting his job, but he couldn't just do nothing. Plus, he liked wine, and he was interested in the science behind it, so he'd thought this could be fun and easy. He was smart, he was a quick study. How hard could slinging wine at a bunch of tourists really be?

Margot glanced in his direction.

"Oh God, so many," she said. "You'll see. Everything from

details about where the grapes come from, to questions about Napa wines versus Sonoma wines and California wines versus French or Italian wines, to stuff about old vintages of ours, to how much money we make, to questions that more or less boil down to 'So, you guys are . . . Black. And you own a winery? Are you . . . sure you own it? Yourselves?'"

He and Marisol both laughed out loud. Margot and Elliot grinned, but she clearly hadn't been joking.

"I actually love giving the tours, even though they take a ton of time that I can't afford anymore. People are usually in great moods and super excited about wine. Some people are interested, some people are nosy, some are nice—sometimes there's the guy who's trying to trip you up, but that's easy to defuse. We won't send you out there alone for a while—you guys will shadow me or other experienced staff until you get the swing of things."

He would shadow her? He tried not to look at her when she said that, but failed. But she'd turned and was looking out the front window.

"Let's take them outside," she said to her brother.

The next hour was like this, with Margot talking the whole time, Elliot occasionally saying something about wine Luke only half understood, Marisol asking smart questions, Luke asking whatever questions he could think of to get Margot to look at him, Margot answering him brightly and never meeting his eyes. She hadn't, at all, since that first shocked look.

Finally, they ended the tour back in the tasting room, just as a woman with light skin and lots of dark curly hair walked through the door.

"Taylor, hi," Margot said. "Our two new members of the Noble team, Marisol and Luke. And we're thrilled to have them here."

It didn't sound like there was sarcasm in her voice, but he couldn't tell for sure.

"Taylor's an expert," Margot said to both of them. "Learning from her will be learning from the best." Margot turned to Taylor. "It should be a pretty quiet day—we only have four appointments, I think. A good way to ease them in."

Taylor laughed.

"I don't know why you even bother to say 'I think' when you and I both know you always memorize that appointment book." She smiled at Luke and Marisol. "Welcome to Noble."

They all shook hands, while Margot slipped behind the bar.

"I say 'I think' just in case a VIP calls me and I have to secretly add an appointment to the book. And then I can say, 'Oh, there were five today, I forgot!'"

She and Taylor both laughed.

Elliot said something in a low voice to Margot and she nodded.

"I'll see you later, Luke and Marisol," he said, and slipped out the front door.

Margot turned back to Taylor.

"Can you start off the training for them? I have a call in a few minutes—sorry about that, I couldn't reschedule it—but I'll join you guys out here after."

Taylor nodded.

"You can count on me, boss," she said, and Margot just laughed.

"Luke, Marisol—I'll have all sorts of fun paperwork for both of you to fill out in a little while. Welcome to Noble, both of you."

And then, before he could say anything, she disappeared through the door labeled STAFF ONLY.

Taylor walked behind the bar.

"Like the boss says, welcome. Noble is a great place to work. Good to have you both here—we've been short-staffed for a while."

"Good to be here," Luke said in unison with Marisol. They looked at each other and laughed, though he was pretty sure she wasn't laughing for the same reason he was. This seemed like a good place to work, if he could judge from the way Margot and Taylor and Elliot all joked around with one another. They seemed relaxed around each other, not tense, or that fake kind of jovial that he was used to in the boss-employee relationship.

He looked at the door that Margot had disappeared behind. He wanted to follow her, with every bone in his body.

He sighed, and turned back to Taylor.

Just as he opened his mouth to ask her a question, the front doors opened.

"Hi," one of the four women in the group said. "We have a reservation at eleven? Cagan?"

Taylor came out from behind the bar and smiled at them.

"Welcome to Noble Family Vineyards," she said. "Please take any seat you like—I'm Taylor, and I'll be right with you."

Taylor turned to Luke and Marisol.

"I'll have you guys tag-team with me on the appointments this morning. Just shadow me and listen and take notes; it's the easiest way for you to learn how we do things here. Luke, why don't you come with me first? Marisol, you can hang out here and read over our brochures and eavesdrop."

The day quickly got busy, with groups of tourists coming in and out, the phone ringing, and Luke trying to remember fourteen different things at every moment. Whenever he'd start to really concentrate, Margot walked into the tasting room to greet people, or check in with Taylor about something, or talk to him and Marisol both—always at the same time—about one of their wines. And every time she walked in, he couldn't take his eyes off her.

While Taylor and Marisol were in the corner with a group of four, Margot walked back in, a stack of papers in her hands.

"Luke, Marisol . . . oh, she's with Taylor, okay." Margot set two stacks of forms on the bar, along with two pens. "Here are employment forms for you to fill out, so we can actually pay you."

She still didn't quite meet his eyes. That was a good sign, at least, that this was affecting her, too, despite how relaxed she'd seemed.

"Sure, of course," he said, and took the papers from her. Their fingers touched, just for a moment, and she flinched. Okay, she was definitely not relaxed.

He was closer to her now than he'd been since they were in the car this morning. Was that bruise on her collarbone from him? A moment from the night before flashed back to him. Yeah, he was pretty sure it was. He fought back a smile.

"Let me know, um, when you're done with those," she said. And she swept out of the tasting room.

He'd finished filling out the forms by the time Taylor and Marisol came back to the bar.

"Marisol, Margot brought some forms for us to fill out." He didn't let himself stop to think about what he was about to do. "I'm done with mine, I'm going to just bring this to her office," he said.

Then he went through the staff-only door to find Margot.

She was sitting in her office, the door open, looking at her computer screen. He stood in the doorway.

"I finished filling out the forms," he said. She looked up at the sound of his voice. He kept going. "You probably also need this," he said, and pulled his passport out of his back pocket.

She reached out a hand, and he walked in and handed her the forms and his passport.

"Thanks." She looked back at her computer screen, clearly ready for him to go. He didn't.

"Are we going to talk about this?" he asked.

She finally met his eyes. The relaxed, cheerful mask dropped from her face.

"Close the door," she said.

He closed it, very gently.

"No, to answer your question," she said as soon as the door was closed all the way. "Other than to say that one, it obviously can't happen again, and two, no one can know it happened. Especially not my brother."

Did she think he was going to spread this around? He wouldn't do that.

"Of course not," he said. "Do you want me to quit? I can just leave at the end of the day and not come back. I'm sure I can find something somewhere else."

Why had he said that? He didn't want to quit. But now he had to if she said yes.

She lifted a hand to her face and closed her eyes. He waited for her answer.

"No," she finally said. Why was he both relieved and disappointed by that? "First of all, it would probably violate some sort of employment law if I said yes. And we've been short-staffed, it's been a challenge to hire people who are both intelligent and likable, and my brother actually liked you, which is rare. I'll feel way too guilty if we lose you because of me."

"Okay," he said. He turned to open the door, and then stopped and turned back around. "I have one question to ask you, though. Were you going to text me?"

She looked in his eyes, for one long moment.

"I think it's best if I don't answer that question."

She turned back to her computer screen. Okay. He got the message.

He opened her door and walked back out into the tasting room.

Well, this wasn't how he'd expected his first day at work to go.

But damn it. He wished she'd answered the question.

Four

MARGOT FLED FROM THE winery that evening like she was escaping something. Which was more or less true. Luke had left before she did, but by the time she got in her car, hours before she usually left the winery, she felt like she couldn't be inside the building for another second or else she'd explode.

Why? Why why why did the guy she'd had fantastic sex with all night have to be her new employee? What had she done in this life, or a previous one, to deserve that kind of karmic punishment?

Thank God, at least, that Elliot was so focused on wine that he never noticed anything and hadn't seemed to pick up on the way she and Luke had stared at each other when they'd walked into her office that morning. Or the way she'd tried to avoid looking at him after that first shocked moment.

Should she have told him to quit, when he'd walked into her office later that day, for the confrontation she'd known they had to have? She still wasn't sure. Yes, obviously, she didn't want him working at the winery, what a fucking HR minefield that was. Especially with the way he'd looked at her, first in the tasting room and then right before he'd left her office. It had made her remember the night before—and that morning—all too well. It had made her whole body remember how it had felt to be touched by him, kissed by him. He couldn't keep looking at her like that. If he did it again, she'd have to tell him so.

Even though, God, she wanted him to keep looking at her like that.

It figured that this would happen. That as soon as she was feeling confident about her role at Noble, as soon as she'd really settled into the job, felt like she was starting to make it her own, felt like she could actually be good at this thing, something would happen to remind her that she didn't deserve to be there.

Her phone rang. In the second before the number popped up on the screen in her car, she wondered which would be worse right now: Elliot calling, because he somehow knew what she'd done, or Luke calling, because he'd gotten her phone number from somewhere and wanted to, like, talk this whole thing through some more, or something. She let out a sigh of relief when she saw it was Sydney.

"Hey," she said.

"Hey yourself," Sydney said, an amused tone in her voice. "I believe you have a story for me? Meet me for drinks?"

Margot slammed on her brakes for a yellow light.

"How did you know?"

Had Luke told someone, who told someone else, who told Sydney? She knew Napa Valley was just one big sprawling, wine-soaked small town, but this was fast even for the Napa rumor mill. Oh God, then the rest of her staff would find out any second, because Taylor knew everybody.

It would still take Elliot weeks to find out, though—he was so far outside the rumor mill that he didn't even know it existed. But this meant she'd have to tell him.

"How did I know?" Sydney laughed. "Well, I guessed something happened after I saw the two of you walk out of the Barrel together last night, and I saw that very tender way he steered you past those annoying tourists Mark had just dealt with."

Of course. Sydney knew only that something happened last night. She didn't know about today.

"But I guess I was right and there's much more to this story," Sydney continued. "Which (a) I'll take that thank-you anytime you want to give it to me, and (b) why didn't I get a text about this at some point today? Obviously this means (c) we're meeting for drinks within seconds."

Thank goodness it had been Sydney who'd seen her and Luke together last night, and not someone else. But then, if it wasn't for Sydney, she never would have introduced herself to Luke in the first place.

"Re: (a)—that thanks isn't coming for quite a while, and when I explain why, you'll understand; (b) as well. But re: (c) yes, definitely drinks within seconds, but this calls for you to come over to my place. Bring food, I don't care what it is as long as there's a lot of it. I just realized I haven't eaten all day. I'll provide the wine."

She did that sometimes, forgot to eat lunch when she was busy working. She almost always realized she was starving by three in the afternoon and grabbed some cheese and crackers from the tasting room. But even if she'd realized how hungry she was this afternoon, nothing in the world would have made her go into the tasting room.

"I'll be at your place in thirty minutes," Sydney said, and hung up.

Margot had just enough time after she got home to straighten up the living room and open a bottle of wine—one of her good bottles—before Sydney knocked on her door.

"There had better be a really good reason why you haven't thanked me yet, if your story is what I think your story is," she said as she walked in the door and through the house to the kitchen.

Margot poured them both glasses of wine while Sydney took down plates from the cabinet.

"Oh, there is, don't worry," Margot said. She closed her eyes and breathed in. "Whatever you've brought me smells amazing."

"Of course it's amazing, this is me we're talking about," Sydney said. She took a stack of boxes out of the bag she'd carried inside. "I could tell from the sound of your voice that you needed carbs."

She slid a mound of pasta onto a plate, and handed it to Margot.

"Carbonara, like the doctor ordered," Sydney said.

Margot looked down at her plate and smiled genuinely for the first time since Elliot and Luke had walked into her office that morning.

"Carbonara. Yes. This is just what I needed. How did you know?"

Sydney handed her a fork and waved at her to start eating.

"I always know."

Margot sat down on one of the high-backed barstools at her counter and dug her fork into the plate of pasta. She took one very large bite, and sighed.

"I love you so much," she said to her friend as soon as she finished chewing.

Sydney slid her own plate of pasta onto the counter next to Margot and sat down.

"I know you do," she said. "There's also bread and cheese and charcuterie, obviously. But we can't let the pasta get cold. Eat."

Margot ate. The pasta was perfectly cooked, the pancetta was crispy, every single noodle was coated in just the right amount of sauce . . . this was bliss.

She put her fork down after she had inhaled half the plate, and took a sip of wine.

"Thank you," she said to Sydney. "For the pasta, and for letting me eat before I started talking."

Normally, she would have been delighted to tell Sydney about her unexpected hookup with a twenty-eight-year-old. She'd even thought on her drive to work this morning about how fun it would be to spill the details of this escapade to Sydney, to have her cackle and take credit for it and say she told her so. They would have laughed about his *I thought I dreamed you* line, debated whether she should text him or not, Sydney would have toasted her for this, and the whole thing would have felt even more fun.

Of course, it wouldn't have happened exactly like that, since the only reason Margot knew Luke was twenty-eight was because she'd seen his birth date on his employment forms today.

She sighed.

"Okay. So. Yes, I went home with that guy last night. Luke. He kissed me outside of the Barrel." Sydney grinned, and Margot couldn't stop herself from grinning back. "And then I told him that we couldn't do that there, that too many people know me around here." Thank God she'd said that so quickly, at least. "And his place was closer, so we went there."

Sydney shook her head, her smile huge.

"I didn't think you had it in you."

She wished she hadn't.

"Yeah, well, just wait. The sex was . . . great. Unfortunately." Or would it have been more awkward if the sex had been bad and he'd shown up at work today? Yes and no—at least then she wouldn't have felt like her body was on fire whenever he looked at her. "He drove me home this morning—a very gentlemanly move, since he lives only six blocks away, which he knew."

She took another sip of wine. And then another. She needed fortification for this next part of the story.

"And?" Sydney prompted her.

She took a deep breath.

"And. Two hours after he dropped me off here, he walked into Noble Family Vineyards to start his new job as a tasting room associate. The job my brother hired him for on Friday, when I wasn't there."

Sydney's mouth dropped open.

"Yes, that was also my response when he walked into my office with Elliot this morning," Margot said. "Elliot told me he hired a 'William something,' not Luke Williams! Granted, I didn't know his last name until this morning, but still!"

Sydney got up and walked back into the kitchen and picked up the cheese and charcuterie.

"I'm glad I got all of this cheese, we're going to need it after this story." She sat back down and reached for a cracker. "How did he react when he saw you?"

Margot considered that.

"He seemed as shocked as I was." She took another sip of wine. "This afternoon, he walked into my office and offered to quit."

Sydney spread some gooey cheese on a cracker and handed it to her.

"What did you say?"

Margot sighed.

"I said no. What else could I say? I can't tell someone who works for me to quit his job because we had sex—that seems like an employment-law nightmare. And plus, as much as I want him to go away and never come back, Elliot actually liked him, and despite how annoyed I was about Elliot hiring someone without me—which, as we see now, I was correct to think was a disaster waiting to happen—the whole reason we're hiring more staff is because I pushed to expand our tasting room. Though Luke told me last night that he was only in town for a few months; I never would have hired him if I'd known that. But I'm sure if he quit, Elliot would figure out a way to blame this on me." She made a face. "To be fair, he would be right to do so."

Sydney looked at her hard.

"Do you really want Luke to go away and never come back? I saw that way you smiled when you talked about last night."

Margot let out a long breath.

"Of course I do! Do you think it's going to be fun for me to have him around? At the winery? With my brother there? Because I can tell you right now, today was the opposite of fun." She stared down at her plate of pasta. "He gave me his number this morning. Right before I got out of the car. Told me to text him, said he wanted to see me again."

Sydney set her glass down.

"Were you going to text him?"

Of course she was going to ask that question.

"I had decided not to," she said. "I think."

But . . . if Luke hadn't walked into her office today, and she'd gotten into bed alone tonight, and thought about the night before, what would she have done? Would she have pulled that number out of her wallet? She didn't know.

"He asked me that, too. After he offered to quit." She saw the question in Sydney's eyes. "I told him it was best if I didn't answer."

Sydney laughed.

"I can just hear the way you would have said that, too. With your firm, CEO, taking-no-shit voice." The smile dropped from her face and she pushed the garlic bread toward Margot. "I'm sorry. This sucks. And it was my fault."

Margot shook her head.

"It wasn't your fault. How could you know the guy you dared me to talk to was my new employee? Plus, I'm the one who demanded to go home with him." She dropped her head into her hands. "But wow, I can't even describe how I felt when Luke and Elliot walked into my office this morning." She sat back up. "Calling it a nightmare doesn't even do it justice. It felt like one of the worst kinds of anxiety dreams. You know the ones, where you're back in high school and you have one more class to take before you can graduate and you're trying to figure out how you messed up your life so much that you're back in that terrible place? Except this was me, in my office this morning, in a great mood after last night and a good work call this morning and with this little secret smile on my face and hum in my body, and then the reason for the smile and the hum walks into my office with my *brother* and he's my new employee." She grabbed the garlic bread and tore it in half. "Business school did not prepare me for this."

Sydney grinned. "Okay, but you say that every week about your job."

Margot took a bite of garlic bread that was at least seventy percent just roasted garlic.

"I know, but when I said it those other times, I meant they

need to do a better job prepping people to work in small businesses and on shoestring budgets and to figure out how to deal with natural disasters. Now I mean it on a more . . . global scale."

Sydney was silent for a while. She ate cheese while Margot demolished the garlic bread. What if she asked her favorite business school professor, whom she'd reached out to a number of times with questions, about this?

Hi, Professor Karlan,

Hope you're well! Just a quick question today. What would you advise if—unbeknownst to me—I slept with my newest employee the night before he started work at the winery?

Thanks so much for any assistance! Can't wait to host you in the tasting room soon!

Margot Noble

She tried to picture the look on her professor's face upon receipt of that email, and failed completely.

Margot let out a sigh and turned to Sydney.

"How did I get myself into this? No, wait, that's the wrong question, I always get myself into things like this. Better question: What am I going to do?"

"What you always do," Sydney immediately replied. "Put your game face on, get up and go to work tomorrow, and make the world bend to your will."

Margot laughed.

"I love that you see me that way." She only wished Sydney's vision of her was the true one. "And thanks. I hope I can do that." Oh hell, if she couldn't say this to Sydney, who could she say it to?

"The thing is. The problem with that plan is that. You see. The sex was very good."

Sydney sat back.

"Ah. That is a problem." She laughed when Margot glared at her. "No, I swear, I'm not being sarcastic. Normally I would be, if you said something like that! Normally that would not be a problem at all! But now . . ."

Margot closed her eyes.

"I swear to God, Syd, when he walked into my office this afternoon, I almost had to take a step back, so I didn't throw myself at him. I didn't move—toward him or away—and obviously I won't do anything, but holy shit this is unfair."

Sydney got up and went back into the kitchen.

"It's very unfair." She flipped open a pastry box, cut two slices of pie, and put them on plates. "I think I have a solution, though." She got a pint of ice cream out of the freezer. "I think the next time you come to the Barrel, you have to say hi to whichever cute man is sitting next to you again. Use this good sex energy on someone else."

Sydney set a plate in front of Margot, and Margot took the spoon she handed her.

"Absolutely not," she said. "You see what happened when I said hi to a stranger last night: utter chaos. From now on, I'm only talking to people I've known for at least five years."

Sydney raised her eyebrows.

"You've only known me for three years."

Margot waved the spoon at her.

"You don't count, obviously. It *feels* like I've known you for, like, fifteen."

Sydney nodded.

"Okay, what about at work? All the tourists who come in? And almost everyone who works in the winery who isn't your brother?"

"Look, I didn't invite you over here to parse all of my words, did I? You know what I meant." Margot took a big bite of the pie. "Oh God. This pie is incredible."

Sydney was already halfway through her slice.

"I know. I made it this afternoon—I was going to bring it to a meeting tomorrow, but this was an emergency."

Margot took another bite.

"Thank you for understanding that."

Sydney sat back and looked at Margot.

"This is going to be okay. You know that, right?"

Not really, no.

"What if my brother finds out, Syd?" Margot closed her eyes. "I . . . It'll just confirm all of the worst things he thinks about me, and my commitment to the winery, and my ability to handle this job without fucking it up. I don't . . ." She took a breath. "I don't want that to happen."

Sydney put her arm around her.

"Do you need me to tell you all of the ways in which you've been incredible for that winery and your brother should thank his lucky stars every single day that you are his partner, and also list the hundreds, if not thousands, of ways that you've shown your commitment to the winery and to this community? Because I will, you know."

Margot knew she would.

"That's very tempting, but what I really want is for you to bring me another piece of that pie and then for me to take one bite and say, 'Oh God, I'm too full to eat any more!' and then for you to not yell at me for that."

"I can do that." Sydney got up and picked up the wine bottle. "This is empty. Do you need more wine?"

Margot shook her head.

"I'm too old for that now. If we open another bottle, I'll feel it far too much tomorrow morning." She picked up her glass and swirled the wine left in it. "I may accidentally fuck my employees, but as God is my witness, I will never show up to my winery hungover!"

She and Sydney both cracked up.

—————

LUKE COULD BARELY BELIEVE what had happened to him in the last twenty-four hours. Okay, so, he'd met a hot woman at a bar near his new apartment—not something that happened every day, but within the realm of possibility. He'd kissed her outside of the bar—again, more rare than he would like, but not, like, ridiculous. She'd come back to his apartment—usually something to celebrate, and he had last night, and again this morning. He'd even wanted to see her again!

And then, not two hours after he'd dropped her off at her house—her house that was exactly six blocks from his apartment—he'd walked into her office to be introduced to his new boss.

Why hadn't she told him her last name last night?

Well, if she'd done that, he probably wouldn't have ended the night with her naked in his bed, and that truly would have been a shame. But now he had to work under Margot Noble, while all the time thinking about what it had been like to be literally under Margot Noble, and if he'd thought his old job had been a struggle, that would be nothing compared to how this was going to be.

And now he had to go have dinner with his mom and Pete, and try to explain to his mom why he'd quit his very prestigious and well-paying tech job, and why he'd moved—at least temporarily—back home to Napa and was now working at a winery. She would be so shocked and horrified. But even worse, she'd be so disappointed in him.

God, he was dreading this.

Unfortunately, his mom and Pete's house was only about ten minutes from Noble, which meant he wouldn't have the advantage of a long drive to clear his head before this dinner.

Why was he acting like such a child about telling his mom he'd quit his job, anyway? He was an adult! He would be thirty in a little over a year! He was a college graduate and accomplished in his field!

And that was the exact problem. His mom was so proud of him, for all of that. For how hard he'd worked, for all that he'd accomplished.

He still didn't know if quitting had been the right decision. Probably not. When he remembered the relief he'd felt on his last day, he was so glad he'd quit. But when he thought about how impulsive his decision had been, that he had no idea what to do next, he doubted it.

He wished he could just . . . not tell his mom about this. But he'd fucked that up on his own by deciding to move back to Napa, and then getting the damn job at Noble so he'd have something to do all day.

But then, he couldn't have blown off Avery like that when

she needed him. She'd been his best friend since high school; she'd been there for him for everything both good and bad for well over a decade. Her breakup had hit her hard, and now that he could actually be there for her at a difficult time, he was glad he was able to do it. She so rarely ever let anyone know she actually needed help, and he couldn't regret being here for her, when she'd been so relieved that he'd been there to help her move, and she'd seemed so happy to make plans with him for tomorrow night. And she hadn't even flipped out about him quitting his job, and had even seemed happy for him.

At least, he'd have a story for Avery when he saw her. He laughed. She would freak out when he told her about Margot.

When he got to his mom's house, he walked up the path to the front door and knocked firmly on the door. This wasn't the house he'd grown up in; his mom had sold that house and moved into this smaller one when he'd been in college, and Pete had moved in here a few years later. She'd used some of the money from the old house to help pay Luke's tuition, which was one of the many reasons he felt guilty for quitting his job.

His mom threw open the door, a huge smile on her face, and he smiled back at her. He hadn't seen her in a few months; he hadn't realized how much he missed her. Now he felt bad for how much he'd been dreading this.

"Hey, Mom," he said, and pulled her into a hug.

She gave him a very tight hug in return and then took a step back.

"To what do I owe this pleasure?" she asked, with that look on her face that he knew meant she was trying not to smile at him. "Dinner with my son, on a Monday night, when it's not a holiday?"

He followed her into the house. This might not be the house he grew up in, but it smelled like home.

"Something smells incredible in here," he said, bypassing her question for the moment. "Don't tell me you made short ribs?"

She took the lid off the big pot on the stove and gave it a stir.

"Well, I know they're your favorite, and even though it's the end of April, there's still a chill in the air in the evenings, so I thought we'd all like something cozy tonight. And you gave me enough warning that you'd be up here so I could start this early and have it simmering all afternoon."

Luke lifted his hand to Pete, who was standing by the refrigerator. His mom and Pete had met because of him—he'd worked for Pete one summer in high school, and then a year or so later, his mom and Pete had started dating.

"Hi, Pete," Luke said. "Good to see you."

It was true, even though he'd had a full year there—at least—when he'd been furious at Pete for dating his mom. And furious at his mom for dating Pete, though he'd been more mad at Pete. At that point, it had been only a few years since his parents had gotten divorced and his dad had moved away. His parents were much better as friends than as a married couple, but he still hadn't liked the idea of either of them with anyone else. But he'd moved past that eventually. It had helped—once he'd gotten over himself—to see how happy his mom was around Pete.

"Hey, Luke," Pete said. He opened the refrigerator and pulled two beers out. "Want a beer?"

Luke grinned at him.

"Sure, thanks." Though a beer made him think about the bar last night, which made him think about Margot, which made him think about things he did not need to be thinking about right now.

"Need any help, Mom?"

"No, no, it's almost ready," she said as she drained a pot of potatoes.

Within minutes, she'd mashed the potatoes, tossed the salad and ordered Luke to put it on the table, and dished up bowls of short ribs on top of creamy mashed potatoes for all three of them. Luke's stomach rumbled as he carried the food to the table.

"So?" she said as soon as they all sat down. "Are you going to tell us what you're doing in Napa on a Monday night? Is there a conference or something?"

Luke picked up his fork. And then he lost his head.

"I'm on sabbatical, so I moved back up here for a little while."

Why had he said that? He wasn't on sabbatical!

His mom raised her eyebrows.

"Sabbatical?"

Now he just had to go with it.

"Yeah, we can take sabbaticals after five years, and I'm overdue for one." What was he even saying? "And I came up last week to help Avery move, and well, one thing led to another, and—"

A wide smile spread across his mom's face.

"Oh, really? You and Avery? Oh, I'm so glad."

She beamed at him.

Shit. His mom thought he meant he'd gotten back together with Avery?

"Oh, that's not what I—"

"I should have known you two were back together when I saw that smile on your face. What a great reason for you to be back in town."

Oh no, she looked so happy. He and Avery had dated for like five minutes when they were teenagers, and then had been best friends ever since, but his mom had hoped for years that they'd get back together, even though he'd told her a million times they were just friends. He had to correct her.

"Mom, it's not—"

"I know, I know, I won't get my hopes up that it's forever," she said. "But I have a good feeling about this. And the timing is perfect, with your sabbatical! And I get to have my son back in town for a while? I didn't know they gave you sabbaticals there. What a great company that is. Do you want some water?"

She got up and bustled into the kitchen for water, before he could respond. Luke stared down at his food. He couldn't let her keep thinking that he was dating Avery. He had to tell her the truth, about that, and his job.

But. What if he didn't?

Just for the next week or so, while he got settled in, and figured everything out, and decided how he would tell her what had really happened at work, and started to make a plan for what he would do next. Then he could say, *Oh, the Avery thing was all a misunderstanding*, he didn't realize she thought that, and then present her with his great new plan for his life.

Because right now, she hummed as she came back to the table and had a smile on her face instead of that disappointed look that he'd been dreading.

No, he couldn't lie to her like this. He was an adult! He was too old to lie to his mom, come on. He'd tell her. Right now.

"More mashed potatoes, Luke?" she asked.

"Yes please," he said.

Avery was going to kill him for this.

Five

MARGOT GOT TO THE winery on Tuesday morning earlier than usual. She needed to get herself in the flow of things before she had to face Luke again. She needed to remind herself that she was more than the woman who had slept with her newest employee, whom she was still, unfortunately, wildly attracted to. She needed to sit down at her desk, throw herself into some spreadsheets and emails and metrics, try to remember that she was good at this job, that she genuinely loved this job. Because for the past twenty-two or so hours, she'd felt like an extreme fuckup.

She had to get back to Margot Noble, CEO and co-owner of Noble Family Vineyards. Fake it till you make it—hadn't that been her motto for the past few years? She hadn't made it yet, but at least she'd gotten good at faking it. And she needed to pull herself together before she saw Luke again. Before he said anything to her, in that voice he'd used to whisper in her ear in bed, before she heard his laugh from across the room, that laugh that had made her lean over just a little closer when they'd been at the Barrel. Before she saw those long, neat fingers of his carefully picking up wineglasses in the tasting room, with the same care he'd used to run his fingers up her . . . No. What was she doing? She had to stop thinking about this.

The party, that's what she had to think about. She should have spent yesterday making initial plans, doing some research into when other wineries were having their events, what caterers she could get when, but no, she'd spent it obsessing about Luke. Maybe she should obsess about the party instead.

She wanted this party to be a true celebration of the winery, of all that Uncle Stan and Elliot—and she—had accomplished. Even more, she wanted it to be a sign of bigger things to come. She wanted more sales, more publicity, more attention for their winery. To fill their coffers, yes, but also to put them securely on the Napa Valley map. They were on the cusp of so much, she could feel it. She wanted it all to happen.

At ten forty-five, she heard someone drive up to the winery, and glanced out her window to see who it was.

Luke. So he had come back today.

She shouldn't be relieved. She should be disappointed—if he'd disappeared and never come back, she wouldn't have to deal with that particular stress anymore.

But she *had* wanted to hire before things got—well, hopefully got—busier this summer. And she'd already been able to tell from yesterday that Luke would be good at this—she'd been able to tell by his interactions with customers and the way he'd listened to Taylor and Elliot.

And fine, she'd been able to tell by the way he'd listened to her as they'd talked and laughed and flirted at the bar on Sunday night. She'd wondered later if he'd just listened to her so well to get into her pants, if his whole goal in asking her questions and laughing at her stories was to get her in his bed at the end of the night. If that had been his goal, then wow, that had worked out well for him, but after seeing the way he'd chatted with customers the day before, she thought this kind of thing just came naturally to him.

Why had he come back today? Why had he applied for this job in the first place? After seeing his résumé—and his car—she was pretty sure he didn't need the money.

See, this was why she shouldn't have done that no-talk-about-work bullshit at the Barrel on Sunday night. Yes, sure, she'd been sick of work, and she'd wanted to relax, but if she'd just said where she'd worked, she would have had a short, professional, friendly conversation with her new employee, and then she would have gone home and cuddled with her favorite vibrator, instead of fucking Luke all night.

Oh God, she had to stop thinking about her vibrator and the sex she'd had with her employee, when said employee was about to walk into the building. She did not want him to see that same look on her face when she unlocked the door to let him in for his second day of work as he had on Sunday night when they were both naked in his bedroom.

She forced her face into a professional smile and unlocked the winery doors.

"Good morning, Luke," she said.

He smiled at her, with a slight question in his eyes. Did he wonder if she wanted him to come back?

"Good morning. Looks like today is going to be busy; I took a glance at today's schedule yesterday."

No, of course he wasn't thinking about her. Why did she think she knew his facial expressions like that? He was talking about work. She should do that, too.

"Yes, a lot busier than yesterday." She walked over to the bar and pulled up the schedule, and he followed her. "Our first appointment isn't until eleven thirty, but after that, we'll be going almost all day." She stared at the schedule again. Before they'd hired extra staff, when there were this many appointments on the schedule, she'd have to pitch in almost all day to help out. Today she'd still have to, but eventually the new staff would mean she'd have more time and space to devote to the actual running of the winery.

"Am I the first one here?" he asked.

She nodded.

"Taylor should be here any minute, and then Daisy will be here this afternoon—you haven't met her yet, she's great. It's good we have so many people here today, it's a packed schedule for a Tuesday."

He took a step closer to her as if to glance at the schedule, but then stopped, still a few feet away. Yeah, that was for the best. Just the idea of him standing so close made a shiver go down her spine.

He looked at her for a moment, still a few feet away, and she looked back at him. Then, almost simultaneously, their faces both relaxed from their polite, tense smiles, into grins.

"Hi," he said.

"Hi," she said.

"This is going to be weird, isn't it?" he asked.

She nodded.

"Yeah. Probably. At least for a while." Maybe it was easier to talk about this, at least briefly, than to avoid it. "I'm sorry," she said.

He shook his head.

"You have nothing to apologize for." He glanced around the room, then back at her. "I'm going to try my best to not make it weird, but these first few days might be a challenge."

She laughed. At least she wasn't the only one who was feeling like this.

"I was just about to say the same thing."

"Good morning!" Taylor said as she opened the front door.

Margot turned in her direction. A few moments ago, she would have jumped guiltily at being caught in here alone with Luke, like she was doing something wrong just by looking at him. But their brief conversation and acknowledgment that they were both struggling with this made her feel almost as relaxed as she sounded.

"Hey, Taylor, good morning. I was just going over the schedule for the day with Luke."

Taylor came over to the bar and glanced at the schedule.

"Is he going to shadow you on that tour and tasting at one?"

It did make the most sense for him to do that, but Margot hadn't wanted to suggest it herself. She raised an eyebrow at him, and he nodded.

"Good idea," she said. "Don't worry, Luke, you'll get lots of training before we send you out to do tours on your own."

He gave her a wry grin.

"Was it so obvious that I was worried?"

She and Taylor both laughed.

"Oh, I forgot to tell you this yesterday—maybe Taylor did?—but there's always coffee in the kitchen in the back, and often baked goods. The vineyard manager's husband loves to bake, so he's always bringing stuff in. Today there's coffee cake."

Taylor immediately turned toward the employees-only door leading to the kitchen.

"Be right back," she said. They both laughed when the door closed behind her. And then they turned to face each other again.

"If you don't want to shadow me today, I understand," Margot said in a low voice.

Luke shook his head.

"It's fine. Don't worry about that."

She glanced back at the schedule, then stepped out from behind the bar.

"Okay, thanks. Just . . . let me know, okay? If it's ever a problem."

Luke nodded.

"I will."

Taylor walked back into the tasting room, a square of coffee cake in her hand and a blissful expression on her face.

"I know that man is happily married, but I swear I want to marry him. Have you tried this coffee cake?"

Margot laughed.

"Wouldn't Gemma have a problem with that?" Taylor's girlfriend worked at a winery down the road.

Taylor waved that away.

"She would be fine with it if she got coffee cake like this. Luke, you should go get some."

"That sounds like an order." Luke disappeared through the door.

Margot turned to Taylor.

"Let's hope that within a few weeks he and Marisol will both be able to take tours on their own, and I'll be able to get some other work done."

Taylor brushed sugar off her fingers.

"Oh, I bet he will—he's a quick study. He was pretty good with the guests yesterday. Where did you find him?"

At the bar at the Barrel, and then I went home with him and we had sex for hours.

"I didn't," she said. "Elliot found him. Incredible, right?"

Taylor's eyes widened.

"Incredible, yes."

Just then, Luke walked back into the tasting room.

"What do you think of the coffee cake?" Taylor asked.

"I think I'm going to fight you for him," Luke said. "It could be a slightly awkward workplace issue, especially on my second day, but I hope the boss will understand."

Margot locked eyes with him, and then all three of them laughed.

"YOU SLEPT WITH MARGOT Noble? The night before you started work at NOBLE?" Avery's eyes were wide open.

"Shhh! Keep your voice down!" he said.

She looked around.

"Luke. We're sitting inside a parked car with the windows up, and no one is around us. No one can hear me." She turned to look directly at him. "I wondered why you made me come get in your car when we were supposed to be meeting for dinner. I assumed you wanted to show me some fancy thing about your car, but this is definitely more interesting." She rubbed her hands together. "I'm so glad you moved back here."

Avery had that grin on her face she always got when he told her anything about his love life. He hated that grin.

But he was glad to see her smiling, after how sad she'd looked last week when he'd helped her move. If his ridiculous story could bring her some joy, he supposed it was worth her making fun of him.

"I'm glad the roller coaster of my life is entertaining to you. But this has felt sort of like those roller coasters where someone promised you it was just a regular ride, so you got some really great ice cream right before you got on, and then you get on and there's a huge drop and then it gets stuck and you feel like there's no escape and also you're going to throw up. That kind of roller coaster."

Because when he'd woken up with Margot in his bed on Monday morning, he'd thought this impromptu move back to Napa was going to be great. He'd had great sex; he hoped to have more of it; he had a new, fun job very different from his old one; he'd have some space to figure out his next steps. But instead, the woman he'd had the great sex with was his new boss, more sex with her was definitely off the table, and that all made his new job much more stressful than he'd planned on.

Stressful, but also very enjoyable. Because God, that day at work, while he'd been shadowing Margot on that tour, he hadn't been able to keep his eyes off her. He'd been glad that they'd given him a job where he was supposed to look at her, listen to her, pay attention to her, because that's all he'd wanted to do.

It was good that they'd had their brief clearing of the air that morning—that had been much better and less stressful than their conversation yesterday, when both of them had still been in shock from waking up together that morning and then seeing each other at work a few hours later (and with some pretty excellent morning sex in between).

Should he have quit? Even though she'd told him not to, should he have not gone back that day? He flashed back to that look of pure horror on her face when he and Elliot had walked into her office the day before.

The problem was, he didn't want to quit. Was that so wrong? That he didn't want to lose the chance to see her every day? Plus, what else was he going to do all day if he didn't have this job? He needed to look for a new real job, he knew he needed to. But he'd put that off for the past two weeks—the idea of it seemed so stressful, so overwhelming. He'd been almost relieved when Avery had needed his help. He felt bad thinking that way, but her crisis had given him something to do. And then, after he'd sublet his old place and moved back up here, he'd applied for the job at Noble on a whim. He'd thought it would be so much less stressful than his old job.

He would have quit if Margot had asked him to. But she hadn't.

Avery laughed at him again.

"What's so funny?" he asked her.

"Do you really need me to answer that?" she asked. "Because this whole thing is hilarious, and you know it."

He let himself smile, a tiny bit.

"Look, I suppose if it was happening to someone who wasn't me, I would be able to find the humor in it a little more."

She patted him on the arm.

"Ahh, there's the real Luke Williams. I was also laughing because this whole thing is so not you. You always do the right thing, never get into trouble—hell, I'm surprised that you even went out the night before you started a new job. Honestly, if you found this as funny as I did, I would be concerned that you'd been replaced by some sort of impostor."

His small smile turned into a grin.

"This whole thing is all your fault; you're the one who pointed out the Barrel to me when we drove by my building." He looked around at the parking lot. "But you have to keep this a total secret, okay? I shouldn't have even told you, but honestly there was no way I could meet you for dinner tonight and answer questions about how my first day of work was and keep this in." He shook his head. "I should have known this would be a problem after I kissed her outside the bar and she said we couldn't do that there, that too many people knew her around here. Do you know the kind of women who say things like that? The kind of women who end up being your new boss, that kind."

Avery laughed again, and this time he laughed along with her. It was funny. He supposed.

"I gave her my number. Monday morning, after I drove her home," he said.

Avery stopped, her hand on the car-door handle.

"Wait. I thought this was just a one-night stand. You were going to see her again?"

"I wanted to," he admitted. "She was . . . We had a great time." Avery got that grin on her face again. He was suddenly irritated, far more than he probably should have been. "That's not what I mean." Well. Not *just* what he meant. "We talked, for a long time. At the bar, I mean. I really liked talking to her. She's smart, funny, interesting, easy to talk to. We had fun."

Avery's eyes were wide.

"Did you want to *date* her?"

He shook his head.

"Date her, no, I'm not going to be up here for that long. But I thought maybe Margot and I could be . . . friends." He couldn't hold back a smirk. "The kind of friends who have really great sex sometimes."

Avery made a face.

"Ewww, I wasn't asking for details, but okay." She opened her car door. "Now can we please go inside and get some drinks and food? I need wine after that conversation."

Luke laughed and got out of the car.

"How'd your mom take the news?" Avery asked after they sat down at a table and ordered drinks. "Of you quitting your job and moving up here and all?"

Funny that she asked.

"Mmm. About that. I didn't . . . quite . . . tell her that I'd quit."

Avery raised her eyebrows at him.

"You didn't 'quite' tell her you'd quit? What did you tell her?"

He sighed.

"I told her I was on sabbatical. Which, yes, was a total lie. It's just . . . it had already been a long day, what with the Margot thing and all, and my mom is just so proud of me, and I didn't want to . . ."

Avery put her hand on his arm.

"You didn't want to disappoint her. Especially since you feel bad about quitting in the first place. I get it."

He looked up at her.

"How did you know I felt bad about quitting in the first place?"

Avery rolled her eyes.

"Luke. How long have we known each other? Come on." She patted his arm. "What did your mom say to the sabbatical thing? Did she believe it?" She looked at him and then narrowed her eyes. "Oh no. What's wrong?"

Avery really was going to kill him.

"The thing is . . . when I told her I'd come up here to help you move, and everything"—Avery looked away at the reminder of her breakup, and he quickly rushed on—"I—accidentally—said something that led her to believe that we were together. You and me, I mean."

Avery's eyes widened.

"Your mom thought we were dating? Oh no. She must have been even more disappointed when you told her it wasn't true."

Luke looked down at the table.

"LUKE."

He cleared his throat and looked up. She was giving him her fiercest glare.

Where were mashed potatoes when he needed them?

"I didn't . . . exactly . . . tell her it wasn't true."

Avery kept staring at him.

"See. It was just that . . . her whole face lit up when she thought I told her we were together. She didn't question the sabbatical thing at all."

Avery picked up her glass of wine and took a long gulp. Luke sighed.

"I know, I know. I lost it, Avery. I should have prepared a better story to tell my mom about why I suddenly quit my job and what the hell I'm doing with my life and I'd planned to figure all of that out on Sunday night and Monday and then Sunday night I met a hot woman at a bar and Monday I found out she was my new boss and that drove everything else out of my head so I was vastly underprepared for that dinner with my mom and so when she beamed at me like that when she thought I said you and I were dating I just went with it."

He shook his head and took a breath.

"I'm not usually like this. I procrastinated applying for new jobs for weeks, I lied to my mom—I don't do things like this! What's wrong with me?"

Avery patted his hand.

"You're having a quarter-life crisis. I didn't expect it to happen to you, of all people, but that's exactly what this is."

"A quarter-life crisis? I'm twenty-eight. Exactly how long do you think I'm going to live?"

She brushed that off with a quick flick of her hand.

"That job did a number on you! Those people sucked, that job destroyed your confidence, it made you feel unworthy, which you're not, but I know you won't believe me." He tried to smile at her, but she just shook her head. "I'm glad you're going to be up here for a while—you need to get your swagger back."

He hoped his face looked as skeptical as he felt.

"How long have you known me? I don't think I've ever had 'swagger,' Avery."

She rolled her eyes.

"You know what I mean."

Yeah, he knew what she meant.

"I did sleep with my new boss the other night, if that counts?"

Avery giggled.

"Good point, but that feels like an isolated incident. More of that, though."

He laughed, and then sighed.

"Anyway, I'm sorry for involving you in all of this, even though I did it accidentally. I feel like such a child, lying to my mother about all of this."

Avery shook her head.

"Luke, you're talking to someone who still hasn't told her mother that she broke up with Derek. I just have to text her and get it over with, but I'm dreading it. I get it." Her face relaxed into a grin. "But you and me? Gross."

"I'm a little offended that your reaction to the idea of dating me seems to be abject horror," he said.

Avery rolled her eyes again.

"Yeah, yeah, you're a great catch, I love you with my whole heart, and I can't wait for you to date a woman worthy of you, but we all know it's not going to be me. It's still hilarious to me that your mom keeps wanting us to get back together. While we were dating, I thought she hated me."

Luke laughed.

"Yeah, well, she's mellowed some over the years." He paused. "About some things."

Avery looked at him over her wineglass.

"Okay. I owe you one. After last week, and everything. You can keep up this pretense with your mom—I won't blow your cover."

He shook his head.

"Avery, no, you don't have to do that. You don't owe me anything. I did all of that for you because I'm your friend and I love you."

She touched his hand, for just a second, and smiled at him.

"Fine, I don't owe you anything. But I'll do this for you anyway. Because I'm your friend and I love you. Not like your mom wants me to, but still. We'll let her think so for a little while."

Was she sure about this?

"You don't have to do this, just because I'm a coward."

She narrowed her eyes at him.

"One, you're not a coward. Two, if you tell your mom you quit, you're going to try to rush yourself back into another tech job, and you need a break. Let her keep thinking this for a while, chill out, work at Noble, lust after Margot. Okay?"

Well. That last part wouldn't be too hard.

He nodded.

"Okay. And Avery? Thanks."

"You're welcome." She took a sip of wine. "Just promise me you'll let me know if you're cheating on me with your boss."

He thought about Margot, smiling at him as they walked back from the tour today.

"If only."

Avery grimaced, and he laughed.

Six

ON SUNDAY EVENING, AFTER the tasting room was closed, Margot rummaged through the hall closet at the winery. She should be getting ready for the staff dinner that night, but she wanted to find that old landscaping plan for the winery she was sure she'd seen in Uncle Stan's office years ago. She knew she didn't have to do the landscaping just the way he'd wanted, but she wanted to at least see what he'd wanted. And maybe then Elliot would be happier about this work, and her plans, and the party. Or, at least, less unhappy.

She grabbed two big boxes from the back of the closet and brought them into her office to look through. She kept getting sidetracked from her search as she flipped through all of these papers—handwritten notes from Uncle Stan from the early years of the winery, ancient bills for a fraction of what everything cost now, old newspaper clippings about Noble Family Vineyards. She should pull all of this stuff out, get some of it framed to hang on their walls.

Finally, right along the bottom of the second box, she found it. There was his sketch of the winery building, the barn, the vineyards in the distance. Oh wow, he'd wanted paths around the lawn and to and from the winery building just like she did, and he even had a little garden there, next to the winery building, with chairs and tables, like she'd told Elliot she wanted. They'd had a makeshift outdoor seating area in that space for the past year, but she wanted to improve the seating, make it feel like a real part of the winery. Maybe Uncle Stan had wanted it to look like she did.

She could picture the winery like this, see it in her head, just from seeing these plans. The back lawn, green and well taken care of, brand-new paths around it leading to the barn, to the winery building, to the parking lot, to the garden. Flowers everywhere, chairs and benches around, with the vineyard in the distance.

"Why are you all covered in dust?"

She blinked away her daydream and looked up to see Elliot in her doorway.

"I found them!" She beckoned to him. "Those old landscaping plans of Uncle Stan's."

She wasn't sure if Elliot would care about this, but he came right over to her desk.

"Oh wow, you actually found them. I was sure they were lost."

They stood there and looked down at them together for a few moments.

"He wanted a garden back there, just like you do," Elliot said finally.

She'd thought he hadn't been paying attention when she'd told him.

"Yeah," she said. "He did."

They smiled at each other for a second. Her eyes were suddenly full of tears. She blinked them back so they wouldn't drop down onto the plans.

Elliot turned away and walked to the door.

"Granted, we can't get the garden done by your party, of course. And we can only get the other stuff done if we can find a good landscaper in time."

Of course he had to say "*your* party" like that.

"I know," she said. There was no point in saying more. She didn't want to fight about it now. "We should get over to the barn, it's almost time for the staff dinner."

A staff dinner every six months, where the staff could learn about and taste all of the wines, had been Margot's brainchild the year before, and it had been one of the few of her new ideas for the winery that Elliot had embraced. But then, if there was one thing Elliot cared about, it was their wine, and he wanted anyone who spoke for the winery to know the wines well.

Elliot sighed. "Oh, is that tonight?"

At least, she'd thought Elliot had embraced it. Apparently not. Why did it still hurt so much, when he did things like this?

"Yeah, it's tonight," she said. "The food got here a few minutes ago, Taylor brought it over to the barn."

Elliot just nodded. "Okay. Meet you over there."

Margot watched as Elliot walked out of her office. Sometimes, when she let herself, she missed how it used to be with Elliot. Before Uncle Stan died, before they were business partners, when they were just brother and sister. When they'd been able to kid each other and laugh at each other and relax with each other without his resentment and her hurt and their reluctant partnership that overshadowed everything. She sighed, and went to the bathroom to dust herself off.

By the time she got over to the barn, Elliot was all smiles with the staff. Well, as "all smiles" as he ever got, anyway. When she'd come up with this idea, sure, partly it had been because she wanted to make sure that the new employees really knew their wine, but it was more than that. She wanted them to feel like they were part of this place, that she and Elliot valued them, and for them to understand what Noble Family Vineyards was all about. And now that they'd added Luke and Marisol, she wanted them to care about this place the way the rest of their staff did.

Well. Luke might feel slightly different than the rest of the staff.

Margot shook her head at herself, pulled out her phone, and snapped a few photos for their social media.

"Hey, boss," Taylor said. "Have you decided when the anniversary party is going to be?"

Taylor, at least, was excited about the party.

"I was going to make an announcement about this later: it's the last weekend of June, so save the date. I know that's soon, and I have a ton of planning to do for it, but I think it'll be great." Could she really pull this off in two months? God, she hoped so. "I've reached out to some people I know who've done a lot of these, and I have some breakfast and coffee meetings this week to ask them a bunch of questions." Luke and Finn walked over just then and joined them. "I'm hoping we can get some work done on the lawn and the rest of the property before the party. If you know any good landscapers, let me know."

"Actually," Luke said. "I might know someone."

Margot glanced at him. For the past few days, she'd tried to avoid doing that for longer than a few seconds. It had been less awkward between them, yes, but still, if she looked at Luke for too long, her mind went to places it shouldn't go when she was at work. And looking at her employee.

Places like the way his fingers had felt on her skin; the way he'd looked at her after he'd kissed her in his apartment for the first time, so full of heat; the way he'd laughed with her and then rolled on top of her; the way he'd . . . She snapped herself back to the present.

"Really?" she asked. "You know a landscaper? Here?"

He nodded.

"My mom's partner. Pete Smythe. Give him a call—tell him I sent you."

"Will do," she said. "Thanks, Luke."

Taylor took a sip of wine and turned to Luke.

"So you've never said what made you leave one of the biggest companies in Silicon Valley—if not the world—and move to Napa to work in a tasting room," she said to him.

Margot wanted to know the answer to this question, too. She knew that he used to work in tech, obviously, from the hoodie he'd been wearing that night at the bar, but because she'd so stupidly closed off all conversation about work, she had no idea why he'd left. She knew he'd grown up here in Napa, but that was about all. At the bar he hadn't talked in much detail about why he'd come back here—he hadn't seemed to want to, and it wasn't like she was going to press a stranger at a bar to talk about something they didn't want to talk about. But now, she was so curious about him. She wondered if he would blow off Taylor's question; she wouldn't blame him if he did.

But he took a sip of wine and considered it.

"Mostly I was tired of being one of the only Black people in the whole place. And I was really tired of all the bullshit," he said.

Margot and Taylor both burst out laughing. Luke looked on with a surprised grin on his face.

Margot lifted her glass to him.

"Well, congratulations," she said. "I think—I hope—we have a lot less bullshit here. And I'm sure we have a much higher percentage of Black people here."

Their eyes met again as he touched his glass to hers, and a shiver went down her spine. The way he looked at her, all warm and intent like that . . . she could really fucking get used to that. *Damn it.*

"Thank you." His voice was low. He could have said that in a joking way, to make this whole conversation feel less serious, less real, but he didn't. He seemed pleased that she'd congratulated him. "And I know you do. You might even come out on top on sheer numbers."

They both laughed.

Why were they standing so close? When he'd come over here, Luke had been on the far side of Taylor, she was sure of it. But now he was right next to her, so close they were almost touching. She hadn't even noticed him move. Or had she?

She made herself walk away to get some food. For the rest of the night, as she circulated and sipped wine and chatted and took photos, she forced herself not to turn in Luke's direction. She'd already looked at him too much while she was talking to him and Taylor—she'd probably spent too long with them as it was. She had to keep it strictly professional between the two of them. Especially around Elliot.

At the end of the night, she made a little speech to the whole group about how much she and Elliot appreciated all of them, after which everyone applauded, and then Elliot said, "Yeah, what Margot said," which made everyone laugh as the party broke up.

The prearranged cars showed up to shuttle everyone home, grouped by the city they lived in. Taylor and Finn were both in St. Helena, Daisy and Marisol were down in Vallejo, and . . . oh no. She should have thought of this.

"Margot, you and Luke are both in Napa," Taylor said. *Damn damn damn.* She should have said she was staying at the winery to do more work and would get a ride home later, but it was too late now. If she tried to make up an excuse not to share a ride with Luke back down to Napa, it would too obviously look like she was avoiding him, especially since she'd had no time to plan this.

"Great," she said. She glanced over at Luke and tried to make the look on her face as *benevolent boss* as she could manage. "Let me just make sure everyone else gets off okay and then we can go."

He nodded as she turned away, wishing she could go hide in the basement. *Gets off? Really, Margot? Did you really need to imply that you get all of your employees off?* If her cheeks were red, she hoped everyone blamed all the wine, even though she'd been careful to drink no more than a sip or two from each glass. She couldn't be the drunk boss, or even the tipsy boss. She was already the boss who'd accidentally fucked one of her employees—she couldn't take it further than that.

She made sure everyone was in their cars, texted Elliot that she was leaving—he'd already disappeared back into the barn; see, he had the right idea—and then gave Luke a bright smile.

"Ready?"

Luke opened the back door of the car as an answer, and she

got inside. He walked around the car and got in the other door, and the driver looked back at Margot.

"Going to the same place?"

"No!" she blurted out. She took a deep breath. "Um, I mean, I'm on Washington Street, and— Luke?"

She could see Luke's grin in the dark, but he didn't let the amusement show in his voice when he gave the driver his address. The car pulled out onto the road, and they drove in silence for a few minutes.

"I could easily have been insulted by that 'NO,'" Luke murmured.

Margot couldn't help but smile, but she didn't let herself look at him.

"But you weren't," she said.

"No," he said. "I wasn't."

———

THEY WERE SILENT FOR a few minutes, but it wasn't the awkward silence from when they'd first gotten in the car. He tried not to look at her, like he'd been trying all night. But like he'd done all night, he failed.

This would all be easier if he weren't more and more attracted to her every day. Their night together kept coming back to him at odd moments—the look on her face when he'd kissed her against the door of his apartment; the way they'd laughed together at the bar; that low, almost guttural moan she'd made when he'd brushed his thumb over her nipples in the morning; that soft, clinging kiss goodbye when he'd driven her home; that kiss that had made him want so much more.

Damn it. And now he wanted her even more. The way she'd made those speeches to the staff tonight that got everyone laughing; when she'd had that long conversation with Elliot's assistant, Finn, who Luke had thought didn't actually speak to anyone; the way she'd ordered everyone at the winery around, sometimes directly, sometimes in a way they didn't quite notice. He always did, though. And the contrast between how soft and pliable she'd been in his arms that night, and how firm and steely she could be at work . . . God, it made him want her so much it was all he could do not to reach for her right now, while they were alone, in the back seat of this dark car.

"I understood what you meant," she said, startling him. "About your old job, I mean. Being sick of all the bullshit. And being sick of being one of the only ones. My last job—before I came to Noble, I mean—was like that. I felt . . . Well, I know how it feels, to get out of a place like that."

He could tell she really did understand.

"Yeah," he said. "I didn't realize it was bullshit at first. When I started, I bought into all of it, you know. I went there straight from Stanford, I felt like one of the chosen ones, I absorbed the whole mindset, not just of the company, but that whole Silicon Valley ethos. About, like, grit and whatever, how tech was better than anything else, how we were changing the world." He rolled his eyes. "Do you know the number of times I've seen some pasty dude in a hoodie—or sometimes a fleece—declare he was changing the world? Thousands, I'm sure."

She laughed.

"I'm sure," she said.

He shook his head.

"And it's not like I'm not used to being the only one—I grew up here, after all. But it was different there. The week before I quit, my boss made a crack at a meeting about a neighborhood where I'd met a friend for lunch that day. 'Look at you, making a trip to the ghetto! I've always wanted to go to that place—if I go, I'll have to take you with me for safety!'"

"Wow," Margot said. "Is that why you quit?"

He shrugged.

"That played a role, yeah." That was partly true, he supposed.

"I know how working at a place like that can be," she said. "It's demoralizing."

He'd told her only a tiny piece of the story. But she'd gotten that right.

"Yeah," he said. "Demoralizing is exactly the right word. For . . . so much that happened there." He laughed. "At least I managed not to quit until after the bulk of my options vested."

She turned, then, to face him, though he could barely see her eyes in the dark.

"I'm glad you got out," she said. "I'm also glad you waited until your options vested, for your own sake."

He grinned.

"It means that now I have the freedom to do things like this." He gestured to the vineyards lining the road.

Which was both true and not true. He had a lot of money saved up, he probably didn't have to get any kind of job for at least a year if he was careful. He could do things like sublet his old place, move back to Napa, get a job working at a winery. But he still felt guilty, embarrassed, about what he'd done. And hadn't done.

"Why this?" she asked. "Not just why Noble, but why any winery job, when you could be doing anything at all?" She sat back against the seat. "I understand if you don't want to answer that, I am your boss, but I truly don't mind whatever your answer is."

He shrugged. "Mostly, it was just an impulse. My best friend convinced me to move back up here, for kind of a break, while I figure out what to do next, but once I got to Napa, I realized I'd be bored as hell here without something to do all day. I've always been interested in wine, the science of it kind of fascinates me, so it felt like a fun option. And—please forgive me for this—I thought working at a winery would be easy. Don't worry, I no longer think that."

She laughed. "What did it for you, that bachelorette party on Thursday, or the eight cases of wine you had to load into a Honda Civic on Friday?"

He shook his head.

"Neither of those things—finding all of those bottles on Tuesday! Taylor just pulled them out, like they're color coded or something, where I had to read labels and try to remember vintages and varietals and . . . this is a lot harder than I thought."

Margot laughed again. Fuck, he needed to stop making her laugh. That low, throaty laugh of hers did things to him. It made him feel like it was a private laugh, just for him. That laugh of hers had been one of the things that had first drawn him to her at the bar that night. He had to stop thinking about that night.

"Can I tell you a secret?" she said to him.

"Always," he said. He shouldn't have said that, but he couldn't help it. Luckily, she didn't really react.

"It's a lot harder than I thought it would be, too," she said. "The stuff you do, I mean—the stuff we do, I guess. The business stuff I knew would be hard, I was prepared for that, and the wine stuff—even though I'm not that involved in it, I know some about it just because of Elliot, though a lot of it is still a mystery to me. But I figured the tasting room stuff, the customers, the tours, all of that, I figured it would be easy. How hard could it be, just serving some wine to some tourists who want to spend their money? The answer is: very."

"Very!" he said, and this time they both laughed.

"Thank you for telling me that," he said. "I was feeling kind of like an asshole—I grew up here, I should have known that nothing about this business was easy. But I always thought of the winery people as the rich people, you know? It all seemed so snooty. I thought they had an easy life. I was wrong about that, too."

He was glad they were talking in this normal, relaxed way with each other. At work, after that first day, it hadn't been awkward between them, but it had been almost worse. Margot had looked at him, talked to him, like he was anyone else in the winery. She'd smiled easily, she'd been businesslike and matter-of-fact, she'd looked neither at him nor away from him in a way that would seem unusual. He'd hated it. It wasn't like he wanted her to be unprofessional or anything like that—he'd just wanted some sign that she thought about him like he thought about her.

He wasn't exactly getting that tonight, but at least right now she was being casual with him, relaxed. She was laughing in that way she'd laughed at the bar, and not the more cheerful, less sexy laugh she gave customers.

"You weren't totally wrong about that," she said. "Some of them are definitely snooty. Especially the big, very expensive ones. Most of us, though, are just small businesses, where our product happens to be something people imbue with all of those elite markers. I'm happy to do it sometimes, too, when it gets Noble where I want us to be, but I do have to remember most of it is bullshit. People have been drinking wine since the beginning of time! Literally! It's great, don't get me wrong—I love wine and I love our winery. But still."

The car stopped with a jerk, and Luke looked away from Margot for the first time since they'd gotten in the car.

"Oh," he said. "We're at my place."

She looked out the window, too.

"So we are." She didn't sound embarrassed at that—was he glad about that? He wasn't sure. She didn't sound anything. He wished she'd sounded something.

He opened his door.

"Well, good night, Margot. See you tomorrow."

Did she remember that this time last week, they were sitting next to each other at the bar, her leg pressed snugly against his, just hours from that kiss outside, and then that electric walk back to his place, and then . . .

"Good night, Luke," she said quietly.

The car drove away as soon as he got out. He stared after it for a few seconds before he sighed and went inside.

Seven

"YOU DROVE HOME ALONE with him?!" Sydney said. "Was that really the smartest thing to do?"

Margot took a sip of her martini and sighed.

"No, of course it wasn't the smartest thing to do," she said. "But I'd left it to Taylor to organize getting the cars to take everyone home, and I forgot—or, maybe, didn't even realize—that we were the only two people who live in Napa. And by the time I realized it, it was too late. What was I supposed to do, say 'Oh, guys, I can't be alone in a car with Luke—exactly a week ago, I slept with him, you see, and I'm still wildly attracted to him, no matter how much I try not to be, and I'm afraid I might jump him in the back seat of this car'?"

"Well, at least you didn't jump him in the back seat of the car." Sydney grinned as she picked up her negroni.

Margot looked around. It was Monday night, Sydney's night off, and they'd gone to a restaurant they both liked, up in St. Helena. They were sitting along the wall, by the window, with no one around them. She was sure they would run into someone they knew there; they always did. But at least no one could over-hear them for now.

"Yes, thank God for that. But . . . honestly, it was almost as bad, Syd. Okay, no, obviously not anywhere near just as bad, but like, we talked the whole way home. We lost track of time, talk-ing. Like we did at the bar that night, but even more so, because now we know each other better. It was . . . bad. I need to make sure I'm never in a car alone with him again."

Sydney raised an eyebrow. "You just . . . talked? That's what was so bad?"

"Yes!" Margot realized, by a few turned heads, that she was just slightly too vehement. She lowered her voice. "Sydney. I like him. That's dangerous. I'd forgotten that part. I'd just remem-bered the sex, and how great it was, and how much fun we had, but like, I've had great sex before. I figured I'd make myself find someone else to sleep with, get him out of my system, and every-thing between us would be no big deal. But I forgot that part of the reason—probably, the whole reason—I went home with him in the first place was because I liked him. And the more time I spend with him, the more I like him. It sucks!"

"Well . . . you could still fire him, so you can go out with him?" Margot rolled her eyes, and Sydney laughed. "Kidding. You could hope he quits?"

Margot sighed.

"He will eventually, of course—he's only in Napa Valley for a few months, he told me so at the bar that night. But that means that when he quits it will be because he's leaving town, so that doesn't really advance my cause." She took another sip of her drink. "I don't even know why I'm talking like this—it's not like the two of us would eventually ever really date. He's far too young for me, first of all. This is just a very unfortunate crush I have on someone who happens to be one of my employees. Like all crushes, I'm sure it'll go away as soon as I find out more about him. He's probably a jerk to waiters or a troll to women online, or tells women he likes them better without makeup, or something."

Their server set their appetizers down in front of them, and Sydney divided their salad onto two plates.

"Yeah, I'm sure you'll get bored by him if you know him better," she said. "What was it like at work today?"

Margot shrugged.

"Fine, normal. We were totally civil, even friendly. I tried not to react too much when he made me laugh. He's really good at the job, though—totally charmed a group of retired women who had an early-afternoon appointment, they stayed for hours and bought a case of wine between the three of them. Taylor told me that. She likes him, too."

Margot looked at the expression on Sydney's face.

"I know what you're going to say—I didn't ask her about him, she volunteered it! She likes Marisol, the other new person, too; although she's not as good with the customers, she's great with learning the wines and inventory and stuff. But Taylor thinks she'll get there with the customer service."

Sydney scooped some burrata onto a piece of bread.

"That's great, but unless you also slept with Marisol the night before she started her job, I don't really care how much Taylor likes her."

Margot dissolved into giggles. This was why she kept Sydney around—she could make even the worst things funny.

"I did not, thanks for asking. She *is* my type, but don't worry—I will now never have sex with anyone before finding out exactly where they work. Maybe even where they might hope to work sometime in the future."

Sydney lifted her glass.

"I'll toast to that. But I also think your idea of sleeping with someone else and getting this guy out of your system is a good one. And don't worry—I'm sure he'll show his asshole side at work soon. Men always do."

Sydney was almost certainly right about that. She was definitely kind of a misanthrope, after years of working in, and now owning, restaurants, but many of her pessimistic pronouncements about men had proved themselves to be correct.

"Good point," Margot said. "Anyway, enough about me— How's the restaurant been this week? Sorry I haven't been by—between trying to figure out some initial details for this anniversary party and all of the other winery stuff, I've been swamped."

"Don't worry about it—you aren't obligated to come in to test our new recipes, you know."

Margot grinned at her.

"I know, but your chef trusts my palate more than anyone else."

Sydney sighed.

"Unfortunately for your ego, that is correct. But to answer your question, things have been good this week—for the past month, really. Business is looking up."

"Really?" Margot asked. She knew how touch and go the last year had been for Sydney. "Oh, Syd, I'm so glad."

The proud, relieved expression on Sydney's face made Margot so happy.

"Yeah," Sydney said. "Me, too."

They clinked their glasses and grinned at each other.

"How are plans for the party going?" Sydney asked. "I can't

believe you managed to convince your brother that it was a good idea."

"He doesn't quite think it's a good idea, but he's at least resigned to it now." Margot made a face. "I think."

"He'd better be," Sydney said. "Obviously, you know we're in, right, to do some food for the party? Just let me know what your budget is and Charlie will come up with a great snack to serve."

She could always count on Sydney.

"Thanks. I really appreciate it. I'll get you numbers this week so you two can plan."

The server came over to clear their appetizer plates, when something made Margot look up.

"What is it?" Sydney asked.

Margot shook her head.

"Nothing. I . . . Nothing." She must really be around the bend if she was hearing Luke's voice out of the blue. Plenty of men had voices that sounded like his.

"Oh, and speaking of the party . . ."

Her voice trailed away. The hostess was walking toward her. And behind the hostess, obviously going to their own cozy table for two, were Luke and a woman. Clearly on a date.

Shit, this wasn't just *a* woman. This was Avery Jensen, an event planner Margot knew casually and was supposed to have breakfast with later this week to ask her questions about details for the party. Oh God.

"Margot?" Sydney said.

Margot didn't have time to warn Sydney. Luke would notice her any second. She just had to trust in Sydney's poker face.

Yep, there it was. He saw her.

"Margot, hi," he said. He and Avery stopped in front of their table.

"Hi, Luke," she said, in what she was surprised to hear was a normal voice.

"I . . . um, how are you?" he asked. "Having dinner?"

He was already fucking going on dates? And with someone she knew? See, she should have done that, instead of making excuses about work.

"Yeah, I love this place," she said. "And hi, Avery, good to see you. Looking forward to our breakfast later this week."

Luke turned to Avery for a half second. Margot could see the *You know each other?* question on his face, but he didn't ask it.

"Hey, Margot, me, too. And hi, Sydney," Avery said. "How are you guys?"

Margot smiled. At least, she hoped she did.

"Oh, good!" She gestured to Sydney. "Luke, my friend Sydney, she's a local restaurateur. Sydney, this is Luke Williams, he's one of our new tasting room staff at Noble."

Sydney gave Luke a very bland smile, and Luke smiled back. Did he recognize her from the restaurant that night? Margot couldn't tell.

"Hi, Luke," Sydney said. "And hey, Avery."

"Hi, Sydney. Nice to meet you," Luke said. He—very slightly—raised his eyebrows at Margot. Okay, maybe he did recognize Sydney.

Damn it, why was he giving her secret little eyebrow raises when he was on a date with another woman? She tried not to let her expression change.

"Are you—" Luke started, but just then, their server came over with their entrées.

"Oh! I'm sorry, are your friends joining you?"

"No," Margot said, she hoped not too sharply. "Thank you."

Luke took a step back.

"We shouldn't keep you. I, um— See you tomorrow, Margot. Nice to meet you, Sydney."

Margot nodded, and tried not to look at him.

"Yeah, see you tomorrow. Talk to you soon, Avery."

They walked away, presumably to another table, though Margot forced herself not to turn her head to see where they were, and just concentrated on the steak in front of her.

"Okay," Sydney said after about thirty seconds. "They're out of earshot."

Margot's head shot up.

"Are you sure? Like, positive?"

Sydney nodded.

"I mean, if you start shouting again, then no, but yes, we can carry on a low conversation about what the fuck just happened without them hearing us."

Margot took a gulp of her drink.

"Great, because what the fuck just happened, Syd? Did my employee, who I—accidentally—slept with, and now can't fucking stop thinking about, much to my dismay, just walk in here on a motherfucking date? With Avery Jensen, of all people?"

Sydney cut a scallop in half.

"Yes to all of those things, but why 'of all people'? I thought you liked Avery?"

Margot cut into her steak, probably more vehemently than the steak deserved.

"I do like her! She's great! She's also young and skinny and has gorgeous hair and probably perfect perky boobs, all things I do not!"

Sydney paused, her scallop halfway to her mouth.

"Hey. You have great boobs. And fantastic hair."

Margot rolled her eyes.

"Yes, when I work at it. Avery has that effortless sun-kissed-curls thing going on. When I try that, I just look bedraggled." She grimaced. "See? I should have tried to go out on dates to get him out of my head! I should go pick up a stranger at a bar, or something, and make it even better than last time, so I know the magic is in me, not fucking Luke Williams."

"In a manner of speaking," Sydney said.

Margot glared at her.

"I didn't say anything," Sydney said.

"That's what I thought," Margot said.

Margot stabbed her steak again.

"You know it's killing me that my back is to them, right?"

"Oh, I know," Sydney said. "You're doing great at not turning around, though. I'm really impressed."

"Thank you. I appreciate that." Then suddenly she grinned, and Sydney grinned back at her. And then they both started laughing.

"Only me," Margot said, when they finally subsided.

Sydney shook her head.

"Oh God no, definitely not. Do you know how small Napa Valley is? Things like this happen all the time. Everyone knows each other."

Margot sighed.

"I know. Did I tell you . . . when he kissed me, outside the Barrel that night, that's what I told him—that we couldn't do that there, that too many people know me."

Sydney laughed again.

"Well, that's both absolutely true and a very slick way to invite yourself back to his bed."

Margot shook her head.

"No, no, I would have invited him back to mine, but his place was closer!"

And then they cracked up again.

"'HAVING DINNER?' DID I really say 'having dinner' like that?" Luke asked Avery.

She nodded, a huge grin on her face.

"You did indeed."

"Why would I ask that question? Like it's not completely obvious they're having dinner, when they're at a restaurant table at seven thirty p.m.? What else would they be doing? Plotting to overthrow the government? Baking a cake? Watching a movie? What is wrong with me?"

Luke glanced over at Margot and Sydney's table. They were diagonal from them in the restaurant, but Margot's back was to him. From the look on Sydney's face, though, they were having a great time.

"Nothing's wrong with you," Avery said. "You were just a little taken aback, that's all, by running into your boss outside the office."

Luke glared at her.

"Okay, fine, you were a little taken aback by running into your boss who you slept with the night before she became your boss outside your office. Better?"

"And that same morning, too," Luke muttered.

Avery made a face.

"Please, no more details. But you recovered from it quickly!"

He absolutely had not. He still wasn't recovered from it, as a matter of fact. Because not only did he have to deal with the shock of seeing Margot, he'd also quickly recognized that Sydney had been the bartender at the Barrel that night. She must own it; that must be what Margot had meant by *local restaurateur*.

But also . . .

"When were you going to tell me that you and Margot were meeting for breakfast? I didn't even know that you two knew each other," he said. He tried to keep his voice casual, but by the way her eyes swooped up from the menu, he'd clearly failed.

"Everyone up here knows each other, you know that," she said, a little defensively.

He just looked at her.

"Okay, fine, yes, I should have told you I actually know her, but I didn't want you to be self-conscious or think I was going to say something to her. We're not, like, friends or anything, but . . . friendly acquaintances, let's say."

"Friendly acquaintances who have breakfast together?"

"It's a work breakfast! She wants to get some advice for that anniversary party Noble is going to have, get some event planning tips, that's all." Avery grinned again. "It's too bad I don't know Sydney well enough to bond with her over how both awkward and hilarious it was to be with two people who desperately want each other and are also desperately trying to pretend they don't."

Luke's head shot up.

"What do you mean, 'two people'?"

The waiter came over just then to take their drink order, while Luke stared at Avery. She glanced at the menu like she hadn't just said something impossible to him.

"I'll have the Brown Sauvignon Blanc. Luke?"

He very much did not want to make any decision about wine right now.

"Yeah, sure. Me, too."

As soon as the waiter walked away, he asked again.

"What do you mean, 'two people'?"

Avery rolled her eyes at him.

"Oh please, you're not going to try to pretend that you aren't still completely hot for Margot, are you? That was obvious to everyone in the restaurant."

He didn't think it had been *that* obvious, but he'd let it slide for the moment.

"No, I'm not saying that. What I'm saying is that it's obvious to me that she doesn't feel the same way."

Avery laughed. He couldn't believe she was laughing at him now. Actually, no, of course he could believe it.

"You are one of the smartest people—if not the smartest—I know, and yet you sit here and say something so silly to me? And with a straight face? Come on." She took her glass of wine from the server while Luke stared at her. "That breakfast is going to be very awkward now, after Margot saw us on what very much looks like a date tonight."

Luke looked over at Margot's table. Neither she nor Sydney seemed to be interested in anything other than their own conversation.

"We clearly aren't on a date, but Margot wouldn't care about that. Margot could not care less about me, other than my value to Noble Family Vineyards. I mean sure, she likes me fine, but it's all business with her. Other than a few tiny things—which are clearly just her being paranoid that someone will find out, or feeling awkward about this whole situation—she treats me like I'm any employee."

Luke looked again. Margot was laughing, her head thrown back. He could hear her laugh even over the music in the restaurant and the din of all of the voices.

Avery narrowed her eyes at him.

"Okay, *first* of all, aren't we supposed to be pretending that we're dating?"

Right. He'd forgotten about that.

"Only my mom would believe that the two of us were dating," he said.

Margot couldn't have thought that. Could she?

"No one who *knew* us—other than your mom—would think that, but Margot doesn't know us. And please, that woman so has the hots for you. I saw the way she looked at me, right at first, before she recognized me. That was not an *Oh, my new employee is here, that's nice* look. That was a *I can't believe this motherfucker is on a date with this bitch* look. Don't get me wrong, I respect that. And then she was so extra gracious to you. Obviously, it's because she can't let you know how she wishes she was at this table with you right now, but I promise you, that's exactly what she wishes."

Luke dropped the menu that he'd been gripping since they sat down and stared at Avery. Then he shook his head.

"I know you're just saying that to make me feel better, but please don't bullshit me here," he said.

Avery laughed at him.

"Oh God, you have it bad, don't you? But I'm not bullshitting you." She looked around, and then lowered her voice. "Margot Noble does not have normal boss-employee feelings for you, that much was *very* clear to me."

Could Avery be right? Luke thought about the night before in the car, their warm, friendly conversation. Their completely-devoid-of-flirting conversation. There had been that moment at the beginning, when they'd gotten in the car, sure, but that had just been a shared joke. After that, there had been no undercurrents, no significant eye contact, not even when they'd pulled up in front of his building, the one she'd walked into with him almost exactly a week before.

He shook his head.

"You're wrong. She doesn't act like that to me at all. She's just friendly, professional, like she was tonight. There's never any sign from her that anything ever happened between us."

Or could ever in the future. Unfortunately.

"Luke. You were too busy being in shock that she was right there in front of you to see the way she looked at us when she noticed us. She *definitely* thinks we're on a date, and she's *definitely* pissed about it." Avery raised an eyebrow at him. "Do you want her to keep thinking that? I'll pretend for Margot, as well as your mom, if you want."

He didn't even have to think about it.

"No." He sighed. "Not like it matters, she's made that very clear, but . . . still no."

"That's what I thought." Avery picked up her wineglass. "See, Luke, this is why I adore you. Some men would want her to think that, to make her jealous, make her more interested, or whatever. You've never been like that."

A genuine compliment like this from Avery was rare. She usually just made fun of him. Her breakup had clearly had an effect on her. Speaking of.

"Enough about me. How are you doing?"

Avery flashed him a smile.

"I'm fine."

"No, really," he said. "How are you?"

She picked up her menu.

"I'm fine. Really." Okay, she obviously didn't want to talk about it. That was like Avery. He wouldn't push her.

"Okay, how's work going?" he tried.

Avery perked up, like he knew she would.

"Really well, actually. Things have gotten so busy I might have to hire my own assistant. And speaking of your mom, she sent me a couple who got engaged at the inn—I don't do a ton of weddings these days, but they were so nice that I couldn't say no to them."

"Oh, that's great," he said. "I'll tell her that."

Avery smirked.

"Oh, I can tell her that, in my new role as your fake girl-friend." She took a sip of her wine. "And don't worry: when I meet Margot for breakfast, I'll make it clear to *her* that you and I are just friends and were definitely not on a date tonight."

He did not want Avery discussing him with Margot.

"Please don't," he said.

"But you said you didn't want Margot to think we were dating!"

He never should have said that.

"I don't, but—"

"Well, I'll make sure she doesn't."

If Margot knew he'd told Avery about the two of them, she'd be furious.

"Avery—"

She waved a hand in the air.

"I swear, I won't drop the slightest hint that I know what hap-pened between the two of you, okay? I will just casually mention that you're an old friend from high school, make it clear you and I could not be less interested in one another."

Luke looked over at Margot and Sydney's table. They were laughing again.

"There's nothing I can say to keep you from doing this, is there?"

Avery grinned at him. He didn't like that grin at all.

"Absolutely nothing, no." She picked up her glass of wine. "It's very funny to me that I have to make it clear to your mom that we *are* dating, but also make it clear to your boss that we are *not* dating." She rubbed her hands together. "This is going to be fun."

He dropped his face into his hands.

"Fun at my expense, you mean," he said.

"My favorite kind," Avery said.

Eight

THURSDAY MORNING, MARGOT DROVE over to the upscale bakery/café where she was meeting Avery for breakfast. She was very glad she'd had lots of experience forcing a warm professional smile onto her face at all times, because she still couldn't fucking believe she had to have breakfast with Avery a few days after she'd seen her on a date with Luke.

"It's not like you're dating him," she reminded herself out loud in the car, for the twentieth or so time. "Or that you were ever dating him. You don't even want to date him! He's too young for you, remember? And he's leaving Napa Valley in a few months, he told you that. And even if he wasn't, I'm sure he wouldn't want anything serious—guys like him never do. And I don't know why you're even saying any of this to yourself because he is your employee!"

She let out a long sigh, pulled into a parking space, and touched up her lipstick. Sure, she wasn't dating and couldn't date Luke Williams, but if she had to see his new girlfriend or whatever right after she'd seen them on a date together, she was at least going to look fantastic.

She walked into the bakery and looked around. Avery wasn't there yet. Maybe she'd forgotten about their breakfast date. Maybe Luke had distracted her. Maybe she was in bed with him right now. *Oh God, stop it, Margot, what is wrong with you?*

She went up to look at the display case, but heard her name a few seconds later. Avery walked up to her, a smile on her face.

"Hi, Margot, there you are. I highly recommend their apricot croissant if you haven't had it yet this spring."

Margot smiled at her.

"I haven't, but I'm a real sucker for their ham and cheese croissant. I think I have it every time I come here." She looked back at the bakery case. "Let me get one of the apricot ones for my brother, he loves those." She waved toward the case. "Is that what you want? This is on me, you're doing me a favor here."

"Oh, I'm happy to help, but if you insist, yes, an apricot croissant and a large coffee," Avery said. She glanced around the room. "I'll grab us a table while you order."

When she got to the front of the line, Margot ordered the pastries and their coffees. She really *did* appreciate Avery taking the time to talk to her, even though she wished they'd done this before she'd seen Avery and Luke together. Avery had been doing event planning for years—first with a local wedding planner, then bigger corporate events, many of which were at wineries. If Margot could have afforded to hire Avery to plan the party, she would have, but she was doing it all herself, so she was trying to glean all of the information she could about how to do this right. Avery didn't have to take time out of her schedule to give Margot advice.

Damn it.

Margot caught Avery's eye when she brought their coffee over to the milk station, and Avery shook her head at the milk, but nodded at the sugar, so Margot brought a few packets over to the table, after she stirred some milk into her own coffee.

"Thanks again for meeting me this morning," Margot said when she sat down. She pulled out the new notebook that she'd designated as The Notebook for this event. "I'm really excited about this event, but I have to admit that I'm starting to feel a little in over my head."

Avery laughed.

"Oh, that happens to me every time, but don't worry, you have lots of time. All you really need is to have obsessively organized spreadsheets, and this will go great."

"Avery, that's music to my ears," Margot said. "If there's one thing I know how to do, it's obsessively organize spreadsheets."

They both laughed, and then got down to details.

"Okay, so that's all of the most important stuff," Avery said, thirty minutes later. "I'm sure I'll think of other things, but like I said, the key is hyperorganization leading up to the event, and then flexibility on the day of, because everything is going to go a little sideways."

Margot looked up from her notebook.

"This has all been invaluable, thanks so much. Thank goodness for the great community here—between this info from you, the Barrel jumping in already to be one of the food stations, and then hopefully finding a landscaper through someone on my team at the tasting room, I'm starting to feel like we might be able to pull this off."

Avery grinned.

"Oh, did Luke hook you up with Pete?"

Shit. She shouldn't have made a reference to anything having to do with Luke. In her defense, this last hour had been so all about business that she'd almost forgotten about Luke and Avery.

Also, apparently he and Avery had been dating long enough that she was on a first-name basis with his mom's boyfriend. Great.

"Pete Smythe? Yeah, he's coming by the winery later today," Margot said. Time to move the conversation away from Luke. "The party is a good excuse to do this landscaping, I just hope we have time."

Avery took a sip of her coffee.

"I'm sure Pete will be able to get it done for you. He's great— I've known him forever. Luke and I went to high school together, you know."

No, of course she didn't know.

"Oh wow, really? What a small world this place is," Margot said. What else could she say?

"Isn't it?" Avery took another sip of her coffee. Wasn't it cold by now? Didn't she need to be somewhere? But no, she looked perfectly comfortable, like she was settling in for a nice chat. "Luke's great. He's been one of my best friends since we were teenagers. He's like a brother to me." She laughed. "We dated very briefly when we were fourteen, but quickly realized we were much better as friends."

Wait. Did that mean that Monday night hadn't been a date?

"I bet you're glad to have him back up here," Margot said.

Avery nodded.

"Yeah. I had kind of a bad breakup recently, and he helped me move to my new place."

Oh.

It hadn't been a date, then. Margot forced her expression not to change.

"I'm sorry to hear about your breakup," Margot said.

Avery looked sad for a moment.

"Thanks." She sat up straight and smiled. "I'm glad I have Luke. He's a good friend."

Margot took a sip of her own now-cold coffee. Did Avery know about what happened between her and Luke? It didn't seem like it. She hadn't given her that smile last night that said she knew, and there was no knowing glance today. But maybe she just didn't want to make it awkward?

"He's been a great addition to the tasting room staff," Margot said as casually as she knew how. "Even Elliot thinks he's worthy of discussing his wines, and you know how winemakers can be."

They both laughed, and Margot reached for the bag of pastries on the table and dropped it into her tote bag.

"Speaking of Elliot, I should get to the winery."

Avery stood up.

"Yeah, I should get going, too. But seriously, Margot—let me know if you have any other questions. Just text or call."

Margot nodded.

"I will almost certainly take you up on that. And let me know if I can ever return the favor."

They hugged goodbye at the door of the bakery, and then Margot walked to her car. It wasn't until she was a mile into the drive to the winery that she allowed a huge smile to break out over her face.

"I don't know what you're smiling like that for," she said to herself. "It's not like this means anything. It doesn't matter that he wasn't on a date with Avery—he's still your employee, remember? You still can't do one single thing with that man."

But the smile stayed on her face for the whole drive.

LUKE GLANCED DOWN AT his phone when he got in the car to drive to the winery on Thursday morning.

AVERY

Mission accomplished

That was all Avery was going to tell him? Of course it was. He wanted to ask for details, but he couldn't give her the satisfaction.

He couldn't believe that he'd let Avery "make it clear" to Margot they weren't dating. Wasn't he supposed to be pretending that he and Avery *were* dating, in order to get his mom off his back? What had he been thinking?

He'd been thinking that he wanted Margot to know he wasn't dating anyone, no matter how pointless it was.

Luke pulled into the parking lot at the winery and saw Pete's truck there. Right. Today was the day that Pete was coming by to meet with Margot and Elliot.

Pete got out of the truck just as Luke walked by.

"Morning, Luke." He handed him a paper bag. "Your mom gave me this to give to you if I saw you here, and by that she meant I'd better find a way to see you here and give you that, so I'm glad you made it easy."

Luke laughed at that. He peeked into the bag to see two sticky buns, and his smile got wider.

"Thank her for me, please," he said. "If I had known that moving back to Napa meant getting surprise pastry deliveries, I might have moved back years ago." He and Pete walked toward the front door of the winery. "And thanks for making the time to come by here."

Pete shrugged.

"It's no problem. Glad to be able to give you some brownie points, not that you need them, I'm sure." That was debatable.

Luke opened the door for both of them. Taylor was already inside the tasting room.

"Hey," he said to her. "This is Pete Smythe—he has an appointment with Margot and Elliot this morning."

"I'll buzz Margot," Taylor said, but before she could pick up the phone, Margot and Elliot both walked into the tasting room through the front door, laughing about something. Margot had on jeans, boots, and a big sweater, and Luke smiled at the sight of her. She was usually more dressed up than this. He liked those dresses she always wore, but he liked casual Margot, too. But then he'd really liked her in nothing at all.

Fuck. He had to stop thinking about that.

"Hi, Margot and Elliot—this is Pete Smythe, the landscaper I was telling you guys about. I used to work for him, a long time ago, but don't hold that against him."

Margot and Elliot—and Pete—all laughed, and there was a whole round of handshakes.

"Thanks for coming by, Pete," Elliot said. "Why don't we walk you around the property, and you can let us know if you'll be able to execute my sister's vision."

Margot glanced quickly at her brother. She looked irritated, for just a second, before she turned to smile at Pete again.

"Elliot, if you're busy, I can handle this," she said.

Elliot shook his head.

"Oh no, wouldn't miss it."

There was weird tension there. Luke took a step away, but Elliot stopped him.

"Luke, care to join us? That is, if you can spare him in the tasting room, Margot and Taylor? It could be useful to have him as a translator here, since he's done this kind of work before."

Luke looked at Margot. She opened her mouth, he was sure to object, to tell him to stay back in the tasting room with Taylor, but then Taylor piped up behind him.

"It's no problem—I don't need him for the next thirty minutes or so."

Margot smiled at Taylor, and then at him.

"Then let's all go," she said.

No matter what Avery had said to Margot this morning, Avery was definitely wrong about how Margot felt about him. She didn't seem to care one way or another if he was around.

Margot led the way with Pete, while Luke walked along next to Elliot.

"So, you used to work for Pete?" Elliot asked. "You've stayed in touch?"

Luke laughed.

"I worked for him in high school, yeah. But also, right when I graduated from high school, he started dating my mom, and they've been together ever since." He glanced over at Elliot. "So yeah, you could say we've stayed in touch."

Elliot let out a short bark of a laugh.

"That's definitely one reason for staying in touch. And that explains how you were able to get him to return a phone call so quickly."

"Well, also because he likes you guys," Luke said. "He told me you treat your workers well. He wouldn't have come today if he didn't know that about you, no matter how long he'd been with my mom."

Elliot looked embarrassed.

"Well. We don't do anything out of the ordinary. At least, anything that should be out of the ordinary. But I appreciate you saying that." He cleared his throat. "And I hope everything for you so far at Noble has been good?"

Other than how he couldn't keep his eyes off the Noble co-owner, just a few feet up ahead of them, looking really good in those jeans and clearly charming the hell out of Pete?

Though . . . she seemed tense. Was it because he was there? Or was there another reason?

"Everything's been great," he said. "Still settling in some, and figuring out the wines, but those are good lessons to have to learn."

Elliot perked up.

"You know, if you ever want to come by the barn and—"

Margot stopped and beckoned both of them forward.

"Okay, Pete—why don't I show you my vision, and you can let me know what you think? But also, I'm eager to hear your thoughts on what's worked and what hasn't for other wineries, since I know you're experienced at this."

Margot walked with Pete around the lawn between the winery building and the barn, and Luke and Elliot followed at a slight distance. Her voice was animated as she described how she wanted the path to look, where she wanted greenery, and how she wanted to improve and add to the makeshift outdoor seating area.

"But mostly," she said as they stopped on the other side of the lawn and looked back over to the winery building, "I want it to feel warm, comfortable, like the kind of place you could relax and drink wine forever. But also like a home. Not like one of those corporate big wineries, everything all pristine and matching, but like you're in a friend's large, relaxing, lovely garden, drinking excellent wine. Do you know what I mean?"

Luke did know what she meant. He smiled at the picture she'd created for all of them, at how animated she got, how passionate she was about this idea, how happy the thought of it clearly made her.

"That sounds like an excellent plan, Ms. Noble," Pete said.

"Margot, please," she said.

"Margot, then. And one that I think we can accomplish. The timing might be an issue, but I think we might be able to manage it—or, at least enough of it before your event to make it feel good, and we can finish up afterward if there are other pieces of your vision missing." Pete didn't even sound like he was kidding when he talked about Margot's ideas, but then this was his job. Luke was sure he talked about people's visions all the time. "I have to check in with my team and get back to you. Let me take some pictures and give you a call tomorrow, if that works?"

Margot beamed at Pete. Luke couldn't take his eyes off her. Why was she smiling at Pete like that? He wanted her to smile at him like that.

"Thanks so much, Pete. Take all the pictures you need."

On the way back to the winery building, Elliot walked with Pete, and Margot and Luke walked behind them.

"You seemed stressed when we came out here, is everything okay?" Luke asked her. He immediately shook his head. He hadn't meant to do that. "Never mind, I'm sorry. I shouldn't have asked that."

Margot looked at him, a soft smile on her lips.

"Was it that obvious?" She sighed. "It was just that I sort of bullied my brother into this party in the first place, and I started having second thoughts. Not about what I want the wincry to look like and why, but just about—" She stopped herself and shook her head. "Anyway, we'll see if we can get it all done on time."

He wondered what she'd been about to say, but he knew he couldn't ask.

"Well, you can trust Pete to be honest with you," he said. "That plan he had to get back to you by tomorrow was wildly optimistic, just FYI—but he does good work and is reliable."

"Thanks, I appreciate that," she said. "And yeah, I was already thinking it would be more like this weekend when I heard back from him, but I hoped that if he said tomorrow, it really *would* happen this weekend." It had better be by this weekend— if not, Luke would have to call Pete again to check in on this, and he didn't want to have to call this favor in twice. Especially since he didn't want Pete—or his mom—to wonder why getting back to Margot was so important to him.

Why was it so important to him?

She just seemed . . . worried about this party, and everything around it. If he could make this part of it easier for her, then he wanted to.

"So, Pete's your mom's partner," Margot said. "Is that why you used to work for him? In the family business for the summer?"

Luke shook his head.

"No, it's sort of the other way around," he said. "I worked for him one summer in high school, and that's how he met my mom."

"Ah," Margot said. She turned toward him, and he could tell she wanted to ask him another question.

But instead, she paused for a second.

"Well, thanks for sending him our way. I have a good feeling about Pete." She stopped and looked around. "There's so much I want to do here. Let's cross our fingers that we can get it done."

Luke started to respond, but Elliot called Margot, and she hurried over to him and Pete. Luke watched her go, but she didn't look back.

Nine

THE FOLLOWING WEDNESDAY MORNING, Margot walked into the winery early and smiled as she turned the lights on in her office. It had been a good week so far. A long one, but a good one. Lots of appointments at the tasting room, lots of calls, lots of plans for the party, for the future. If she could pull all of it off.

Pete had said he could start on the landscaping work the following week; he thought her ideas to get ready for the party would take only a few weeks and said they could talk about some of the other stuff she wanted to do afterward. He'd quoted her slightly above the budget she'd allocated for the landscaping, but had told her it would be cheaper if she eliminated the planter boxes that she'd wanted to have around the path, and she reluctantly agreed to that. They could make do with old wine barrels full of plants and herbs at the entrance to the barn and get planter boxes another time.

She and Elliot had made a tentative peace about the landscaping, though she was still on edge about how much he would push back about the work being done, the people in his way, and most of all, about her ideas to change the look of the property, the land that was theirs, but that she knew he thought of as his. Finding the old plans had helped with that, but only somewhat.

She looked over the appointments for the day. One appointment had canceled, so they had only five— Did that really justify having both Taylor and Luke on the clock today? Hopefully people would buy a lot of wine and make her feel better about investing in the new hires.

She still felt guilty when she thought about Luke. Mostly because every time she thought about him, or looked at him, or talked to him, she was more and more intrigued by him. Attracted to him, yes, obviously; she'd hoped that would go away with more contact with him, but it had just gotten stronger. But that's not what felt so dangerous to her—it was how much she wanted to know more about him, how much she wanted to tell him more about her, the way he listened when she talked, the way she always knew he was smiling at the same things that made her smile. When they'd talked last week while Pete was at the winery, he'd known she wasn't telling him everything that was stressing her out, and she could tell he'd wanted to ask her more about it. She had wanted to spill her guts to him, tell him about her worries about her place at Noble, her fear that she'd mess this whole thing up, that she wouldn't be able to pull it all together in two months. She'd had the wild impulse, in that brief moment as they'd walked together back toward the tasting room, to talk to him like she didn't talk to anyone around here other than Sydney.

She desperately needed to get out there, that's what she needed. Sydney was right. A night of good sex with a guy who seemed like a good listener was apparently all it took for her to get all swoony and want to bare her soul?

She shook her head at herself. *Focus, Margot.*

Just as she turned to her to-do list, her phone buzzed. Taylor. Was she running late?

"Hey, Taylor, what's up?"

"Hi, boss." Margot groaned internally as soon as she heard Taylor's voice, because she could immediately tell what she was about to say. "I'm sick. I can't come in today. I'm so sorry."

Margot pulled up the calendar.

"Don't be sorry—you're sick, it's not your fault. Take care of yourself and let me know how you're feeling, okay? We can handle it here."

Well, at least she could congratulate herself for hiring more staff. Because a month ago, if Taylor had called in sick, she would have had to cover the tasting room alone all day. Now Luke could cover it. And he'd had weeks of training, so hopefully he could cover it without too much intervention from her.

She walked into the tasting room to unlock the door for Luke, just as he walked up the front steps.

"Good morning," he said.

"Good morning," she said. "Taylor is sick today—do you think you're ready to handle the tasting room on your own?"

He looked startled, but recovered.

"I . . . Sure, okay." He glanced over at the bar. "Let me print out some menus and unload the dishwasher."

As much as she hated to admit it, Elliot had been right to hire Luke. Other than that whole sleeping-with-him thing, he'd been great since he started, with nothing to complain about, and this was another example of it. No panic, and he already knew what needed to be done to get ready for the day.

"I'll print out the menus if you get the dishwasher," she said. "I'll be around all day, so I can help out. I have a few calls later so you might be the only one in here on and off. But obviously, if anything comes up, just buzz me or come find me."

He nodded, a worried look coming over his face.

"Okay, will do. Just . . . chardonnay is the yellowish one, right?"

She felt a brief moment of panic before she saw that tiny crinkle in his eyes. She laughed out loud, and he did, too.

"I almost got you. Admit it."

She tried to tuck away her smile, but it was impossible.

"You did. What can I say, I'm not at my best this early in the morning."

He met her eyes and opened his mouth before he shook his head and closed it.

She blushed and turned away. She hated how much she wanted to know what he was about to say.

"Okay," she said, looking at the computer. "There's a party of four at eleven. But that's it until noon, when there's a party of three and one of four. And then nothing until two, so you can let them linger. But I'll be in and out all afternoon to help out. And really, don't hesitate to let me know if you need me."

He nodded.

"Thanks, Margot. Will do. I think I'll be okay in here—between you, Taylor, and Elliot, I've been well trained over the past few weeks."

She laughed. They certainly didn't leave anything to chance with their employees.

"True. But thanks for stepping up, nonetheless."

She smiled at him, and he grinned back at her. She suddenly realized they were alone in here. She turned away and slipped through the staff-only door and back to her office.

Thank goodness she had these calls today to keep her busy

so she couldn't stay in the tasting room with Luke all day to help out. God, why was she so drawn to this man? It wasn't his looks—yes, Luke was definitely attractive, but she'd never found that sort of tall, scruffy, nerdy type all that appealing before. She tended to like the clean-cut, well-put-together vibe a lot better. But there was just something about Luke.

At least Luke didn't know how much she was drawn to him, how much she thought about him. Well, she hoped he didn't know that. And she thought about that night far too often, especially when she couldn't sleep and she let herself remember every second of that night, starting from the kiss outside the Barrel, and then that silent, tense, anticipatory walk back to his place, and then that kiss at his front door. She especially let herself remember the way his fingers had brushed against her nipples, and then lingered; the way they'd slipped inside of her, later on the bed, followed by his tongue, and then—

Shit. No. She couldn't think about this here, now, of all places. Not with Luke so close. Plus, she really did have that call at eleven, and she had to prep for it. Oh, and she had to print the menus for today, right. She forced herself to put thoughts of Luke to the back of her mind, and turned to her computer.

———

LUKE HOPED MARGOT HADN'T noticed his moment of slight—very slight—panic when she'd told him that Taylor was gone for the day and he'd be all alone in the tasting room. He'd wanted to beg Margot to stay in there with him, tell her that he wasn't ready to do this by himself, but his pride wouldn't let him.

It wasn't that the general duties of working in the tasting room were beyond him. He was smart, he could follow directions, he could pour wine; he'd graduated magna cum laude from Stanford, after all. He opened the dishwasher to unload it, but the glasses in there were still dirty. Whoever had closed up the night before must have forgotten to turn it on. He powered it on and went to check the appointments for the day.

This job, for the most part, was a lot of fun. But it was the questions all of these people asked! That's what had made him bite his lip to keep himself from swearing when Margot had told him he was in charge of the tasting room for today. He'd have to find a way to answer things like how many different kinds of grapes were in each bottle of wine; and where all of those grapes were grown, and if they'd had any issues with smoke taint (a horrifying phrase if he'd ever heard it) because of the fires from the past few years; and how many acres, exactly, of vineyards did the Nobles own; and were their grapes grown elsewhere; and wasn't this Cab Franc a lot more like a Cab Sauv and really, what was the difference between them; and so many other things. And of course, since he was Black, and a man, and many people who came to the winery knew that the winemaker was Black, and a man, they often assumed he was Elliot, and asked him lots of detailed winemaking questions that didn't stop even when he'd made it clear that he was neither a winemaker nor a member of the Noble family.

Up until now, Taylor or Daisy had always been there to jump in when he'd gotten questions he couldn't answer—occasionally Margot was around to pitch in—but today he'd just do what he could to answer and call in Margot only for anything extra tricky.

He knew that was another part of it, of course. He didn't want to have to call in Margot for anything tricky. He didn't want Margot to have to rescue him from questions he didn't know enough to answer. He wanted to impress her. But then, would Margot, being Margot, be far more impressed with him if he admitted to what he didn't know?

He wasn't used to being in an environment like this. He had no idea how to handle it.

He sighed and looked back down at the appointment list.

"Oh no!" Margot stood at the door, a stack of menus in her hands and a panicked look on her face. He turned around to see what she was looking at. Water, leaking out from the dishwasher. He jumped to turn it off, but Margot had gotten there before him.

"It's broken," she said. "Damn it. I'll call the plumber, I guess." She sighed. "This would happen on a day Taylor wasn't here."

He rolled up his sleeves.

"Want me to take a look at it first?"

Margot stared at him.

"What do you know about dishwashers?"

Luke knelt down in front of the dishwasher.

"My mom owns an inn—I had to figure out pretty quickly how to fix most household appliances."

Margot let out that low laugh of hers. Thank God his back was to her.

"I honestly don't know why none of us have ever figured out dishwashers, we certainly wash enough wineglasses every day to need to know this. Between me, Elliot, and Taylor, we know how to fix almost everything else around here, including all of the cars. I think it's just because the dishwasher hasn't broken yet."

He turned around at that.

"You can fix cars?"

She put her hands on her hips, a look of mock outrage on her face.

"Don't look so surprised at that. Don't I look like the kind of woman who can fix a car?"

He had no idea how to answer that, but she just laughed again.

"Well, I am—at least, for the easy stuff." The expression on her face softened. "Uncle Stan taught both me and Elliot about cars, starting with that old truck of his that's still out there."

He'd wondered about that old truck. It looked well-preserved, but it had been in the same place since he'd started here.

He turned back to the dishwasher. He opened it and looked around.

"I'll get the tool kit," Margot said from behind him. He heard her heels clicking on the wood floor as she went into the back and then quickly came back out.

"I may not need it," he said. He moved the float switch up and down a few times and then closed the dishwasher door.

"That's it?" Margot asked.

He laughed.

"I feel like I should pretend there's a lot more to do here, and it's super complicated, so I can get lots of praise, but I'm pretty sure the float switch was just stuck." He looked at Margot. "Okay if I turn this thing on so we can test it out to see if I was right?"

Margot shrugged.

"Might as well, while we're here to watch it. And we have lots of towels at the ready and are close to the water off switch, just in case."

Luke pressed the on button and then held his breath. He *thought* he was right on this one, but it would be just his luck to be very wrong when he was trying to impress a woman. Who was also his boss.

They both stared at the machine as they waited to see what would happen.

"Oh, there you are, Margot, did you get the— What are we looking at?"

He and Margot both turned to see Elliot there, a cup of coffee in one hand and a pastry in the other.

"We're looking at the dishwasher," she said. "It's broken. Or . . . was broken, but Luke may have done some magic with it." She turned to Luke. "I think it's not leaking anymore."

He nodded.

"I think you're right," he said.

"You've saved the day, Luke," Elliot said.

"Not just the day, but he also saved me from having to write a large check to a plumber for about three minutes of work," Margot said. "Thanks, Luke."

He met her eyes. That warm expression was all the thanks he needed.

Well. He probably could have come up with something better. But unfortunately . . .

"No problem," he said. "Happy to help."

Elliot smiled at him and then looked at Margot.

"See? Aren't I good at hiring? On top of everything else, he's good with his hands."

Margot bit her lip, hard.

"Um, you had a question for me, Elliot? Let's head back into my office." She walked toward the door to the back. "Thanks again, Luke."

"No problem." He grinned at her, and she looked away. Were her cheeks a little flushed?

"Hi!" Luke heard and turned toward the front door, and saw a couple standing there. "We have an appointment at eleven?"

He smiled and beckoned them inside.

"Welcome to Noble Family Vineyards. I'm Luke."

The first appointment of the day went great—two older couples, obviously relaxed and happy. The men didn't pay that much attention to him, and the women beamed at him. They didn't ask many questions and then surprised him by buying two cases of wine between them. Okay, at least his first solo appointment was a success.

At ten minutes to noon, while the eleven o'clock appointment was still relaxing and drinking the last of their wine, the front door opened.

"Hi. We have a noon appointment, but we're early," one of the three Black women at the door said. "Is that okay?"

Luke looked down at the reservation list and smiled at them.

"No problem. Monroe, party of three? I'll get you set up over at this nook in the corner, if that works for the three of you?"

"This definitely works for us," the shortest of the three said when they followed him over to the corner. "But only two of us will be tasting today. Is that all right?" She nodded at her friends. "I'm sure these two will more than make up for me, though."

The other two erupted in laughter as they all sat down.

"Look, you were the one who decided to do a spa getaway in Wine Country when you were four months pregnant, okay?" the third one said. "We're just trying to be polite and keep the wine away from you."

"Mmm, polite," the pregnant one said. "That's not a word I usually use to describe you, Maddie."

Luke smiled at the three of them. He could already tell they'd be a fun group.

"Let me get you your first glasses of wine," he said. He nodded at the pregnant one. "And some sparkling water?"

She grinned at him.

"Please. Thank you."

By the time he got them set up with wine and snacks and water, the other noon appointment had arrived. And as soon as they walked in, Luke knew these people were exactly whom he'd been dreading.

Two white couples, male-female pairs, all of whom looked to be around his age or a little older. He could tell a show-off from a mile away—probably because he'd been one for a while there, until the even bigger show-offs he'd worked with had made him see the error of his ways. One of these guys was definitely here to show the world, and especially the people he was with, just how much he knew about wine. Great.

"Welcome to Noble Family Vineyards," Luke said. "Do you have a reservation?"

He hoped the answer would be no, that they weren't the Christopher, party of four, on the schedule, and he could turn them away. But he knew he wouldn't be so lucky.

"Christopher, party of four," the show-off said. Luke almost felt bad about mentally labeling him the show-off until his next words. "You must be Elliot Noble, the winemaker."

Luke could feel the frozen smile on his face.

"Nope, I'm not that fortunate," he said. "I'm Luke Williams, I just work here."

"Oh." He looked taken aback that there were apparently two Black men in Wine Country. "Well, is Elliot here to talk to us? And can we sit at those couches in the corner?" He gestured to the corner where the three Black women were sitting.

"Oh, unfortunately, there's a party already sitting there," Luke said to him in an even voice, like maybe the three women laughing and talking ten feet away from them were invisible to this dude in some way. "I'll see if Mr. Noble is available. Why don't you all sit down here, and I'll get you your first glasses of wine?"

He'd noticed both Taylor and Margot do this, refer to Elliot as "Mr. Noble" around annoying guests who asked to talk to him in that demanding way, like they were summoning him to an audience. To normal guests, they just called him Elliot. No matter what, though, it was rare for Elliot to drop into the tasting room to talk to people—he was usually too busy working.

He saw the irritated expression on the face of the know-it-all and tried to smile at the rest of the party as he poured their wine, and then went over to check on the fun table in the corner, who were, yes, at the best table in the house.

"We were wondering," the know-it-all said when Luke came back to their table with the second bottle of wine. "Are all of your grapes grown here in Napa Valley?"

At least he'd started with an easy one.

"Yes, all of the Noble Family Vineyards' grapes are grown right here in Napa Valley," he said. He might as well answer the guy's next question before he could ask it. "Some—most, actually—right here on our estate, and then a small percentage of our grapes are grown elsewhere in the valley."

It had surprised him, how quickly he'd started saying "our" in relation to Noble Vineyards and everything they made. It was silly, probably. But he already felt like part of this place.

"Where else in the valley?" the guy asked. Of course he did. Luckily, Luke had memorized this.

"A few small estates in Calistoga, one up in the hills in St. Helena, and one large estate in Napa. All of the wines that use one hundred percent of the grapes grown here on the Noble estate are clearly labeled as estate wine. Would you like a pour of our Napa Valley blend? It's the next wine in your tasting—you'll be able to compare it to the estate blend, which you'll be tasting later."

They all nodded, the guy triumphantly, the people with him with some relief that finally he was going to stop talking and they were going to get to drink wine. Or maybe that was just projection, since that's exactly how Luke would have felt.

He knew the guy thought he'd gotten Luke to give him something extra because of all of the questions, when really, they almost always offered people a taste of the estate blend at the end of the tasting.

He stopped over at the table in the corner to move the fun group on to the next wine. Because they were so nice in contrast to Question Dude over there, he gave them—or the two who were actually drinking—heavy pours.

"This one is my personal favorite," he told them. He lowered his voice, "But also, don't rely too much on that—I started working here less than a month ago."

He walked away from the table as all three laughed at that, even the one who wasn't drinking.

The grin on his face faded as he dealt with Know-It-All again.

"Wasn't there a fire here in the year of this vintage?" he demanded. "How are those really Napa Valley grapes, then?"

This guy seemed obsessed with the idea that they were, what, sneaking in grapes from across the Sonoma border? Or from somewhere in the Central Valley?

"There have been fires here in Napa Valley frequently, unfortunately, over the last few years," he said. "Climate change isn't great for the wine business. But fortunately for Noble, we managed to harvest most of our grapes just in time to save them, though there have been a few years where we've lost some vintages."

There he was, saying "we" again, like he'd personally been there to harvest grapes. He should probably dial back his feeling of ownership here—this whole sojourn in Napa was supposed to last him only a few months, remember? Until he had to go back to his real life.

"Are you sure some of the bad grapes didn't just . . . slip in?" the guy said. He lowered his voice. "You can tell me."

This guy had a real attitude.

"Yep," Luke said. "I'm sure."

"Can we taste the difference between the same wine in different years?" He looked around at his group, like he'd just won something. "Just to . . . see."

"We'd be happy to let you taste anything you like."

Luke smiled as he heard Margot's commanding, courteous, and clearly—at least to him—absolutely furious voice coming from behind him. The people at the table didn't seem to notice how angry she was, but he knew, even without turning around.

"Hello. I'm Margot Noble, co-owner of this winery," she said. "Luke and I will get those wines for you to taste. Please let me know if you have any other questions about the integrity of our winemaking."

Luke didn't look at Margot, but looked at the know-it-all to see his response. He opened his mouth, and then closed it, at least four times before he actually got words out.

"Oh, I wasn't saying . . . I was just wondering . . . You hear stories . . ."

Now Luke turned to look at Margot, who smiled oh-so-widely.

"Oh, of course," she said. "No offense taken. I just wanted to offer up my expertise."

Luke hoped Margot never looked at him like that. She definitely wanted to throw that man out the window. Without opening it first.

"I'll be right back with those wines," he said.

Margot turned to him, and her smile changed. It was conspiratorial now.

And so fucking hot.

"Thanks, Luke," she said as they walked together to the bar. "I've got this from here."

He raised his eyebrows at her.

"Oh, I'm sure you do," he said under his breath.

She winked at him.

"You know it," she said.

They locked eyes for a moment. Finally, Margot looked away.

"Go check on that group in the corner. They seem fun. Actually, wait." She went behind the bar and came out with a bottle. "Give them some of this."

Luke took the bottle from Margot and went back over to the fun group.

"Can I offer you three—or you two, rather," he said, with an apologetic look at the pregnant one, "a taste of our 2014 estate Cab? Margot—our co-owner over there—thinks you might enjoy it."

They all giggled.

"If that's an apology for making us listen to that blowhard," the one with the curly hair said, "no need. Not that we'll say no to the wine, obviously, but watching her insult him to his face without him knowing what she was doing was a master class, and I thought I was good at that."

Luke grinned at them as he poured wine into their glasses.

"Wasn't it? I learn from her every day."

"To Margot," the one in the pink dress said, "and to having a built-in designated driver."

The pregnant one rolled her eyes, but drank her sparkling water.

"You two are going to be nightmares later, aren't you?" she said.

They nodded.

"Yep," they said in unison.

Luke laughed as he walked back to the bar.

MARGOT KEPT THE POMPOUS little jerk talking for so long that (a) she barely had to pour him and his silent group any wine, and (b) she made them late for their one-thirty lunch reservation. People like him always overscheduled themselves in Wine Country. Now she'd messed up his carefully crafted day, and he'd be stressed and running behind until dinner. Just thinking about that would make her happy all day. She gave the group a huge, genuine smile as she waved them out the door.

The group of three Black women in the corner who had been laughing and casually flirting with Luke for the past hour got up to leave just after Margot had waved goodbye to Mr. I Bet You Snuck Some Smoke-Tainted Grapes into Your Wine.

"Well, this has been both delicious and very exciting," the woman in the royal blue dress said, "but we've got to motor if we're going to make those spa appointments on time. However, since I'm newly a member of the Noble Family Vineyards wine club, I'd like to take advantage of my discount and buy some of that last wine . . . well, and a few of that second-to-last one." She grinned at her friends. "That phone call in the airport yesterday landed me a new client, I just found out."

The one in the red dress hugged her.

"Great job, Liv!"

Margot rang up the wine and gave the women their discounts and then waved goodbye to them. They talked and laughed on their way to the car, and Luke followed them out, carrying their many bottles of wine. She admired his muscles under his T-shirt for a few seconds before she caught herself and turned away. She glanced at the appointment book. Nothing in there until two, and it was one forty-five. She could go back to her office for the next few minutes, or even for the rest of the afternoon. Luke could handle the afternoon appointments by himself, unless he needed her.

He hadn't really needed her for the noon appointments, but when she'd glanced into the tasting room, just to check and see what was going on, and overheard that guy maligning her brother's character, she hadn't been able to stop herself from butting in. She probably shouldn't have done it—she probably should have gone back to her office and let Luke handle it, or she should have just been bland and politic and tried to sell wine, but she'd honestly wanted to kick that asshole out of her winery, so being rude to him in a way he was too pompous to notice was her compromise.

She walked slowly back into her office, but just as she walked in the door, Luke came in behind her.

"That . . . that was incredible," he said.

She turned around and grinned at him. She couldn't help it.

"What was incredible?" she asked. Yes, fine, she wanted to hear him praise her. So sue her.

He leaned against the doorframe, a grin on his face.

"The way you dealt with that guy. He was a nightmare, and you managed to put him in his place completely. I only wish Taylor could have been there to see that, she would have loved it."

Margot laughed. She had felt pretty triumphant about that, actually.

"I have to admit, it felt pretty great. Maybe that's petty—shouldn't I have taken the high road, and, like, made him fall in love with our wines? What a terrible example to set in front of my new, young, impressionable employee. And yet, it felt so good."

Luke had a huge grin on his face.

"First of all, your new, young, impressionable employee thought that was a very instructive life lesson on how to get rid of an annoying customer. And second, I think you more than made up for any wine that guy would have bought—which, we both know he wouldn't have—by the impression you made on those women. They told me on the way to the car they were ready to join your army. And the three of them joined the wine club—even the pregnant one, who wasn't drinking today. That was all due to you."

Margot sat down on the edge of her desk and laughed.

"Not *all* due to me—they were already in excellent hands by the time I walked into the tasting room, and you get all of the credit for that. You did well on your own."

He brushed that aside.

"Thanks, but I was very glad when you walked in. I could have handled two, maybe three, of the fun tables like those women, but once I get the actual wine people like that guy, my eyes start to glaze over and I forget everything I've ever known about wine—the vast majority of which, by the way, I've learned in the past few weeks."

He grinned at her, and she grinned back. Why was it so fucking easy with him, so natural to talk to him and laugh with him? It wasn't fair.

She glanced around her desk, and then jumped up.

"Oh no, I think I left my phone behind the bar. Let me grab it now, before everything gets busy again."

Luke straightened up as she walked toward her office door. Then, in one quick move, he closed the door.

"What are you—" Her voice died out as she looked up at him.

He put a hand against the wall next to her head, trapping her against the wall with his body. Like he'd done that night. She knew she could get around him, open the door, and leave. But she didn't want to. The proximity to him was intoxicating.

He wasn't touching her, but he looked at her with such heat in his eyes that it felt like his hands were all over her.

She looked back at him. This was a bad idea. She had to leave. She didn't move.

"Margot." He said her name in a low voice, a voice she hadn't heard since that night. "Please tell me you think about that night, like I do. Am I alone in this? Because, my God, I think about it all the time. I think about you all the time. I can't be the only one who feels this, can I? Sometimes—most of the time—I think I am. And then, every so often, you look at me in a way that makes me think I'm not. Tell me I'm not. Tell me you want me."

He held her gaze. She wanted to look away, to deny it all, but she couldn't.

"I can't tell you that," she said.

"Can't, or won't? Can you not tell me that because it's not true, because you don't want me? Or do you just not want to say it?"

If only it weren't true.

"I can't tell you that because I'm your boss," she said in a low voice. "I can't tell you that because that night never should have happened."

She wished she weren't breathing so fast.

He shook his head, but his eyes never left hers.

"You know that's not true," he said.

God, he was so close to her. She wanted to reach for him so badly. She let her eyelids flutter shut. Maybe it would be easier to move away from him if she couldn't see him. But no, this was worse. Now she could feel the warmth coming from his body, so close to hers. She could feel his breath on her face. She could smell him, that smell she remembered from that night, that fresh soap smell, combined with his own body scent. She breathed it in and smiled. Now he smelled a little bit like wine, too.

She could hear him, breathing as fast as she was.

She opened her eyes. He was still looking straight at her.

"You didn't answer my question," he said.

"You know the answer to that question," she said.

A smile touched his lips.

"I didn't, when I came in here. But I do now." He moved closer to her. "So tell me. Tell me you want me."

She tried to look away from him, but she couldn't.

"Why? You know it."

His eyes finally left hers, but it was only to look, slowly, up and down her body. He lingered on her hips, her breasts, her lips, before he looked her in the eye again.

"Because I want to hear you say it," he said. "I want to think about it. Later."

She shouldn't do this. She knew she shouldn't. But that last thing he said broke her. God, she wanted him to think about her later.

"I want you," she said.

He kissed her, hard and fast, just like she wanted him to kiss her. His hand slid into her hair, and she gloried in the feeling of his hands on her, his lips on hers, again, finally. She reached for him, pulled him closer, kissed him harder, moaned into his mouth as he kissed her back.

"My God, Margot," he said.

He brushed his hand over her hair, her cheek, with such reverence. She reveled in his touch.

No. She had to stop this.

She made herself pull away. He immediately stepped back.

"I'm sorry," he said. "I wasn't going to do that. I shouldn't have done that. But holy shit."

She let out a breath and moved farther away from him.

"I wanted you to do that," she said. "I wanted that. But we can't do it again."

"I know," he said. "But—"

She shook her head.

"Go."

He looked away from her, finally. He opened the door and walked out of her office.

She almost stumbled to her desk, sat down on her chair, and dropped her head into her hands. She could still feel the imprint of his hands on her body, of his lips on hers. And the worst part was, she didn't want that feeling to go away.

ten

LUKE LEANED HIS HEAD against the cold tile of his shower, still breathing hard.

Why had he told her to say that?

All he could hear—all he'd been able to hear for the past three hours—was her voice, throaty and hoarse and full of longing, telling him she wanted him.

He'd heard it all afternoon at the winery as he tried to juggle three overlapping appointments, while glancing at the staff door every thirty seconds to see if she'd walked through it. He'd heard it when she eventually did walk through the door, when he was in the middle of checking out a group and all of their wine, and so couldn't look at her. He'd heard it when he finally looked at her, to find her talking to other people and very definitely not looking at him. He'd heard it when Elliot had walked into the tasting room at five thirty and told him he'd take care of locking up, since Margot had an appointment and had left early.

And he'd heard it the whole way home, where he'd immediately jumped in the shower and let himself think about her with abandon, how it had felt to be that close to her again, how it had felt to kiss her and have her respond so passionately. He'd let himself revel in it, in her smooth hands on his skin, her body against his as his own hands moved faster and faster on his cock. And when he came, too fast, he just wished she were there with him.

Fuck. What was he going to do now? Should he quit?

What, and just find another winery job somewhere, to keep up this pretense with his mom that he was up here to date Avery?

He laughed at himself. That wasn't the real reason he wouldn't quit. He didn't want to quit. If he did, he wouldn't get to see Margot all day at work. Even though it killed him to see her and not be able to touch her.

And Margot would be pissed if he quit, he knew that. Noble was understaffed right now—if he hadn't been there today, Margot would have had to cover all of that herself. No matter how much she wanted him, she cared a lot more about the winery than she did about fucking him. If he quit just because he wanted to be able to fuck her again, he probably wouldn't even get to do that.

Well, he couldn't tell Avery about this, that was for sure. Avery had already mocked him mercilessly for sleeping with Margot, and there was no way he could claim that he'd accidentally kissed her. No, that kiss had been very purposeful.

Plus, Avery knew Margot, which he hadn't known when he'd told her about the first time. He couldn't do that to Margot.

He turned off the water and cringed at himself for how much he'd wasted. He couldn't find another way to release his frustration, in the middle of a drought?

He got dressed, sat down on the couch, and then immediately jumped up to look in the fridge. No, nothing had magically appeared in there since the day before.

Okay, fine, that was something to do with this night that suddenly stretched out too long and empty before him. He would go find dinner.

He walked down the stairs and toward his car, then changed course just as he reached for the door handle. No, he'd driven enough today. He wanted to walk.

He didn't even realize where he was going until he stopped in front of the Barrel. He shouldn't go in. He'd seen her afterward, with that bartender. They were clearly friends. Margot must go there all the time. But . . .

He stood there, his hand on the door for a few seconds, then took a step back and turned away.

"Good decision," a voice behind him said.

He turned. The bartender. Of course. She was actually the owner of this place, right. She looked at him with an amused, but severe, expression on her face.

He didn't even pretend not to know what she was talking about.

"Yeah. I guess so. I thought it would be better if I didn't come in, just in case she was there."

She kept her eyes on him.

"But you thought about it."

He sighed.

"Yeah. I thought about it. I—" He shook his head. What was he even doing? "I'm sorry, we shouldn't be having this conversation."

She laughed, and opened the door.

"What conversation?"

He turned to walk down the street.

"Luke."

He looked back. She was out on the sidewalk.

"Go to Fork in the Road—two blocks that way. Great bar, excellent steak, very good burger. Tell them Sydney sent you."

He felt like he'd won her approval, somehow.

"Thanks," he said. "I'll do that."

The steak was excellent, the bourbon was poured with a heavy hand—he was pretty sure because of Sydney's name, which he'd dropped—and he didn't even glance at the people sitting next to him at the bar. He knew they weren't Margot.

MARGOT FELT LIKE A coward as she drove away from the winery that day. A coward and a failure. She'd gone out the back door of the winery and then called Elliot from her car to tell him she had a meeting and he needed to lock up. That first part was true, she did have a meeting that night, but there was plenty of time for it; she didn't have to leave early. But on the other hand, she absolutely had to leave early. She'd waited until the last two people of the day were already in the tasting room, and she'd overheard enough to be sure Luke could handle it on his own, but still. If she'd been strong, if she'd had courage, she would have stayed, gone into the tasting room after it was closed for the day, locked up after Luke had left. But then, if she'd been strong, she wouldn't have allowed anything that went on that day in her office between her and Luke to happen.

She could have stopped it. Luke would have moved away with a single word from her, the slightest sign. She knew that, the whole time. And she hadn't done a thing. She—eventually—did stop it, but that wasn't a comfort. It was the literal least she could do.

And here she was proving Elliot right. Along with the rest of her family, and everyone who had ever doubted that she was good enough, dedicated enough, committed enough to run this winery. She was risking all of this for a guy? And not even a guy she was in an actual relationship with, or who even seemed to want to be in an actual relationship with her, but a guy she'd had a one-night stand with, and now couldn't stop thinking about?

Granted, it *was* gratifying to know that he couldn't stop thinking about her, either. She grinned, even though she knew she shouldn't be smiling about this. It was really gratifying. But that didn't get her anywhere. She couldn't risk her winery just for more good sex.

When, she wondered, had she started to think about the winery as hers? Definitely not at first. For that first year, at least, she'd thought about it as Uncle Stan's winery. A few times, she'd overheard Elliot refer to it as his winery, and while part of her had bristled at that—the part of her that thought Elliot had meant for her to overhear it—another part of her thought it was only right. It did feel like either Uncle Stan's winery or Elliot's winery, for a very long time. But now she understood how Elliot felt. Because yes, while it felt like their winery, theirs together, it also felt like hers.

She wished she could talk to Uncle Stan. Ask him why he'd left the winery to her and Elliot equally. Had he just done it that way because he would have felt bad leaving it to Elliot alone, like it would have hurt her feelings? It would have, a little, but she would have understood, she would have expected it. Had he

thought she would just be a silent partner and let Elliot do everything? She didn't think so—Uncle Stan knew her too well to expect her to be silent about anything—but she wasn't sure. Had he
expected her to sell her half of the winery to Elliot? Elliot had no
business sense—he was just all about the wine. Which made for
excellent wine but would not make for a very successful winery.
Or had he wanted her to actually chip in, become invested in
this place, and in these people, like she had? To do things he
wouldn't have done, and probably wouldn't like that she was doing, like all the social media content, renovating and expanding
the tasting room, this party? She had no idea.

She went to her meeting, paid absolutely no attention for an
hour, and then got in her car and drove home. When she walked
into her house, she stood there and looked around. No. She
couldn't be at home alone all night. She had so much to do for
the party, but all she would do was think about Luke. She texted
Sydney.

MARGOT

Save me a seat at the bar

She texted back right away.

SYDNEY

Someday I'm going to make you make
reservations, like a normal person

Margot laughed.

MARGOT

Never. Be there in ten

When she slid onto her seat at the bar, Sydney raised an eyebrow at her.

"Wine kind of night, or cocktail kind of night?"

Margot let out a sigh.

"Cocktail kind of week, more like."

Sydney poured something or other in a shaker, along with ice, and then strained it all into a coupe glass.

"Here. And food is on its way, I'm sure." Then she inclined her head slightly to Margot's right. "Also. I got you a present."

Margot took a sip of her cocktail—*ooh, tart, and very strong,* just what she needed—and then shifted her eyes to her right, certain what she would find.

A man. She shook her head.

"Why not?" Sydney asked. "It worked last time. Plus, you need a palate cleanser. You told me that you did!"

Margot picked up one of the arancini that landed in front of her.

"It worked *well* last time?"

Sydney laughed.

"I guess that depends on your definition of 'well.' It absolutely worked well until you got to work the next day, didn't it?"

Margot just looked at her. Sydney sighed.

"Fine, just throw my present away like that. But haven't you been saying that this is what you need to get over the last time?"

Sydney walked away without giving Margot a chance to answer.

"I'm not *under* the last time," she muttered. At least Sydney hadn't been able to call her on that lie.

"What was that?"

The man next to her turned to her, a curious, friendly expression on his face.

"Oh." *Shit.* "I was just . . . chatting with the bartender." She sighed. "She's a friend of mine—she likes to push my buttons in the way that friends do."

He laughed.

"I get that." He hesitated, then turned to her all the way. "I'm Matt."

She swore she could hear Sydney cackle. She held back a sigh. Fine.

"I'm Margot." She'd at least ask this question right off the bat. "What do you do, Matt?"

He smiled at her.

"I'm a lawyer. I live in San Francisco, but I'm in town for a conference. I had to escape the conference hotel, you know how it is."

A lawyer. Thank goodness. And he was definitely not the lawyer who occasionally did work for Noble—that lawyer was a woman.

"Oh, I know how it is," she said. "Sometimes you need to get away."

He laughed.

"Yeah—when you're at these things, if you go to the hotel bar, you invariably run into a million people from the conference, and it's just more hours of work. And the networking would probably be better for my career, but tonight I wanted a break from all of that, if you know what I mean."

Oh, did she.

"I definitely do. I live up here, and almost everyone who lives here is more or less in the industry—we don't quite all know each other, but there are a lot fewer than six degrees of separation, let's put it that way." She nodded in Sydney's direction. "As you saw. If I want to take a break from work, I have to leave the state."

He laughed. She did like a man who laughed at her jokes.

"Surely, not the whole state? Can't you just go down to San Francisco?"

She took a sip of her cocktail and shook her head.

"I love the Bay Area, don't get me wrong, but that's work, too—I own a winery up here, so I spend a lot of time down there or in L.A. marketing our wines. Which is great, and we've been successful at that. But that's why I have to get out of California for a true break. No restaurant is safe."

His eyes opened wide when she said she owned a winery. She used to lie about that, or sort of minimize her role there to men. Say she was an executive at a winery, or she worked in sales at a winery, or sometimes just she worked at a winery. All of those things were true, but not the truth. And eventually, she'd gotten sick of it. If men were scared off by that, so be it.

They usually were.

Would Luke have been? If she weren't his boss?

She didn't think so.

"Oh wow, you own a winery?" Matt asked, and leaned in a little closer. Hmmm, apparently he wasn't scared off. "Which one? That sounds amazing."

She tossed her hair back, more for the benefit of Sydney, who she was sure was watching.

"Noble Family Vineyards," she said. "It's a lot of fun, and also a lot of hard work. I don't do it by myself, of course—my brother and I are the co-owners."

"How does that work, to own it with your brother? I can't imagine being in business with any of my siblings," Matt said.

It would be easier if Elliot didn't hate that she was the co-owner. And if he respected what she did. And if he stopped doing things like hiring people without talking to her about it first. God, why did she keep thinking about Luke?

"We have a pretty good division of labor," she said.

She and Matt talked for the next hour, as food kept appearing in front of Margot. Matt seemed like he'd finished eating, but made no motion to leave.

Finally, Margot asked for, and paid, her tiny bill, and Matt did the same.

"I should be getting home," she said.

He stood up when she did.

"So should I," he said, like she'd known he would. "Breakfast session tomorrow morning, unfortunately."

They walked out of the bar together. Margot refused to even look in Sydney's direction, but she knew her eyes were on them.

Matt stopped her on the sidewalk.

"My hotel is this way, if you'd like to walk with me? Maybe have a nightcap?" He took a step closer to her. When she didn't move away, he took another.

"I . . . That sounds . . ."

Before she could finish, he bent down to kiss her.

The kiss was very nice, just like Matt. But after a little while, Margot took a step back.

"I'm sorry, Matt. I should get home. It was lovely to meet you, though. Really."

Matt stepped back and smiled at her.

"It was lovely to meet you, too." He pulled a card out of his pocket. "Just . . . just in case you change your mind."

She smiled at him.

"Thanks. Have a good day tomorrow."

He nodded.

"You, too. Maybe I'll stop by that winery of yours sometime."
She knew that was her cue to give him her card.

She didn't do it.

"I hope you do," she said instead.

She watched him walk away, then went back into the Barrel.

"Excuse my language, but what the fuck are you doing here?"
Sydney asked her when she sat back down at the bar.

"He kissed me," she said.

Sydney raised her eyebrows.

"And?"

"And nothing. Just . . . nothing." Margot sighed. "A perfectly
nice, nothing kiss."

Sydney looked at her.

"And are you sure that nothing wasn't because of you-know-
who?"

Margot stared down at the bar, and then back up.

"It wasn't about him in the way you mean. It's not like I'm
saving myself for him, or anything like that. But . . . I knew immediately, as soon as he kissed me, that it would be good with
him. That it would be great with him. That first kiss, it was . . .
My whole body responded to him. And so when I know it can be
like that, why waste my time with a kiss that feels like nothing?
Why waste Matt's time when I felt nothing?"

Sydney pursed her lips.

"I don't think Matt would have thought his time was wasted."

Margot pursed her lips right back.

"And doesn't that make it worse?"

"Point taken." Sydney lifted her hands in surrender. "Oh
well. You tried."

Margot dropped her head to the bar.

"Yeah. I tried," she said. *God damn it.*

She pulled herself upright and shrugged.

"Okay. I'm going to walk home now."

Sydney shook her head.

"Oh no you're not. Not with that look on your face. Stay here while we close up. I'll drive you home when I'm done here."

Margot sat back down.

"Only if you promise not to make fun of me for all of this."

"I promise," Sydney said immediately.

"Okay," Margot said. Sydney started to walk away.

"He's not dating Avery," she said as she stared down at the bar.

Sydney stopped and turned back to Margot.

"He told you that? Please don't tell me you asked him."

Margot's eyes shot back up to Sydney's.

"No. My God, no. Of course not. And no, he didn't tell me. Avery did. When I had breakfast with her to talk about the party."

Sydney counted on her fingers. Margot knew what was coming.

"You had breakfast with her on Thursday, yes? Last Thursday?"

Margot sighed.

"Yes."

"Mmm," Sydney said. "So how did it take you this long to tell me that Avery Jensen made a point to tell you that she wasn't dating your little fling turned employee?"

Margot tugged her hair up into a bun.

"First, don't call him mine. Second, she didn't make a point to tell me, it wasn't out of nowhere; it was in the context of me hiring his mom's boyfriend to do landscaping. She told me they've been friends since high school. Third, I was going to say some bullshit about how I haven't seen you since last Monday so that's why I haven't told you, but I know exactly what you'd say

to that, so I'm not even going to bother, and I'll say the real reason, which is that I didn't want you to think I cared that much."

Sydney raised her eyebrows.

"But you do. Don't you?"

Margot didn't say anything for a while.

"Yeah," she said finally. "I do."

Sydney took a step away.

"Be right back."

In a few minutes, she walked up, a paper bag in her hand.

"I was right—we did have more of that ice cream you liked in
the back. Let's go."

Margot looked up at her.

"I love you so much."

Sydney dropped an arm around her shoulder.

"Yeah. I know."

Eleven

LUKE WOKE UP SUNDAY morning and checked his phone. A text from Craig? That was a surprise. Craig had been his mentor at work; they'd always gotten along well, but Craig had seemed as shocked and disappointed as everyone else when Luke had quit. He'd been pretty sure he'd never hear from him again.

CRAIG

> Thought you might be interested in this news. Let me know if you want to chat about this. We miss you around here.

Luke clicked on the link Craig had sent him and laughed when he saw the headline. Oh, they'd pledged $10 million toward diversity, equity, and inclusion efforts? And had hired a brand-new chief diversity officer? Right. Of course they had.

He flinched when his phone rang. Craig couldn't be calling

him to talk about this, could he? Did he want Luke to talk to the press, to parade him around in the way they'd done before, this time as a Black former employee who had just loved his time there and didn't experience discrimination at all?

Oh, it was just his mom. Luke was so grateful he immediately picked up.

"Luke! Pete and I are going to that sale and auction you and I always used to go to today. Want to join us? Maybe you and Avery could come along? That is, if you two didn't have other plans today."

This is what picking up the phone got him. And he didn't have to work today at Noble, so he couldn't wiggle out of this that way.

"Sure," he said to his mom. What else could he say? "I don't think Avery can come, but I'll meet you guys there."

Maybe today was a good time to tell his mom the truth about his job. And about this Avery thing. He was feeling better about everything, maybe because he'd been out of that job for over a month, and working at Noble for three weeks now. It was fun, to learn something brand-new, to get to interact with people all day, none of whom seemed to be looking for him to fail. He wasn't stressed, anxious, about work anymore. That felt weird, almost unnatural.

Maybe Avery had been right—it was good to do something so different from his old job, get some distance from it. He was maybe even starting to get his swagger back.

He laughed at himself and got in the shower.

Before he left home he texted Craig back. Partly to stay friendly with him, just in case he'd ever need Craig in the future for a reference. But also because he'd always liked Craig; he didn't want to blow him off.

> Thanks for reaching out—good to see this. Hope all is well with you.

There. That was good enough.

When he caught up with his mom and Pete, his mom grinned at him.

"I can't believe my son voluntarily came to this place that I dragged him to for years when he was in high school," she said.

Luke hugged his mom.

"That's the difference between age fourteen and twenty-eight, I guess," he said. "Just point me toward the rooster."

He and his mom both laughed. Once, in high school, when he'd come with his mom to one of these things, she'd insisted on buying a huge metal rooster for his grandfather's yard; she'd said his grandfather would love it. Luke had hated the thing, and had no idea why his mom was so thrilled with this find, and was furious at his mom for buying it after she'd dragged him along to this stupid event, especially because he knew he would have to be the one to carry it to the car. But then, he and his mom had laughed so hard when he'd tried to wrestle the damn rooster into his mom's tiny sedan for the drive home that he'd forgiven the rooster. His grandfather had loved it, just like his mother had predicted. After his grandfather had died, his mom had called him and told him an antiques dealer had offered her hundreds of dollars for the thing, which had made them both weep with laughter.

His mom pulled him in for another hug.

"It's good to have you so close by, Luke. It's nice to be able to see you more often. When do you have to go back to work? Your real job, I mean. Or are you thinking about staying up here, working remotely?"

This was the perfect opening.

"Actually, Mom, I . . ." He swallowed. "I'm not sure."

He'd chickened out, again. But then, the time wasn't right—he couldn't tell her he'd quit his job and had no idea what he was doing with his life when they were in public. He'd do it later.

She nodded, that smug look back on her face.

"I understand."

She thought he meant Avery. She thought he was waiting to decide because of Avery. He had to tell her that wasn't actually happening.

But if he told her that, then how would he explain what he was doing here?

"Oooh, looks like there are some treasures over there!" she said, and ducked into a booth, leaving him and Pete standing there.

"You, um, liking the job at Noble?" Pete asked him.

A question he could actually answer honestly.

"Yeah, it's been great so far. A nice change from what I'd been doing, that's for sure." He shrugged. "I know it's weird to do it with my background and all, but it's fun, and the people are great. Really supportive and helpful."

"It's a good group there," Pete said.

Pete had been there with his team every day that week.

"Margot seems pleased with how the landscaping is going," Luke said.

Pete nodded.

"She's definitely very particular about what she wants, but I don't mind that. And she doesn't do that thing where she changes her mind after we've already made a decision. When she wants something, she makes it clear."

Luke thought back to that first night with Margot, when they'd left the bar. Yes, when she wanted something, she definitely made it clear. He fought back a grin.

His mom popped her head around the corner of the booth.

"I found a gorgeous set of vintage CorningWare. Can one of you bring it out to the car?"

Luke groaned, then laughed at himself. How did he always revert to teenage Luke when he was around his mom?

"Lead me to it." He reached his hand out to Pete, who was trying to volunteer for this. "I had this job first, Pete. Just give me your keys."

When he walked back to find his mom and Pete, he heard his mom's voice before he saw her.

"Well, Luke has only wonderful things to say, too!" She saw him walking toward her and beamed at him. "Oh, there you are! Look who we found!"

He knew, before she even turned around, that it would be Margot. Had he conjured her up, just by talking about her to Pete?

She turned and smiled at him.

"Hi, Luke," she said. Why was her voice always perfectly normal whenever she talked to him?

Well, not always. It hadn't been, last week in her office.

"Hi, Margot," he said. He looked over and saw Elliot deep in conversation with Pete. "Hi, Elliot." Elliot waved at him and went back to listening to Pete talk about soil.

"Enjoying the fair?" Margot asked him.

He grinned at her.

"Oh yeah, having a blast," he said.

"Don't say it like that," his mom said. "You know you're enjoying yourself."

"I am—somewhat—enjoying myself," he said to Margot. "But please, don't let that get out. I have a rep to worry about, here."

Margot laughed, and his mom just shook her head at him and smiled.

"Your secret is safe with me," she said.

"Pete, good talking to you," Elliot said. He nodded at Luke's mom. "Nice to meet you." He looked at Margot. "There's some equipment that I want to check out in the warehouse."

Margot nodded.

"I'll meet you over there."

Then Elliot turned and raced away. Luke's mom turned to Margot.

"I've met your brother at least three times," she said, a smile on her face.

Margot nodded.

"Yeah, that sounds like my brother." She smiled at the three of them. "Good to see you all. Luke, see you at the winery."

She followed Elliot, and Luke let his eyes linger on her, just for a second, before he turned back to his mom. Wait, would she have noticed that, and wonder why he was staring at Margot like that, when he was supposed to be dating Avery?

He looked down at his mom, but luckily, she wasn't paying attention to him.

"Oh, Pete, look—just the kind of thing I've been wanting for the kitchen!" she said, pointing to a clock.

What was Margot doing here? He hadn't seen her car in the lot—not that he'd been looking for it, so it could very well be here. Had she and Elliot come together? Were they here on some winery business? Maybe, and almost certainly, and why was he wasting time thinking about this?

He knew the answer to that.

———————

AS SOON AS MARGOT had seen Pete, and Pete had introduced her and Elliot to Lauren, she'd *known* that Luke was with them. Why, she had no idea, probably just because it felt inevitable, probably because her worst nightmare was for Elliot to find out about her and Luke.

She'd never met Luke's mom before, but she knew Lauren had always made a point to send people from her inn over to Noble, and Margot always returned the favor. There weren't that many Black-owned businesses in Napa Valley—they had to look out for one another. But it felt surreal, to stand there and smile and chat with Lauren, all the while waiting for Luke to walk up to them. Lauren had even said something about how she was so grateful to Avery, for getting Luke to move back to Napa. She'd had a little smile on her face when she'd said it. Did she think—or hope—that Avery and Luke were going to get back together?

Margot tried to push away all thoughts of Luke, but that was impossible. He'd looked particularly attractive today, with his worn jeans, an old Stanford T-shirt that was just a bit snug on him, and that part-embarrassed, part-defiant, part-pleased, wholly adorable look on his face when his mom teased him. *Damn.* This wasn't good at all.

She shook her head. Whatever. She'd dealt with her attraction to Luke Williams for this long; she could keep dealing with it until he inevitably moved on from Noble and out of Napa Valley. From what he'd said that first night at the Barrel, he wasn't planning to be in Napa all that long anyway, and she wasn't going to fool herself that he'd changed those plans because of her. She knew that Luke was attracted to her, but she didn't think that attraction actually meant anything to him. Men always found her too intimidating as it was; she was sure it didn't help that she was Luke's actual boss.

She found Elliot gazing at some equipment, a weird expression on his face.

"I got it," he said.

"Great," Margot said without any real idea of what he was talking about.

Forty-five minutes later, she knew all too well. A bunch of equipment from a winery that had gone out of business the month before, all of which had to be packed just so in Elliot's truck so nothing would break on the drive back to the winery, along with a pile of scrap wood and various other prizes.

"How are we going to get all of this—plus ourselves—in your truck?" she asked her brother.

Elliot shrugged in that way that had always infuriated her.

"I'll figure it out," he said.

They spent the next twenty minutes trying, and failing, to figure it out. They tried to do it one way, failed, unloaded everything, and tried and failed again.

Margot stood there, her hands filthy, her hair pulled on top of her head, sweat running down her face, and stared at the pile of stuff Elliot had bought.

"Why do we have to take all of this today?" she asked. "Why can't we get most of it and then come back for the rest tomorrow?"

Elliot didn't even look at her.

"We have to get it all by the end of the day," he said. "And there isn't time to do two trips from here to the winery and back before everything is closed up."

That would have been good information for her to know—or for Elliot to keep in mind—before they'd bought all of this.

She wiped her face with the bottom of her shirt.

"Then why didn't you have me take my car so we would have more space?"

He just shrugged and picked up a pile of wood.

"Wouldn't want you to get your car all dirty. Don't worry about this, it's not your kind of thing anyway. I'll figure it out."

Damn it, why did he always have to say things like that? Things that made her feel like she was the interloper who had taken over his winery? She wanted to yell at him, say her car wasn't even particularly nice, that she didn't care if it got dirty, that it got dusty all the time driving the roads around here and did he see her stressed about it? And why did he say it like that, that *he* would figure it out, not that *they* would, together?

Elliot had asked her to come with him just the day before, and she'd said yes, even though she had so much to do to plan for the party. They rarely spent time together anymore outside of the winery; she'd thought it would be fun, a bonding experience even, a time when they could relax in the car together and work together and feel like they were part of a team. Why had she thought that?

Tears sparked in her eyes, which just made her angrier.

"You know, I'm capable of—"

A car pulled up right next to them.

"Need some help?" Luke asked from the driver's side window.

"Luke." Elliot looked relieved. "Just the person we need, if you can spare the time."

Part of her—the part of her that was frustrated and hot and sweaty and mad and didn't want Luke seeing her looking as terrible as she was sure she looked—was pissed that Elliot seemed so pleased that Luke was there, like she hadn't been any help to him at all. But mostly she just hoped that maybe Luke could actually solve this problem, and she could get home at some point, and get in the shower, and be done with today.

Luke jumped out of the car.

"No problem. I just finished helping out my mom and Pete, so I'm all warmed up."

Margot smiled at him and tried to forget how bad she looked.

"I would say you don't have to do this on your day off, but I'm too grateful for the help to even pretend."

And that was true, even though she was also mortified for him to see her so disheveled and sweaty. Her hair was up in a bun, not like, a pulled-together topknot or a sexy, intentionally messy bun, but just a quick double loop with a ponytail holder she'd found in her bag to get her hair out of her face. Her jeans were dirty, her T-shirt was sticking to her body, and she was almost certain her eyeliner was smudged all over her face. Oh well, at this point she was too frustrated to care. Almost.

The three of them managed to load all of the stuff into the truck, and Margot grinned at Elliot and Luke.

"We did it!" she said. That was until she took a step back, and saw the big stack of wood sitting on the far side of the truck.

"Shit," she said, pointing to the wood.

Elliot sighed.

"Damn. It would all fit in the passenger seat. If only I hadn't brought you along with me."

She turned away, but Elliot must have chosen that moment to look at her.

"I didn't mean it like that," he said. Sure he hadn't. "I just meant I wish you had another way back to . . ." He looked from her to Luke. "Luke. Can you drive Margot home so we can put the rest of this in my truck and be done with it?"

Oh no.

"Sure," Luke said, "but we can also just put them in my car, you know."

Elliot shook his head.

"I don't want to get your nice car all dirty, and then you'd have to unload at the winery. You've already done enough work on your day off. But it'll all fit in the truck." He picked up all of the wood and set it inside while Margot and Luke just stood there. "See? So you can drive Margot?"

Margot wanted to say no, there must be another solution, but to protest now would seem churlish. Especially after how exhausted she and Elliot both were. And, at this point, the last thing she wanted was an hour-long car ride with her brother.

Luke looked at her, a question in his eyes.

"As long as that's okay with Margot," he said.

She shrugged.

"Sure. Thanks, Luke. We both really appreciate it."

He shook his head.

"It's no problem. You're just right—" He stopped for a second. "I'm sure it's not too out of my way to take you home," he finished.

Good save, Luke.

Margot rescued her tote bag from the passenger seat of the truck and turned to Luke's car.

"Ready?" Luke asked.

She nodded.

"Yep, I've got everything. Drive carefully, Elliot."

He ignored her, like she knew he would.

She and Luke got in his car and pulled away.

Twelve

MARGOT DIDN'T SAY ANYTHING as they drove out of the parking lot. Neither did Luke. When they pulled onto the main road, as if that was some sort of signal, they both started talking at once.

"I'm sorry if I—"

"I hope it's okay to—"

They both stopped, and then laughed.

"You first," Margot said.

Luke smiled at her, and then his smile faded.

"I was just going to say—I'm sorry if I said yes to Elliot too quickly. I'd understand if you didn't want me to drive you home. I haven't—really—apologized for what happened in your office, and I need to."

She shook her head.

"You have nothing to apologize for. I could have stopped you at any point. I didn't."

He turned and looked at her.

"Yeah, you could have. But still."

She waved that away.

"I appreciate it, but it was my fault, too," she said.

She tugged the ponytail holder out of her hair and let it down. It probably looked terrible, but the breeze from the open windows felt so good.

"Anyway," she said. "You didn't say yes to my brother too quickly. I think we both needed a break from one another. I was going to say that I hope it's okay to impose on you in this way, and on your day off." She untangled her hair with her fingers. "Oh God, I just remembered—you were with your family, you probably had plans for later!"

He shook his head.

"No, my mom had to get back to the inn, don't worry about that."

She relaxed against the seat and closed her eyes. It felt good to sit here, and have someone else be in charge, after a day of working and socializing and being on and dealing with Elliot. She was exhausted.

"Well, thanks again," she said. "A few more minutes of that and Elliot and I might have murdered each other. No, I should be accurate—Elliot is far too levelheaded to do something like murder. I would have been the one murdering him—that's on me."

She must be *really* tired. Luke worked for them, for God's sake. Why did she constantly forget that when she was around him?

"I shouldn't have said that, I'm sorry. That was wildly unprofessional of me. Again. Forget you heard that."

"First of all, I've always thought you and Elliot got along great, and I would never peg you as the killer if Elliot turned up dead," he said.

She couldn't help but laugh at that.

"And second, I can definitely forget I heard that. But also: if we keep tripping over things, and apologizing to each other, and cutting ourselves off, that's going to make this drive really annoying. Feel free to tell me no, this is crossing a line or whatever, but for the purposes of this car ride, can we make a rule that we're just Luke and Margot? That your job and my job don't matter, and I'm just your neighbor giving you a ride home? And everything we say to one another doesn't leave this car? Or we could not do that, and just sit in silence for however long it takes to get home"—they pulled onto the freeway and saw the traffic stretched out in front of them—"but I think that's going to take a while."

Margot thought about that. While she could usually chatter on for way too long with bright, impersonal conversation about the winery, somehow they already knew each other too well for her to talk to him like that. And it had been a long day; she was clearly so exhausted and stressed about Elliot and the party and everything else that she'd already threatened to murder her brother in front of one of their employees. Who knew what else she'd say?

"Okay," she said. "Just Margot and Luke. Cone of silence. Thank you."

She looked over at him. He was concentrating on merging into a lane, but he smiled. She liked his smile way too much. But right now they were just Margot and Luke.

"Honestly, you're doing me a favor," he said. "I spent hours with my mom listening to her talk about vintage kitchen goods or whatever; I need some interesting conversation so I don't go home and start looking up the difference between old Pyrex and new Pyrex, and if you know, please don't tell me; I know it will just lead to more questions, and I'm trying to pull myself out of this rabbit hole."

She laughed, like she knew he wanted her to. She could tell he was trying to put her at ease. She appreciated it. Being in the car with him, being this close to him, made all of her nerve endings feel exposed.

"Okay." He glanced over at her. "I'll go first. Here's something that I absolutely would only tell my neighbor Margot, not my hypothetical boss Margot—I up and quit my last job in a rage. Just got furious one day and quit."

She raised her eyebrows at him.

"Was it because of what you told me on the way back from the staff dinner? The racist thing that your old boss said?"

He shook his head slowly.

"No. Not for that. I'd probably have more respect for myself if that was why." He sighed. "It was something small, stupid. I brought something up in a meeting, an idea I had, and he mocked it. Just totally laughed at me, and got other people laughing at me, too. Which had happened more than once, actually—to me, to other people, he did that kind of thing, to kind of get us competing with each other—but I was just suddenly so fucking sick of it. I drafted my resignation email while I was still in that meeting, and about an hour later, I pressed send."

He wasn't looking at her. His hands gripped the steering wheel tightly. It had been hard, she realized, for him to tell her this.

"Good for you," she said.

He tensed up. She could feel it.

"What do you mean?"

Oh. He thought she was being sarcastic.

"I mean good for you. Really. I'm glad you did that. I've worked in toxic places like that and stayed far too long. Good for you for getting out when you did."

He was quiet for a while. She let the silence grow.

"Thank you," he said finally. "I'm sure everyone else thinks that I couldn't hack it anymore, that I wasn't strong enough to keep going. The only other person I've told—really told, I mean—about how and why I quit was Avery. Avery Jensen, you know her; she's one of my best friends. She also told me I did the right thing. It's not that I don't trust her, I do, but Avery never takes any bullshit from anyone, so of course she would think it was a good decision."

"Avery was right," Margot said.

Luke laughed.

"I won't tell her you said that. She'd lord it over me forever." His smile faded. "Anyway, I haven't even told my mom that I quit. I gave her some bullshit about taking a sabbatical and told her that's why I moved back up here. In an attempt to get her off my back, I found a new job at a winery." He smiled sideways at her.

"Ah, everything makes sense now," she said.

They both smiled for a moment.

His smile faded, and he looked straight ahead.

"I haven't even told Avery this, but sometimes I wonder if I should have just kept my head down, worked harder, had more grit or whatever. Or that the real reason I quit was I just wasn't good enough. I guess . . . I guess I haven't told my mom because I know I'd be disappointing her. She's just so proud of me—you saw her today, she brags about me to everyone like that. And if she knew I failed, like this . . . I just don't want to let her down."

"You didn't fail, Luke," Margot said. Did he want to hear that from her? She wasn't sure, but she had to say it.

He just shrugged.

"I guess. Sometimes it doesn't feel that way, though." She

started to say something else, but he kept talking. "My old mentor there texted me this morning—linked me to this big article about all of their brand-new diversity efforts, said to call him if I wanted to chat about any of that. Said he missed me around there."

She raised her eyebrows at him.

"Does this mean we're going to lose you soon?" She cleared her throat. "I mean, since I'm just your neighbor Margot, are you going to go back?"

He laughed.

"Back there? Oh God no, never. I think I burned too many bridges. Plus, I can't imagine working with that same set of assholes again. I'm sure I'll go back to tech someday, though. I actually liked the work I did, once upon a time, at least. I'm glad someone there seems to still like me, it'll mean a good reference and some good connections, but I can't imagine going back there. Luckily, I saved up enough while working there that I don't have to worry about my next steps for a while." He grinned at her, but it felt like he had to make an effort to do it. "There— that's a good story from your neighbor Luke, who gave you a ride home."

He clearly didn't want to talk about that anymore, okay.

"So is it my turn now?" she asked.

He shook his head.

"No. I mean, yes, of course, if you want, but when I said that I'll-go-first thing, I didn't mean you had to go next. I didn't mean to say all of that, it was just, being around my mom today made me feel . . . Anyway, sorry about that."

Margot waved that away.

"No apology necessary. I'm just your neighbor Margot, remember? Neighbors talk about stuff like this." She paused. "Family stuff is hard sometimes," she said, in a different, quieter voice.

"Yeah," he said. "It is."

LUKE GLANCED OVER AT Margot, who was looking at him with such an open, caring expression that he had to look away. He really hadn't meant to say all of that. Especially not the stuff about how he was disappointed in himself, how sometimes he felt like he'd really left because he couldn't hack it, that he wasn't good enough. Great, now Margot would think he wasn't good enough—that was the last thing he wanted. It was far too easy to talk to her, that was the problem.

"Speaking of family," she said. "You're probably wondering why I was threatening fratricide earlier."

He laughed, glad that she'd broken into his thoughts.

"I mean I was, but really, you don't have to talk about this if you don't want to."

"I know," she said. "But I can't just throw murder out there on the table and then never finish the story. That sounds like the beginning to every murder mystery I've ever read, and I don't want to be cast as the prime suspect." She hesitated. "But . . . if this is weird for you, for me to talk about my brother, since . . ."

"I can't imagine how it would be weird," he cut in. "I don't even know your brother. I'm just your neighbor Luke."

She laughed at that.

"Oh, right. I forgot."

He could tell she needed someone to listen to her. Maybe even that she wanted *him* to listen to her?

"When I—when we—inherited Noble Family Vineyards from

Uncle Stan, it was a shock," she said. "To me, and I think to everyone else in the family, Elliot included. We all expected it to go to Elliot. Just Elliot. He'd worked for Uncle Stan for years, everyone knew he was destined to be the winemaker here someday. Everyone knew—or, I guess, thought they knew—that the 'Family' in Noble Family Vineyards meant Elliot. No one thought it meant me." She shook her head. "That's unfair to Uncle Stan—that makes it sound like he never told me it meant me, too, or that I thought he didn't love me. That couldn't be further from the truth. He was wonderful to me, we loved each other a lot. I spent a ton of time with him at the winery But . . . I just assumed—we all did—that the winery would go to Elliot. Uncle Stan had been sick for a while, but he didn't tell us he was sick until it was pretty close to the end, and the end came faster than he thought it would. He'd said he had something to talk to me about, but by the time I saw him, he wasn't . . . he couldn't really talk about anything."

Luke kept his eyes on the road as she said all of this. He wanted to give Margot her privacy, but he also wanted to know if she was okay. Should he comfort her in some way? Or at least, attempt to? Her voice was steady, but that meant nothing. Margot was good at masking her emotions, he knew that much about her.

He risked a glance over at her, but she was looking away from him, out the passenger-side window, so he couldn't see what, if anything, her face would tell him.

"How did you find out?" he asked her. "About the winery, I mean."

She turned back toward him.

"Elliot told me. The day after Uncle Stan died. He thought I already knew—I think he didn't realize that Uncle Stan hadn't told me. He said something about what 'we' would do with the winery, and I said 'we?' He had a stone face about it, like Elliot does about everything, so I thought he was okay with it. But I was stunned."

She dug down into her bag and pulled out a water bottle and took a sip.

"It wasn't until I overheard him talking to one of our cousins. Someone on our mom's side who's never really liked me. We were all at the winery, after the funeral, and as I was coming out of the bathroom, I overheard Jimmy saying, 'I can't believe Stan left this place to you and Margot. Why would he do something like that?' I probably shouldn't have listened, but I'm sure there isn't a person alive who wouldn't have done the same thing. Elliot said, 'Margot and Stan were very close. He loved her very much.' Which would have been fine. But then Jimmy kept pushing. He said, 'But come on—Margot? You deserve this place, she doesn't! She's not actually going to do anything here. She'll get bored with it in a heartbeat, and then what are you going to do?'"

Margot paused, but Luke could tell something else was coming.

"And then Elliot said, and I'll never forget this, 'Of course she doesn't deserve it. But when that happens, I'll figure it out.'" She let out a long breath. "I didn't think Elliot would say something like that. But Elliot doesn't say things he doesn't mean."

She was silent again. Luke wanted to reach for her hand, but he knew he couldn't.

"I'm sorry, Margot. And you've had to work with him ever since, knowing that? Have you ever talked to him about it?"

She shook her head.

"What would I say? 'Oh, by the way, I know you don't think I deserve this place'? What would be the point? It wouldn't change anything."

"Have you been trying to prove yourself to him ever since?" he asked. And then immediately regretted it. He shouldn't have asked her that.

But she just sighed.

"Yeah, probably. Well—at first, definitely. Who knows, if I hadn't overheard that, maybe I wouldn't have come to work at the winery at all. Maybe I would have just hired someone, dropped by from time to time. Instead, I quit my job and threw myself into being the CEO of Noble, learning everything I could about the wine business. Now for the most part, I'm focused on my work on the business side, and I'm working hard for the sake of the winery, not Elliot. But sometimes . . . now it's less that I'm trying to prove myself to Elliot, but more trying to prove to El-liot that I love the winery just as much as he does. Maybe in a different way than he does, but I love it, nonetheless, and every-thing I do, I'm doing for the good of the winery, even though he has very different ideas on what is for the good of the winery." She sighed again. "I just wish . . . Elliot and I were close, before. But ever since then, there's been a barrier between the two of us. Even with something like today—I thought it was going to be a fun, relaxed day together, and it was, and then he got all closed up and stone-faced, yet again, and I was frustrated, and then he hurt my feelings, and I got angry at him, and wow, I shouldn't have told you a single word of that."

"Margot. I would never . . . This might be a weird thing to say, but you can trust me. I won't say anything about this. To anyone."

She looked at him, for the first time since she'd started this story.

"Thanks. I appreciate that. But that doesn't mean it wasn't highly unprofessional to spill all of my business and my broth-er's business and our business's business to one of our—"

"To Luke, your neighbor," he cut in. "And maybe even your friend?"

She gave him a faint smile, but it was a smile, nonetheless.

"To Luke, my neighbor. And my friend," she said. She looked at him sideways.

"Speaking of friends—you mentioned Avery. You two are close?"

He pushed the next question he was about to ask her away.

"Yeah, she's one of my best friends," he said.

She raised her eyebrows at him.

"Your mom seemed to think there was more going on there."

Oh God, what had his mom said to Margot while he hadn't been there? He made himself laugh.

"My mom would think that. We dated for something like three weeks back in high school, and then we realized we were much better as friends. But my mom has wanted us to get back together for years. I've tried to tell her it's never going to happen, but she won't believe either of us."

Was he just imagining it, or did she relax against her seat when he said that?

"Avery told me she just had a hard breakup? How's she doing?"

Avery must have mentioned that at their breakfast.

"I think she's doing okay, but with Avery, you never know. I couldn't stand that guy, she's way better off without him, which—"

"You *didn't* say that to her," Margot said.

"Which I made the mistake of saying to her right after they broke up," he said. "I didn't realize exactly how much of a mistake that was until she said, 'Do you know how stupid that makes me feel?' and then burst into tears. And while you may not realize what a big deal that is, I'll tell you that in the almost fifteen years we've been friends, I think I've seen Avery cry exactly once before this. I felt . . . so terrible." Avery had forgiven him pretty quickly, at least. "That was partly why I moved back here—she seemed like she could use a friend around. Granted, she didn't *say* that—she said now that I wasn't working, I should move somewhere else for a while, maybe I'd learn how to relax. Which is funny, because I don't think she's ever relaxed a day in her life."

They both laughed.

"So have you?" Margot asked. "Learned how to relax, I mean?"

He shook his head. "Absolutely not."

Margot grinned at him. "I didn't think so."

Luke knew he was smiling, far too big, but he couldn't make himself stop. He knew, actually, that he shouldn't even be doing this right now. It was his fault, this warm, close, intimate conversation he and Margot were having, where they'd both shared so much with each other, things neither of them meant to say. He'd started it, with that whole *in this car, we're just Luke and Margot* thing. Because the problem was that they weren't just Luke and Margot, and they both knew it.

He was just happy, right now, in this moment, with Margot sitting next to him, so close to him, and smiling at him in that way that had attracted him from the very first moment he'd seen her.

They finally passed the accident that had made the delay so intense for the past forty-five minutes, and the traffic got a lot lighter. They talked about other things, less heavy things, for the rest of the drive—their last vacations, favorite restaurants, what they'd both been reading. And all too soon, he pulled off the freeway.

Margot lifted a hand and pointed.

"To get to my house, you turn—"

"I know how to get to your house," he said.

"Oh. Right." After what she'd said about Elliot, he'd worried that she was embarrassed by what had happened between the two of them. But she still had that smile in her voice, and—he saw when he glanced over at her—on her lips.

A few minutes later, he pulled up in front of her house. And then he turned to face her, to see her smiling at him. But her smile was different from what he'd seen before. Not flirtatious and confident, like the night they'd met; not cool and professional, like at work; not even that friendly smile she sometimes gave him at work, when they managed to be normal and relaxed with each other. The smile on her face now was warm, trusting, open. It was his favorite way she'd ever looked at him.

"Thanks for the ride," she said. "And . . . for listening."

"It was my pleasure," he said. "Really. And thank you, too."

She didn't move to get out of the car. They both just sat there, looking at each other, until he lifted his hand and cupped her face. God, her skin was so smooth. He made himself drop his hand, before she could pull away. Everything in him wanted to kiss her.

"I hate this, you know," he said.

"I hate this, too," she said in a low voice. And then she turned and got out of the car without another word.

Thirteen

MARGOT PULLED ON HER black wrap dress on Monday morning, this time with flat caramel sandals, a denim jacket, and simple gold jewelry. It would be too hot for the jacket by eleven, but for now it was still just overcast and cool enough that she needed it. It was going to be a busy day today; she had a bunch of calls, appointments back-to-back all day, and a few tours, one of which she'd let Marisol do, and another she might let Luke do.

Luke. She sighed. What had she been thinking the day before, telling him all of that about her and Elliot? Talking to him like she had? Looking at him, right before she got out of the car, like she knew she had.

She knew what she'd been thinking. That she was frustrated and needed a sympathetic ear, and that Luke had appeared out of nowhere with those thoughtful eyes and that kind smile and that warmth in his voice for her. Everything had come spilling out, and it had felt so good to say it all out loud, to voice the resentment and frustration and confusion that she usually kept bottled up inside. And Luke had just listened. He hadn't given her advice, or told her it would all be okay or that maybe she'd heard Elliot wrong or that maybe he hadn't really meant it, or tried to play devil's advocate, or any of the things that would make her regret having told him. He'd just listened. That's why she'd looked at him like that. That's why she'd wished they were actually just Margot and Luke.

She usually rolled her eyes when men said "you can trust me" like Luke had. It was usually one of many signs that you absolutely should not trust them. But with Luke . . . it felt different.

She'd thought, for a moment there in the car when he'd dropped her off, that he was going to kiss her. He'd looked at her like he wanted to. But he hadn't done it, hadn't even tried. If he'd tried, she would have had to stop him, and it would have ruined the bond they'd woven together during the course of that car ride. If he'd tried, she would have known he hadn't listened to her when she'd said not to do it again. If he'd tried, they would have had to become boss and employee again, and said goodbye to Luke and Margot, friends. That look on his face when he'd wanted to kiss her, but hadn't, had been one of the most attractive things she'd ever seen. That he hadn't kissed her made her feel closer to him than if he had.

Margot sighed again and got in her car to drive up the valley.

As soon as she got to the winery, she was so busy it felt like she never stopped moving. She was on one call even before she walked in the door, a returned call from a restaurant owner in L.A.; she had to remember everything about his account on the fly, which she did, but barely. She was just off that call when Pete called; when she saw his number, she was sure it would be a crisis, him canceling the rest of the work he was supposed to do for them—but no, it was just to tell her he and his guys would be there early the following morning and hoped to finish up this week. She'd just had time to get coffee when Taylor buzzed her to say that some VIPs had stopped in without an appointment, so she had to check her lipstick and then breeze into the tasting room to charm them and ply them with the best of Noble's wines. They left an hour later, after messing up her whole schedule for the day, but also after buying three cases of wine.

She was so busy that day that whenever she saw Luke in passing, all she could do was smile or nod in his direction, and all he could do was smile or nod back. That was for the best. It felt different between them now. It had been one thing when they'd had sex, or kissed; that had been purely physical. But in the car together, they'd talked. Talked in a way that they hadn't before. That she hadn't with someone before, not in a while. She hadn't even gotten that vulnerable with Sydney in months—it had felt easier to just push all of those difficult emotions away, not talk about them, not deal with them. But she'd talked to Luke, and he'd talked to her, and they'd felt like friends. She didn't want to disturb that closeness between the two of them. But she also knew that it was exactly because she didn't want to that she had to ignore it, put it away from her. If she were smarter than she was, she would do something to shatter it, show Luke she was one hundred percent his boss, not his friend. But then, if she were smarter than she was, she never would have allowed that closeness to grow in the first place.

Margot went back into her office to check her email. She jumped when Elliot knocked on her door.

"Sorry, I didn't mean to scare you," he said.

"It's no problem," she said. "I was just . . . in the middle of something. What's going on?"

Elliot usually didn't come by during the day unless something was wrong. Though he'd been coming by the winery building more, recently.

"I just came by to check to see that you got back okay," Elliot said. "Yesterday, I mean. Since there was all that traffic on the way back up here."

What? He was checking on her now? Did he suspect something about her and Luke? No, that didn't make sense—he'd been the one to volunteer Luke to bring her home, anyway.

"Um, yeah, it was fine. A long drive, but no big deal."

He nodded.

"Okay, just making sure. Also, I know you said it was too expensive for Pete to get planter boxes. I was thinking that I could use some of that scrap wood I got yesterday to make some. If you wanted."

This was a surprise. Margot looked at Elliot, but he was looking at the old plan that she'd tacked up on her office wall.

"I'd love that," she said, carefully. Like if she talked too fast, it would scare him away. "If you have time, that would be amazing."

Elliot turned from the wall to look at her.

"I know there isn't time before the party to put vegetables and stuff in them, but we could get herbs, flowers, some things like that. I'll check with Pete about it all."

This was one of the only times he'd ever brought up the party himself.

"That sounds great," she said.

He turned to walk away. Then he turned back.

"I hate those things, you know. The auctions."

She had no idea.

"No, I didn't know," she said.

He nodded quickly.

"Makes me feel like a vulture, grabbing up everything from a winery, from people who tried their best and failed. It just makes me think . . . I'm always in a bad mood, after. I thought maybe bringing you along would help, but I . . ."

Her phone buzzed, and Elliot took a step back.

"You're busy, you probably have to get that. Talk to you later." He walked away, and left Margot staring after him.

Was that his attempt at an apology? If so, it actually did make her feel a bit better about Sunday. And explained why things had felt good between them early in the day, and it had all gone south later.

At the end of the day, she stood in her office, staring at the wall she'd devoted to the party, with her many lists, the old plan, and her own bad sketch of what the property would look like, so she could envision the layout of the party.

Taylor knocked on her open door.

"I think we're done for the day, boss, if you— What are you staring at?"

Margot laughed.

"Just trying to figure out how I'm going to arrange everything, and what the schedule is going to be. We're only a month out now, and I know that sounds like a lot of time, but . . ."

Taylor stared at the wall.

"This has gotten significantly more complex since the last time I saw it. I'll be right back." She disappeared out the door and came back a few minutes later, with Luke and Marisol in tow. "You guys, look at this wall!"

"This wall has really . . . expanded over the past few weeks," Marisol said.

"That's putting it mildly," Taylor said. "Has Elliot seen this? It's incredible."

"Is this your conspiracy wall?" Luke asked. "All you need are little red and green and blue strings to connect all the dots, and . . ."

"Enough out of you three." Margot fought back a grin. "But, if you know where to get strings like that . . . just let me know."

They all laughed. Margot met Luke's eyes, just for a second, and they grinned at each other. *Motherfuck*, that grin of his was dangerous. Margot swung her eyes back to the wall.

"Now that I have you three in here, you might as well help me with something. Okay: The party is over a three-hour time period—ideally, there will be plenty of food for at least the first two hours. The goal is to have people be able to taste a variety of different things, so there will be reasons for them to stay and chat and taste more wine and then also buy more wine. These are the potential food choices, and I have to decide on them soon." Margot gestured to the list on her second whiteboard. "We want them staggered, not ready all at once. I want everything to work together, but also not be too similar, and to have a good variety—for vegetarians, et cetera—and I can't decide. I've been staring at this board for hours, please help."

"This sounds like a standardized-test problem." Luke rubbed his hands together. "I loved those."

Everyone in the room turned and stared at him.

"What?" he said. "I was a real dork in high school. I think we've established that?"

Taylor and Marisol burst out laughing, and Luke grinned at them. Margot felt a stab of jealousy at the way they all laughed together, at their casual ease with one another, at this inside joke she wasn't a part of.

Oh no. She wasn't jealous of Taylor and Marisol because she thought there was anything going on with either of them and

Luke—she was jealous because they got to talk to him all day, they got to hear his stories, they got to know him better. That time in the car hadn't been enough for her. She wanted more.

She cleared her throat.

"Well, then, it seems like I've come to the right place," she said. "Any ideas?"

Luke looked at the board for a moment and then turned to her.

"Do you have any index cards? We need index cards."

Index cards. Why hadn't she thought of that?

"You're brilliant."

Margot grabbed a pack of index cards from her supply closet and tossed them to Taylor, who wrote all of the options down and put them up on the corkboard.

"Tacos should go second," Marisol said. "You don't want them first—you want everyone smelling them for a while and getting hungry, especially those people who planned to just stop in for a minute on their way to somewhere else. Then they'll stay, and eat tacos, and taste more wine. And buy more wine."

"Okay, but where does that put the wood-fired pizza?" Luke asked.

They debated and argued about the food for the next ten minutes, as Margot moved the cards around. And then, finally . . .

"I think we have a lineup," she said, with a smile at the corkboard and another at her staff. "Everyone happy with it?"

They all nodded, satisfied smiles on their faces.

"Good job, team," Margot said. "Thanks for your help, I never would have managed that without you. Now, everybody, go home, it's late."

They all grinned at her as they left her office.

"That was fun," Marisol said.

"Agreed," Luke said. "Let's do that again. The next time you need to work on the conspiracy wall. We're here for you, Margot."

He turned and met her eyes just before walking out of her office.

"Brilliant, huh?" he said under his breath.

She had said that to him, hadn't she?

"Don't let it go to your head," she said, trying not to smile.

He didn't even try.

"Oh, don't worry. It already has."

———

THE NEXT MONDAY MORNING, Luke left home earlier than usual so he could drop by his mom's place with flowers for her birthday on his way to work.

Craig had texted him again today. They'd texted a few times over the past week—just about what was going on with him, how Craig was doing, stuff like that. It was sort of weird, to get reminders of his old job. He hadn't been gone for even two months, but it felt like forever. Especially after working at the winery, which felt so different from his old job. *He* felt so different about it. Like, he was eager to get to work, every single day. It almost felt . . . too easy? Too good?

Of course, he knew part of the reason he was eager to get to work every day was Margot. He'd worried that things with her would be awkward after their car-ride confessions on Sunday, that she'd be stiff and uncomfortable with him, like on his first day at work. He'd been embarrassed that he'd told her how he felt about quitting his old job—he was still embarrassed about that. Would she be self-conscious about talking to him like she had? But on Monday, she'd smiled at him like she was happy to see him, and he'd smiled back in the same way, because he sure as hell was happy to see her. And then she'd called him brilliant in her office that day. Ever since, things had been easy between them. Friendly. Good.

I hate this, too.

Had she meant that when she'd said it? Really meant it? He had. He wasn't sure how much longer he could take this. Because as much as he loved working at the winery, he hated that it meant nothing could happen between him and Margot. If she even wanted anything to happen, which he had no real idea about.

He shook thoughts of Margot away as he parked a few doors down from his mom's house.

When he knocked on the door, Pete opened it.

"Oh good, you're here," he said, and turned and walked toward the living room.

That was a weird reaction.

"Hey, Mom. Happy . . ." His voice trailed away as he saw his mom, sitting on the couch, her arm in a blue cast. "What's wrong? What happened?"

She looked startled to see him, and then smiled at him like nothing was wrong.

"Oh, Luke, look at those flowers! They're beautiful! Thank you!"

He set the flowers down on the coffee table.

"Oh no, don't put them there, you should get them in some water, the vases are in the—"

"Forget the flowers," Luke said. "What happened?"

"Oh." She looked away from him. "Nothing major, it's really no big deal. I'm fine, I really am."

He looked at Pete, who shook his head.

"Lauren."

His mom sighed.

"I really am fine."

"Mom." Luke sat down next to her, and she winced. Shit, he should have sat down a lot slower. "Why is your arm in a cast?"

"I got in a—very minor—car accident last night. That's all."

"What?" He stood back up, and his mom winced again. This time he moved to the other side of the room. "You got in a car accident, and no one told me?"

"It was late at night," she said. "I was going to call you this morning."

"I wanted to call you last night, but your mother didn't want you to worry," Pete said. "I'd just finished telling her she had to call you this morning when you got here."

"It really was very minor!" his mother said. "Someone making a left turn hit me, they weren't going that fast, I'm fine! I just have a broken wrist, that's all."

"And a totaled car," Pete said.

She glared at him.

"We don't *know* the car is totaled." She turned to Luke. "Just because the airbag went off, Pete thinks it must be. Anyway, I'm going to be fine. And I *was* going to call you this morning, I just had to call Beth to make sure she could get to the inn early today since I won't be in."

"Or for the next month," Pete said.

Luke turned to Pete.

"Month?"

"Pete, I really don't think—"

Pete broke in.

"The doctor said that she shouldn't drive for three weeks minimum, maybe six weeks. Or more. It's more than just a broken wrist, she has a few sprained ribs, too." Pete glared at Luke's mom. "And she said you had to rest."

"I know," his mom said, "but I have the inn, and while Beth is lovely, and I like her so much, she's still new. I have to be on hand to do all of the hard stuff. I'm just not confident enough in her, that's all."

Pete shook his head.

"Well, you need to get confident. I don't want you to run yourself down, Lauren." He turned to Luke. "Your mother wants me to drop her off at the inn every day. Maybe she'll listen to you."

Unlikely.

"Mom, if the doctor said that you should rest . . ."

His mom sighed.

"I know, I know. If only I had Samantha still, but she moved to Los Angeles. She was so detail oriented."

Pete frowned at her.

"What if you call Samantha? See if she could come back up here, fill in for you for the next month or so?"

His mom brightened up.

"Oh, that's an idea. And I bet she could live with her sister."

And then it hit him. The solution to both of their problems.

"I have a better idea," Luke said. "Mom, what if I took over for you at the inn for the next month? I already know how stuff works there—well, most stuff—and you trust me to take care of things. Would that keep you at home, make you rest?"

Her whole face relaxed, and then she shook her head.

"Of course that would be wonderful, but you can't do that. You're working for Noble—I'm sure they need you, too."

He tried to keep his face neutral.

"I'm sure the Nobles will understand. I'll talk to them. What do you think?"

He could see the relief in her face.

"If you're sure, then . . . yes, that would be perfect. You'll check in, let me know how everything is going, right?"

He nodded at his mom as Pete clapped him on the back.

"Thanks, Luke." He lowered his voice. "She never would have agreed to take the time off otherwise."

"I heard that," his mother said. "But Luke, promise you'll tell me if the Nobles need you?"

He nodded.

"Yeah, I'll tell you."

Thirty minutes later, he walked into Margot's office. How would she feel about what he was going to tell her? Had he just made a bet that he was going to lose?

Margot and Elliot were standing in there, laughing together. If he hadn't desperately wanted to see Margot alone, he'd be glad to see that, after everything Margot had told him last weekend.

"Oh good, I'm glad I found you both here together," he said. What else could he say?

Margot turned and smiled at him, and then her smile dimmed, maybe because Elliot was there next to her, maybe because of the way Luke was looking at them; he didn't know.

"Hi, Luke," she said.

"Hi, Luke," Elliot said. "Come on in. What's up?"

Luke took a deep breath.

"I'm really sorry to do this to you two," he said. "But I have to resign."

He looked at Margot and saw a brief flash of something in her eyes. He didn't know if it was shock or sorrow or anger or happiness. God, he wanted to know. He turned to Elliot so he wouldn't betray himself.

"I wouldn't do this for any other reason," he continued. "But

I have to help my mom out; she got in a car accident last night—she's fine, but she has a broken wrist and some sprained ribs, and she can't work for the next month or so. Her front-desk staff at the inn is pretty new, so I said I'd help her out, but I'm really sorry to—"

Elliot cut in.

"Of course you have to help your mom," he said.

"Yes," Margot said. "Of course you have to help your mom."

She said it casually, with a smile on her face, but it wasn't that friendly smile she'd given him when he'd walked in the door. It was her boss-to-employee smile.

"We'll miss you around here, but the rest of us can pick up the slack in the tasting room," she said.

"If we get desperate, I can help out," Elliot said.

Luke and Margot both burst out laughing.

"No offense, Elliot," Margot said, "but that's a terrible idea."

"Do you see what I have to put up with here?" Elliot asked Luke.

Luke grinned.

"The thing is . . . she's right."

Elliot sighed. "Yes, of course she is."

Margot turned to Elliot, a look of sheer glee on her face that almost made Luke laugh out loud again.

"Did he really just say that?" she said out loud.

Elliot either didn't hear that or heard it and ignored it. He walked over to Luke, his hand out, and Luke shook it.

"Don't be a stranger, okay?" Elliot said.

Margot nodded at him, but didn't come over to shake his hand.

"It's been a pleasure having you at Noble," she said. She said it in such a formal way, like she'd say it to anyone.

Luke nodded at both of them.

"It's been a pleasure being here. I've really learned a lot from this place." He turned to the door and winced. "I have to go tell Taylor now, don't I? She's going to kill me."

Margot and Elliot both laughed as Luke walked out toward the tasting room.

Later that evening, after a long day at the inn, getting up to speed on everything and fielding what felt like dozens of phone calls from his mom, he got in the car to drive home. And he could think about only one thing.

Margot wasn't his boss anymore.

Was she thinking about that? Would she care about this as much as he did?

He had no idea. But he had to find out.

Fourteen

MARGOT GOT OUT OF the shower and wrapped her longest, plushest bath towel around her body. She'd given two tours that day and pitched in for an hour in the tasting room, in between many phone calls and emails and voice mails. She had needed at least an hour of undivided time alone to commune with her spreadsheets for the party, update her to-do lists, stare at her conspiracy wall and check things off, and she hadn't gotten it. The party was less than a month away, she had so much to do, so much was riding on it. So when she'd gotten home, hot, sweaty, and sad for reasons she didn't want to think about, she'd dropped her laptop on the coffee table, pulled her hair into a bun on the top of her head, and gotten straight into the shower. She'd get work done after she felt like herself again.

After she dried herself off, she pulled on her favorite silk robe to cheer herself up. What she needed cheering up from, she didn't have the time or inclination to dwell on just now.

He'd walked out just like that. Out of her office, where she'd been standing with Elliot and couldn't really say anything to him, and then out of the tasting room, and had driven away. Had he walked out of her life, too? He didn't smile at her or give her any looks like he wished she were alone in her office, or like he wished . . .

No, she wasn't going to think about this now. What did it matter, anyway? They weren't anything to each other, really. She should think about her robe. Wearing it did help. She'd splurged on it the year before, with visions of herself swanning around her house in it, lounging and drinking champagne and entertaining gentleman callers. It was deep red, with a floral pattern, and looked great on her. She rarely wore it, though. When she was at home, she was usually either working or snacking or both, and it felt too nice to wear while working, and she didn't want to get pasta sauce or olive oil or Cheeto dust on it, so she usually kept it in her closet. But it wasn't like she was going to change her work habits anytime soon, and it felt like a shame to let it just hang there in her closet. What good did it do her, just gathering dust? Absolutely none. Even if she got potato chips on it, she'd at least get the joy of wearing it.

She got a glass of water and sat down on the couch, her laptop in front of her. Was that a knock at her door? Sydney had texted that she might drop by with the sweater Margot had left at the restaurant the other night; it must be her. She was the only person who dropped by Margot's house, anyway. Margot had assumed she was at the restaurant by now, but maybe she'd had time to come by with a snack from Charlie—who Sydney was convinced had a crush on her—or some hot gossip she wanted to share in person.

Margot should be mad at the interruption; she'd wanted to get this work done all day. But right now, her heart wasn't in it.

She opened her front door, and then stopped.

"Luke."

He was leaning against the side of the porch. It was dusk, and the porch light wasn't on yet, so she could barely see the uncertain look on his face.

"Hi, Margot," he said.

At first she just stared at him.

"Um. Do you want to come in?"

He nodded, and she opened the door wider. So many questions jumbled around her mind, flew through her head, it felt like they were thought bubbles above her head, racing around and disappearing and reappearing at breakneck speed. She knew she should make them stop, take a breath, think, ask him, ask herself some of those questions.

But she didn't.

As soon as the door closed behind him, she reached for him. And then she kissed him. She kissed him how she'd wanted to kiss him in the car the week before, how she'd wanted to kiss him every day for the last month. Her lips on his, her body pressed against him; her desire for him, her sheer want for him, no longer hidden, but there for him to see, to feel, to taste.

He kissed her back immediately, at first with a sigh of relief that made her smile, then with determination. His hands moved slowly, possessively up her body, first skimming over her breasts, her waist, then gripping her hips and pulling her closer to him. She could feel the imprint of his fingers on her skin, through the thin silk of her robe. She held on to him tighter.

Finally, they broke apart, gasping for air, and she rested her head on his chest. After a moment, she looked up at him.

"Do you know what?" she asked him.

He smiled down at her and traced her eyebrows with his finger.

"What?"

"You don't work for me anymore."

His smile got wider.

"No," he said. "I don't."

And then he kissed her again, kissed her like he'd dreamed of this, or maybe she just thought that because she had. It felt like coming home, with his hands on her and his body against hers and that way he sucked her bottom lip, just the way she'd thought of and fantasized about for weeks.

Eventually, they stumbled to her couch and sat down. He took her hand and played with her fingers.

"I hated the way I had to leave today," he said. "With you and Elliot both there, I mean. I was glad that I could tell him directly, and that he didn't seem to be pissed at me—"

"He's not," she interrupted. "He meant what he said."

"Good," he said. "But to be honest, I don't give a fuck how Elliot felt about me leaving. I only care how you felt."

She touched his cheek.

"I was . . . I didn't . . . I wasn't sure how to feel, actually. I didn't know if you'd—"

He laughed, and pulled her closer.

"Are you kidding me? I have wanted you since the moment I first saw you, and then every single moment since, and you didn't know what I was going to do as soon as I wasn't working for you anymore?" He traced the neckline of her robe with his finger. "When you answered the door in this," he said, "and you clearly weren't expecting me, I was consumed with jealousy, you know. I thought you were expecting someone else."

She laughed softly. That would have never occurred to her.

"That's very flattering, but I haven't thought about anyone

but you since that night." She kissed him softly. "I shouldn't say that, I know, I should play it cool, pretend I haven't been thinking of you, of that night, for so long. But I'm not good at that."

He dropped light kisses along the neckline of her robe.

"That's the biggest lie you've ever told, Margot Noble, because you've seemed excellent at it to me. Here I've been staring at you all day at work like a lovesick puppy, and you barely glanced my way." He loosened the tie of her robe and pushed it off one shoulder. "I know you didn't look at me, I was checking."

She couldn't believe she was really allowed to do this. Kiss him, like she was doing now. Slide her hands up and down his body. Breathe in his scent. Luxuriate in the way he looked at her, touched her, with his hands, his lips, his tongue.

"I had to pretend," she said as his fingers circled her nipple. "But my God, I wanted you. I wanted this."

He pushed her slowly back on the couch.

"I just need to look at you," he said. "Then I'll believe this is really happening."

She should feel self-conscious, with all the lights on, as she lay here, half-naked—more than half, really—with him staring at her. But she didn't feel that way at all. Maybe it was because they'd done this before, maybe it was because she felt so comfortable with him, but all she could do was glory in the way he looked at her. That look of pure need. He'd looked at her like that in her office the day they'd kissed. She'd almost thought she'd imagined it until now.

She reached for the bottom of his shirt and pulled it up over his head.

"Until that time in my office, I really wasn't sure that you—"

"That I wanted you—that I want you—so much I could barely

function?" He lowered himself on top of her, and she reveled in the feeling of his body on hers, his warm and smooth skin against hers, his breath on her chest, her cheek, her neck.

"Do you know what I thought about, later that night, after I kissed you in your office?" he said in her ear. "I heard your voice, over and over, saying you wanted me. I thought about how much I wanted you, what I wanted to do to you, what I wanted you to do to me." He opened the robe all the way.

She reached for his belt.

"So did I."

He looked at her, so intently, and smiled.

"What did you think about? What did you want me to do to you? Because, I promise, I am down for it all."

She could feel how hard he already was. She wanted him inside her right now, but she also wanted this moment to last forever.

She took his hand from where it rested on her shoulder.

"I thought about you touching me here." She moved his hand to her breast. "You came so close, in my office that day, and I wanted it so much."

He squeezed her already-hard nipple between his finger and thumb.

"You stopped me," he said.

"I know," she said. "But I didn't want to."

He leaned down and sucked her nipple in between his lips. She closed her eyes, and let her head fall back against the arm of the couch.

"God, I love when you do that," she said.

She could feel him smile against her skin.

"I can tell. I love that I can tell." One of his hands was at her waist, and she covered it with her own.

"Do you want to know what else I thought about?" she asked him.

He lifted his head to look at her.

"Absolutely I do."

Had anyone ever been this laser focused on her? Not that she could remember.

She slid his hand down.

"I thought about you touching me here," she said, moving his fingers between her legs. He dipped one finger inside of her, and she watched his smile widen.

"Were you this wet, when you thought about that?" She moved her hand out of the way as he pushed her knees wider.

She shook her head.

"Not until I thought about how much I wanted you to put your tongue there."

Now his grin was very wide.

"Have I ever told you that I like the way you think?"

She shook her head. She couldn't believe she'd waited so long for this.

"You haven't, as a matter of fact." She ran her fingers up and down his arms. She couldn't stop touching him. Maybe, eventually, she'd believe this wasn't one of her fantasies.

"Well." He slid onto the floor and swung her legs wide. "I like everything about you."

She looked down at him as he pressed kisses from her knee all the way up her thigh. She wasn't sure she'd ever seen anything so arousing. When he was almost there, almost where she wanted him, he moved to the other side, with a little smile on his face. She reached down and played with his hair, so springy under her fingers. He moved slowly, teasing her a little. It was agonizing. She loved it.

Finally, oh God, finally, his tongue slid inside of her, and she let her eyes flutter closed. She'd wondered if she'd just made up how good he was at this, built it up in her mind, because she had to see him almost every day, because she'd wanted him so much. She'd wondered if maybe she'd pretended to herself that he—that this—was more than what it actually was.

But somehow, it was even better. As she gripped his hair, as he kissed and licked and squeezed and sucked, as she sighed and gasped and opened her legs wider and wider, it felt so good that it felt almost impossible, that nothing in the world could ever feel this good. And then he moved, just in the right way, and her fingernails dug into his shoulder, and he kept doing that, just the way she liked it, faster and faster, and she came so hard she almost forgot to breathe.

When she opened her eyes, he was sitting up on the couch again, with her legs draped over him, smiling at her.

"That was . . . holy shit," was all she could say.

He laughed. He'd somehow lost his pants, thank goodness. She took his hands and pulled him toward her. He understood, and crawled up her body, to lie half next to her, half on top of her, on the couch.

"Can I tell you something?" he said in her ear. She nodded.

"Every time I would walk by your office and see you sitting in there, at that big desk, I would think about how I wanted to crawl underneath it, and push your legs apart, and slide my tongue inside of you, and make you come, just like that."

She trailed her hand all the way down his chest, down to his cock, which was hard as steel. He took one quick breath when her fingers landed on him, and then he moved slightly, to give her more access.

"You know that means I'm never going to be able to sit at my desk again without thinking of you underneath it, with my legs wide open to you, right?"

She looked up at him, and he smiled, but his eyes were on her fingers.

"That wasn't my intention in telling you that, but wow, is that an excellent side benefit for both of us."

She started to move her hands faster, but he stopped her.

"I need to be inside of you." He kissed her, hard, and moved his hand back to her nipples. "As soon as possible."

Then he dropped his head back against the couch.

"Shit. I came here straight from the inn. I didn't plan . . . any of this when I left my house this morning. I don't have any condoms."

She pushed him back up.

"Bedroom is that way. Nightstand, bottom drawer."

He jumped to his feet.

"Oh, thank God."

She smiled as she watched him race into the bedroom. She could have just moved this whole operation in there, she realized. But she was too relaxed, too content, to think about doing anything but staying right here and waiting for him to come back.

Which he did, very quickly, and with a big smile on his face.

"That's a very interesting bottom drawer you have there," he said as he came back to the couch.

She laughed, and blushed a little. She'd been so single-minded in her quest to get condoms that she'd forgotten what else he'd see in that drawer. It was a little early in their relationship—if this was a relationship—for that, but he certainly didn't seem to mind.

"Too much for your youthful eyes?" she asked him as he knelt on the couch above her.

He opened his eyes wide.

"Oh yes, absolutely. Why, I don't even know what some of those things actually do." He leaned forward, and whispered in her ear. "I might need you to show me."

She hadn't been sure, after he gave her that incredible orgasm, if she'd be up for more tonight, or if she'd be too blissful to really get into it. Well, that little whisper took care of that particular worry.

She put her hands on his knees, and ran them up to his thigh, and then onto his hard cock.

"After you kissed me in my office that day," she said, "when I got home that night, I opened that drawer right away."

He froze.

"Holy fuck, Margot. Please tell me you're serious."

She nodded. He licked his fingers and rubbed them over her nipples. She smiled.

"I felt so guilty about it. But it was all I could think of. I wanted your hands on me and your body against mine and to feel you inside of me, so I had to . . . imagine."

He tore open the condom packet in his hand and rolled it over his cock.

"That is the hottest fucking thing I've ever heard. The previous record, by the way, was held by a woman who, just about a month ago, demanded to know how close my apartment was, because we both knew we needed to get each other naked as soon as possible."

She laughed out loud as he pushed her thighs farther apart.

"I was pretty aggressive that night, wasn't I?"

He moved his hands down to her hips.

"I fucking loved it."

And then he thrust himself inside of her.

"Oh God, Margot. You feel so good."

As he drove himself into her, she moved back against him, arched her back, gripped him, in search of just the right angle. They found it together, and he moved harder and faster, and she clutched at him as the waves of pleasure went through her, and they kept going, until he collapsed on top of her with a low moan.

He pulled himself off her, with clear effort, and went to the bathroom to throw away the condom. Then he came back to the couch, and she pulled him down to her.

"Well," she said. "I'd say that was worth having to hire a new employee."

He bit her ear, and she laughed.

———

THEY STAYED CURLED UP together on the couch like that for a while, until his stomach growled. Margot giggled. Luke didn't think he'd ever heard her make such an undignified noise. Well, other than about five minutes before.

"Is that your way of telling me you want dinner?" she asked.

He lay back on the couch and pulled her on top of him.

"Absolutely, though I'm going to tell you right now, I refuse to go to the Barrel with you. Your friend Sydney intimidates me."

She giggled again.

"She intimidates everyone. But no, we absolutely can't go there right now. First, I don't want to put clothes on, but second, okay, yes, Sydney will take one look at us and alert the entire bar."

She pulled herself up, despite his attempts to keep her on top of him.

"I'll make us pasta."

He got up, too, and followed her to the kitchen.

"You don't have to do that, we can order something."

She was already filling a pot with water.

"I know, but in the time it'll take for it to get here, I could make us pasta twice over."

Well, he wasn't going to complain if a hot, naked woman he'd just had excellent sex with wanted to make him dinner. She bustled around, taking eggs and cheese out of the fridge, and garlic out of the pantry.

"What can I do?"

She smiled at him.

"You can pour us some wine. There's a bottle open in the fridge."

He found the bottle, and then dodged around her to reach the wineglasses.

"What else?" he asked as he set her glass on the counter at her right hand.

She looked at him for a second.

"Please don't take this the wrong way, but you can sit at the counter there and talk to me, and—"

"And get out of your way?" he finished, moving out of the kitchen to sit at the counter.

She laughed.

"Yes, thank you. This kitchen is too small to have more than one person in it at a time."

He looked at her, standing next to the stove, a glass of wine in one hand, a knife in the other, as she sliced garlic, and bacon sizzled next to her.

"Um. Can I also do one more thing?" He went back in the living room and picked up the silky, clingy, incredibly sexy robe she'd been wearing when he came to her door. "Not that I *want* you to put clothes on right now," he said, when he came back into the kitchen, "but I've quickly become very attached to those breasts of yours. I don't want them to get burned."

She grinned at him and slid the robe on.

"Better?" she asked as she took a sip of her wine and stirred the bacon in the pan.

He shook his head.

"I mean, yes and no. That seems a lot safer, but I miss the view." He bit his lip. "Though . . . you look pretty fantastic in that robe, I'm not going to lie."

She'd tied it very loosely. He liked it that way.

"See, if we'd gone somewhere, or ordered food, at least one of us would have had to put actual clothes on, and that would have been terrible." She giggled again. "I just imagined the look on Sydney's face if I'd walked into the Barrel to pick up takeout in this robe."

He looked up from her cleavage.

"Did she tell you that I went there, looking for you?"

Why had he just blurted that out? If Sydney had told her, which was likely, there was no need to talk about it right now.

She put down her wooden spoon and looked at him.

"No. When did you go to the Barrel looking for me?"

Oh.

"I assumed she told you. It was after that time in your office. Later that night." She lowered her glass to the counter. "I walked over there, thinking maybe you might be there. I wanted to . . . I don't know, see you, talk to you, apologize, something. And then I stood outside for a while and decided that if you were there, you wouldn't welcome me coming to find you. So I turned away. Sydney saw me. I think she approved."

Margot had an expression on her face he couldn't decipher.

"Yeah, she would approve," she said finally. A tiny smile came to her lips. "So do I."

The water boiled over and hissed on the stove. Margot grabbed a big handful of pasta and dropped it in the pot and gave it a big stir.

"I think Sydney feels . . . responsible," she said. "For what happened that first night."

He laughed.

"Responsible? Why?"

She looked up at him from under her lashes.

"She kind of . . . dared me to hit on you that night. She was *very* proud of herself when we left together." She made a face. "That was, until I talked to her on Monday."

Luke laughed.

"Ah, that's why you said 'responsible' like that. I was going to say, 'responsible' means it was something bad, and that night certainly wasn't."

Margot laughed, and then sighed.

"No, but I felt pretty guilty, and Sydney knew it. I didn't even tell her about that kiss in my office, you know. But she knew I was . . . having trouble not thinking about you. That's probably why she reacted the way she did to you when you went to the Barrel. She even—"

Margot stopped, and turned the temperature down under the bacon. It wasn't until she reached for the tongs that he realized she wasn't going to finish.

"She even what?" he asked her.

She stirred the pasta with the tongs, not looking at him.

"Nothing." He didn't think it was nothing, not by the way she avoided his glance. She finally looked up, and laughed at the look on his face. "Fine. She sort of dared me to hit on someone else. Later that same night."

He tried not to let her see the wave of jealousy that hit him when she said that.

"Did you do it?" He shouldn't ask. It wasn't any of his business. Margot had been his boss then.

But he hated it when she nodded.

"I felt like I needed to do something to . . . get you out of my system." She shrugged. "It didn't work."

"Oh?" He wouldn't ask any more questions. He was glad Sydney's stupid plan hadn't worked, obviously, but he didn't want to know the details.

"Yeah. He kissed me, outside the Barrel." Great. She was telling him the details anyway. "But I felt nothing at all. So I turned around and went back inside."

He couldn't hide his relieved grin.

"Nothing at all, huh?" He took a sip of his wine. "That poor guy."

He didn't mean it, though. He didn't feel sorry for that guy at all.

A few minutes later, Margot set a big bowl of pasta in front of him.

"You are a goddess, Margot Noble," he said.

She laughed and sat down next to him and stuck a fork into her own pasta.

"You are easy to impress, Luke Williams."

He shook his head.

"No. I'm not."

He looked at her—hair piled on top of her head, her cheeks pink from the heat of the kitchen, that soft smile around her lips—and smiled.

They both dove into their pasta. When he was almost done, he thought of something he really should tell her.

"Avery knows. About that first night, I mean. I had no idea you two knew each other when I told her. But I'm sure she hasn't told anyone."

"That's okay." She laughed. "That does explain why she made it a point to tell me that the two of you were absolutely just friends."

He pushed her robe to the side and put a hand on her thigh.

"She told me she thought you were jealous when you saw us together at dinner, but I didn't believe her."

She leaned closer to him.

"Oh, she was right."

He couldn't help himself from smiling at that.

"I can't tell her that, I'll never hear the end of it," he said. "But I'm glad you told me."

She smiled as he played with the sash of her robe.

"Oh, are you?"

He nodded, and moved his hand up higher.

"Mmmhmm." He looked at her. "I don't—quite—understand why you have clothes on right now."

She shrugged. The neckline of her robe almost—but not quite—fell off her shoulders.

"Apparently, someone was concerned about me cooking in the nude. I was a little worried that meant he didn't want to see me naked, but—"

He kissed her, hard, before she could finish that sentence. He pushed her legs apart and slid his fingers inside of her, and she gasped against his mouth.

"Do you need me to tell you how I feel about seeing you naked?" He untied her robe and stared down at her. "Do you need me to tell you how often I fantasized about just that, how clearly I remembered this mole, right here?" He licked that hollow between her breasts and sucked on the mole in the center. "Because I can, if you want. But also, that big bed of yours looked very enticing. I have a feeling we can have a lot of fun there."

Margot stood up, leaving the robe behind.

"I'm not sure this has to be an either-or," she said.

He followed her into the bedroom.

"You're absolutely right. One question: Are you really as flexible as I've remembered? And if so . . ."

———

MARGOT WOKE UP EARLY the next morning. She could sense Luke's presence in her bed, even though they weren't touching. Her back was to him, but she could feel his warmth behind her. The sound of his regular breathing relaxed her. Even though she had no real idea what was next for them.

Was this just another one-night thing? Just to get each other out of their respective systems, so they could stop thinking about how it would be (fantastic) and wondering if the first time had been a fluke (absolutely not) and then go forth and forget about each other since they didn't have to see each other every day anymore?

She hoped not. She didn't know what she wanted from Luke, but she knew that she wanted more than one more great night.

She had to tell him that. She'd had enough of all of this uncertainty and pretending.

His slow, even breathing changed. She felt movement behind her. And then a gentle kiss on her shoulder blade. And then another. And then another.

She turned over and smiled at him.

"I thought I dreamed you," she said.

He burst out laughing, and kissed her cheek.

"Good morning to you, too." He put his hand on her waist and pulled her closer. He didn't move his hand up, or down; all he did was hold her like that and kiss her shoulder. She leaned her head against his chest and relaxed into him. When was the last time someone had held her, just like this? Without asking for anything in return, but just because? She couldn't remember. She hadn't realized how much she'd wanted this. Needed it.

"I hate to ask this," he said after a few minutes. "But what time is it?"

She reached for her phone, which she kept on her bedside table overnight. It wasn't there.

"I think I left my phone in the living room." She looked up at him. "I must have had my mind on other things last night."

He grinned at her. His cheek was creased from the pillow, his eyes were still only half-open, and he was the best thing she'd seen in the morning for a very long time.

"You must have."

He kissed her cheek and then pulled himself out of bed.

"Let me grab mine. I'm sorry, I wouldn't even bother, but you see"—he shook his head—"I have this new job now, I have to get there a lot earlier than my old one."

She laughed as he walked out of the room.

He was back in a few seconds, his phone in one hand and his clothes in the other.

"I have time to go home and change and get to the inn on time, but I have to leave"—he looked down at the phone in his hand—"in only a few minutes, which does not give me the time to do what I want to do right now, with you all warm and naked and luscious."

Had anyone ever described her in such complimentary terms before? Certainly none that made her feel this good.

"That's unfortunate," she said as she watched him pull his clothes on.

"It really is," he said, his eyes on her.

When he was almost dressed, she got out of bed and slid into the robe hanging on the back of her closet door. Not her silk one, that was in the living room still . . . or maybe the kitchen? She needed to remember to hang it up. Maybe get it dry-cleaned. It had done so much for her.

She smiled at the disorder in her house as they walked to the front door. Pasta bowls, forgotten in the kitchen. Her robe, on the kitchen floor. Her laptop and phone, on the corner of the coffee table. The couch cushions everywhere.

He turned to her when they got to the door. She had to do this now, before she lost her nerve. She opened her mouth, to tell him that she wanted to see him again, that she didn't want this to be like last time, when he touched her bottom lip with his fingertip.

"When can I see you again?" he asked.

A spark of joy flamed in her chest. She must have looked surprised, because he laughed.

"I haven't lusted after you for the past month to let you get away with this only being one night, you know. Not again."

Lusted after her. She liked the sound of that.

"Plus," he said, "don't you want to find out if this is something?" He looked at her for a long moment. "I do."

She reached for his hand and smiled at him in the way she'd wanted to, but couldn't, for the past month.

"Yeah," she said. "I do, too. Tonight?"

He smiled back at her.

"Tonight's great."

She pulled him against her body and kissed him, and it was so easy, so perfect, so good. After too short a time, he took a step back.

"I want to stay here all day, but . . ."

She dropped her hand.

"I know. You have to go."

He opened the door and took a step outside, before he stopped and turned back around.

"Do you think that maybe now you'll give me your number?"

She burst out laughing and held out her hand for his phone.

"I don't think I've ever had to work this hard for one woman's number," he said as she typed her number in.

Then his eyes skimmed over her, from head to toe, and back up.

"It was all worth it, though."

She laughed again.

"Save that charm for the guests at the inn today, you've already gotten me into bed."

He grinned at her.

"True. But I hope to do so again. Without as much time in between as last time."

She laughed again and waved him out the door. When she closed it behind him, she leaned back against the door and smiled.

Fifteen

ALL LUKE WANTED, ALL day Tuesday, was to be with Margot. He felt silly about it—like it was the first time he had sex, and all he wanted was to do *that* again. Ridiculous. He smiled. And yet.

He even texted her as soon as he got to work.

LUKE

> Just checking to make sure this is really you

She texted back, but not for thirty agonizing minutes.

MARGOT

> Who's this, again?

> ☺

> You forgot your belt

He shook his head and grinned.

LUKE

You're cruel, do you know that?

He wished he was at the winery, where she was just a few steps away, where at any point during the day, he'd be able to see her, talk to her. Instead of here at the inn, where he was fielding calls to the front desk asking for extra towels or more toilet paper or directions to restaurants or whether it was true that harvest wasn't until the fall.

But if he were at the winery, and not here, last night never would have happened. And tonight wouldn't be happening, either.

He answered the next call with a much bigger smile on his face.

And then, at lunchtime, it hit him.

He had to figure out what to do with Margot tonight.

This was their first date, after two nights and many days spent together and one long, intense, excellent car ride. And he'd said that thing this morning, kind of impulsively, that he wanted to see if this was something. And it was true, he did, but if he'd thought about that more, he probably wouldn't have said it.

But then, she'd said she did, too. Maybe his impulse was correct.

He'd known how to do first dates before. Back in his old job. He met women on apps, almost exclusively; he suggested one of, like, five bars, though occasionally they suggested somewhere else; he would drink a beer or two; if it went well, they'd order food; if it went very well, he'd end up in bed with them a few hours later. Like he had with Margot, that first night, but also, completely different. Everything with Margot was different. She just . . . had a way about her. Something that drew him to her, right away. And, unbelievably, she seemed to be drawn to him, too.

But what was he going to do for a first date with her tonight? He now knew a handful of bars in their neighborhood, none of which felt right for this, and he definitely couldn't take her back to the Barrel. And he knew Margot well enough now to know that she had very particular tastes, so he didn't want to just pick a restaurant without consulting her. Nor did he want to just leave it up to her, which would be far easier, but then she'd think he didn't care about tonight, and he didn't want her to think that.

Avery would know where he should go. But this time he should probably check with Margot before telling her anything about them.

Wait. He had an idea. He pulled out his phone.

LUKE

1) Long story but I'm filling in for my mom at the inn for the next few weeks—she's fine, but she got in a car accident and broke her wrist and can't drive for a while

2) I don't want to bother her with this or she'll think the place is falling down without her but one of the guests wants to know a good place for a romantic dinner tonight that might still have reservations? Good food is important, he says. Help me not send this guy to a tourist trap!

Avery texted him back a few minutes later.

AVERY

> 1) I'm going to kill you for not telling me your mom got in a car accident. Just for that, I shouldn't answer this

> 2) But because I'm incredible, I will: for romance and good food, I'd go with Verdant, Yard and Vine, or Zuzu. Oh, or maybe Carina

Thank goodness for Avery.

LUKE

> You're the best. And I know I know, I'm sorry. She didn't tell me until the next day either, if it makes you feel any better

Two of her options had openings. He made reservations at both, then texted Margot.

LUKE

> For tonight: Yard and Vine at 6, or Verdant at 8? Neither is also a perfectly fine answer if you're in the mood for something else

He thought of how he'd woken up that morning, with Margot next to him. When he'd pulled her close, she'd nestled into him with a little sigh. He wished he'd been able to stay longer.

His phone buzzed.

MARGOT

> Verdant at 8 sounds great. That'll give me time to get home from work. And I've been wanting to go to that place

Bless you, Avery.

LUKE

> Perfect. Pick you up at 7:30?

She texted back right away.

MARGOT

> Sounds great. See you then

He knocked on her door at exactly seven thirty that night. She laughed as she opened it, her jacket in her hand.

"It's good I know that you're terminally punctual; otherwise, I would be alarmed that you're already here, and I also would be at least five minutes from being ready. Luckily, I remembered."

He smiled down at her. She was wearing a clingy emerald green cotton sundress, and her hair cascaded over her shoulders. She seemed lit from within, with the way she smiled and laughed at him.

"You look incredible," was all he said. That didn't feel like what he meant, but then he wasn't exactly sure he knew how to say what he meant.

She looked suddenly almost shy. He never would have thought to describe Margot Noble as shy, but it was true.

"Thank you." She picked up her bag and slid on sandals. "Shall we go?"

He glanced sideways at her as they walked down to the car together. She looked so elegant tonight, in just a simple sundress and jewelry. He suddenly felt too young, too unseasoned, to be walking next to Margot. He knew he was younger than her, but he wasn't quite sure *how* much younger. Did she know? Did she care? If he asked her how old she was, she would think he cared about her age, which he didn't. Well, not like that—he just wanted to make sure she didn't care. See, this was why he couldn't ask her, because even in his head he sounded like he cared for all the wrong reasons.

He opened the car door for her, and she smiled at him. He realized what would help him stop overthinking this.

He got in the driver's side and unbuckled the seat belt she'd just put on.

"I meant to do this at the door," he said, "but you in that dress got me all flustered."

She laughed as she turned to him.

"Did I? What did you mean to do then?"

He took her face in his hands.

"This." He leaned forward to kiss her, just as she reached for him. The kiss felt familiar now—he knew the way her lips felt against his, the way her body dipped and curved under his hands, how smooth her skin was. But it still felt so exciting, so hard-won, that he could just reach for her like this, and kiss her, and have her meet him kiss for kiss, touch for touch, with that soft sigh and gentle tug that thrilled him so much.

Finally, they pulled apart, and he touched her bottom lip with his thumb.

"Hi," he said softly.

"Hi," she said. They smiled at each other as she put her seat belt on again.

———

LUKE DIDN'T REACH FOR her hand as they got out of the car and walked inside Verdant. Margot was both disappointed and relieved about that. She didn't—exactly—want to walk into the restaurant holding his hand. It wasn't anything about Luke; he was great. She was actually worried that he was too great, that this whole thing was some sort of a trick, or mirage. But that wasn't why she'd been relieved.

She was sure she'd run into someone she knew tonight—it was almost impossible not to, these days. And she was worried she'd run into someone who knew that Luke had been her employee up until yesterday. Or even someone who thought he was still her employee, currently. And that then they'd tell her brother.

She should have thought about this earlier today, when Luke had asked if she wanted to go to Verdant—one of the hot new restaurants in the valley—for dinner.

But all she'd thought when she'd gotten that text was how it had been years since someone had put thought into a date with her, planned something for her like that, and how wonderful and surprising and disconcerting it was. When she'd said "tonight" that morning to Luke, she'd just expected him to come over for sex again, maybe buy her takeout for dinner, if he really gave it some forethought. She hadn't expected a real date.

He'd obviously gotten advice from Avery on where to take her, which was so fucking sweet it made her want to lean over and kiss him right here, in the doorway of the restaurant. She didn't do it—she didn't even reach for his hand—but just thinking of it made her almost not worried about whether she'd run into someone she knew.

"We have a reservation at eight—Williams, party of two," Luke said.

The host smiled at them.

"Margot! Good to see you."

Margot almost laughed, it happened so quickly. This host had worked at the Barrel last year for a few months.

"Hi, Sean. Good to see you, too. I didn't realize you were here now."

He picked up two menus and tapped something at the computer before he led them to their table.

"Yeah, I've been here since they opened. Sydney helped me get this job, I owe her one. Tell her I say hi."

Margot apparently had a great deal to tell Sydney the next time she talked to her.

"Will do."

Luke laughed after Sean walked away.

"Do you know everyone in this town?"

Margot shook her head.

"Not at all—I'm brand-new here, by the standards of Napa Valley, but I've tried hard to remember names, it makes a big difference when you're trying to establish yourself. But the thing is, as you know, there aren't all that many Black women in Napa Valley, especially not Black women winery owners, so everyone seems to know *me*. Which definitely keeps me on my toes."

"Ah." Luke smiled at her, with a little glint in his eye. "So you weren't just saying that, that first night. About how too many people know you around here for me to kiss you on the sidewalk."

Margot tried to keep a straight face.

"Excuse me, are you trying to tell me that you thought I was just making that up to try to get in your pants? That it was a handy excuse to invite myself back to your place?"

Luke twitched his eyebrows at her.

"It's honestly kind of an ego blow for me to realize you were just telling me the exact truth." His leg touched hers under the table. "Though to be fair, you didn't immediately invite yourself back to my house—you clarified first whose place was closer."

She laughed.

"Oh, that's right, I forgot that part."

"If I'd been a little farther away, you would have just turned toward your house, and I would have run right after you."

She liked that he said that. She'd always thought of herself as the aggressor that night. That was one of the things that made her feel even more guilty that she'd slept with her employee, accidentally or not, when she agonized about everything in her life at two a.m. But he *had* been the one to kiss her. And he'd seemed just as eager for that night to continue as she had.

They smiled at each other, and the lingering nervousness that she'd felt about this date fell away. She thought maybe Luke had been nervous, too, because he seemed less tense than when they'd walked in together, or when he'd walked up to her door. Maybe she'd just imagined that, though, with her whole fit of first-date jitters. She had no idea why she'd been so nervous— she'd already slept with him! Multiple times now! She knew he liked her. Well, she knew he lusted after her, at least—maybe that had been why she'd been so nervous, because in addition to lusting after him, she already knew she liked him. And she wasn't—totally—sure if he liked her, too.

This morning, he'd said he wanted to see if this was something. What did he mean by "something"? She knew what she wanted him to mean by that, she knew what she hoped he meant by that, but maybe he'd just meant *If we keep getting along well and having great sex*, that's all. He was only twenty-eight; men that age didn't care about real relationships, at least not in her experience.

Oh God, now she was nervous again. *Margot, chill out, this is only your first real date, after all.*

Luke cleared his throat.

"So, Margot. What do you do?" he asked in a slightly deeper voice than normal.

She raised her eyebrows at him, and he looked back at her straight-faced, but with a glimmer of a smile in his eyes.

Oh. This was their first date. So he was making first-date small talk. How . . . adorable.

"I work at a winery," she said. His eyes widened, in fake surprise, and she forced herself to keep a straight face. "Actually, I'm the co-owner of a winery; my brother and I own it together. I'm on the business side, he's the winemaker. What about you?"

"What a coincidence—I very recently left a job at a winery," he said. Margot picked up her wineglass to hide her smile. "I was just in the tasting room, though. I loved working there; it was a ton of fun. How'd you get into the winery business?"

This whole first-date thing was kind of fun. Well, a first date with Luke was.

"My Uncle Stan—my dad's brother—was a winemaker, and he

started a winery in Napa Valley when I was a kid," she said. "My brother, Elliot, and I spent a lot of time down here with him. He died a few years ago and left the winery to the two of us. So I quit my old job and moved up here to run the winery."

"Oh, really? What did you do before moving up here?" he asked.

They'd never really talked about this, had they?

"I worked in marketing at a handful of big companies in the Bay Area and in L.A. I kind of miss living in big cities sometimes, but I get to visit a lot, and I love my current job, so it all balances out." Now it was her turn. "You said you recently left your job at a winery—what are you doing now?"

He almost, but not quite, winked at her.

"Now I'm helping my mom out at her inn. She got in a car accident the other night; nothing serious, but she can't work for a while. But before I was at the winery, I was a software engineer at a big tech company."

"Oh? How'd you like that kind of work?" she asked, and then almost immediately regretted it. She knew exactly how he felt about his old job.

He half smiled, half shrugged.

"The work itself, I actually really enjoyed. When it was good, it was like a fun puzzle, where I learned something new every day and got to exercise my brain in all kinds of ways. I actually really miss that." He'd never really told her about the parts of his old job that he'd liked. That was good to hear. "But I got a new boss about two years ago, and it stopped being quite so fun." The smile left his eyes for a second. "But now I'm back home in Napa, and glad to be here."

"Oh, Napa is home for you?" she asked. "Did you grow up here?" She knew he'd gone to high school up here, and that his parents were divorced, and that was about all.

He nodded.

"For middle school and high school, at least. We used to live down in San Jose, and then moved up here for my dad's job. My parents split up when I was in high school and he moved back down there, but my mom loved it up here, and I stayed here with her. I still saw my dad a lot, though." He raised an eyebrow at her. "What about you? Did you grow up here in Napa?"

"No, I grew up in Sacramento. My parents still live there."

He hadn't actually known that, she realized by the look on his face. There was a lot they still didn't know about each other.

"Oh, that's interesting," he said. "You went to high school there? When did you graduate?"

She had to smile at that question.

"Is that your subtle way of trying to ask me how old I am?"

He grinned at her.

"Apparently not all that subtle," he said.

"I'm thirty-four," she said. Was that a problem for him? That she was so much older than him? Did he care?

"Ah," he said. "Well, I'm almost twenty-nine. So . . . pretty much the same."

She smiled slowly.

"Yeah," she said. "Pretty much the same."

WHEN THEY GOT BACK to Margot's house, he reached for her hand as they walked up to the door. He'd felt a little silly at first, when he'd made first-date small talk with her, mostly to shake off his own—and, he sort of thought, her—first-date jitters. But she'd clearly been just as amused by their fake getting-to-know-each-other conversation as he had. And they'd both learned things about each other they hadn't known.

After they got inside, Margot looked over at the door, and then at him.

"You're going to stay, right? Tonight."

Luke smiled at the matter-of-fact way she'd said that. A few days ago, he never would have believed he'd be staying over at Margot Noble's house as a matter of course.

"Yeah," he said. "I'm going to stay."

She looked him up and down.

"Well, you're not exactly wearing your work clothes tonight, and this morning you had to leave kind of abruptly to go shower and change at your house, and the thing is, there's a shower here, but—"

"But I didn't bring anything to change into," he finished.

He'd thought about it, when he'd gone home from work to change for tonight. But he'd worried that might make him seem too sure of her (which he wasn't) or too into her (which he was) and so he'd abandoned the idea. Now that felt ridiculous.

"I only live six blocks away," he said. She looked disappointed when he said that, until he moved to the door. "Be right back."

She looked confused for a second, and then laughed.

"Excellent idea. And you'd better mean that."

He turned, his hand already on the front door, and smiled at her.

"My car can go very fast."

Luckily, he didn't have to run any red lights on the way to his apartment building, but he blew through a few yellows. He threw jeans, boxers, a shirt, and socks into his bag, along with a razor and a handful of condoms, and in less than fifteen minutes, he was back at Margot's front door.

She opened the door almost as soon as he knocked, which was very gratifying.

"Hi," she said.

He kicked the door shut behind him and dropped his bag.

She'd changed. She was wearing another silky robe, like the night before, but this one was a lot shorter, and a lot more sheer, than the one from last night. It was black, trimmed in lace, and was tied, very loosely, at her waist.

And it was very evident to him that she had nothing on underneath it.

"Wow," was all he could say.

That put a very wide smile on her face.

"I hoped you would like this."

He trailed a finger along the neckline of her robe.

"I honestly don't think I could have lived another minute without seeing you in this."

She laughed, that throaty laugh that had driven him wild, the times he'd overheard it at the winery. And he realized again that he didn't have to hide his reaction to her anymore.

He let his hand move slowly down her body, from her neck to her waist, and then pulled her closer to him.

"Do you have any idea," he said, "just how much I've wanted you? Every time I looked at you, all I could think of was just how fucking incredible you are. In many ways, but specifically right now I have to tell you how hot you are. And all I wanted was to be able to touch you like this."

Her hands were on his chest, and a look he'd never seen before was in her eyes.

"And now you can," she said.

"And now I can," he said. And then he bent down to kiss her.

They stood there for a while, kissing, touching, whispering to each other, in the middle of her living room. Unlike last night, he didn't want to rush this. They had all night. They had as much time as they wanted. He wanted to relax into this, linger in it, revel in it. He wanted her to enjoy this, thrill in it, the way he was.

"Let's go in the bedroom," she said, low in his ear, after they'd stood there together for a while. "I want you."

He kissed her harder when she said that. When she'd said it the first time—in her office, with the two of them almost wild with pent-up desire—he'd thought he felt triumphant. But that was nothing compared to how he felt now. Now she said it with no prompting; now she said it just because she wanted him to know it. Before, he'd wondered after if she hadn't really meant it, at least, not the way he meant it. Now he didn't doubt her.

He took her hand.

"Yes. Let's go to the bedroom," he said.

When they walked into the bedroom, he reached for the sash of that robe, but she dodged him.

"Not yet."

She smiled as her eyes raked over him.

"I can't argue with you when you're looking at me that way," he said. If she wanted to put lacy robes on like that, and unbutton his shirt so slowly like this, and then unbuckle his belt like that, as her fingers brushed up against his rapidly hardening cock, who was he to stop her? He was pretty sure she was enjoying this just as much as he was.

She pulled his belt out of his pants and dropped it to the floor, and then tossed his shirt after it. She let her fingernails skim over his chest. The friction felt so good he reached for her again, and again she stopped him, that smile still on her face.

"You'll have your turn later," she said.

Her eyes were locked on his as she slowly, so slowly, unzipped his jeans. Had he wanted this to go slow before? *Why?* Because right now, he was ready to explode, and she'd barely even touched him yet.

She tugged his jeans down, and he kicked them to the side. She smiled down at the bulge in his boxer briefs.

"Mmm. There you are," she said. She hooked her thumbs under his briefs at either side of his waist, and with one tug, pulled them down to the floor. Maybe she was getting impatient, too.

She knelt down in front of him, in that sexy-as-hell robe, where he could see the darkness of her nipples, and the curve of her belly, and he thought he might come just from how hot this moment was.

Then her hands and mouth were on him, at first slow, too slow. She was teasing him, he could tell by that tiny smile on her lips. And then she moved faster, and stroked harder, and his hands were in her hair, and holy shit it was good, and then she scraped her teeth against him, in just the way he liked, and he couldn't hold back anymore.

She stood up, a grin on her face, while he collapsed on top of her bed.

"You couldn't have let me sit down first?" he said when he could talk. "Because I was this close to falling over."

She shook her head as she stood in front of him.

"I wasn't worried," she said. "You're young and strong and agile, I knew you'd be okay. Plus, I liked it like that. But I mean, if you didn't . . ."

He grabbed her by the waist and pulled her to him.

"Is there any possible way that you don't know just how much I liked that?" He tugged the neckline of her robe down to expose one of her breasts. "Because if so, we have a serious communication problem here."

His face was almost exactly level with her breasts in this position. He liked that a lot, too.

"I think the two of us are communicating just fine," she said.

"Mmm, me, too."

He sucked her nipple into his mouth, and she laughed out loud.

Sixteen

WHEN MARGOT WOKE UP the next morning, she could feel the smile on her face. At first she couldn't remember why. And then she opened her eyes.

"Good morning," Luke said, his hand moving gently up and down the side of her body. "I was hoping you would wake up before I had to leave."

He looked so good right there. In her bed, against her pillows, with his warm brown skin and wide chest and big eyes and soft smile and low voice. And that smile on his lips and in his voice was for her.

"Good morning," she said. This thing between them had felt so impossible, for so long, but she'd wanted it for just as long. Did she really have it now?

She had to pull herself back. It had been only two days. She needed to slow down, take this one day at a time, not sweat the small stuff, all of those aphorisms that were so contrary to her very being. She always thought far in advance, she always jumped to conclusions, sweating the small stuff was in her job description. But right now, she didn't want to spoil this. She just wanted Luke.

"Would it be pushing things to ask if I can see you tonight?" he asked.

She smiled and shook her head.

"It wouldn't be pushing things at all," she said. *Wait. Shit.*

"Oh no, I just remembered—I have a dinner tonight over in Sonoma. I'll be home pretty late, I'm sorry."

He kissed her softly on the lips.

"That's okay." He slid his hand down the curve of her back. "I mean, that's okay in the abstract, like, you don't need me to approve of where and when you have dinner, but also I very much wish you were having dinner with me tonight instead."

"Maybe you could come over, after?" she said. Then she regretted it immediately. She shouldn't sound quite that eager. This thing was brand-new, she should—

"Yes, please," he said. "Text me when you get home?"

She pulled him closer and kissed him hard.

"Will do."

He got up and got in her shower. She pulled on one of her much more practical robes than the one she'd worn last night and went to make coffee.

He came into the kitchen a little while later, fully dressed and rubbing his head with her towel.

"I realized that I don't know how you take your coffee," she said. "I've known you for a while now, but there are still so many gaps in my knowledge."

He picked up the mug she'd poured and took the milk she handed him.

"A lot of milk, a little sugar," he said. "I learned how to drink coffee from Avery in high school, and while she's become more grown-up in her coffee tastes, I have not, unfortunately."

Margot laughed.

"I'm surprised Taylor didn't make fun of you for that. She's a coffee purist, you know."

He made a face.

"She did indeed make fun of me for this. You just never overheard it, thank goodness. I would have been mortified."

She laughed as he put sugar in his coffee.

They drank coffee together for a few minutes, while she checked her emails and texts that had come in overnight. She'd gotten a few texts from Sydney. She hadn't told her, yet, about what had happened with Luke the other night. She'd almost told her the day before, but she'd held off. She'd wanted to wait, until she knew what this was, until she knew if it was just a second one-night stand or something else.

Luke set his mug down on the counter.

"I hate that I have to go now."

He stood up and bent down to kiss her. She twined her arms around his neck and held on.

"I wondered, you know," he said, his mouth just inches from hers, "if that first night, that night at my apartment, was as good as it could get. If maybe I'd built up this thing between us so big in my mind that I'd invariably be disappointed if it ever happened again." He kissed her, so hard it made her breathless. "But the opposite is true. It only keeps getting better."

It felt almost absurd to her that she felt the same way. That the hunger she'd had for him hadn't dissipated, but had increased. And that not only did he feel the same way, but he was saying this to her.

"I know," she said. "It does."

He kissed her again and then took a step back.

"Okay. Talk to you soon, then."

She followed him to the door.

"Yeah. Talk to you soon."

He flashed one more smile at her before he walked out her front door.

She poured more coffee into her mug and prepped a fresh pot. And then she picked up her phone.

MARGOT

> Come over for coffee. Bring pastries.

Sydney texted back moments later.

SYDNEY

> Have you been kidnapped?
> it's 7:30 am. i don't leave my
> home before ten unless it's an
> emergency.

Margot grinned as she took a sip of her coffee.

MARGOT

> Luke quit two days ago.
> Coincidentally, he just left my
> apartment for the second morning in
> a row.

She didn't have long to wait.

SYDNEY

> You fucking bitch. Ham and cheese croissant?

Margot laughed out loud.

MARGOT

> Yes please! See you soon.

She put her coffee down in the kitchen on the way to the bathroom. She probably had just enough time to shower before Sydney got here.

FRIDAY, MIDMORNING, AVERY WALKED into the inn, two cups of iced coffee in her hands.

"What are you doing here?" Luke asked her.

She set one of the cups on the desk and grinned at him.

"I knew you had a weakness for the iced coffee from Eden's and I had a meeting this morning, so I thought I'd drop by with a treat for you."

He reached for the cup.

"Bless you. Especially since the air-conditioning in this place could use some tuning up. I'm dying here." He took a sip and sighed. "Oh, man, I haven't had one of these in years. They're as good as they used to be."

Avery gave him a wide smile.

"I thought you'd appreciate that. Now. Tell me all about your big date with Margot on Tuesday. I would have come by sooner, but I've been booked solid all week."

He let out a long sigh.

"How did you know?"

Her grin got even wider.

"I believe the traditional answer in this instance is 'You just told me.'" She laughed at him. "Come *on*, Luke. You just happened to ask me for restaurant advice for a 'hotel guest,' the day after you quit your job at Noble, when Margot was no longer your boss? I know you far too well for that."

Why did he even think he would be able to get away with that lie to Avery? She did know him too well for that.

"Just be quiet about this, okay? I was her employee as of just a few days ago, and no one else really knows that anything's going on between us." He glanced around the lobby. "Plus, my mom still thinks . . ."

Avery rolled her eyes.

"Yes, yes, your mom still thinks the two of us are dating, which is ridiculous. But I get it, I won't tell the world about your scandalous affair with an older woman who was very recently your boss. But you didn't answer the question. How was the date?"

He smiled. The date had been so good. And then the rest of the night had been—

"Okay, that smile is quite enough, thank you," Avery said. "I don't need to know all of the gory details! But like . . . is this going to be a thing between the two of you?"

God, he hoped so.

"I think so." He held up a hand. "Don't get too excited—I don't know how long it's going to last, or really, anything else. We're taking this day by day."

Avery looked closely at him.

"You really like her. Don't you? Like, this is more than just sex."

"Yeah," he said. "I really like her. She's . . . gorgeous and smart and thoughtful and interesting and—" Avery was grinning at him, so he trailed off. "Anyway. Yes, I like her. But I'm not counting on anything. I'm just going to enjoy this for now, okay?"

Avery still had that smirk on her face.

"Okay. Sounds good."

She turned to leave, but he stopped her.

"Wait. Avery. How are you doing? Really doing, I mean. No 'I'm fine' bullshit this time."

The smile dropped from her face as she looked at him.

"I'm okay," she said finally. "Really, I am. The past few weeks have been . . . hard. Not in the way I really expected, though."

"What do you mean?" he asked.

She let out a breath.

"The breakup itself obviously sucked. But after that . . . I thought I would miss him a lot. But I haven't really, at all. And I've felt pretty bad about that."

He didn't understand.

"Why have you felt bad that you haven't missed him? That's great."

She looked away from him.

"I mean yeah, it is great. Sort of. It's felt so good, to be without him. And I've felt bad that it's felt so good, that I'm not a good person, that I should have loved him more, cared about him more. And also, that I should have realized how I felt so much earlier, and that I'm so stupid for not seeing that, and after I did see it, I was so stupid for not doing something about it for so long." She tried to smile. "I feel bad about one of those two things most of the time, they switch back and forth."

"I'm really glad it's felt good to be on your own," he said. "I just wish you didn't feel bad about it." He felt especially guilty now about things he'd said to her about her ex. "I'm really sorry if I—"

She shook her head.

"It's not your fault. But the good thing is that every day I feel a little less bad about both of those things, and a little—sometimes a lot—happier about being on my own now. So I really meant it when I said I'm okay."

He looked closely at her. He could tell she was being honest with him.

"I'm glad," he said. "You'll let me know if you need anything at all, right?"

She smiled at him.

"You know it." She let out a dramatic sigh. "And—look, you know I'm not one for mushy stuff, so I'm only going to say this once—it's meant a lot to have you here. I know you moved up here only because you were worried about me, and you didn't have to do that, but it's been . . . really great to have you nearby. So. Thanks."

"You're welcome," he said, "but you know you would do the same for me."

She laughed.

"I wouldn't help you move, I'd just buy you an enormous amount of fried chicken and let you watch all the bad movies you wanted."

He rolled his eyes.

"Just because you don't like horror movies doesn't mean they're bad, you know."

Avery opened her mouth to respond, when his mom came in through the front door.

"Luke! Oh, and Avery! So lovely to see you!" She looked from Luke to Avery and beamed.

Oof. It felt even weirder now for his mom to think he and Avery were together.

"Mom, what are you doing here? You're supposed to be at home, resting."

She looked around the lobby. He knew she was making sure it was as clean and well organized as she usually kept it.

"I know, I know, but I hadn't left the house all week, so I got Pete to bring me along with him in the car today when he had to stop by a client's, and it was nearby, so I just thought I'd come in and say hi!" She turned to Avery. "It's so good to see you, Avery. How are you doing?"

"I'm doing really well, Ms. Williams—Lauren," Avery said. "I was so sorry to hear about your accident, but I'm glad it looks like you're healing okay. And thanks again, for sending that couple my way for the wedding—it's been a real pleasure to work with them so far."

His mom smiled at Avery and then raised her eyebrows at him. Was she expecting him to *propose* to Avery? *Oh God.*

"Of course, of course, I was glad to be able to do it. They seemed like such a nice couple," she said to Avery.

Avery picked up her drink.

"I have to run—I was just driving by and stopped in to say hi, but I have a lunch meeting coming up. Talk to you soon, Luke."

He nodded at her.

"Talk to you soon."

His mom beamed at him when Avery walked out.

"So . . . things are going well there?"

It had been easy, up until now, to pretend to his mom that he was dating Avery. But after the past few days with Margot, after leaving her bed this morning and thinking about her all day and telling Avery that he actually really liked Margot, it felt impossible to seem even a tiny bit interested in any other woman.

But he couldn't confess everything to his mom now. She was injured, and stressed about the inn. He didn't want her to be upset about his job, too. And plus, like he'd said to Avery, he still didn't know how long this thing with Margot was going to last.

"Yeah, Mom," he said, looking down at the computer. "Things are going well there."

Why did he feel so guilty when he said that?

LUKE SPENT THE NIGHT at Margot's house every night that week. Margot knew they should hold off, that they should take breaks from each other, that she shouldn't let herself get too attached too fast, but every morning when he left he said, *See you later?* and every time she said, *Yes, see you later.* She couldn't help herself. She liked him, she liked everything about him. She liked the way he asked her questions about her day and listened, really listened, to her answers; she liked the stupid jokes he cracked when he could tell something had gotten her in a bad mood; she liked the way he smiled at and chatted with their waitress at the burger place they went to on Thursday night after work; she liked the huge tips he left, without calling attention to them; she liked the way he talked about his mom, exasperated but loving.

And she liked—she really liked—the way he looked at her, the way he talked to her, the way he touched her. Like she was the only person he'd ever looked at in that way, like he'd been waiting all day to talk to her, like the ability to touch her, to kiss her, was a privilege.

But every night? She had to stop this. It was too fast. She would get sick of him, or he would get sick of her, more likely. She decided this on Thursday, on Friday, on Saturday, all during the day at work, but every night right when she was about to leave the winery, he would text her, or she would text him, and he would be waiting at her door when she got home.

On Sunday, she decided for sure. They'd both been working hard all week, not sleeping enough; they probably both needed a break from each other.

No, they definitely did. Plus, she hadn't been by the Barrel in way too long. She would go, sit at the bar, talk to Sydney. And then she'd go home and get work done—she still had so much to do for the party, so many tiny details to figure out so it would be perfect. She could see Luke Monday. Or even Tuesday. This thing between them couldn't last too long; she didn't want herself to get too attached. Luke was only up here in Napa Valley temporarily, she knew that. He wasn't looking for anything serious, she assumed. She would still enjoy the hell out of this as long as she could, obviously. But she didn't want to make it into something it wasn't.

She didn't text him before she left the winery that night. She didn't even check her phone. She parked at her house, walked over to the Barrel, and slid into her regular seat at the corner of the bar.

"Excuse me?" she said to Sydney's back. "Can I get some service over here?"

Sydney turned around and gave her a wide smile.

"Welcome to the Barrel! Can I interest you in some wine? We have plenty of local Napa Valley vintages. Are you visiting the area?"

Margot pursed her lips.

"Come off it, Syd."

Sydney opened her eyes wide.

"Oh! It's you! Margot Noble, as I live and breathe! It's been so long, I barely recognized you. How have you been?"

Margot just stared at her and did her best not to smile as Sydney's grin got wider.

"Don't even remember how you've been? The sex is that good, huh?"

"Sydney!"

Sydney laughed, and Margot couldn't help herself from laughing, too. Sydney pulled out a bottle of sparkling wine, poured a glass, and set it in front of Margot.

"There. My penance, for making fun of you."

Margot picked up the glass.

"Thank you. And the answer to your question is yes."

Sydney grinned.

"I thought so. Where is lover boy tonight? Is he joining you here soon?"

Margot shook her head.

"No. And I don't know where he is. I decided we needed a little break from each other tonight."

She fought herself not to pull her phone out to see if he'd texted.

What if he hadn't texted? Or what if he had, and was waiting outside her house for her? She should check, just to make sure.

"Why?" Sydney asked.

Margot looked up at Sydney.

"What?"

"Why?" Sydney repeated. "Why did you decide you needed to have a break from each other tonight? Did you have a fight?"

Margot shook her head.

"No, nothing like that. It's just . . . we've been together every night all week. It's good to have breaks, right? I don't want to get too . . ." She couldn't say *attached*; Sydney would think she was already attached, which she wasn't. "Too overexposed."

Sydney raised her eyebrows as a salad of little gem lettuces and fresh peas landed in front of Margot.

"Overexposed? This isn't business, Margot. What does that even mean?"

Margot turned her attention to her salad.

"You don't have to parse all of my words. Can't I just come to my friend's restaurant to hang out with her? I don't have to spend every night with Luke."

Sydney didn't say anything to that. Finally, Margot looked up from her salad—it was delicious; she should tell Charlie that—to find Sydney smiling at her.

"Thank you for coming to your friend's restaurant to hang out with her," Sydney said. "As you can see, Charlie has missed you."

She glanced over Margot's shoulder, and seconds later Margot had a plate of grilled calamari with lemon and artichokes in front of her.

"I missed Charlie, too," Margot said.

Sydney looked closely at her.

"But things are good? With you two?"

Margot looked down at her plate.

"Yeah. Things are good." She thought of the way Luke had kissed her that morning, over coffee in her kitchen. He'd taken the mug out of her hands and pulled her close and . . . She shook that off and looked at Sydney, who had an indulgent smile on her face.

"It's not serious, of course," she said quickly. She didn't want Sydney thinking she was expecting anything out of this. "He's a lot of fun, and he seems interested now, but I don't know if I can trust him. I probably can't."

Sydney shrugged.

"Probably not. But do you like him?"

Margot sighed. Then nodded.

"Yeah. I like him a lot."

Sydney looked over Margot's shoulder again.

"Hold on, be right back."

Sydney handled an issue at the front door, came back behind the bar to help the bartender pull together drinks for a big party, and then chatted with Margot for a few minutes before she had to rush off and deal with something else. That had never bothered Margot before, the way Sydney jumped around the restaurant the whole time she was there, but tonight it made her fidgety. Usually she would sit here and do some work on her phone, scroll social media, occasionally read a book, but tonight she hadn't brought a book with her, and she'd banned herself from looking at her phone. Even though it felt like it was glowing there, in her bag. She knew if she pulled it out, she'd either see a text from Luke and she wouldn't be able to help herself from texting back, or she wouldn't see a text from Luke and she'd be disappointed.

She dug through her bag and found a magazine, left over from when a guest had left it at the tasting room weeks ago and she'd tossed it in her bag on the way out the door. She flipped through it, looking for something to entertain her, to keep her attention, to keep her from thinking about Luke and why she'd had this stupid idea to spend a night apart in the first place.

Sydney walked in her direction, and Margot looked up with relief.

"More bubbles?" she asked as she filled Margot's glass.

Margot laughed.

"What if the answer was no? It is sometimes, you know."

"I know," Sydney said. "But those times you tell me when you sit down. 'Only one glass, I have work to do tonight.' Do you forget how well I know you?"

Margot sighed and picked up her glass.

"Occasionally, yes."

Sydney looked over Margot's shoulder again. More drama by the front door, probably.

"Fancy seeing you here tonight," she said to someone, with a grin on her face.

Margot turned.

"Hi," Luke said. "Is this seat taken?"

God, she was happy to see him.

"It is now," she said. "What are you doing here?"

He sat down next to her, and she reached for his hand.

"I got a text from Avery to come here."

Oh.

"Did you have plans with her tonight?"

He shook his head.

"No, I was just at home—I hadn't heard from you, so I figured you were busy, and I got that text from Avery." He looked around and let go of her hand. "Is she here? I got distracted when I saw you, but I guess I should find her."

Margot looked up at Sydney.

"You're welcome," her friend mouthed, with a very smug grin on her face.

Margot tried to glare at her, but she couldn't keep the smile off her lips.

"Sorry I didn't text," she said. "Avery's not here. I think this is a situation where my friend conspired with your friend to get us together tonight, and I can't be mad about it at all."

Luke laughed and reached for her hand again.

"Well, I guess I need to thank them both, then."

Margot picked up her champagne glass. She suddenly felt very silly about coming here, ignoring her phone, ignoring him. It would have been one thing if she'd made plans with Sydney on purpose, but she'd just done this to prove a point to herself, and to Luke. A stupid point.

"I should have texted," she said. "I, um, thought we maybe needed a night off. I didn't want you to get tired of me."

Luke laughed again, but stopped when he looked at her face.

"You're not serious?" He looked at her for a moment. "Is that a nice way to say that you needed a break from me? Because if so, you can just say that."

She shook her head.

"No, that wasn't it." That's why she hadn't texted him that she had other plans, she realized. Because she'd wanted to see him. "I didn't. I don't. But it's been every night this week, and I didn't want us to—" She didn't know how to finish that sentence, not in a way that wouldn't reveal too much. "I thought maybe you'd be busy. Or that you might want to spend a night in your own bed."

He laughed.

"Why would I want to be alone in my bed if there was the slightest possibility I could be with you in yours?"

He said it so casually, like it was obvious that's what he would want. This man made her feel so good.

Sydney strolled up to them and set a glass down in front of Luke.

"Let me know if there's anything else you want, Luke. I remember you liked Uncle Nearest last time."

It felt really good, to be here with him at the bar, with his hand in hers, and her friend grinning at them.

"You have an excellent memory," he said. "And thank you. For the drink and everything else."

Sydney smirked.

"Anytime."

Luke looked down at his drink, but Sydney kept looking at Margot.

"Not serious?" she mouthed.

Margot did glare at her this time, and Sydney just laughed.

"What?" Luke asked.

"Nothing," Margot said.

Seventeen

A WEEK LATER, LUKE lay in Margot's bed while she got dressed. He was usually up and gone before Margot, but his mom had ordered him to take the day off. He'd already taken full advantage of getting to stay in bed with Margot.

"You look very smug, all tucked in my bed like that," she said.

He rested his hands behind his head.

"I feel very smug, now that you mention it. That was a very promising start to a workweek, don't you think?"

She grinned at him.

"I do think."

They smiled at each other for a while before she turned to her closet.

She pulled on that black wrap dress of hers, and he smiled.

"Ah, your Monday dress," he said.

She stopped, midway through tying the knot at her waist, and stared at him.

"No one has ever noticed that I wear this dress every Monday," she said.

"I notice everything about you," he said.

She stared at him for a few more seconds, an uncertain smile on her lips, before she turned back to the mirror.

"I wish we could spend the whole day together," he said. "I can't believe I have the day off but you'll be at work all day."

She looked at him in the mirror.

"I wish we could, too," she said.

He sat up in bed.

"Why can't we? You're the boss—can't you take today off? We could stay in bed all day, or take a road trip. Go down to San Francisco, or to the beach or something."

Her eyes lit up.

"The beach?" She sighed. "Wouldn't that be nice?"

She picked up her mascara. She didn't think he was serious.

"Well? What winery emergencies are going to come up that you can't solve if you're twenty or so miles away?" She just laughed. "No, really. When's the last time you took a day off? Like, didn't go into the winery at all, didn't turn on your computer, didn't take a bunch of calls, for a full day?"

She thought for a second.

"Well, the last day I didn't go into the winery at all was the day before I met you."

They grinned at each other.

"See, you're trying to get me sidetracked here," he said. "Weren't you on a work trip then?"

She sighed again.

"Yes. Okay, fine, I was still working that day. I don't know, maybe sometime in January?"

He got out of bed and went over to her.

"January? It's June! You haven't taken a day off in almost six months? Mondays are quiet at the winery anyway. Is Taylor working today?"

He reached for the tie of her dress, but she put her hand on his to stop him.

"Yeah, but with the party coming up, and everything, I just have so much to do." She raised her eyebrows at him. "Why do you have today off, anyway? Is your mom well enough to drive now?"

He dropped his hand from her dress. Right, of course she'd ask that.

"Oh. It's . . . my birthday."

She looked startled.

"Your birthday? Today? I didn't know."

He nodded.

"I know—I don't like to make a big thing about it. But my mom ordered me to take today off, said Beth could cover and could call her if there was a crisis." He grinned at her. "It already started off great, though."

"Well, happy birthday." She wiggled her eyebrows. "Glad I could start your birthday with a bang. So to speak."

He laughed, and so did she.

"Your birthday," she said again. She bit her lip. He could tell she was thinking. "Well. I guess I will take the day off, then."

"Does this mean you think Taylor and Elliot can handle everything for one day?" he asked her.

She smiled.

"Well, the last time I left Elliot in charge, he hired you."

He dropped a kiss on her lips.

"We both know what happened after that. Do you regret leaving him in charge that day?"

He'd said it as a joke, but now he wanted to know how she would answer. Did she regret that? Did she regret sleeping with him that first night, which she definitely wouldn't have done if she'd been at the winery that day? Did she regret letting Elliot hire him in the first place, so she'd have to work with him? Because despite how much every moment of that time, of having to stay an arm's length from her, had killed him, he didn't regret a second of it.

"No." She pulled him closer. "I don't regret leaving him in charge that day."

"Excellent," he said. "Let's go to the beach." His hands went to her waist again. This time she let him untie her dress. "This dress, as much as I love it on you, is not beachwear."

She smiled at him.

"It's going to be foggy at the beach, you know."

He stepped closer to her and slid his hand around her waist.

"That's okay. We can huddle for warmth."

She burst out laughing as he kissed her neck.

"The beach it is, then. It's your birthday, after all. Let me call Taylor. And Elliot."

In less time than he would have expected, they were in his car, on the way to the Sonoma coast. He kept waiting for Margot to say no, wait, she had a call she had to take at the winery that day, there were VIPs coming that she had to do a meet and greet with, but she seemed content to sit in the passenger seat of his car, with the windows down and the music up.

Granted, she checked her phone more than once, but he'd expected that.

"Speaking of that first night, which we were an hour ago," he said, when they were on the way, "I've been wondering. Were you ever going to text me?"

He felt her eyes on him, but he didn't look at her. He knew she would tell him the truth either way, but it might be easier if he wasn't looking at her.

"I hadn't decided," she said. "I mean, I was still deciding, when you and Elliot walked into my office." He waited. He knew she wasn't done. "But probably not."

"Why not?" He looked out at the vineyards lining the roads, forced himself not to look at her, tried not to care too much about her answer.

"That night was—talk about taking a break—that night was the first time in a long time I felt like I had a real break. I had a great time with you, but it was more than that. I didn't think about the winery the whole time we talked at the bar, that whole time at your apartment, not until morning. And you were so . . . The whole night just felt perfect. And I didn't want to spoil it. To text you and have you never text me back, or for you to end up being an asshole, or not actually like me, once you got to know me. So. That's why I was leaning against it."

He wanted to respond to everything she said, argue for past Luke and why she should have texted him, but he pulled himself back.

"Then I'm especially glad that you left Elliot in charge at the winery that day."

She grinned at him.

"How long do you think you'll be at the inn, anyway?"

He shrugged.

"Depends on how quickly my mom gets better. At least another few weeks, maybe a month." He sighed. "After that, I suppose I'll have to look for a real job." He grinned at her. "Maybe I can come back to the winery? I miss being around you all day."

She just laughed at that.

He knew that as soon as his mom was better, he *would* have to look for a real job. Life had been far too easy for the past few months. Too easy and too fun. He'd slept a lot, watched a lot of sports, worked at jobs that he'd enjoyed, and had a whole lot of great sex. But he knew this wasn't real life.

He was dreading going to another toxic, stressful place where he would wake up every morning depressed about going to work. At least he thought he could count on Craig for a good reference.

They stopped on the way to the beach—first at a bakery to get coffee and pastries, and then, when they were closer to the beach, at a deli to get sandwiches and snacks. They didn't talk as much on the drive, not like that long drive from a few weeks ago, where they'd talked the whole time, but this time he knew he could touch her, knew he could kiss her, like he'd wanted to that other time. When he reached over and took her hand, she slid her fingers through his and rested both of their hands together on her bare knee. A little while later, she leaned her head back against the seat and closed her eyes. She stayed like that, still holding tight to his hand, for a while.

She opened her eyes when they slowed to a stop in traffic, and looked over at him.

"I haven't been doing a good job of entertaining you, have I?"

He shrugged.

"I don't need entertaining. You seem like you needed a rest."

She pushed her hair back from her face with her free hand.

"Yeah. I guess so. It's not that—" She sighed. "I love the winery, I do. But planning for this party is a lot. I was probably too ambitious, to do it this quickly, and with the budget I had."

He shook his head.

"The party is going to be great. And you don't have to tell me you love the winery. I'm not going to think you don't love it because you need a break from it."

"I guess I just feel defensive about it," she said. "Maybe I also feel like I shouldn't need a break from it if I love it. Elliot doesn't seem to."

"You're not Elliot," he said. "You don't have to be."

"Thanks." She squeezed his hand. "I'm glad we did this today."

"We haven't even gotten to the beach yet," he said.

She smiled.

"I know. I'm still glad."

THEY GOT TO THE beach just before eleven. They got one of the last parking spots in the lot, but the beach wasn't too crowded. Luke carried their food and drinks, Margot carried the blankets and her tote bag, and they made their way from the parking lot down onto the sand. She lay the oldest of the blankets she'd brought along with her out on the sand, and then they set up the food and her bag and their shoes at the corners.

She really shouldn't have taken a day off today, not with the party only two weeks away, and the tourist season in full bloom, and so much to do. But she'd been so touched by that look on Luke's face when he'd said he wanted to spend the whole day with her. And when he'd said it was his birthday, there was no way she could say no. It was his birthday, and he wanted to spend it with her. And she wanted to spend it with him.

She'd looked at his birth date on his employment forms his first day, just to see how old he was, but she hadn't remembered today was his birthday. She felt bad about that, for a moment. But back then, she hadn't had any reason to remember the date.

"I have to get in the water, even though it's freezing," she said. Luke grabbed her hand.

"I'm coming with you."

They ran to the water, first stumbling in the deep, uneven sand, and then going faster as the sand got wet and compact, until the icy froth of the ocean touched them. She looked out at the sun breaking through the clouds and shining on the water, and then turned and looked at Luke, who was smiling at her.

"Should I have quit right away?" Luke asked, like they'd been in the middle of this conversation. Maybe they had. "After that first day, I mean."

She thought about that for a second.

"No. If you had, it wouldn't . . . we wouldn't have gotten to know each other." That's not quite what she meant, but she wasn't sure how to put into words what she meant. If he'd quit right away, she wouldn't have cared about him. He would have just been that guy that she'd had the great one-night stand with. "I'm glad you quit when you did, though."

He put his hand on her waist.

"Me, too."

She leaned in to kiss him when a wave hit them and splashed them both chest-high. They both burst out laughing, and she turned back to the water, still giggling.

"At least the sun is coming out," Luke said. "We'll dry off."

She grinned at him.

"Yeah, we will." Then she stood up on her tiptoes and kissed him on the cheek.

They walked back to their blanket after a few more minutes and sat down. She hadn't worn a swimsuit under her dress—it was usually too overcast at the beaches here for that—but Luke was right: the sun was coming out, they'd dry off. Eventually.

He sat behind her, put his arms around her, and pulled her into his chest. She sighed, and relaxed into him.

"We aren't going to dry off like this," she said.

"I know," he said. "I don't care."

They sat there for a while, not talking, not reading, not doing anything, but doing so much at the same time.

"Do you remember," Luke asked after a while, "how I said I wanted to find out if this was something?'"

"Yeah," she said. "I remember."

"This is something," he said. "Don't you think?"

She put her hands on top of his.

"Yeah," she said. "I do."

She slid her hand into one of his and kissed his knuckles, like he'd done to her in the car. He tightened his grip around her and kissed the top of her shoulder blade.

"Something good," she said.

He kissed her hair, the back of her neck, her cheek, and then, finally, when she turned around to him, her lips.

"Something good," he said.

Eighteen

WHEN MARGOT GOT DRESSED the next morning, Luke assumed she would pull the black wrap dress back out of her closet,
but she reached for a blue-and-white-striped dress instead.

"You're not wearing the black one?" he asked.

She turned to him, a horrified look on her face.

"It's *Tuesday*," she said. And they both burst out laughing.

He and Margot left her place at the same time that morning.
Usually, he left much earlier than she did, but today she'd wanted
to get to the winery early, he guessed because she'd taken the day
off before.

He got to the inn, said hi to Beth, and checked if any reservations or emails had come in overnight. Then he went into the
office; he was trying to take this opportunity to update all of his
mom's software and get all of her systems working right, which
he'd longed to do for years.

A few hours into the morning, Beth poked her head into the
office.

"Is it okay if I take my break now?" she asked. "I was going to go on a coffee run."

He stood up.

"Sure, no problem. I'll take over the front desk."

A few minutes after Beth left, the chimes dinged over the front door.

"Welcome to the Punchdown Inn, I'm Luke. How can I help you?" he said as he glanced up at the couple who walked in.

"Yeah, we're checking in, last name Jordan—wait a minute. Luke Williams?"

He looked at the guy and sighed inwardly. He used to work with this guy. Grant Jordan. Perfectly fine coworker, but kind of a jackass.

"That's me. Hey, Grant, how've you been?"

"You're working *here* now?" Grant stared at him for a moment and shook his head. "How did *that* happen?"

Luke kept a smile on his face.

"My mom owns this place. Just helping her out while she's recovering from an injury." He took Grant's driver's license and credit card.

"Oh, that makes a little more sense, but . . . but still. Wild." His eyes widened. "I knew you left, but to do this? How the mighty have fallen, huh?"

Luke gritted his teeth and ran Grant's card through the machine.

"Oh, hey—did you hear that Brian is leaving?" Grant asked.

Luke looked up. Brian, his old, loathed boss.

"Really? No, I had no idea. I've been in touch with Craig, but he hasn't mentioned it."

Grant smirked.

"Yeah, guess he wouldn't."

Luke kept his face blank and gave Grant his room keys.

"Glad to have you here at the inn," he lied. "Room Five, it's right off the pool. Let me know if you need anything."

He didn't mean that. If Grant asked him for help with his luggage, he'd just want to kick it down the stairs.

"Sure, yeah. Thanks, man."

Grant walked off with the blond woman next to him. Just as they got down the hall, Luke heard him say in a low—but not that low—voice, "Wonder what the real story is there. I heard some rumors that guy got fired, but I was sure they were all wrong. Guess he just couldn't hack it."

Luke felt a flash of rage, the kind of rage he hadn't felt in months. There were rumors that he'd been fired? Who had started them, he wondered? Brian, who hadn't liked him, but had also been pissed when he'd quit? Or that dude who'd never liked him, ever since that time he'd corrected him in a meeting and his boss's boss had praised Luke? Or . . .

The inn phone rang, and he turned to answer it.

"Good afternoon, Punchdown Inn. Can I help you?"

"Yeah, we're running out of toilet paper in our room. Can you make sure housekeeping brings us some?"

"We'll get you that toilet paper right away," he said. "Please let me know if there's anything else we can help you with."

He winced as he hung up the phone. How the mighty have fallen. Grant might have a point.

IT WAS A PACKED week at the winery. And that was great, it really was; obviously that's what Margot had been working toward for the past three years, to have almost every appointment of the day full, to be busy with visitors and tours and emails and reservations and inquiries about the party and press calls. But when she'd been working toward all of this, she hadn't realized it would all feel so fraught. It felt like they were right on the edge, like the next few months might be huge for them—but that was only a *might*. The next few months could also all fall apart. The party could fail, the interviews could come to nothing, the sales could slow down, the appointments could all stop, and they'd be right back where they were before. But it would be worse, feel worse, because she would know what it felt like to almost succeed.

She felt all week like she was scrambling to catch up, to return all of the emails and phone calls, and check in with everyone, and smile at everyone, and get the whole place organized, and get the party planned just right, and it felt like she would never get there. That day at the beach with Luke had been wonderful, but she felt like it set her back, like the deep breaths she'd managed to take then and the relaxation and peace she'd felt for a few hours hadn't been worth all of the work she hadn't done. How could it be worth it, when she still had so much to do?

Tuesday night, Luke came over, but not until late, because she'd stayed later than usual at the winery to catch up on things. Wednesday she told him not to come over—she stayed at the winery until after nine, returning emails and pulling together her spreadsheets for the party. Sure, she could have done some of that at home, but it was easier in her office, with her two big monitors and all of her notes around her . . . and without the distraction of Luke there.

But that night, when she walked into her dark house at almost ten, with a take-out bag in her hands, she wished she hadn't told Luke not to come over that day. She wished he were there with her, to entertain her with stories from the inn from that day; to joke her out of her bad mood; to sit with her on the couch, his arm around her, and listen patiently while she ranted about the annoying guy who'd called her that day; to kiss her after she stopped ranting and make her forget she was upset at all.

She couldn't call him now, though. She would feel like an asshole, changing her mind like that, and plus, he had to get up far earlier than she did to work at the inn. He might already be asleep. He would probably come over anyway if she called—he was a red-blooded male, after all—but that would be unfair of her.

And also . . . what if he didn't come over if she called? She would understand, of course she would, but she didn't want to deal with how bad that would make her feel.

Plus, she would see him tomorrow night. She'd make sure of that.

She woke up Thursday morning and immediately missed him there in her bed with her. She turned over in bed and reached for her phone to text him. But he'd already texted her.

LUKE

> I think the pillows at your house are significantly better than mine. That must be the reason I didn't sleep well last night

She could feel how silly the smile on her face was, but she couldn't help it.

MARGOT

> That must be it. Weirdly, I didn't sleep that well last night either. I think it was a full moon

LUKE

Maybe tonight we'll both sleep better? I've arranged for the moon to not be full, just for you

MARGOT

You're so good to me. I'll text when I'm leaving the winery

That day was full of stupid, tiny little things that went wrong. She broke a wineglass in the tasting room that morning—it was fine, no big deal, these things happened, but it felt shitty in the moment. Someone had written down the wrong time for the appointment for a party of four—either on their side or the guests' side, it didn't matter—and so the tasting room was packed full of people all afternoon, and she had to pitch in, and she could tell Taylor and Marisol were just as stressed about it as she was. Some asshole had posted on Instagram complaining about his visit to Noble and how it had been so rushed, and she had to respond to it and say something gracious even though she'd wanted to remind him he'd been forty-five minutes late for his appointment. And everything was so busy that day that she hadn't been able to finish drafting the monthly newsletter to the wine club, and she'd wanted to get it done today so she could send it on Friday. It was the last one before the party, and she needed to encourage more people to come—RSVPs had been strong, but not as strong as she'd hoped. Oh well, she'd just finish it when she got home.

Damn it, Luke was coming over. Well, no, not damn it; she

wanted him to come over, she'd been looking forward to it all day. Maybe she could get her work done before he got there, or after they ate dinner, or something. She didn't want to tell him to come over late, not after how last night had gone. She texted him when she got in her car.

MARGOT

Leaving the winery now! Just fyi, I have a little work to get done tonight

LUKE

No problem, see you soon. I'll bring dinner

Okay, great—she could get home in like twenty minutes, and it would probably take Luke twice that to pick up takeout and get over to her house. She'd have time to at least make some headway on the newsletter.

And then, of course, there was an accident on the road, halfway between her house and the winery. At the first opportunity, she turned down a side road and cut over to the other way to get home, but that was the even-more-congested way, so by the time she got home, Luke was waiting outside.

"Sorry," she said when she got out of her car. "There was an accident and then traffic and today has been . . . Anyway, sorry I'm late."

He shrugged and followed her up to her door.

"No problem, I figured." They walked straight to her kitchen, where he set down the bag he was carrying, and she opened a bottle of wine. She took down two glasses and then turned to hand him a glass, to find him looking at her.

"What's wrong?" Did her hair look that bad? She hadn't looked at herself in the mirror all day. Maybe this dress was a mistake? It was snug—was it too snug?

He took a step closer to her and tucked her hair behind her ear.

"Nothing's wrong," he said. "Except that it's been a day and a half since I've gotten to kiss you, and I don't think I can last another minute."

She leaned against him and felt some of the tension from the day seep out of her body. As soon as she felt his lips on hers, she strained to be closer to him, to feel more of him. His hands moved up and down her body, and she kissed him harder. She felt him smile as he moved his hand around the curve of her ass, and then she smiled as she pushed her fingers underneath his shirt. Finally, she dropped her head back onto his chest.

"I missed you," he said in her ear, his arms still around her.

"I missed you, too," she said.

She lifted her head and smiled at him.

"Let's eat," she said. "I'm sure you're hungry, and I haven't eaten since . . ." She thought about that. There had been a muffin that she'd grabbed from the kitchen that morning, and she'd eaten some cheese that afternoon, but . . .

"Okay, if you have to think that hard, it's a problem," Luke said. "Let's eat."

She poured the wine, he piled food on both of their plates—he'd gotten noodles and dumplings—and they sat down at the counter and ate, and drank wine.

"How was your day?" Luke asked.

She knew talking about it would make her more irritable, so she just shrugged.

"How's work been this week?" she asked him, instead of answering.

He shrugged.

"Oh, fine. Small plumbing crisis, but luckily we resolved it." He hesitated for a second. "I found out the other day that my old boss is leaving. At my old job, I mean."

She laughed.

"Good riddance, right? Didn't you say they're doing a whole diversity push? If you were still there, maybe they'd try to make you take that job. Thank God you left."

He looked down at his wineglass and nodded.

"Yeah. Thank God."

"What did you do last night?" she asked.

He looked up at her.

"I had a late dinner with Avery," he said. "She's still kind of getting over her breakup, so it was good to have time to catch up with her and see how she's doing."

So he'd found a replacement for her so quickly, then. When she was working late, and then sitting at home wishing he were here, he was out with Avery. Great.

She was being stupid. She knew that. She made herself smile.

"Oh good. How is she doing?"

They'd both already finished eating, so Margot got up to go into the living room, taking her wineglass with her. Luke followed her.

"Really good. I'm so glad she broke up with that guy. She said she ran into him the other day and she was wearing her good jeans, whatever that means."

Margot pulled her laptop out of her bag.

"I know just what that means. Good for her." Something suddenly occurred to her. She turned to Luke. "Are you coming to the party?"

He shrugged.

"Depends. Do I have to pay?"

She couldn't tell if that was a joke or not.

"No, I'll put you on the list. But if you have to work, or—"

He laughed.

"Of course I'm coming to the party. Whether I had to pay or not." He raised an eyebrow at her. "Does Elliot—or anyone else at Noble—know about us?"

She was surprised he'd asked that.

"No," she said. He had a weird look on his face. "It's only been a few weeks since you quit, and you know things with Elliot are complicated."

He nodded.

"I figured. I just wanted to know for sure, since I'll be there for the party."

She pulled up her draft of the newsletter. She'd gotten only this far? She could have sworn . . . No, she'd just planned to work on it more, and then her phone had rung and she'd abandoned it. *Great.* So much was riding on this; she should have prioritized it this week. Damn it.

"Do you want more wine?" Luke asked.

She nodded, and he got up and got the bottle from the kitchen.

Okay, she had to bring up the expanded hours again—she'd mentioned that in the past two newsletters, but you never knew who actually opened those—it would always be news to someone reading; she had to hype up the party; oh, and she needed a more interesting subject line. That social media person she'd consulted had told her that. What kind of subject line would make people click on this?

Luke sat down close to her and ran his fingers through her hair.

"What are you working on?"

She pulled the ponytail holder off her wrist and put her hair up.

"The newsletter."

He put an arm around her.

"I like that dress. It's very . . . eye-catching."

He moved his hand from her shoulder down her body. She pulled away.

"Give me a minute, okay? You'll get what you came over for soon."

Luke dropped his hands. And then, after a few seconds, he stood up.

"I'd better go."

She was so irritated and frustrated, she didn't even look at him. She kept her eyes on her computer screen.

"Fine."

Out of the corner of her eye, she saw him grab his bag and slide his shoes on. And then, her front door opened and quietly closed.

She looked around at her empty house, at the two wine-glasses on the coffee table, at the meal in the kitchen Luke had brought over for her.

She put her laptop on the coffee table, ran to the door, and flung it open. He was almost at his car.

"Luke!"

He stopped, but he didn't turn around. She ran barefoot down the path. When she was almost to him, he finally turned.

"That's not what I came over for," he said.

"I know," she said. "I'm sorry. That's not why I wanted you to come over, either. Come back inside?"

He had a severe look on his face. She couldn't tell if he was angry or hurt. Or both.

"Okay," he said.

They walked back up the path together and back into her house.

"I'm really sorry," she said once they were inside. "It's been a rough couple of days at work, I was in a bad mood, and I took it out on you. I shouldn't have."

He kissed her cheek.

"It's okay," he said. "I'm sorry, too. I was also in kind of a bad mood. I knew you had work to do, I shouldn't have pushed."

They sat back down on the couch, and she went to close her laptop.

"What are you doing?" he asked.

She turned to look at him.

"I feel like I should let this go until the morning."

He shook his head.

"Oh no, please finish this tonight. If you don't finish, you'll just stress about it and get fussy again." She couldn't even take offense at that description of her, especially when he said it with that tender smile on his face. She smiled back at him.

"Is that what you guys would say about me in the tasting room? 'Oh, is Margot getting fussy again?'"

He shook his head.

"Absolutely not. Everyone loves you there. I tried to never talk about you at all, if I could help it—I didn't want to make it quite so obvious how I felt about you." He put his arm around her. "Can I help? Not to hurry you up, but you had that look on your face like you were stuck, and sometimes it helps to bounce things off someone else."

She put her hand on his cheek.

"I'd love that, thank you. And I know it's not just to hurry me up, you didn't have to say that."

She pulled him close and kissed him. Softly, tenderly, with all of the longing that she'd felt for him, last night and this morning, when she'd missed him so much. She'd been sort of scared of those feelings, she realized now. Scared that she'd become so used to having him around that she'd missed him that much when he wasn't there. She rested her head on his chest. He wrapped his arms around her and held her there.

"You've had a tough week, haven't you?" he asked.

The concern for her in his question, in his voice, made tears spring to her eyes.

"Yeah," she said into his chest.

She usually didn't admit this. She acted like—she felt like she had to act like—everything was fine, easy, perfect. That she was working hard and loving every moment of it. But she could tell Luke the truth.

"It's just that . . . so much is riding on this party, and it's all on me, and sometimes it feels overwhelming."

He kissed the side of her head and pulled her closer.

"I'm sorry it's been so hard," he said.

She just wanted to stay there forever. For the first time in a long time, she felt cared for. It almost scared her, how good it felt. How much she craved this feeling.

Well, not almost. Okay, she'd have to deal with that fear, and why she was like this, in therapy. At some point.

For now, she turned back to her computer, but stayed close to him.

"We should finish this newsletter so I don't get fussy again."

He kissed her cheek.

"Let's take a look at it."

She set her computer on a pillow on her lap, and he peered over her shoulder.

"Oh no, we have to fix that subject line," he said.

She sighed.

"I know. What was I thinking?"

"You were thinking that you're exhausted and you've been working very long days this week, that's what you were thinking." He dropped his arm from around her shoulders and then nudged her legs. "Swing those up on the couch."

She did what he said. He pulled the cardigan off her shoulders.

"Now. Let's get this newsletter done." He put his hands on her shoulders and pressed his thumbs deep into her upper back. She let out a moan, and he stopped. "Too hard?"

She shook her head.

"No, that's perfect. But how do you expect me to do any work when you're doing that?"

He dropped a quick kiss on the back of her neck.

"We're both good at multitasking. Plus, what you have right now is too boring, matter-of-fact, corporate. You want this newsletter to feel relaxed, fun, even a little sexy, don't you? You've got to get in the mood to write it."

The whole time he was talking, he massaged her shoulders, her upper back. She'd thought she'd known what his fingers could do to her—apparently she had whole new avenues to discover.

"Number one, you're absolutely correct about the newsletter, and what was wrong with it," she said. "Number two, that feels incredible. I can't believe you've kept this talent from me for so long."

He kissed her neck again.

"I apologize. Now, let's get to this newsletter before we get too distracted."

***

THEY STAYED THERE ON the couch for the next hour, as he gave her a massage and she rewrote the newsletter, with occasional interjections from him on things to add or change.

Luke had been pissed, really pissed, when she'd made that crack about what he'd come over for. It wasn't until they were back inside, and she'd kissed him like that on the couch, that he realized why. He loved having sex with Margot, fucking loved it—it got better every time; he still felt lucky that he got to do it, that he got to kiss her and touch her and hear how she responded to him and got to feel her hands and lips and tongue on him. But that wasn't why he'd rushed over to her house that day. Or any other day. He just wanted to be around her, be with her, talk to her, hold her, make her feel good, make her happy. The way he felt when he was with her.

And in that moment, when she'd said that to him, he'd worried that she didn't feel the same way. That all she wanted from him was sex. That *had* been all she wanted that first night, she'd been pretty clear about that. But he didn't think she felt like that anymore. Even though she hadn't told anyone at the winery about them. Of course she hadn't—why had he even asked that? He had been her employee only a few weeks ago, and he knew things were weird between her and her brother. It was fine.

He'd almost told her about seeing Grant at the inn, but something had stopped him. If he did that, he'd have to talk about what Grant had said, and how he'd been irritated about it all week. And he didn't want to talk to Margot about that; he was still embarrassed that he'd told her in the car on the way back from the auction why he'd quit, and that he sometimes felt like he hadn't been good enough, strong enough, for that job. He didn't want her to think that, too.

He dropped another kiss on the back of her neck. She let out a soft sigh, pressed a few buttons on her laptop, and closed it.

"I think I'm done for tonight." She set the laptop on the coffee table and turned all the way around to face him. "I'm really glad you're coming to the party."

He pushed her hair back from her face.

"I wouldn't miss it."

She leaned forward and kissed him hard.

"You know . . . while I know *that's* not why you came over, I still like *that* a whole lot."

He laughed and put his hand on her waist.

"I really hope I didn't give you the impression *that* isn't important to me, because it is, very much so. Especially when you look at me like you are right now."

She reached for his belt.

"Does that mean I can take off your pants?"

He leaned back on the couch.

"You can do whatever you want to me."

She smiled, her fingers already pulling his fly open.

"Whatever I want?" She had a glint in her eye that he liked an enormous amount. "I'm going to keep that in mind. However." She pulled his pants all the way down and tossed them to the side, and then she stroked the length of him. He'd be embarrassed at how fast he responded to her, if he didn't know how much she liked it. "We'll do whatever I want next time," she said. "What do you want? Right now?"

He knew she knew the answer to that question. He smiled at

her as she hooked her fingers under the waistband of his boxer briefs.

"I want your mouth on me," he said. "Right now."

She tugged his boxers down and knelt over him on the couch. And then she sucked him into her mouth, and he couldn't help the low moan he let out.

He kept his eyes open so he could watch her. He liked how intent she got when she did this—she worked her tongue, and her teeth, and her fist hard, and she looked so fucking hot while she was doing it. It felt so good that soon he couldn't think about what she was doing, but was just trying to hold on, make it last longer. But then she moved faster, and he came so hard he couldn't think of anything at all.

She crawled up and laid her head on his chest, and he wrapped his arms around her.

"I did not come over for that," he said. "Or, rather, *just* for that. But I'm really fucking glad it happened."

She laughed and moved one of his hands down to her breast.

"That was a remarkably chaste massage you gave me, you know," she said. "But despite that . . ." She pulled her dress down, that tight dress that clung to her boobs and ass, and moved his thumb over to her nipple. "These have been hard for the past hour."

"Mmm, I'm very glad you told me that," he said. "I have a feeling that the next massage I give you will be significantly less chaste." He pushed the straps of her dress off her shoulders and reached around to unclasp her bra.

"Bedroom," he said. "Now."

When they got into her bedroom, he pulled her dress all the way off, tossed her bra on the floor, and pushed her underwear down and kicked it aside. Then he backed her onto the bed and pushed her until she fell onto it. She lay there and looked up at him.

"I like it when you tell me what to do," he said. "I like it a lot. But now, it's my turn to be in charge."

He saw from the look on her face that she liked that.

"Well, then," she said. "What are you going to do with me?"

He looked down at her, naked in front of him. He wanted to touch her everywhere. He wanted her to think of him, and this night, every time she looked at her left knee, or touched that dimple in her thigh.

He put a hand on the arch of her foot, ran it all the way up the inside of her leg, and then down the other side.

"Everything," he said.

Nineteen

THE FOLLOWING WEDNESDAY, LUKE had just pulled into the
lot at the inn when he got a text from Craig.

CRAIG

> Hey Luke—Brian's leaving, his job is
> opening. Interested? Let me know if
> you want to talk about this

Craig wanted to know if *he* was interested in Brian's job? He
was stunned. He never would have expected this two months
ago. Hell, he never would have expected this five minutes ago.
He'd assumed his bridges there were all burned, but even before
that, he'd assumed that no one there particularly valued him, or
his work. Hadn't they all thought he wasn't smart enough, tough
enough, good enough? Was he wrong about that? He must have
been, if they wanted him to even apply for Brian's job.

He wasn't sure how to feel about this. Six months ago he

would have been thrilled. He should still feel that way, shouldn't he? He guessed he sort of did. Flattered? Yeah, definitely. Triumphant that they'd come back to him, after everything? Yeah, that, too, he supposed. Nervous? Suspicious? Maybe a little angry, all over again, at how they'd treated him?

All of that, too.

Was this for real? Craig had always been good to him. He wouldn't have reached out if they already had someone else in mind and this was just some bullshit fake interview, right?

He walked into the inn, but before he could set his coffee down and figure out how to reply to Craig's text, his mom walked in with Pete.

"Before you yell at me, I'm only here for a second to sign those checks," she said.

"I was going to bring those to your house later on today, you know," he said. He knew she was only here because she couldn't stay away.

"I know, I know, but you've done so much for me already. Plus, Pete had to take me to the doctor today, so it was on the way." He just looked at her. "Well, okay, not that far out of the way."

"I tried," Pete said.

He looked at Pete and they both laughed.

"But look, I have a new cast!" his mom said. "A lighter one!"

"You're still supposed to rest for the next few weeks, that's what the doctor said," Pete said.

She made a face.

"I will, I swear. But I've missed this place." She looked around the lobby, a smile on her face. "How was your weekend?"

He'd spent every moment of it that he could with Margot. She'd been at the winery a lot, but they'd been together every night and every morning. She'd cooked an elaborate meal for him the night before, and he had leftovers for lunch.

"It was great," he said.

His mom beamed at him. *Oh. Oh no.* He could feel that smile that had been on his face. It had been involuntary—it must have just appeared there when he'd thought about Margot. And his mom must think . . .

"You spent it with Avery, then?" she asked. "Good, I'm glad she got some time off, too. That girl works too much."

He wanted to correct her, tell her that no, he hadn't been with Avery, he'd been with Margot. That he wasn't *with* Avery, he was with Margot.

He couldn't tell her that, though. He was stuck now, in this lie that he'd been stuck in for weeks. At first, it had felt harmless, even kind of funny. A joke between him and Avery, a silly story to his mom, but one that was no big deal, one that he'd correct eventually, once he figured out what he was doing next.

But now it felt so false, when he was smiling like that about Margot, for his mom to think that it was about Avery. It almost felt like a betrayal of Margot. It definitely felt like a real lie, not just the fudging of the truth it had been at the beginning, where he mostly just hadn't corrected his mom. And he really fucking hated it.

And he'd done this to himself, all because of that job?

"Lauren, we really should get you home," Pete said.

His mom sighed.

"I know." She leaned over and gave Luke a hug. "Thanks again, Luke. I don't know what I'd do without you. On sabbatical from your big-time job and you jump in to help your mom. How did I get this lucky?"

Luke gave her a tight squeeze.

"Just get home and get some rest." He looked up at Pete. "Let me know if I can bring over anything, okay?"

Pete nodded.

"Will do."

Luke watched them walk out, his mind still on everything his mom had said. On sabbatical from his big-time job. Right. He had to do something to end this farce. And plus, he had to see if this whole thing about interviewing for Brian's job was for real.

He pulled out his phone.

LUKE

Hey Craig—I'd love to chat. Let me know when is good for you.

SYDNEY CAME BY THE winery the Friday before the party, ostensibly to see what the Barrel's setup would be, but Margot knew it was really to give her some last-minute help. She was grateful for it—all of the folding tables and chairs had been delivered the day before and were stacked in the barn, but she wanted to get everything else they needed over there before the end of the day. Thankfully, Taylor and Daisy had everything covered in the tasting room, and she could throw herself into party details.

"Charlie wanted to come today but couldn't," Sydney said when they walked out to the lawn, boxes full of wineglasses in their arms. "But they told me to make sure that we have a table out of the direct sun. You know how pale they are."

Margot laughed.

"I do, but no need to worry, we rented shade umbrellas for

that reason. I didn't want anyone getting heatstroke at our party; that would be a nightmare."

Sydney shuddered.

"You'd lose it." She looked around the grounds. "It all looks great back here. I'm really impressed at how much you got done in such a short time."

Margot looked around, too. Everything was green and flowering and fragrant. It looked just how she'd wanted.

"I know. I'm really pleased with it. Pete and his team did all of the hard work. And Elliot made the planter boxes." She grinned. "I just told everyone what to do."

Sydney patted her on the shoulder.

"Well, you're *very* good at that."

Margot brought her into the barn, and they set the wineglasses on a table just inside. Margot looked around, but Elliot wasn't there. Even so, she beckoned Sydney back outside before she said anything else.

"I'm sure my brother is about to explode with how I've taken over part of his domain here for this party that he didn't even want to have, so I'm trying to keep things organized in there."

Sydney waved that away.

"He'll be fine. Is he going to behave tomorrow?"

Margot sighed.

"I hope so." She really wanted to check in with him and ask him to please be nice to people tomorrow, but she had a feeling it would backfire if she did. She'd barely seen Elliot in the last week, but he'd been around last night when all of the supplies had gotten delivered, and had helped them get everything into the barn.

Margot gestured to the corner of the lawn.

"I have you in the corner there. We'll keep this path clear, and have the food all along the far edge of the square, so there will be space in the middle for people to eat and drink and mingle. The wine stations will be right by the barn, partly for flow, partly because then it's easiest for us to restock." She turned to Sydney. "I'll bring you into my office—I have a whole sketch of the setup on the wall, along with all of my other plans. My staff makes fun of me for it."

"I definitely want to see this, and I will definitely make fun of you for it, too," Sydney said. "But when you said your *staff* makes fun of you for it, you had that little smile on your face. Don't you mean your former staff, your current—"

Margot tried to hide her smile, but she couldn't.

"Yes, fine, okay, I meant him, too, but the rest of them also make fun of me for it."

Sydney raised her eyebrows at her.

"Is he coming to the party tomorrow?"

Margot nodded.

"Yeah, he'll be here." She would have been so sad if Luke wasn't going to be there. She'd been working on this so hard, it would have felt awful for him to miss it.

Sydney gestured back toward the winery building.

"Do any of them know about the two of you?"

Margot shook her head.

"No. I'm sure Elliot would think that I pounced on our employee as soon as he was out the door. Or worse." To be fair, Luke had technically done the pouncing, but she'd basically dragged him into her house when he'd shown up at her door. "I'll have to tell him eventually."

Sydney shrugged.

"How often do you tell your brother about guys you're just sleeping with, anyway? This thing between you and Luke is no big deal, right?"

Margot didn't say anything, and Sydney grinned at her.

"Unless you're not just sleeping with him? You didn't answer that other question I asked. Your current . . . what, exactly?"

Margot could feel that smile on her face again.

"I . . . We haven't exactly put a title on that, but fine, I'm not just sleeping with him."

Sydney cackled.

"Finally, she admits it! What happened to 'I don't know if I can trust him' and 'It's not serious,' hmmmm?"

"Well, that was all bullshit, but you knew that already," Margot said. "It's only been a few weeks, though. I shouldn't get in too deep. But . . ."

Sydney threw an arm around Margot.

"But you did anyway. You're happy. I'm glad. Just as long as he knows that if he hurts you, I'll destroy him."

Margot laughed.

"Oh, don't worry, he knows." She turned Sydney back toward the winery building. "Come on, let's go get more wineglasses."

Twenty

MARGOT TOLD LUKE NOT to stay over the night before the party. She knew she wanted to be up and at the winery super early that morning. She'd set her alarm for six, but she woke up at five and decided to just go with it. She was the first person at the winery that day, for maybe the first time ever. Either even Elliot usually wasn't there before six a.m., or he didn't care enough about the party to get there early.

She walked in and started the coffeemaker in the kitchen, and then, with a full cup of coffee in her hand and her coziest sweater on, she stared at her conspiracy wall. Maybe if she looked at it hard enough, all of her plans would work out just as she wanted them to.

She felt silly for being so obsessive, so stressed, about this party. Lots of wineries did parties like this for their anniversaries, for their wine clubs, etc. Some people she'd talked to seemed so casual about them—oh yeah, there was food, people came, drank some wine, no big deal.

But this was the first time that Noble Family Vineyards had ever thrown itself a party, and it had to be perfect.

Thank God she'd put *make coffee* on her to-do list. It felt good to check something off by six a.m.

From there, she took a deep breath and started going. She checked for any last-minute RSVPs, made sure the spreadsheet had autopopulated with them like it was supposed to, and made sign-in sheets for the people who would just show up. She'd counted the linens and glasses and chairs three times the day before to make sure they had the right number. She didn't need to double-check on the wine. Did she? No, no, they'd all gotten it ready and waiting over in the temperature-controlled area of the barn the day before.

Five minutes later, on her way out of the winery building, she ran, almost literally, into Elliot.

"Oh! Hi, good morning," she said. "I was just . . ."

He smiled at her.

"Going to double-check on something? The tables? The chairs? The wine? The in-case-of-rain tents?"

She laughed.

"I did *not* rent in-case-of-rain tents, even I wasn't that pessimistic—or, I guess, depending on your thoughts on the drought, optimistic. Those are umbrellas for shade, Elliot! It's going to be in the nineties today!"

He fell into step next to her.

"So?"

She sighed.

"Fine, yes, I was going to check the wine. Just to make sure we have enough of each kind—I don't want to make anyone have to go running around to get it during the party! Plus, I couldn't remember if I'd increased the amount of rosé we should have on hand—it's going to be hot, you know everyone wants rosé when it's hot."

He put his hand on her shoulder.

"I'm not going to stop you from double-checking. But I was there last night, too, remember. You consulted that list like a drill sergeant as we got all of the wine in the right locations, and I absolutely heard you tell Taylor you'd upped the amount of rosé to put in the fridges. I'll come with you to check, but have a muffin first? You've probably had a lot of coffee already; you need something else in your system."

He took a muffin out of the shoebox he was carrying and handed it to her.

"It's still warm," she said. "Where did you get these?"

She took a bite, and sighed.

"Oh, this is so good. So many blueberries. And is that a little lemon? Just like—"

He smiled.

"Yeah, just like those old muffins of Mom's. I got her to dig up the recipe. I made them this morning."

Margot almost dropped the muffin.

"You made these? Since when do you bake?"

He laughed.

"Since this morning, that's when." He shrugged. "Or, okay, since a few days ago—I had to make a test batch just so I didn't ruin these, which was a good idea, since I did indeed mess up the first batch. These are pretty good, I think. You like them?"

Margot reached into the box and took another.

"Like them? I might eat all of them."

Elliot looked both pleased and embarrassed.

"You can have as many as you want, though I'm warning you, Finn may fight you for them."

They went into the barn, double-checked all of the wine—which was all exactly as it should be—and then Margot looked around. At the barn, the winemaking equipment on the far side, the barrels in the back, and then, outside, the beautifully landscaped grounds, thanks to Pete. They didn't look manicured—that's not what anyone had wanted—but they were full of greenery, shrubs, flowers, and other pollinators. And the raised beds that Elliot had built on the path from the winery building to the lawn looked perfect, all full of fragrant herbs.

She smiled as she looked at everything. It looked like a small, flourishing, beautiful winery. It looked just how she'd imagined. Better than she'd imagined.

"It looks good today," Elliot said.

"Yeah," she said. "It does."

She pulled out her phone and snapped a picture of the winery, in the gorgeous morning light. She wished she'd been able to hire a photographer for today, to get good pictures for brochures and social media, but she'd pushed up against her budget as it was. She should have prioritized that, though. Oh well.

"There you both are," Taylor said, walking from the winery to them. "Are we ready to start setting up?"

"We are," Margot said. "Thanks for getting here so early, Taylor. Elliot made muffins."

Taylor looked from her to Elliot.

"*Elliot* made muffins?"

He held out the shoebox.

"What a banner day." Taylor grabbed a muffin. She turned to Margot. "What's the first thing on that list of yours, boss? Tables or signs?"

Margot took the last sip of her coffee.

"Tables. Let's do those first, then signs. Then . . . everything else."

The next few hours flew by, with setup and extra staff arriving and the food vendors making last-minute calls to her with questions and more RSVPs coming in every time she looked at her phone.

Margot looked around the lawn. The pizza guy was here and setting up, Sydney and Charlie were at the table for the Barrel, and the taco women were at their station. But where was the guy with the tiny cheeseburgers?

She pulled her phone out of her pocket. Missed call, from an unfamiliar number. She checked her voice mail. And then she took a long, deep breath.

She went to find Taylor.

"Hey—the burger guy isn't coming. His power went out last night, all of the meat spoiled. Let's take down his table and put some seating for guests over there, before anyone gets here."

"Okay," Taylor said. "Want me to fix the menus and print new ones out?"

This was why she adored Taylor—she never panicked about anything.

"Thank you, that would be fantastic."

When Taylor came back, Margot took the stack of menus from her and set them in the barn.

"Hey. Can you hold down the fort for like"—she looked at her watch—"ten minutes? I have to change and put some makeup on."

Taylor waved her away.

"Make it fifteen. I've got this."

Margot glared at Taylor.

"Are you saying that I look so bad right now that ten minutes isn't enough to fix this?"

"Don't look a gift horse in the mouth, okay?" Taylor grinned at her. "Go."

Margot went.

She jumped into the tiny shower in the winery bathroom, showered faster than she ever had, and pulled on the red sundress she'd bought just for the party. She'd almost worn black—it made more sense for a day when she'd probably be moving stuff around and spilling things everywhere. But she knew that people would be pointing her out all day from a distance—at least, if all went well they would—and so she decided to take a lesson from Queen Elizabeth and wear a color that made her easy to spot in a crowd.

She laughed at herself. Was she literally thinking of herself as a queen? No, but look, despite the many problems of the monarchy, the woman had some good ideas, okay? Plus, that would be a good fantasy, if today went poorly—she could just pretend she was on some royal holiday somewhere.

No, she couldn't think like that. Today wasn't going to go poorly. Today was going to be great.

However, today was also going to be far too hot and frantic for a lot of makeup. She swiped on a few coats of waterproof mascara, put her longest-wearing red lipstick on, and called it a day. She put the final touches on her hair, sprayed it with an enormous amount of hairspray, and checked her phone. Twelve minutes. Not bad. That meant people would start arriving . . . any minute now.

She smiled at herself in the mirror to make sure there was no lipstick on her teeth, and then she took a deep breath. It was showtime.

When she walked back out toward the lawn, the first person

she saw, walking toward her with a huge smile on his face, was Luke.

"You're here early!" she said. "I didn't expect you here until later." She wanted to reach for him, but she didn't. Not here. She and Luke had been together for almost a month now, and she was going to have to tell Elliot about it sometime, but she didn't want him to find out like this. Not today especially.

He beamed at her, but he didn't reach for her, either.

"Avery called to see if she could get a ride here, since her car was in the shop, and we thought it would be best to get here early, to get parking."

It wasn't until then that she noticed Avery was with him. Margot smiled at her.

"Hi, Avery," she said. "Thanks so much for all of your advice for the party. You're on the list, you know. This is on me."

"Thanks, Margot, but it was my pleasure," Avery said. "I can't wait to see what you put together." Then Avery looked from her to Luke, and smiled indulgently at them. "You two are so cute."

Margot blushed. Luke grinned.

"I . . . um—"

Avery laughed.

"I'm not going to embarrass you anymore—if I do, this one will murder me," she said, pointing at Luke.

Luke nodded.

"It's true, I will."

Margot laughed at both of them.

"Come this way and get some wine, both of you."

Luke walked next to her, and Avery dropped a few steps behind. After they'd walked for a few seconds, he leaned down and whispered in Margot's ear.

"You look beautiful."

She blushed again.

"Thank you." She touched his hand, just for a second. "I'm really glad you're here."

"Of course I'm here," he said.

Her cheeks got hot again, and she looked away from him as they turned the corner to the back lawn. Taylor was walking right toward them. Margot took a step away from Luke.

"There you are, Margot. Luke!" She grabbed him and gave him a hug. "We miss you around here, you know."

He grinned at her.

"I miss this place. I fully expect you to start ordering me to wash glasses and pour wine today, just out of habit."

Taylor laughed.

"I never ordered you around! Well . . . not exactly."

Luke burst out laughing.

"Oh, really? What do you call it, then?"

Taylor turned to Margot.

"Do you see this, Margot? Do you see how he's talking to me, now that I'm not in charge of him anymore?"

Margot grinned. Luke wiggled his eyebrows at her, where Taylor couldn't see.

"I do see that," she said. "I always knew this one was trouble. Remember, Elliot hired him, not me."

They all laughed, Luke and Avery a little harder than Taylor.

"You were looking for me, Taylor?" Margot asked.

"Right—the pizza guy says he has to start a little later than scheduled, but I know that you had a whole plan."

"Okay. I'll go talk to him." Margot turned to Luke and Avery. "Taylor, can you make sure these two get some wine?"

"Absolutely," Taylor said.

Margot made her way across the lawn to the pizza guy.

"Hi," she said. "I'm Margot Noble—you were looking for me?"

He nodded.

"I'm going to need thirty extra minutes to get the oven hot enough—sorry for the delay."

He didn't sound particularly apologetic, but what could she do?

She took a few deep breaths. This was fine. This would be fine. She'd known this wouldn't go exactly according to her plan; she'd built in some wiggle room for everything. This was no big deal.

"Okay, thanks for letting me know," she said. "Let the staff here know if you need anything, or if you have any questions for me, they'll find me." She smiled at him. "Can I bring you a glass of wine?"

He nodded to her.

"Sure."

She walked off to get his wine, trying to tamp down her irritation. She went back to the barn and sent Marisol over to the pizza guy to give him a glass of wine. She didn't want to tempt fate by talking to him again.

By now, more people had started trickling in—they came down the path from the parking lot looking excited, which was exactly how Margot wanted them to look. The signs pointed them to the barn, to check in with Taylor and her guest list to get a wineglass. People could also pay—and join the wine club—at the door.

She joined Taylor at the check-in table.

"Hi, I'm Margot Noble, welcome to Noble Family Vineyards,"

she said to the most recent group who came up to the table. "Would you like some wine?"

"I'd love some!" the woman at the front of the group said.

Margot stepped over to the bar and grabbed the open bottle of rosé.

"Why don't I start all of you off with a glass of rosé? It goes great with all of the food we're serving, and then you can ease into our other wines. Here's a list of everything we're pouring today, all the snacks that will be available, and also all of our wine that's for sale. Please let me or any of the staff know if you have any questions."

"Perfect, thank you!" the guest said. She turned to her friends. "See? I told you this was a good idea."

Margot grinned at the group and poured tastes of rosé for all of them. When they moved on, she greeted the next group.

"Hi, I'm Margot Noble, welcome to Noble Family Vineyards."

The next hour flew by. She poured rosé until Marisol came to relieve her, then she did a circuit of the party and tried to say hi to anyone she recognized from the tasting room or from around the valley, and introduce herself to anyone whom she didn't recognize. She snapped pictures and uploaded them to Instagram, with the caption she'd drafted the night before. The food all smelled good, even though there were no burgers and the pizza wasn't ready. There was nothing she could do about that—she couldn't dwell on it now. She hadn't tried any of the food yet; she was too busy talking to have food in her hands, and was too paranoid about getting anything on her dress to eat while standing. She'd brought along an emergency second outfit (another not-as-good-but-still-fine red dress) just in case, but still.

Every few minutes, she looked around for Luke. He was all over the party—chatting with Elliot, who was actually smiling at him; running errands for Taylor; bringing tacos to Marisol; replacing ice in the coolers at the rosé and white wine stations; and eating pizza with Avery. Every time she looked for him, he caught her eye and grinned at her, and she smiled back. That smile of his, the way he always found a way to see her from a distance, cut the tension in her shoulders by at least a quarter.

Wait! Luke was eating pizza! That meant the pizza guy had finally started serving—he'd said it would be thirty minutes late, it had been more like forty-five minutes late, but who was counting?

She was, obviously.

Huh, why was there suddenly no activity over at the tacos? She walked over to check in.

"Margot, I was just coming to find you. We ran out of tortillas—I must have forgotten to pack the rest of them. My sister just left to pick up more."

She smiled at Luciana, who looked so apologetic.

"It's okay," she said. What else could she say? "Thanks for letting me know."

Thank God for Sydney and Charlie—their food table was the only one that hadn't had a crisis today. Although did that mean they were going to run out of food soon? Sydney looked over at her and gave her a thumbs-up. Okay. She could rely on Sydney.

She went back over to the barn to take over from Taylor.

"Go get something to eat. You need a break or else you're going to collapse," she said to Taylor.

Taylor narrowed her eyes at her.

"I could—and will—say the same about you, you know."

Margot took the bottle she was about to open out of her hands.

"Go. I'll be fine."

Taylor rolled her eyes, but walked over to the line for the pizza. Margot opened the bottle of wine as a couple approached the table. She looked up to greet them, wine bottle in her hands, and froze.

It was Pete. And Luke's mom.

She'd put Pete on the guest list, and he'd RSVP'd with a plus-one, but somehow she'd forgotten—or blocked out—that his plus-one was Luke's mom.

Did Luke's mom know she and Luke were together? She didn't think so. He probably would have told her if he'd told his mom about them, right? When they'd had that conversation about Elliot? But she wasn't sure.

She forced herself to be calm. This was more than she'd bargained for today—a day she already had a whole lot to deal with—but she could handle it.

She hoped.

"Hi, Lauren! And Pete! Welcome to Noble Family Vineyards. I'm so glad you could make it today. How's your wrist?"

Lauren smiled as Margot handed her a glass of wine. She hadn't even asked if Lauren wanted it, she realized. But then, Lauren took it with a smile on her face.

"Thank you, Margot. My wrist is a lot better, thanks for asking. We can't stay long—I'm still recovering, and Pete here is a nightmare about making me rest, but I wanted to see the results of his hard work."

Margot hoped her smile looked normal and didn't broadcast *I'm sleeping with your son! And he's here! And so are you! Do you know that I'm sleeping with him? I don't think so, but I don't know for sure* to Lauren.

"The grounds look beautiful, don't they?" Margot looked at

Pete, who seemed embarrassed. "Pete succeeded beyond my wildest dreams. And we have some more plans for after the party."

Lauren beamed at her, while Pete shook his head.

"Now, Margot, don't make me blush. Where's that brother of yours? I have a question for him."

Margot looked around.

"Oh, there he is, talking to those people in the back." She pointed to the far side of the barn. That was interesting—Elliot was talking to a group of six people, and he seemed totally engaged with them. She'd expected to see him—if she saw him around the party at all today—hiding behind a stack of wine barrels.

Pete grinned.

"I'll go say hi to him," he said, and walked off toward Elliot.

Margot turned back to Lauren. It had been nice to have Pete there as a buffer for this conversation.

"There's lots of food—right now, there are risotto balls, pizza, the empanadas should be out shortly, and the tacos will be ready in a little while. And that's our rosé," she said, gesturing to the glass in Lauren's hand, like it wasn't obvious there was rosé in it. "It's a good first taste, but if you'd like something else, just let me or one of our staff know, and we'll pour it for you."

Lauren smiled at her.

"Thanks, Margot. I can't decide what I want to try first." She looked over to the other side of the lawn, where the food all was. "Ahh, there they are."

Margot poured a glass of rosé for another guest who came up to her.

"There who are?" she said as she tried to smile at the other guest and also smile at Lauren.

"Luke and Avery. Don't they make such a cute couple? I've been wanting this for years, you know."

Margot spilled wine on the table and reached for a napkin to clean it up.

Why was Luke's mom under the impression that he was with Avery? She'd said something like that when Margot had seen her at the auction, but when Margot had brought it up to Luke on the drive home, he'd laughed it off. But she didn't say it like something she was just *hoping* for, she said it like she knew Luke and Avery were dating. Why did she think she knew that?

"Oh?" What else could she say?

She looked over at Luke and Avery. They were standing there, chatting and laughing with Taylor, who had just gotten a slice of pizza and seemed to be making fun of Luke to Avery, who was laughing hard.

"Oh yes," Lauren said. "Anyway, I'm sorry that he had to leave you and Elliot like that; I hope you know I didn't tell him to quit! But I'm very grateful to have him up here, even if it does end up only being for a little while."

Only for a little while?

Margot opened her mouth to ask Lauren what she meant, when someone else stepped up to the table. She wanted—she really wanted—to continue the conversation with Luke's mom, but her professional instincts clicked on.

"Hi!" she said to the newcomer. "I'm Margot Noble, welcome to Noble Family Vineyards. Can I pour you a glass of rosé?"

"I'd love that, thanks so much. I'm Aurora."

Margot smiled and reached for the bottle of rosé, even though she felt like there had just been a tiny earthquake that only she'd felt. Because this woman in front of her was a writer for the *San Francisco Chronicle*. Margot had made it her business to know what everyone who wrote for the food and travel pages looked like, just in case they ever came through the tasting room. And now one of them was here, at the party. She must not have RSVP'd—or done it under a different name—if she had, Margot would have noticed. She'd planned this party, down to the second, but if she'd known this woman would show up, she would have planned it better, done more, made sure they never got off schedule with the pizza, or the tacos, or the burgers . . .

She forced a bright smile on her face and handed Aurora her rosé.

"Enjoy! Here's what we're pouring today, and here's a list of all of our wines for purchase. There's pizza, and arancini, and empanadas . . . oh yes, they're just serving them now. More tacos should be available shortly. My brother, Elliot—the Noble Family Vineyards winemaker—is in the barn, if you have any questions for him."

Did she manage to be friendly and informative and the perfect winery owner and hostess without being over-the-top about it? Maybe. Probably not? Was she smiling too hard? Almost certainly.

She reached for another bottle of wine as Taylor came up to her, two plates of pizza in her hands.

"The pizza is great, boss," Taylor said. "Luke said he knew you hadn't tried it yet, so he had me bring a slice over to you before the pizza man is all sold out."

Margot concentrated on opening the wine, so she wouldn't smile that goofy smile she knew she got whenever she thought about Luke. Sydney had taken a picture of her last week when she'd been smiling like that.

"That was nice of him," she said to the wine bottle. "He seems to be making himself useful today—did you remind him he doesn't work here anymore?"

Taylor laughed and started to answer as Margot looked up. She saw Aurora walking across the lawn in the direction of the pizza, sipping her rosé. She hoped there was enough pizza left for her.

"Taylor," she said in a low voice. "Do you see that woman over there, in the denim shirt and dark hair? She writes for the *San Francisco Chronicle*. Make sure she gets . . . I don't know, our very best service."

Taylor grinned at her.

"We give our best Noble service to everyone."

Margot made a face at her.

"You know what I mean." She looked around. "That reminds me—I have to make sure Elliot knows so he doesn't disappear or anything while she's here. I bet she'll want to talk to him."

She hoped this didn't make Elliot revolt. He'd so far been a lot better today than she'd expected, but she knew that couldn't last.

She put the wine bottle down and turned toward the barn.

"I'll be right back."

She turned and looked for Luke again, just as a guy in a white baseball cap gestured too widely and knocked a glass out of someone's hand. It fell onto the lawn, but didn't break, thank goodness.

Ah, there was Luke. He was standing over by the table for the Barrel, chatting with Sydney and Charlie. He looked up and grinned at her, and she grinned back at him. He gestured to her, like he wanted her to come over there, but she had to go to the barn to talk to Elliot. She'd come back and find Luke afterward.

Wasn't there something she had to talk to him about? She'd remember later.

———

FOR ABOUT THE TENTH time that day, Luke walked toward Margot just as she turned and walked in a different direction. No, it was probably at least the twentieth time; he'd lost count. Any other day, he'd take it personally, except she'd barely stayed in one place for more than five minutes for the entire party. Plus, he'd managed to make it over to her at least three times—each time they'd had only the chance to smile at each other and quickly check in before she'd rushed off in another direction, but just being around her made him happy. And today, unlike the many other times they'd been together at the winery, when he'd looked around for her, she'd looked back at him and given him a quick, tiny smile.

He walked over toward Taylor, a plate of food in his hands. Margot wasn't in sight anymore; Taylor would know where she was. Or, at least, in which direction she'd gone.

"Hey—Sydney sent me over here with food for Margot. Do you know where she is?"

Taylor looked down to see the pizza he'd sent over for Margot still behind the table.

"Good idea. She went to find Elliot, but she could be anywhere now. Though that red dress does make her easy to find."

Luke turned to go find her, and then stopped.

"Before I forget: That guy over there, with the white baseball cap and the blue shirt? I don't think he needs any more wine."

Taylor looked where he'd gestured, and nodded.

"Good catch," she said. "I think we've all been too busy to really keep track. Thanks, Luke."

He shrugged.

"No problem. Be right back."

He probably could have left the food for Margot at the table—Taylor would have made sure she got it—but he wanted to give it to her himself. She hadn't eaten all day. And he'd barely talked to her all day. He wanted to check in, see how she was doing, how she thought the day was going. He thought she'd be pleased—there were a lot of people here, the food was great, the music was fun, everyone seemed happy—but he didn't know if there had been problems below the surface that he hadn't noticed.

He went into the barn to see if Margot was there, and stopped just inside the door. She was over in the corner, with Elliot and a woman with short hair and glasses. Elliot was talking animatedly—which was surprising—and Margot was smiling, but something in the nature of her smile and the way she was standing made it clear to Luke that this was a high-pressure conversation, for Margot, at least.

He waited for her to notice him, which she did after about a minute. She nodded at him, and after another minute or so, put her hand on Elliot's arm.

"I'll leave you two to this. Aurora, please let me know if you need any more wine, though I'm sure Elliot can take care of that. I'll be back outside if you have any questions."

She walked toward Luke, a smile on her face, and an anxious look in her eyes. Luke handed her the plate when she got close enough to him.

"Charlie sent this to you," he said as they walked together out of the barn. "I think they might have me drawn and quartered if I didn't deliver this plate safely. And Sydney gave me these napkins for you."

Margot laughed, but it was her practiced, professional laugh.

It felt weird, to both be here, to be acting so formal and distant with her, when their relationship had changed so much over the past month. Maybe that was why they'd barely interacted during the party: He didn't want to hear that friendly, distant tone to her voice. Like she was talking to anyone.

Why had she kept their relationship a secret from the people at Noble? He knew it was partly because of Margot's baggage with Elliot, but he hadn't pushed her on that. He hadn't really felt like he could, since his mom was still under the impression that he was dating Avery. He planned to tell his mom the truth about that. It just had its own complications.

He and Margot walked out of the barn, and she inclined her head to the far side of the barn. As soon as they were out of sight of the party, she turned to him, her eyes lit up.

"That woman in there!" she said in a low whisper. "In the barn, talking to Elliot! She writes for the *San Francisco Chronicle*! I've been hoping someone from there would come to the tasting room this summer. They've occasionally written about our wines, but not enough, and never about visiting the winery. And now she's here! At the party!"

Margot's professional mask was gone, and she was talking to him like she did when they were side by side at the bar, or at her house on the couch, or in bed. He didn't know why he felt so relieved.

"That's fantastic!" he said. "How did it go with her? Wait, eat those risotto balls before you answer that. And yes, I recognize Charlie is trying to steal you away from me with this food, but the least I can do is to make sure you actually eat today."

Margot rolled her eyes, but blushed.

"Not you, too," she said. "You've been listening to Sydney too much." But she picked up one of the—now probably cold—risotto balls and popped it in her mouth. "Happy now?" she asked when she finished chewing.

He nodded.

"Very. But tell me more about this Aurora person."

Margot grinned.

"I can't believe she's here. She's been on our newsletter list for a while—I've double-checked to make sure she was still on it—and every so often I see her liking our social media posts, but then, lots of people do that, so I wasn't sure it meant anything. But then she showed up today! And Elliot was great with her—she asked him a few really smart questions about wine, and then he was off."

Luke put his hand on the middle of her back and grinned at her.

"She's been on the newsletter list, huh? Maybe it was that newsletter I helped with that inspired her to come."

He'd been joking, but Margot's eyes widened.

"You're probably right!" Her grin got a little wicked. "Mmm, I might have to reward you for that later." She popped the last risotto ball in her mouth and turned to walk back toward the party.

She stopped and touched his elbow.

"Have I told you how nice it is to have you here today?"

The way she smiled at him blew him away.

"Yeah," he said. "You have. Every time you look at me like that."

"Oh, Margot, there you are!"

They both turned to find Finn there.

"Taylor sent me to find you—it's getting crowded at the pouring station."

Margot nodded.

"Right. Coming." She walked back toward the party, Luke behind her.

He stopped when they got back onto the lawn and saw what Finn had meant. Taylor was alone at the white and rosé table, and the guy that Luke had noticed earlier—the one who seemed like he'd had at least two or three glasses too many—was there, with a woman next to him. He no longer looked just drunk. He looked drunk and angry.

"Who are you to say I can't have any more wine?" he yelled at Taylor. "I'm a wine club member here! That means I can drink however much wine I want! All of this wine is partly mine, I can drink it whenever I want!"

As Margot hurried toward the fracas, Taylor grabbed one of the ice buckets with open bottles of wine and moved it off the table, out of his reach.

"Fine, then. I'll just take it!" He tugged at the table, just as Margot got there. She reached for the table, a second too late. The tablecloth, with the second ice bucket full of wine, and two full wineglasses, flew off the table toward the drunk man, who tripped over backward. The tablecloth, glasses, wine, and the drunk man all crashed onto the ground.

Luke ran and was at the man's side before he sat up. Elliot was there only a few seconds later. Luke had thought he was still back in the barn.

"Excuse me, sir," Margot said in her most polite, furious voice. "I'm going to have to—"

Elliot put his hand on Margot's shoulder.

"I'll handle this. Go settle everyone else down." Elliot bent down to the drunk guy and grasped his shoulder. "Let's get you out of here."

Margot straightened up, and Luke saw an expression of mingled rage and humiliation on her face, right before that friendly, professional mask dropped back over it.

"Thanks, Elliot."

She turned back to the table, where Taylor was spreading out a new tablecloth and Finn was filling the ice bucket back up. Luke wanted to help her, but instead looked down at the drunk guy. The best way he could help Margot right now was to get this guy out of here.

Elliot already had the guy off the ground and held him firmly by one arm. Luke took the other.

"Do you know who he was with?" Elliot asked.

Luke nodded toward the woman standing a few feet away.

"Can you come with us?" Elliot asked her. She sighed and fell into step with them as they walked toward the winery building.

"Can you let us know your friend's name?" Luke asked her. "Did he drive here, or can we call the two of you a cab?"

"My name is Porter Eldridge," the drunk man said. "I am a member—"

"A member of the wine club, yes," Elliot said. He wouldn't be a member of the wine club for much longer, Luke was pretty sure. "This isn't a collective, you know; you don't own a piece of the winery."

"He drove us here," the woman said. "But I don't want to get in a car with him again. I can get myself home."

"We can take care of getting you home," Elliot said.

"Come with us," Luke said. "Hold on."

He and Elliot got the guy into the tasting room, where the guy sat down on one of the couches and immediately passed out. Elliot stood watch over him, while Luke went behind the bar to find the number of the tow truck company they used. Then he texted Margot.

LUKE

> He's passed out in the tasting room—
> his date says they drove here. I'll get
> his car towed somewhere and get a
> taxi for him

She texted him back so fast he was sure she'd been waiting for it.

MARGOT

> Perfect. Thank you for handling this.
> Make sure to get his name.

When he got off the phone, Elliot was coolly sliding the guy's wallet back into his pocket.

"His name really is Porter Eldridge," he said. "Incredible."

It was all fixed within twenty minutes. Porter Eldridge and his car were both off the property—the car attached to a tow truck, an angry Porter in a taxi—and he was off the wine club list, his fee refunded. His date had refused to let Noble pay to take her home, but had bought half a case of wine as a thank-you and had taken off in a rideshare. By the time Luke walked back out to the party, it was like nothing had ever happened. Margot was chatting and laughing with some latecomers, Taylor was pouring wine and talking to Avery, and the woman from the *Chronicle* was eating tacos.

Luke looked closer at Margot. Okay, it wasn't quite like it had never happened. He could sense the tension in her, from all the way across the lawn. He could sense it in the way one of her hands was in a fist at her side, in the way she glanced down at her phone with narrowed eyes, in that forced, fake laugh she let out.

The party was supposed to be from noon to three, but at three, there were still plenty of people there. The food tables were all cleaning up, and Taylor and Daisy had disappeared into the barn to pack up wine for guests, but there was still some food left over that the guests were nibbling on as they hung out in the sun and drank wine. Luke checked to see what Margot was doing: still chatting with people who looked like VIPs, and it seemed like she'd be doing that for a while. So he went to go help Taylor and everyone else with the wine.

"You shouldn't be doing this," Taylor said when he picked up a box. "You don't work here anymore, remember?"

"I know," he said. "Where do you want these?"

She sighed.

"The boxes of wine that guests bought today should go by the door to the barn, so we can easily bring them out to their cars when they leave. Make sure there's a name on each one."

Eventually, the guests all got the hint and started filing out, most of them with at least one box of wine tucked in the trunk of their car.

Margot walked over to Taylor just as Luke picked up a guest's wine. She was still smiling, but Luke didn't believe that smile.

"Thanks for taking over the cleaning up," she said to Taylor. "Sorry, I was occupied, I had to talk to Elizabeth—she was a friend of Uncle Stan's. I'm just going to—"

Luke didn't hear the rest of what she said as he followed the guests to their car. He loaded the wine into their car, thanked them for coming, and went back to the lawn. He was worried about Margot. He needed to try to get her out of here, see if she'd go home, relax, maybe even get some sleep. He knew she'd probably gotten here before sunrise.

He also knew that she wouldn't leave here until everyone else was gone.

He looked around for her when he got back to the lawn, but he didn't see her anywhere.

"Where's Margot?" he asked Taylor, who was closing up all of the folding tables with Avery. Avery grinned at him.

"She said she had to grab something out of her office," Taylor said. "She'll be right back. Was someone looking for her?"

He was.

"Yeah, but I can see if one of us can answer their question," he said.

He turned toward the winery building. He couldn't get that look out of his mind: that look on Margot's face when Porter Eldridge had made a scene, that look of despair in her eyes. He didn't really care if people wondered why he went after her. He just knew he had to find her.

He walked in the back door and made his way to Margot's office. The door was closed, but he knew she was in there.

He knocked softly.

"Margot," he said. "It's me."

She opened the door, and the sad, broken look on her face tore at his heart. He stepped inside, kicked the door closed, and pulled her into his arms.

She let out a sob and dropped her head onto his shoulder.

"I knew I wouldn't be able to pull this off, I knew it," she said. "Oh, Luke . . . I can't believe . . . Why didn't I see . . ."

She was crying so hard, he could barely understand her. All he could do was hold her, stroke her hair, and let her cry.

After a few minutes, she took a long breath, and her sobs slowed down. He let go of her for a second to grab a few tissues from the box on her desk and hand them to her, but he put his arms back around her as she wiped her eyes.

"It really wasn't that bad," he said. "Only a handful of people really paid him any attention, and we got him out of the way pretty fast."

Her eyes welled up again and she shook her head.

"This was exactly why Uncle Stan never wanted to have parties here. He didn't want us to become one of those wineries where people would go just to get drunk and make scenes. That's not who Noble is. I'm sure Elliot will remind me of that any second now. And plus, it doesn't matter how many people saw it—and I think most of the party did—people took videos of it, they've already put them online. They were kind enough to tag us as they stood there at our party, drinking our wine. Everyone is going to think . . . And with that reporter right there."

She sat down on the edge of her desk. She looked so heartbroken. God, he hated seeing her like this. He took her hand.

"But everything else went so well," he said. "I don't think one guy getting drunk is going to be the thing everyone is going to remember from this party."

She shook her head.

"So many things went wrong. That was just the cherry on top." She put her head on his chest. "Was it obvious how upset I was?"

He wrapped his arms around her.

"I don't think anyone else could tell. I don't think even I would have been able to tell, except I was looking at you right when it happened. But I swear, this isn't as bad as you think—it barely made a blip in the party. And it wasn't your fault, there was nothing you could have done."

She shook her head.

"Everything that goes wrong here is my fault, it's the nature of the job. But this was very definitely my fault. I noticed that he was drinking too much. I should have cut him off way before we got to that point. But I didn't. And we see what happened."

He wanted to argue with her, try to convince her she was wrong on this, that she shouldn't be so upset, but he knew that wasn't what she needed from him. So he just held her.

After a few moments, she stood up.

"I should . . ." She let out a breath. "I should go back out there. There's so much left to do. I just had to . . . not be on for a few minutes, that's all." She smiled at him, and her eyes welled up again. "But thank you, for coming to find me. It really helped, to have you here."

He squeezed her hand.

"What else do you need? What can I do?"

There was a knock at the door.

"Margot?" It was Elliot.

She dropped Luke's hand and closed her eyes for a second.

"Yeah," she said when she opened them. "I'm in here."

Twenty-One

MARGOT TOOK A DEEP breath and stood up to face her brother.

"Do you want me to stay?" Luke asked in a low voice.

"No. Thanks." She was too close to the edge to look at Luke right now. It would just make her want to lean on him, want to cry again, when she had to be strong for this conversation with Elliot. She'd known it was coming, she just hadn't realized he'd come find her this soon.

"Okay." He took a step away from her as Elliot walked into her office. "Um, I'll go help Taylor."

Elliot laughed.

"You don't have to do that, Luke—did you forget you don't work for us anymore? We're so grateful for your help, especially with our friend Porter, aren't we, Margot? But you should take off, we can handle this from here." Margot tried not to wince at the mention of the drunk guy, but she could tell Luke noticed her reaction. She had no real choice but to agree with Elliot here, even though she wanted Luke to stay.

"Yeah, Luke," she said, trying to make her voice even. "Thanks so much for all of your help today, but we don't want to put you out."

Luke kept his eyes on her, but she looked away from him.

"Congratulations on a fantastic party, both of you," he said. "I'll see you soon."

Margot met his eyes for a second at his last sentence. He raised his eyebrows at her, and she nodded. She dreaded this conversation with Elliot so much, but at least she knew that afterward, she'd get to see Luke.

He closed the door behind him when he walked out, and she turned to Elliot. Might as well get this over with.

"Come to gloat?" she asked.

She hadn't meant to sound so bitter, but she couldn't help it. Elliot hadn't been able to wait until she'd dried her tears to get his *I told you so* in, could he?

He looked surprised.

"Gloat? About what?"

He was going to make her spell this out for him, wasn't he? Elliot usually wasn't an asshole like this, but he'd apparently been even more resentful about this party than she'd thought. Fine.

"The party? How it was everything you said it would be? Your friend Porter Eldridge, who turned Noble into exactly the kind of party winery you—and yes, our uncle—didn't want this place to be. Until, of course, I, who didn't deserve to inherit half of this winery, insisted that we have a party and proved you right? You don't have to say any of it. You were right, I get it."

Elliot took a step toward her.

"Is that how you think I feel? That one drunk guy ruined the party? I came in here to congratulate you. And to apologize, for what a killjoy I've been about this whole thing."

She stared at him.

"Congratulate me? After what happened? That was my fault. I should have cut him off before he got to that point. And the pizza was late, and there wasn't enough food, which is probably part of what caused him to get so drunk so fast, I should have—"

Elliot shook his head.

"You're being too hard on yourself, Margot. Every party has a drunk guy. You were doing a million things today, it's not your fault that one guy tried to make a scene. It wasn't a big deal; we got him out of the way. Most people at the party barely noticed."

That's what Luke had said, but he'd just been trying to make her feel better. Why was Elliot saying this, too?

"Lots of people noticed," she said. "And then there's the Internet—people have already posted videos of the whole thing online."

Elliot brushed that off.

"Aren't you the one who always tells me that all publicity is good publicity? Plus, it's Porter who should be embarrassed by that, not us. That's not going to make people think any less of us, Margot." He gestured toward the lawn. "The people here today were great. Most of the ones I talked to, at least. I didn't want a party because I thought it would be full of Porter Eldridges, but these were all people who are just interested in wine. I probably should have realized that, if I'd thought about it—it was the same kinds of people who come to taste at our winery, something else I complained about and was wrong about. But there were also people who have been in our wine club for years, who just wanted to say hi, tell me how much they liked Stan, thank me—thank us—for carrying on his tradition. I didn't realize how much I would enjoy hearing that, and talking to them." He shrugged. "I even liked that reporter. She knew what she was talking about, and asked great questions."

Margot sat back down on her desk. That was the longest speech she'd heard from Elliot in years. She could barely comprehend what he was saying, it was so unlike what she'd expected. She felt full of adrenaline, ready for this fight that had been brewing forever, but Elliot wasn't giving it to her. She didn't understand.

"Yeah, she seemed good," she said. "And I know what you mean, about the people who came for Uncle Stan—they seemed happy to be able to celebrate him." Her eyes filled with tears. Was Elliot mocking her, when he said all of that about how well the party went, and how he liked the people? "Even though I failed him today."

Elliot shook his head again.

"Why do you think that? And why did you say that, when I came in here? About not deserving to inherit the winery. You know that's not true."

She rolled her eyes at him. It felt juvenile, but she couldn't help it.

"Oh, come off it, Elliot. We both know that's how you feel, no matter how nice you've decided to act today."

He stared at her.

"That's not how I feel. Why do you think I feel that way?"

She was so tired of this. Tired of this constant low-level conflict, tired of feeling less than, tired of always pushing herself and always coming up wanting.

"I think you feel that way because that's what you said! But even if I hadn't heard you say it, I'm not stupid, you know, even though you seem to think that. You've made your feelings about this—about me—crystal clear."

"I don't think that!" Elliot never raised his voice like this. She always wished he would, wished she could get a rise out of him, but she never could. Until now. "I don't think you're stupid, how could I? You run this whole place! And I don't think you didn't deserve to inherit the winery!"

The memory came back so sharply she had to fight back tears again.

"I heard you say it! At the funeral. Right there in the hallway. Talking to Jimmy."

Elliot sighed. He sank down in the chair in front of her desk.

"Oh. I'd forgotten about that. I wish you hadn't heard that."

She got up and moved to the chair behind her desk, just to get some distance from him, to feel in command of this situation, at least for a moment.

"Why? I'm glad I heard. At least I knew what I was getting myself into."

He shook his head.

"No, Margot, you don't understand. I—"

"You're not going to try to tell me that you didn't mean it, are you?" she asked him. "Because I heard you. I could tell you meant it."

He looked down at his hands for a moment.

"No," he said quietly. "I'm not going to try to tell you that. I meant it. Then. I was angry then, at Uncle Stan, and yes, at you. I was angry and bitter and grieving and confused. I did mean it then."

He looked up and across the desk at her.

"But Margot, I haven't felt that way for a long time. You work your ass off for this place, you understand things I would never be able to figure out in a million years, you understand *people*. I know that I've fought you on so many things, but you're usually right. That doesn't stop me from fighting you, but I've gotten better about it . . . at least somewhat. Just look at today—yes, you're right, I didn't want to have this party, and it was great. Even I could tell that, and I don't like parties! All of these people were excited to be here, our staff was happy, it was a good day. You should be proud of yourself." He smiled at her. "Uncle Stan would be. Is."

The tears started falling from her eyes again, but this time they felt so different.

"But I thought—" She reached for her tissue box. "For the past three years, I've thought . . ."

Elliot rubbed his hand over his face.

"That's why you've been so weird and prickly with me. I just thought you didn't want to hang out with your big brother anymore. I wish you'd said something."

She wiped her tears.

"Me, too."

Elliot shook his head.

"But when were you supposed to say something? In the hallway at the funeral, with Jimmy there to overhear you yell at me and me just getting quiet and mean? That would have made things even worse between us."

She laughed at the accuracy of how they both would have acted, and then sighed.

"I know. But some other time, I should have found a way, instead of just silently seething."

Elliot stood up.

"Instead of getting mad at ourselves for the past, how about we agree to never do that shit again? Either as business partners, or family?"

She stood up, too, and walked around the desk to him.

"Let's shake on it." She held out her hand and grabbed on to his. They shook hands, and then he pulled her into a hug.

"The handshake is for my business partner. The hug is for my sister. I'm sorry, Margot."

She hugged her brother tight.

"I'm sorry, too, Elliot."

He took a step back.

"Now—how about we go back out there and finish cleaning up from this great party? There are a bunch of open bottles of wine—I hope it's okay that I told the staff to take them home."

She grinned.

"As long as 'the staff' includes me. I've been looking forward to drinking some wine on my couch tonight all day."

He put his arm around her as they walked out of his office.

"Well, I'll have to check with our CEO on that. She's very strict about these things."

She laughed as they walked back to the lawn. She couldn't wait to drink that wine on the couch. With Luke.

———

WHEN LUKE LEFT MARGOT'S office, his first impulse was to stand outside of her door and listen to whatever went on between her and Elliot. So he could burst in and protect her from her brother if he said something mean to her? No, Margot would hate that. He made himself leave the building and walk out to the lawn.

But on the way, he texted her.

Text and let me know you're okay?
See you later, just let me know when

He hung around outside for a few minutes after he went back out there, helping Taylor pack up, but when Margot and Elliot didn't come back after five minutes, he looked over at Avery.

"I'm going to take off—did you want a ride home?"

He figured that after Elliot had told him to go home, it might make things even more complicated between Margot and her brother if he lingered just to see how she was doing.

Avery looked surprised, but nodded.

"Let me just finish this."

She set the last few wineglasses on the counter into a box, and then stood up.

"Let's go."

He hugged everyone goodbye, and Avery followed him out to the parking lot. She turned to him as soon as they got in his car.

"Is everything okay? Between you and Margot, I mean," Avery asked.

He hadn't expected that question.

"Yeah, of course. Why?"

She shrugged.

"I didn't expect you to leave until she did, that's all. And she disappeared a while ago, and then you did, and now you're leaving and she's still nowhere to be seen, so . . . I just wondered if you had a fight."

He shook his head.

"No, we're fine. Better than fine. She's just—" He couldn't tell her about the Elliot stuff. "I was worried about her, I knew she'd be upset, after that thing with the drunk guy, so that's why I went looking for her. She's talking to Elliot now, so I wanted to give them some space. I'll see her later, though."

Avery sighed.

"Poor Margot. That drunk guy was nothing, there's always one, I should have told her that when we met to talk party planning. But this was her first big event, of course she would think that was the end of the world. I hope Elliot is telling her it's no big deal."

Luke tightened his grip on the steering wheel.

"I hope so, too."

Avery looked sharply at him. *Damn it*, he didn't want her to know there was any friction between Margot and Elliot.

"Elliot doesn't know about you and Margot, does he?"

Well, okay, that wasn't quite the topic he would have picked, but at least it wasn't exposing a secret that wasn't his to tell.

"No, he doesn't know," he said. "Margot felt weird about it, because of the whole she-used-to-be-my-boss thing. No one from the winery knows—at least, I don't think so."

She raised her eyebrows at him.

"Is that weird for you? That she's keeping it a secret?"

He shook his head.

"It's not a secret," he said. Avery just looked at him. "It's not! Lots of people know. We go out together all the time. She just hasn't told her brother, that's all. It's complicated there."

Avery put her hand on his shoulder.

"Okay. I'm just worried about you. I saw the way you looked at her today. And I especially saw the way you looked when she backed away from you when Taylor came over."

He brushed that off.

"I don't know what you mean. She's just been so stressed

about this party that it didn't make sense to deal with anything else until it was over. Plus, I haven't—"

"Yes, I was just about to say, you've let your mom keep believing this ridiculous story about the two of us dating. She came up to me today, and I swear she was about to ask me when the wedding date was!"

Luke laughed.

"Sorry about that. I had no idea she'd be there today. And yeah, I'm going to have to come clean to her soon, I think. About everything." He sighed. "Especially with this interview next week."

"Interview? What interview?" Avery asked.

He'd forgotten that he hadn't told Avery about this yet.

"My old boss is leaving, and Craig—my old mentor there—reached out to me to see if I wanted to interview for the job. They've made a bunch of changes there, so I thought it was worth having a conversation. I was kind of suspicious that the whole thing was bullshit, but when I talked to Craig, he talked a lot about how much everyone there liked me, and then Brian's old boss called to say how great my work had been, and how glad he was that I was interviewing for that job. Granted, it would have been nice if he'd said any of that while I was actually there, but whatever. I'm feeling cautiously optimistic about my chances." He grinned. "Even a little smug, that after everything, they still want me."

"When did this all happen?" Avery asked.

"Just earlier this week," he said. "Everything has moved pretty quickly—I'm heading back down there for an interview on Thursday. It would be a big pay bump, and a level up. And it would be kind of fun to prove something to all of those people who thought I wasn't good enough."

He hadn't told Margot about the interview yet. He'd almost

told her a few times that week, but every time, something had stopped him.

"Oh wow," Avery said. "Well, congratulations, I guess. Let me know how it goes."

He nodded.

"I will."

"And like I said before," she said. "I'll keep up this pretense with your mom as long as you need me to, because I'm your friend, but as your friend, I have to tell you: You have to tell her the truth. Interview or no interview. After all, you have a real girlfriend now—that should make her happy."

He laughed.

"It should, you're right, but you know you've always been her favorite."

Avery tossed her hair back.

"Well, obviously." She looked at him sideways. "Don't think I didn't notice that you just let me call Margot your girlfriend. You didn't even try to deny it."

He actually hadn't noticed that. He'd try to play that off with most people, but Avery knew him too well for that.

"We actually haven't really talked about that, but . . ." He grinned. "We're usually too busy doing other things to talk much."

That wasn't true, but he knew what Avery's reaction to that statement would be. She didn't let him down.

"Ewww! I told you I didn't need to hear the details!"

He laughed again as he pulled up in front of her apartment.

"Have a good night, Avery," he said as she got out of the car. "Talk to you soon."

He checked his phone as soon as Avery went inside. Margot had texted back.

MARGOT

I'm ok. Better than ok, actually. We'll talk later; I'll text when I'm leaving here

He felt a rush of relief, along with another emotion he didn't have words for right now.

LUKE

I'm glad. See you soon

Twenty-Two

WHEN MARGOT LEFT THE winery, she was exhausted. It was the kind of bone-tired that came from waking up at five a.m., walking and standing and smiling and laughing all day, occasional physical labor, sobbing on Luke's shoulder, and a very emotional and cathartic confrontation with her brother, which had upended so much of what she thought she'd known.

She didn't know if she should trust Luke's and Elliot's versions of how the party had gone. She was still getting a ton of social media notifications, but she was too tired to check them to see if they were good or bad. And anyway, the proof would be in how much money they'd made, how many new memberships they'd gotten, what their press would be, how sales would be over the next few weeks and months. She wouldn't know some of that for a while, and she didn't have the strength—or the energy—to stay at the winery that night and look hard at the numbers from the party.

She couldn't wait to get home, hop in a hot shower, take off her bra, and put comfortable clothes on. But most of all, she couldn't wait to be with Luke.

She texted him when she locked up the winery.

MARGOT

Leaving now. Meet me at my place?

Can't wait to see you

She normally would have hesitated to send that last text, to let Luke know how much she looked forward to seeing him, how important he was to her. But after today, she just wanted to be honest. It felt almost too good to be true that she was going home to him now. He almost felt too good to be true.

She got right in the shower as soon as she got home. Just as she got out and wrapped herself in her fluffiest robe, her doorbell rang. She pulled her shower cap off and opened the door to Luke, his arms full.

"What's all that?" she asked as he walked in and set everything down on the counter.

He started opening boxes full of food.

"I thought you might be hungry," he said. "You barely ate anything today, at least that I saw, and I bet you were too stressed this morning to do anything but drink an enormous amount of coffee."

She smiled at how well he knew her.

"I also ate a muffin, but point taken," she said. The smells coming out of those boxes made her swoon a little. Or maybe it was that they were here, in her kitchen, because Luke had brought them to her. She opened the boxes and grinned at him.

"Meatballs, garlic bread, and burrata? This is perfect. I have the total inability to make any more decisions today. Thank you."

She sat down at the counter.

"And"—he flipped open the pizza box that she hadn't even noticed—"that potato pizza you like so much."

He went into the kitchen and opened the silverware drawer.

"Don't worry about plates," she said. "No one needs to deal with all of that right now."

He laughed and handed her a fork.

"Dive right in."

But instead of doing that, she waited for him to sit down next to her.

"Thanks for bringing me dinner," she said. "And for everything else today. It was a really long day. It was great to have you there."

He kissed her on the cheek.

"I'm glad I could be there."

She leaned her head against his chest for a moment. Then she sat up, cut into a meatball, and popped some of it in her mouth.

"Oh God, this is so good."

He picked up his own fork and then started to stand up.

"Do you want wine?"

She laughed.

"I was so looking forward to relaxing and drinking wine tonight, but actually . . . no, I really don't want any. Don't ever tell anyone I said this, but just the thought of wine right now turns my stomach. I have poured more glasses of wine today than ever in my life, I held the same glass of wine for many hours and only took about three sips of it, and I've been so surrounded by the scent of wine all day that I feel like it's coming out of my pores. All I want is ice-cold sparkling water, which, thank God, there's plenty of." She got up and went over to the fridge. "But you should have wine, though, if you want."

He picked up a slice of pizza.

"I don't need any wine. Water is fine. Though—"

She grabbed a glass out of the cabinet.

"You don't like sparkling water, right." She poured a glass for him and sat back down.

"I could have done that," he protested.

She nodded.

"I know. But you brought me a whole perfect dinner, I think I could handle getting you a glass of water."

He put an arm around her, and she relaxed against him.

"I was so . . . When Elliot came in, when you left, I was anticipating the worst."

"I could tell," he said.

It was such a relief to be able to talk to him about Elliot. She didn't have to give him the backstory. She could just talk to him.

"Yeah. But that conversation with Elliot was nothing like what I expected. I thought he would be smug, gloating, sneering at me about Porter Eldridge and how he'd ruined our party." She shook her head at herself. "Even though Elliot has never gloated about anything, that's not how he is. Somehow, in the last few years, I built up this version of my brother who doesn't really exist. But after today, I actually have hope that we can break through all of that."

She told him the whole story. His eyes were on her the whole time, and his hand in hers.

"Oh, Margot," he said, when she finished. "You must be so relieved."

She nodded slowly.

"I think I don't quite believe it yet?" She reached for a slice of pizza. "Maybe the relief will come, after a little while. It's not that I don't believe what Elliot said. I do, intellectually. But . . . it's been so long." She took a bite of the pizza. "I still think it's possible this whole day was a dream, or maybe I just blacked out after our friend Porter made that scene and everything since then is just my fantasy, and I'm going to wake up on the floor of the barn soon with Elliot mad at me and with no delicious meatballs in front of me."

Luke shook his head.

"The floor of the barn? Come on, Margot—if you'd passed out because of Porter, Taylor and I would have made sure you made it to the couch in your office, at least. Give us some credit! I can't believe you'd think we would leave you on the floor."

She bent forward and kissed him softly on the lips.

"You're right, you would never do that," she said. "Now I'm wondering if I passed out in the shower the morning that you quit, and everything since then has been a dream." She thought for a moment. "Or maybe it goes back further than that, and I got in a car accident on my way home from the winery that Sunday night, and I've been in a coma ever since, so you are entirely a figment of my imagination."

He pushed her robe aside and slid his hand up the side of her leg, from her knee to her thigh to her hip.

"I promise, I am flesh and blood," he said.

She reached for the bottom of his shirt and pushed it up.

"I think that's exactly what a figment of my imagination would say."

He untied her robe and moved his hand up the side of her body, until he cupped one of her breasts.

"I am well aware of your excellent imagination." He moved

his thumb and index finger to her nipple and circled it. "I am very grateful for it, as a matter of fact. But do you think that a figment of your imagination would do this?" He pulled her nipple firmly, and her eyes closed.

"Mmm," she said. "Maybe. You see, the problem is that I would imagine someone who would do everything I like the most, and I happen to really like that."

"Oh no." He pushed her legs farther apart and slid his free hand between them. "That means that if I do things like this"—he slid a finger inside of her, and she gasped—"because I know you really like it, it'll prove I'm not real. I guess the only thing I can do to prove myself to you is to do things you don't like." He stilled his finger. And then he grinned. "But where's the fun in that?"

———

LUKE STILL COULDN'T BELIEVE sometimes that he could just do this. That he could sit here, with Margot, and kiss her everywhere he wanted, pull her clothes off, put his hands all over her body, and see all of her. And the best part was that she gloried in it. She reached for him as quickly and eagerly as he reached for her, she kissed him as hard as he kissed her, she sighed and moaned and gasped when he touched her everywhere he was touching her now. He couldn't get enough of it.

"You know," he said, as he pushed her robe all the way open. "I truly do love taking your clothes off, I love it a lot. But I also really love it when I get here and you're wearing a robe and nothing else."

She laughed. She looked so relaxed, so happy, right now. Even with how exhausted she was after the party, the lines of stress had fallen away from her face. He'd known she was worried and upset about everything going on with her brother, but he hadn't really understood the extent of how hard it was on her, until he'd walked in tonight and seen how happy she seemed, how free she looked.

"You seem to make a habit of walking in here when I'm wearing nothing but a robe, it's true," she said. "But thank you for telling me that—it helps to justify my robe purchasing habit. Now I have a reason to wear them all."

He pushed the rest of the robe off her shoulders and played with her nipples again. He loved how responsive her body was to him, how as soon as he took her nipples between his fingers or into his mouth, he could feel her whole body quiver.

"I will happily be your excuse to buy as many robes as you want," he said. "I will appreciate every single one of them." He ran his hands along her thighs, up her stomach, back to her breasts. "And I will appreciate you, inside—and outside—of them."

He stood up and pulled her up with him.

"Come with me."

She followed him into her bedroom. He'd loved that room from the first time he'd walked inside of it, on his quest for condoms when he'd seen her very intriguing bottom drawer. But he loved it for more reasons than that. The huge, comfortable bed; the crisp, hotel-like bedding; the dark walls; all this made it seem like a refuge. From the first time he'd entered it, he'd wanted to stay there with Margot, for a whole day, just in bed with her, around her, sleeping and having sex and talking and sleeping some more and having more sex, from sunup to sundown. Maybe now that the party was over, and that things with Elliot were better, it could happen.

He kissed her. She pulled his body against hers immediately. She was so soft and warm and strong. He loved the feeling of her body against his, her lips on his, her skin under his lips, his tongue.

"Lie down."

She lay down on her bed and smiled up at him. He loved that she didn't cover herself up, but just lay there, blissfully, perfectly naked, so he could look at her. He dropped his pants to the floor.

"I love the way you look at me," she said, staring back at him. "It's . . . It makes me feel so good."

He pulled his shirt off.

"Margot Noble, do you have any idea what you do to me? What you've always done to me, since the very beginning?"

Were those tears he saw in her eyes? It was dark in here; he couldn't really tell.

"I . . ."

He knelt on the bed above her, so he could still look down at her.

"Apparently, I need to do a better job of showing you."

He kissed her neck, the hollow between her breasts, her arms, her belly, and up and down her thighs. He could feel her straining for him. He knew she wanted him to kiss her lips, her breasts, between her legs, but he wanted to draw this out, make her feel this everywhere. He licked her neck and moved down and down, very slowly, until right before he reached her pussy, and then he stopped and moved down more. She let out a little frustrated huff, and he laughed softly.

"You are such an asshole," she said.

"I know," he said.

Finally, he let his tongue dance around her entrance, and she opened wider for him. He licked her clit once, and she sighed, and then he looked up.

"Oh, is that what you wanted?"

He could feel her smile as one of her hands left his shoulder and pushed at his head. He laughed as he moved to where she wanted him.

He didn't tease her anymore. He slid a finger inside of her, and then two, as his tongue went to work, pushing her to her limits, and she moaned and sighed underneath him. He fucking loved this. The way she let herself go with him; the way she was always so formal and professional and businesslike with everyone, but how he could make her fall apart like this; the way he knew exactly when she was starting to get there by how her body would respond to him, how she would get quieter, not louder, how she would let out those tiny gasps, how her fingertips would dig into his shoulders, his arms, his scalp. He moved faster, and she moved faster along with him, and then he felt her whole body spasm. He kept pushing her, kept sucking her, kept touching and rubbing her in that same way as she thrashed against his hand and his mouth, and then finally went limp underneath him.

"Holy fuck, Luke." Her eyes barely opened as he scrambled for a condom.

Normally he waited for a little while until she had a chance to recover more, but he was so hard, so turned on after that, after touching her and listening to her and making her come, that he didn't want to wait.

"Margot—"

She must have heard the urgency in his voice, because she reached for him.

"Yes. Now."

He barely got the condom on before he thrust himself into her. She cried out, and he made himself stop, but she squeezed his ass.

"No. Don't stop."

So he did it again, harder, and she wrapped her legs around him. He slammed himself into her, again and again, and she met him, thrust for thrust, until he felt her start to quiver again. He tried to hold back, to give her time. But she arched up to meet him, and whispered in his ear.

"Harder."

That whisper pushed him over the edge, and he exploded inside of her.

He collapsed on top of her, and kissed her hair, her cheek, her lips.

"That was incredible," he said. "You are incredible."

She laughed against him.

"*We* are incredible."

Twenty-Three

MARGOT WOKE UP THE next morning with a jolt. It was too bright outside. She should be at the winery already to get ready for the party. Why hadn't her alarm gone off?

And then she heard Luke's even breathing next to her and woke up all the way.

The party was over. Many things had gone wrong, but many things had also gone right. She was here with Luke. She could stop thinking, stop worrying, at least for a little while.

She turned over to face him, and put her hand on his chest. His arms went around her. She smiled and fell back asleep.

She woke up a while later to feel his hand on her ass. She nestled into his chest and moved her hand to his waist.

"Ahh, she's awake," Luke said in her ear. "I've been . . . anxious for you to wake up."

She moved her hand lower.

"Mmm, I can see that," she said. "We should do something about that."

She grabbed a condom out of her nightstand and rolled it over him.

"You worked very hard last night," she said. "Today, you get to relax."

She lifted herself on top of him and straddled him. He grabbed her hips and pulled her down on top of him, until he was deep inside of her.

"I like to be able to see you like this," he said as he reached for her breasts. She loved it when he touched her like that, like he couldn't keep his hands off her, like all he wanted was to touch her, please her, make her feel good.

She looked down at him and took a quick inward breath. Last night they'd both wanted to stretch every bit of pleasure out of each other, and that had been amazing. But right now, she knew they both just wanted it fast and hard. She quickened her pace as she rode him, and they both came within minutes.

They fell asleep again, and when she woke up, it was to find him smiling at her again.

"I wanted to let you sleep, because I know you need the rest, but it's after ten. Are you going to the winery today, or are you going to stay here in bed with me all day?"

She sat up with a jerk.

"Oh my God, it's after ten?" Then she laughed. "I guess you're right, I did need the rest. I'd love to stay here in bed with you all day, but the staff worked just as hard as I did yesterday. I don't want to bail on them on a busy Sunday."

He sat up behind her and kissed her between her shoulder blades.

"Okay, but promise me that one day soon we both can take the day off and you really will stay in bed with me all day?"

That sounded wonderful. And from his voice, it sounded just as wonderful to him, too.

"I promise," she said. "But how are you going to explain to your mom why you need the day off?"

He laughed against her skin.

"I'll find a way."

She suddenly remembered something, and turned to him.

"Oh. Speaking of. Something weird happened yesterday. I was talking to your mom at the party, and . . . Why does she seem to be under the impression that you and Avery are to-gether? She said something like that, too, when I saw her at the auction, remember?"

He looked down.

"Yeah, I remember that. About that."

Had anyone ever said *about that* in that tone of voice and had it preface something good? She sat back against the head-board and pulled the sheets up to her chest.

"About that?" she repeated.

He looked up at her.

"My mom thinks that Avery and I are together because . . . I may have given her that impression."

She blinked. Once. Twice. Had he really just said that?

"May have? Or you did?"

He sighed.

"I did. But it was before you and I were together! Long be-fore." He shrugged. "After that first night, but you know what I mean. The thing is, I didn't want to tell her I quit my job, I told you that. It feels stupid, but she was just so proud of me, proud of that job, and I knew how disappointed she was going to be. I was going to tell her, though, but when I said something about how I helped Avery move, she kind of jumped to that conclusion—she's always wanted us back together—and then I just . . . didn't correct her. And then it kind of . . . kept going."

What the fuck? Margot took a long breath. And then another. But no, the deep breaths weren't working this time to calm her down.

"I see. One question: Does Avery know about this, or will she also be surprised when your mom mentions it to her?"

He laughed. Did he . . . think this was funny?

"Oh no, Avery knows. I told her right away. She said she'd play along."

Margot folded her hands together tightly. Was he really just telling her this, like it was no big deal?

"Let me get this straight. Your mom has thought for the past two months that you're dating Avery. You told Avery this right away. She agreed to this. And then, a month ago, you and I got together. At what point did you plan on telling me that you're supposedly dating Avery? Because I asked you about this back when your mom first mentioned it, remember? And you brushed it off. Or am I just not important enough to be in on this little scheme? Not like Avery, right?"

His face fell. He put his hand on her shoulder. She pulled away.

"No, Margot, that's not it! I just kept forgetting to tell you, that's all—it's not that you weren't important, it's that this wasn't important enough for me to mention it to you. I should have told you, I know that—I shouldn't have even done this in the first place, it was stupid, I obviously know that, too. I was just embarrassed and stressed and in too deep, and the longer it went on, the harder it was to tell my mom the truth."

"Okay," she said. "I get all of that. Sort of. But look at this from my perspective for a moment. Imagine how it felt for me, to be standing there at the party yesterday talking to your mom, who looked over at you and Avery and started talking about what a cute couple you were. I was uncomfortable when I just assumed it was wishful thinking, but now I find out she thought that because you told her so? And you've let her keep thinking that the whole time we've—"

She stopped. That they'd been what, sleeping together? It was far more than that to her, and she'd thought it was more than that to Luke, too. Had she been wrong? She was annoyed to feel tears come to her eyes. She hoped Luke didn't see them.

"I'm so sorry," he said. "This had nothing to do with you and me, I swear. I'm with you. I never should have lied to my mom. And I should have told you about this a long time ago. I should have told you in the car that day. But I didn't want you to think that I'm the kind of person who lies to his mom so he doesn't have to tell her he quit his job and feels like a failure. Please forgive me?"

She was still mad. And hurt. But she couldn't say no to him when he looked at her like that, with those kind, worried eyes, and so much emotion on his face.

"Okay," she said. "But can you please stop this pretense? Like, immediately?"

He nodded.

"Yeah. I'll tell my mom right away. That the Avery thing wasn't true, but also about you and me."

He put his arm around her, and she leaned into his chest. She'd panicked, for a moment there. For longer than a moment. That everything between them was fake, that she was wrong to trust him, that everything she'd been so happy about last night and this morning had turned to dust.

He kissed her on her shoulder blade, and she let herself breathe again.

"Are we okay?" he asked.

She closed her eyes and breathed him in. She felt a lot more uncertain of him than she had twenty minutes ago, but she didn't want to throw all of this away just because of a stupid thing he'd done before they'd gotten together. And she knew that he'd been telling the truth when he said it had nothing to do with them.

"Yeah," she said. "We're okay."

HE PULLED HER CLOSE. He'd been terrified for a moment there that he'd fucked it all up.

"How's your mom going to take it when you tell her that you aren't on sabbatical, but you quit your job?"

Well, now he had to tell her about the interview.

"A lot better now than she would have a few months ago. They're trying to get me to go back. I told you that my old boss is leaving. Well, I have an interview there this week for his job."

After the stuff he'd told her about that job, he wasn't sure how she'd react. She looked stunned.

"They're trying to get *you* to take that job? You're interviewing for it this week?"

Why had she said *you* like that? Like it was ridiculous for them to want him?

"Yeah, well, I've been texting back and forth with my old mentor for a while now, and last week he reached out to see if I was interested. Big pay increase, a level up, a better title, and from what I can see online, the people who most annoyed me are gone, so I wouldn't have to deal with them on my team. From what he said, it's mine if I want it, but I'm not counting on that."

She pulled away from him and turned to face him. She still looked stunned, but also angry. Was she still mad about the Avery thing?

"Wait, last week he reached out to see if you were interested? And you said yes?"

He shrugged.

"I mean, I've been thinking about my next steps for a while, so when he texted, I figured I should at least talk to him about it. He was really complimentary about my work and what I could bring to the team, so anyway, long story short, I have this interview on Thursday."

She pulled the sheets tighter around herself.

"You've been thinking about your next steps for a while? You've known about this interview since last week, and you're just telling me about all of this now? The last we talked about this, you said he'd texted you, and I asked if you'd ever go back there and you laughed and said never."

Oh, right, he had said that to her on the drive back from the auction. That felt like forever ago.

"Yeah, but . . . things have been changing there, and I figured I might as well give them another shot, right? Plus, my mom will be better soon, I'll need to find another job anyway. The devil you know, right?" He grinned at her, but she didn't grin back. Was she upset because she thought he'd be moving? "Don't worry, I don't have to move back down there—I can do most of the job remotely."

He reached for her, but she pulled away.

"That's great, but if you've been thinking about this for a while, and talking to your old mentor and other people about an interview, why is this the first I'm hearing about it? Why didn't you talk to *me* about it?"

Was she actually pissed about this? Why wasn't she excited for him?

"I don't know, Margot. Maybe because I knew you'd say something like 'They're trying to get *you* to take that job?' like it's absurd for them to actually want me, to think I'm competent, like I'm good enough to do it."

She shook her head.

"You know that's not what I meant. Why didn't you *want* to talk to me about this? This is a huge surprise to me—you've been thinking about this for weeks, you completely changed your mind about this major thing in the course of a month, and you didn't feel like talking through any of that with me?"

"I didn't think I had to talk to you about it," he said. "I thought you'd be excited for me!"

Why wasn't she excited for him? Why was she reacting this way?

"You didn't think you *had* to talk to me about it?" Oh, great, now she looked pissed. "Oh, I see. Just one question: Did you tell Avery about this?"

Shit. He couldn't lie to her about that, not after the conversation they'd just had. And by that hurt, angry look on her face, he could tell she already knew the answer.

"Fine, yes, I told Avery, but that's not a big deal! There's nothing going on between me and Avery, I'm with you!"

She looked down and didn't say anything for a moment.

"I know there's nothing going on between you and Avery," she said quietly. "But are you really *with* me? If you've spent the whole time you've been up here pretending you're with someone else, and you make this huge decision without even wanting to tell me about it, that doesn't sound to me like you're exactly *with* me. What else haven't you told me?"

Why was she making such a big deal about this?

"That's not fair. You know the Avery thing had nothing to do with you."

She shrugged.

"Sure, okay, then let's talk about what does have to do with me. Let's see: you told me on the way back from the auction that you'd never go back to that job; you blew me off when I asked why your mom thought you and Avery were together; oh, and you asked me when we were on the beach if you could come back to Noble after your mom was better."

She was going to bring *that* up? They both knew he wasn't serious then.

"You know I didn't really mean that, I was just saying it! I meant I missed being around you all day! You *knew* that."

She nodded.

"Sure, of course, that makes sense. What else did you 'just say' to me that you didn't really mean?"

Oh, come the fuck on.

"Are you going to twist everything I'm saying here? You're overreacting again, just like you did yesterday about the party. Me not telling you about this doesn't mean anything about how I feel about you! The interview isn't until Thursday. I'm telling you today, aren't I?"

She shook her head.

"If you could spend the past two months pretending to your mom that you were with Avery, including when you were with me, and you could make a big decision, like going back to your old job, the one that you quit because they made you feel terrible, without even wanting to talk to me about it, that makes it clear to me what a small part of your life I am." Her voice caught. "I have . . . You have been a part of my whole life. I thought—"

He couldn't let her get away with that.

"You and I both know that's not true," he said. "How was I a part of your whole life? You didn't tell your brother we were together. You didn't tell anyone at the winery! And the winery sure as hell is your whole life. I asked you about it, and you gave me some bullshit about how I used to work for you and the party and everything. And then yesterday you flinched away from me as soon as you heard Taylor's voice, like you were ashamed of me."

She glared at him.

"We talked about that. You were my employee—I didn't want them to think our relationship overlapped your employment at Noble."

She'd given him this excuse too many times now.

"I haven't worked for you for a month, Margot, come on."

He hadn't realized until now how upset he'd been about that. How much he'd hated hiding their relationship at the party, how much he'd wanted her to tell Elliot about them.

"You knew it was complicated between me and Elliot," she said. "There were a lot of things that made me want to wait to tell him about you."

He nodded.

"Sure, just like there were a lot of things that made it complicated for me to tell my mom about you. You keep bringing up Avery: Avery has been my best friend for years! I'm not going to apologize for talking to her about something important going on with me."

And Avery had congratulated him for the interview, wished him luck. Unlike Margot.

"I'm not asking you to apologize for that!" she said. "I'm asking why I'm not important enough for you to want to talk to me about that. But I guess I don't have to ask, there's my answer." She looked away from him. "I don't even understand why you're thinking about going back to that job in the first place. I thought you never wanted to go back there. I can't believe it's more important to you than me."

"Oh my God, Margot, it's not a choice! Why are you being so irrational about this? I don't try to make you choose between the winery and me, do I?"

She shook her head.

"That's different."

He laughed.

"Why, because I'd always lose?"

She jumped out of bed, grabbed a robe from her closet, and wrapped it around herself.

"You told me this, between us, was something. My life includes you; you are a part of my life. I thought I was a part of yours. I guess I was wrong."

He shook his head.

"You can't spare one moment, one *second*, to be excited for me about this? To say 'Congratulations, Luke, how exciting'? Getting this interview is a big deal. I worked my ass off, and I thought quitting would put me behind; instead, I'm getting offers like this out of the blue. But you're not even happy for me."

He got out of bed and started pulling his clothes on.

"You don't think I'm good enough for a job like this, like everyone else. That's it, isn't it? You only think of me as your 'young, impressionable employee,' an extra set of hands in the tasting room, that guy who's helping out his mom, who's available at your beck and call whenever you happen to have time to see me. That's why you haven't told anyone about us. You don't care about me, or what I want. It's all about you, Margot, isn't it?"

Margot stepped back. She had a blank, empty look on her face.

"Is that what you really think of me?"

He picked his belt up from the floor.

"Maybe I didn't tell you because I didn't think you'd be supportive," he said. "Or that you'd care about me, instead of only about yourself. And I was right."

"I guess there's my answer," she said right before he slammed her front door.

Twenty-Four

MARGOT DIDN'T GET TO the winery until well after eleven that day. What with Luke, and the sex, and the fight, and the worse fight, and all the crying she did in the shower after he stormed out of her house, she'd been a little delayed that morning.

She wished she could rewind, go back to that morning, to how happy they'd been. How did that fight get out of hand so quickly?

How could he walk out of her house, just like that? When he'd told her about the interview, so casually, right after telling her he'd been pretending to date Avery for months, she'd lost it. She'd tried to stay calm about the Avery thing, even though it freaked her out. She could have taken one of those hits alone. But both of those things, back-to-back, had been too much for her to handle. They made her realize how absolutely not casual she was about him, how important he was to her, how central he'd been to her life over the past month.

She should have just been happy for him, like he'd wanted her to be; congratulated him about the interview; asked more questions. And then, later, she could have asked him what this meant for the two of them.

Why didn't you tell me? she'd whined, like Luke owed it to her to discuss every single thing with her. He didn't! He hadn't wanted to tell her!

But that was the thing, wasn't it? He hadn't wanted to tell her. She wasn't important enough for him to want to tell her this major thing in his life, about how and why he'd changed his mind so quickly, so completely. He hadn't trusted her to talk to about something like this.

They'd only been together for a month; that wasn't that long. Just because she'd gotten herself in so deep, so fast, that didn't mean he had.

But it felt like it had been more than a month. It felt like they'd been together since that very first night.

She wanted to call him, apologize, start over. But when she thought about some of those things he'd said that morning, she stopped herself. No. She had too much pride for that. Plus, if they could have such a big and terrible fight like that after only a month, there was no hope for their relationship. This should be the honeymoon period, right?

She was at the winery; she couldn't think about Luke. She had a million things to do today, little things to wrap up after the party; there were guests coming to the tasting room all day, she already felt guilty for how late she was, she had to be on, bright, smiling, welcoming, all day. She couldn't let Luke distract her.

Like he'd been distracting her for months. Ever since that first night, she hadn't stopped thinking about him. She'd thought about him every single fucking day since then. He'd put her off her game. Yes, the party had gone okay, but just think how much more organized she would have been if he hadn't been around, doing things like causing her to zone out in the middle of the day thinking about him and making her decide to stop working at six instead of eight and bringing her dinner and giving her massages and putting her in the right frame of mind to write the newsletter so people would open it and come to the party and—

She had to stop thinking about this. She needed to get her head in the game, forget about him, at least for the next few hours while she was at work. She could wallow later, at home.

She went into the winery through the back way, so she could avoid talking to the guests in the tasting room. It usually put her in a good mood to walk through the tasting room in the morning when there were already guests there—she got to greet everyone, smile at them, see how much fun they were having. It usually gave her a little boost to start her day. But right now, she needed some time. She'd go in later, say hi to whoever was there, make sure the staff knew she was around if they needed her, thank them for their hard work yesterday. But she needed a moment to turn herself back into Margot Noble, co-owner of Noble Family Vineyards, and not the Margot who sobbed in the shower this morning.

She sat down at her computer and flipped it on. She automatically checked the sales for the last day, like she did every morning.

Wow.

Either people had gone home from the party and decided to order even more wine, or all of the posts on social media—including the ones about Porter Eldridge—had boosted their profile, or something else, but their sales had risen dramatically last night and this morning, even excluding the wine they'd sold at the party. And a bunch of people had joined the wine club overnight.

Whatever had inspired this, she'd take it.

She spent the morning replying to emails and calls from VIPs and friends of hers and Uncle Stan's who had been at the party and wanted to congratulate her, or who had missed it and wanted to apologize. She managed to convince most of that second group to make it up to her by buying wine. She got off one of those calls with a smile on her face. See? That was better.

When she went out into the tasting room, Taylor and Marisol both grinned at her and beckoned her over to meet the guests. She laughed and flirted and complimented them and recommended other wineries for them to visit, and they all laughed and smiled along with her. Okay. She could do this. She loved this. She didn't need Luke.

She walked over to Taylor and Marisol, both pouring new flights at the bar, before she went back to her office.

"Hey, you two. You all, the whole staff, did an incredible job at the party yesterday, and I'm so grateful. Take a day off this week or next—paid, I'll cover your shifts. Just let me know what day."

Taylor glared at her.

"Shouldn't you be the one taking some time off?"

Margot waved that away.

"I will, I will. I'll plan an actual vacation soon."

Eventually. Once she had time and mental space to plan something. When that would be, she had no idea, but she'd figure it out someday.

Taylor turned to Marisol.

"What day works best for you?"

"Is next Friday okay?" Marisol asked. "It's my birthday, and I wasn't going to ask, but . . ."

Margot smiled at her.

"Of course it works! That's perfect—have a great birthday." She turned to Taylor. "I'm not letting you off the hook here."

Taylor sighed.

"Fine, I'll do this Thursday. My sister wants me to go wedding dress shopping with her, which . . . whatever, but now she won't be mad at me."

Thursday. The day Luke would be at his interview, for the job he cared about more than her. She'd take over for Taylor, be in the tasting room all day; that was just what she'd need.

"Perfect. Thanks again, guys."

Margot walked back toward her office, still thinking about Thursday, and Luke. She supposed it would be better to be here and busy in the tasting room all day that day, than to be in her office most of the day, on calls and looking at spreadsheets and getting distracted by why he was going down there for the interview and why he'd told Avery and not her and why she wasn't as important to him as he was to her and why her too-good-to-be-true life had fallen apart in a matter of hours.

Why had she even thought it could be true? She'd known Luke would leave, she'd known this was only a temporary thing for him, she'd known that from the very beginning. He'd told her at the bar that first night that he was only in Napa for three months, max. How had she convinced herself otherwise? How had she let herself think he would change all of his plans for her?

She went back to her desk and stared at her computer. Congratulatory emails were still pouring in, sales numbers were great, and huh, there was an email from Elliot, forwarding her a question from a journalist. This was all that really mattered; this was everything important to her. If three months ago she'd been able to see her inbox today, she would have been over the moon.

So why did it feel so bad?

THURSDAY MORNING LUKE WALKED through those gleaming glass doors again. It felt like he'd never left, but it also felt like it had been years since he'd been there. So much had happened in his life since then. With all that time in Napa. And with Margot.

He'd been furious when he'd left her house on Sunday morning. Angry and hurt that she'd turned this whole thing around on him, made it a bad thing that he'd gotten this interview. He'd hoped she would be excited for him, impressed, that she'd congratulate him for this achievement.

Margot was probably just pissed about the Avery thing, which, fine, he'd been stupid about that. But he'd apologized, and she'd said they were okay. And then she'd exploded on him five minutes later about his interview? It made no sense.

Why wasn't she happy for him? This was a big deal. She knew that! He'd told her how bad he'd felt about quitting—she should have been thrilled for him that they'd tacitly acknowledged how wrong they'd been to treat him the way they had. That they knew how good he was.

But he hadn't heard from her since he left her house on Sunday morning. She hadn't even texted him this morning to say good luck. He'd checked his phone again, right before he'd walked inside, and nothing.

His former grandboss—a term he'd always found revolting, but that people insisted on using—came out to get him.

"Luke! Glad to have you back, we've missed you around here." He had a bigger smile on his face than Luke had ever seen before. Okay, they were definitely giving him special treatment here.

They went straight into a conference room, where four other people—three of whom he knew—were waiting for him. There was a quick preamble of greetings, but as soon as he sat down, they started peppering him with questions. But he was ready for them.

He was glad he'd spent all week, when he wasn't at the inn, prepping for this interview. See, it was good he hadn't had Margot around; he wouldn't have had time to really throw himself into planning for this.

He spent almost all day on campus, talking to different groups, standing in front of too many whiteboards, having lunch, chatting with former coworkers. It all felt so familiar that when he was finally on his way back home, he almost took the wrong freeway exit, to drive back to his old place, instead of to Napa.

He was sitting in traffic when Avery called.

"Hey! How'd it go today? Do you want to get a drink and fill me in? Or do you have plans with Margot?"

He'd ignore that last question.

"It went well," he said. "And sure. But I'm still on my way back and there's a ton of traffic, so give me an hour or so?"

"Okay," she said. "But if it went well, why does your voice sound like that?"

"Like what?" he asked.

"Like you've been kidnapped and this is a hostage phone call and you have to tell me it went well because they have a gun to your head," she said. "What's wrong?"

"I don't know what you're talking about," he said. "Nothing's wrong. I was great, they were all excited to see me back. Way more excited than I expected, actually. I think I have a pretty good shot at the job."

He finally got past the accident that was slowing everything down, and sped up.

"Then why did you just sigh like that when you said you have a pretty good shot at the job?" she asked.

Huh. He hadn't done that on purpose.

"Oh. I didn't mean to." He sighed again and caught himself. "It's just . . . I don't know, it was weird to be back there."

"Weird how?" Avery asked.

Weird to drive back into that parking lot; weird to have that complicated interview, which tested him on nothing important; weird to have to say hi to people he'd thought he'd escaped forever.

"I just . . . didn't expect to be back there, I guess. But they seem excited about me for the job. It's a big deal: lots of money and a big title, and I'll be able to—"

"What does all of that matter if you hate it?" she asked him.

That question threw him.

"Why are you assuming that I'll hate it?" he asked.

"Um, maybe because you hated working there before?" she asked.

"I didn't hate working there before. I just . . ."

He stopped.

"Yeah, you did," she said.

Yeah. He had, he supposed. But so what if he did?

"Whatever, it's fine. I liked it at the beginning, didn't I? I can like it again. All of those other people are there, they don't hate it, they can handle it. I just need to—"

"Need to what?" Avery asked. "Work harder? Get a thicker skin? Show them how good you are, how smart you are? And then what? What's that going to get you? It's not going to make you happy. I know you liked it at the beginning, but that was forever ago. You haven't liked it for a long time."

"It doesn't matter. It'll be fine, and I'll—"

"Yes, it does matter!" Avery yelled. "What's wrong with you, Luke? I thought you were coming to your senses."

Now Avery was going to be mad at him, too?

"Coming to my senses, how? Nothing is wrong with me! I need a job, don't I? Something more than working at a winery, or the inn! And going back there will be good for my career."

Why was everyone being shitty to him about this?

"Oh, Luke." Avery sighed. "I get it, I do. I get why you think you need this job. But we can't spend our whole lives chasing someone else's approval. Your mom's, your mentor's, people you don't even like."

"That's not what I'm doing! I'm trying to make a success of my life, why can't anyone understand that?"

This was the most frustrating conversation he'd had since . . . Sunday.

"You don't have to be unhappy in order to be successful in life!" Now she was yelling again. "You liked your job at the winery a lot! And yes, some of that was because you had the hots for your boss, but it wasn't all Margot—I saw you at the party, you *like* all of those people. You even like your job working for your mom—at least, you like it better than your old job, which, again, you hated!"

He shouldn't have picked up the fucking phone when she'd called.

"Avery, I'm really not in the mood for this right now. Can we just—"

She ignored him.

"Do you remember when you told me you always hated Derek, after we broke up, and I started crying?"

Fuck, she had to bring that up now, didn't she?

"Yeah, of course. I'm really sorry that I—"

"I know you're sorry. The thing is, I was *miserable* with him. I hadn't been in a real relationship for so long when he and I started dating, and when he wanted me, it felt like okay, great, I have to hold on to this one, what if I don't have another chance? But I wasn't happy with him. I was so *unhappy* with him. You saw it, you knew."

"Yeah. I knew," he said.

"And I knew you hated him, of course I knew that. But I thought it didn't matter. I thought it was fine. But my confidence was shot, I felt like a different person, I didn't feel like me."

He saw where she was going with this.

"Avery. It's not the same."

She kept talking.

"And I've been so happy since we broke up! Yes, it's been really hard, and I've felt scared, a lot. But I've also been so much happier, Luke. I've felt guilty for how happy I've been. And I know you've been so much happier since you quit that job, don't even try to pretend you haven't been."

He had been. But that had mostly been about Margot.

But . . . not all about Margot.

"Wait," Avery said. "Did Margot want you to take this job? What did she say about the interview?"

He'd always fucking known Avery was a mind reader.

"Do we have to talk about that now?"

"Oh no," she said.

"What does that mean?" he asked.

"What did you do?" she asked.

"Why is that the question?" he asked. "Why is it what did *I* do? Couldn't she have done something? Why aren't you asking me, your best friend, what she did?"

"Luke. What did you do?"

He cut over into a faster lane.

"Nothing! She got pissed at me, just because I hadn't mentioned the job interview to her until last Sunday morning." He sighed. "And I sort of hadn't told her that I led my mom to believe you and I were dating."

"WHAT?" He was surprised no one in the cars around him turned at Avery's yell. "You didn't tell her about that!?"

He should have known she would react like this.

"You don't have to say it like that. I meant to tell her, I just . . . forgot."

"I can't believe you didn't tell her that," Avery said. "I can't believe I was out there pretending to be your girlfriend and your real girlfriend didn't even know! I was a fake other woman?"

He laughed, despite himself.

"You were not a fake other woman. She didn't think we were actually together. But . . ."

Avery sighed.

"Okay." Her voice was brisk. "Come straight here."

He didn't want to be an asshole, but there was no way he could go over to Avery's place and have a heart-to-heart about all of this right now.

"Thanks, really, but . . ."

She cut him off.

"I'm leaving now to get the fried chicken. Think about what movie you want to watch. See you soon."

Oh, thank goodness.

"Spicy please, dark meat only, and so many biscuits my stomach will hurt tomorrow."

"Do you think you have to tell me any of that?" She hung up.

He rolled down his windows and turned up the music. He hoped Avery got them potato salad, too. Maybe that would solve all of his problems.

Twenty-Five

THE TASTING ROOM WAS booked solid with appointments on Thursday, and with Taylor gone, Margot didn't sit down all day. She chatted and laughed and smiled with guests, encouraged them to have another sip, buy one more bottle, relax with a glass of wine on the new Adirondack chairs out on the grounds. It was a relief, to be around people all day, to be busy from when she walked in the door, to not have to be alone with her thoughts. She was successful, she was thriving; there was no need to think about Luke, why she hadn't heard from him, how lonely she'd been all week, how she'd almost texted him that morning about his interview and had chickened out.

At six that evening, when everyone was gone, she locked up the building and turned off the lights in the tasting room. But instead of getting in her car to go home, she went back to her office. She might as well get more work done, since she was here, and she'd been terrible this week about getting work done at home. At home there were reminders of him everywhere, all of the places she normally worked: her couch, her kitchen, her bedroom.

She looked at her phone, which she'd planned to ignore all day. She hadn't, exactly, but at least she hadn't checked it as obsessively as she had all week. Nothing from Luke. Sydney had texted, though.

SYDNEY

Come by tonight? Charlie has a new menu item you'll love. Or I could bring something by after work?

She'd told Sydney everything on Monday night, over an enormous amount of pasta, and Sydney had very reassuringly been out for Luke's blood. That had been great, to feel angry at Luke, instead of sad. But tonight, Margot couldn't handle Sydney's concern for her and urge to destroy Luke. She loved her for it, very much, but right now, she needed to just be.

MARGOT

Working late tonight, maybe tomorrow

Tell Charlie I said thank you.

She worked for a while before she got up to go to the bathroom. Oh, and wait, had she gone through the whole closing checklist before she'd locked up the tasting room? She hadn't closed up in a while.

She went back in the tasting room and looked around. The bar was cleaned up, the wine was all put away, the dishwasher was loaded, but—*oops*—she'd forgotten to turn it on. She did that, and then had a sudden vision of Luke, his sleeves rolled up, fixing the dishwasher.

"Fuck!" she yelled to the empty room. Did he have to be everywhere in her whole fucking life? She'd known this man for only two fucking months!

She took a glass down and pulled out one of the bottles they'd opened that day at random. What was the fucking point of owning a winery if you didn't get to drown your sorrows in wine at least once?

She poured a glass and then sat down on one of the couches by the window.

His interview had been that day. She'd tried, so hard, not to let herself think about it, but she had. All day. He'd said she was being irrational to be so angry, to feel so betrayed that he'd decided to do this without telling her, that he'd decided to do this at all, and maybe he was right. But for the past month, almost as soon as they'd really gotten together, he'd been completely woven into her life. Okay, fine, almost completely—he was right, she hadn't told Elliot about him, or anyone else at the winery. But she'd talked to Luke about so much. She'd told Luke about all of her conflicts with Elliot, about what he'd said at the funeral, about how hurt she'd been, then and since; she'd sobbed like a baby on his shoulder at the end of the party; she'd told him everything she and Elliot had talked about after she'd come home. She'd thought of him—she'd treated him—as someone she could share her whole self with, without having to edit herself, without having to hold anything back. And she'd believed he thought of her that same way, too, especially after that car ride when he'd told her about leaving his job. She'd trusted him with everything, in a way she rarely trusted people.

She got up, opened a new bottle, and poured herself more wine. This time, she brought the bottle back to the couch with her.

She stared at the sky out the window, the faint orange and pink and purple of the approaching sunset. Sunset was so late this time of year.

Had Luke spent all of this time with her thinking about his next move, his next step, the rest of his life, without sharing any of that with her? They'd been dating for real for only a month; this was probably her fault for expecting too much of someone far too young for her, of thinking that he wanted the same things she did. Sure, he was twenty-nine, but in man years, that was more like nineteen. She should have known that. He'd said that he thought they were something, he'd seemed to care about her, but he'd decided to go back to a job he'd hated, without even talking to her about it. And he'd walked out on her and hadn't come back.

She felt tears fall down her face, for the first time since Sunday morning.

Had he cared, the way she'd thought he had? The way she'd cared? Even when he'd told her about that stupid lie he'd told his mom about dating Avery, the way he'd said *I'm with you* had seemed so definite. But maybe that meant something different to her than it did to him. Maybe they just thought of their relationship differently, wanted different things. He had been pretending to date someone else the whole time, after all. Maybe she shouldn't have built this whole relationship up in her head with a twenty-nine-year-old guy she'd been dating for only a month who had told her at the outset he wasn't staying in Napa for long. Maybe this was all her fault, not his.

It probably was. She was too much for most people. For most men, especially. She wanted too much, she talked too much. She cared too much. Luke was probably just done, and this was his way of telling her that.

Her wine on the coffee table seemed very far away. Why was this coffee table so low, anyway? You had to sit all the way up and then reach all the way forward for the wine—she should do something about that.

For now, it was far easier to just sit on the floor, where she could have her wineglass right next to her. And then she could pull her legs into her chest and drop her face on her knees.

She poured more wine into her glass and took a gulp. Had she been unfair to Luke? Irrational, like he'd said she was being? Probably, but everything about their relationship had been irrational! Had it been rational for her to sleep with him that first night? No! Had it been rational for her to lust after him every fucking day when he was working for her? No! Had it been rational for her to pull him into her house and kiss him just hours after he'd quit working for her? Absolutely not!

She reached for her wineglass again. Then she looked up with a jerk as the tasting room door opened.

"Margot?"

It was Elliot.

"Yeah," she said. "I'm in here."

Elliot took another step into the tasting room.

"There you are. I had a question for you." He walked over and looked down at her. "Is there a reason you're sitting on the floor in the dark with a bottle of wine in front of you?"

She stared at the bottle.

"It seemed logical at the time," she said.

Elliot stood there, staring down at her, for a few seconds. Then he went over to the bar, took down a glass, and sat down next to her.

"What's going on?" he asked as she poured the rest of the bottle into his glass.

She was too sad and too drunk to tell him anything but the truth.

"I had a fight with the guy I was dating," she said. "We haven't talked since. I guess I'm at the sitting-on-the-floor-in-the-dark-drinking-wine stage."

Elliot looked up from his glass at her, in that serious, thoughtful way he had.

"Luke?"

She sighed.

"Yeah, Luke. Was it that obvious? I didn't want to tell you because he used to work here, and I thought you'd think . . . but we didn't start dating until after he quit." She sighed again. "Right after. But still."

Elliot nudged her with his knee.

"Come on, give me some credit. You don't have to tell me that, I know you wouldn't do that. And no, it wasn't obvious. But when you said you'd been dating someone, I remembered the way he looked at you in your office on Saturday. And I did kind of wonder why he was working so hard during the party, when he doesn't actually work here anymore." He grinned. "Plus, I always sort of thought he had a crush on you."

She sighed and picked up her wineglass.

"Well, it was more than that. At least, I thought it was more." She shrugged. "I guess I was wrong."

She took a gulp of wine.

"What happened?" Elliot asked.

She shook her head.

"It's a long story. It was probably all my fault for thinking there was more to the relationship than he wanted. I thought we were . . . We had a fight, Sunday morning. I think we broke up. I don't know. It started with one thing and then there was another thing and then it spiraled and we both said terrible things to each other and I haven't heard from him since then. Why would he say things like that? Or tell me that it wasn't a big deal when it was a very big deal! I know they weren't together for real, but why didn't he tell me? And . . ." She looked down at her wine. "I'm sorry, I'm not making sense. But that's why I'm sitting in the dark getting drunk on your wine and not at all doing it justice."

Elliot put his arm around her.

"Our wine. And what's the point of owning a winery if you can't take advantage of it once in a while?"

"Our wine. You said 'our wine.'" She burst into tears. "I know on Saturday you said . . . I think it really hit me, just now. I'm sorry, I'm a mess."

Any other time, she wouldn't have let herself fall apart around Elliot like this. He'd always hated it, when they were kids, teenagers, when she got all emotional. He never did. She half expected him to get up and leave, maybe toss her a box of tissues. But he just sat there with her, not saying anything, but with his arm tight across her shoulders, until she stopped crying.

"Will you let your big brother give you some advice?" he asked her after a few minutes.

She nodded.

"As you can see, I need all the advice I can get."

He laughed softly.

"I know that's not true. But—does Luke know how much you care about him? I don't have to ask if you care about him a lot. The Margot Noble I know would never sit on the floor of her winery crying about some guy she didn't care a whole lot about."

"Our winery," she said. "And . . . I think he knows. I mean, it's only been a month. But . . ." She dropped her head into her hands. "I miss him so much. I'm still so mad at him, but I miss him so much."

"If the answer is just 'I think so' then you have to talk this out with him," he said. "Don't make my mistakes. Don't wait until it's too late."

Margot turned to look at Elliot. What mistakes was he talking about?

He shook his head.

"Long story," he said. "I'll tell you, sometime. But for now—you should at least see if there's a way to work this out. Don't let it fester."

Elliot was right. Of course he was right.

Margot started to get up, to go find her phone. Elliot pulled her back down.

"Not *now*. Not while you're drunk, and still mad at him. That story never ends well. Take some time to think about it, but not too much time." He stood up and reached for her hands to pull her up. "Here. We need to get some french fries in you."

"French fries!" Margot let him pull her up. "Oh God, I could eat an entire bucket. Do you remember how—"

"How we would sneak out and get fries and Mom would yell at us because she could still smell them in the car the next day? Of course I do."

He put their wineglasses on top of the bar.

"Wait here."

He went into the back, and came out a minute later, her bag and phone in his hands.

"I turned off your light, you're clearly not doing any more work tonight." He opened the front door. "First fries, and then I'm going to get you home. How exactly did you plan to get home, after drinking almost a whole bottle of wine while sitting on the tasting room floor?"

She followed Elliot out to his truck.

"I would like you to know that I started off drinking wine on the couch, I only later moved to the floor. And I hadn't gotten that far—I think after the second glass I had some idea of sleeping on the couch in my office? But that would have been deeply uncomfortable, now that I think about it."

Elliot laughed, and helped her into the truck. Why did they make trucks so hard to get into?

"Can we write it into our partnership contract that anytime one of us is at the drinking-wine-on-the-floor stage, the other one will come bring them fries and drive them home?" Elliot asked. "Because I know my time will come."

She reached out a hand to him.

"Shake on it."

He grabbed her hand, and they shook hard.

LUKE GOT TO THE inn early Friday morning. He did not feel entirely . . . well after everything he'd eaten at Avery's house the night before, but it was high tourist season, there would be a ton of check-ins and checkouts and questions from guests today, and he had to be ready for all of that.

Avery hadn't tried to get him to talk about everything, for which he'd been very grateful. But when he'd left, she'd given him a big hug and then said, "Think about what I said, okay?"

She was obviously some sort of witch, because he hadn't been able to stop thinking about what she'd said since then.

My confidence was shot, I felt like a different person, I didn't feel like me.

That's exactly how he'd felt at that job.

But, like he'd said, it wasn't the same.

Midway through the morning, he felt his phone buzz in his pocket.

CRAIG

> Expect good news in the next few days

He should be excited about this. Just like he'd told Margot, it was a level up, more money, and aside from either of those things, it was proof to anyone out there that he could hack it, that he was good enough. Better than good enough.

LUKE

> Great! Thanks for the update.

But everything Avery had said kept running through his mind. She had been miserable with that guy, and he'd known it. He hadn't understood why she'd been with him, why she'd stayed with him so long.

But this was different. Wasn't it?

Margot had said something like that about his job, too, but he'd been so angry and hurt that he hadn't really paid attention.

He walked out into the reception area a few minutes later with a question for Beth, and saw his mom walk through the door.

"Don't worry, I'm only here for a little while. Pete came home for lunch, and I convinced him to drop me off while he's at a job nearby." She grinned at him. "But the doctor said that I can drive soon. Well, we also have to get a new car, but that should happen next week."

She looked so happy. He gave her a hug.

"That's great, Mom."

She hugged him back, and then grinned as she looked around the lobby.

"I've missed this place."

He laughed.

"You've managed to stop by so often, I'm surprised you had time to miss it." He had to do this now, didn't he? He'd told Margot that he'd tell his mom right away, but then after their fight on Sunday, it hadn't felt as necessary. But he'd avoided this conversation long enough. "Come back into your office and sit down, I'll go make you some tea."

When he came back, he set the tea in front of her. Then he closed the door.

"Um, Mom—I've been meaning to talk to you about something."

She looked at him as he sat down.

"Is something wrong?"

He let out a breath.

"Not . . . exactly. Well, yes, but not in the way that you mean. I didn't really tell you the truth about why I moved back up here. I'm not on sabbatical. I quit that job." She opened her mouth to say something, but he held up a hand. He had to get this all over with. "And I'm not with Avery. I didn't move up here for her, at least, not in the way that you thought. She had that breakup, she knew I'd just quit my job and was stressed about everything, so she said I should move somewhere else for a while, and I moved up here, partly to keep her company, but we aren't together. We were never together. You assumed that, and then I let you believe it because I . . ." He swallowed. "I didn't want to tell you how difficult everything was at that job. And I didn't want to tell you I quit. I thought you'd be upset, ashamed of me. I guess I was ashamed of myself. So when you brought up Avery, like you always do, I let you think it was true. And then . . . I kept letting you think it."

His mom looked shocked, which is about what he'd expected.

"Why, Luke?" she said. "Why would you think I would be ashamed of you? Why would you ever think that?"

He'd thought she'd be upset about the job, or the Avery news, but not that.

"You were so proud of that job," he said. "You told everyone about it. You were so proud of me, for having that job."

She shook her head.

"No. I mean yes, sure, I was proud of you for having that job, but I've been proud of you every day of your life. I'm proud of you because you're my son, I'm proud of you because you're a good, kind man, who treats people well. I'm so sorry that I ever made you think that you had to do anything special, have any job, or title, or degree, to make me proud. I tell everyone about you because I love you, that's all. Do you know how many people I've bragged to that my son is helping me at the inn right now? I think half of Napa Valley knows about it."

He laughed, because that sounded so much like her. And yeah, he'd known she'd told everyone he was working at the inn right now, but he'd thought . . . He didn't even know what he had been thinking.

Was that true, what she'd said?

Of course it was true. He knew it as soon as she said it. He knew that despite how much his mom had always pushed him in school and in everything else, she'd always been as proud of him as when she'd cheered for him, louder than any of the other moms, at the second-grade spelling bee, when his name was called for the first time. He'd gone out in the second round, but she'd given him a huge hug and taken him out for ice cream afterward.

"I shouldn't have lied to you. I think I just felt so bad about myself, and it made me think you'd feel the same way. I wasn't even going to tell you that I'd quit, because they want me to come back, for a bigger title, more money; I interviewed down there yesterday. But I knew I had to tell you about the Avery thing, and I thought it was better to be honest about everything."

She put her mug down and looked at him.

"You interviewed there yesterday? Why did you quit in the first place? You always said it was your dream job."

"Because I hated it." He hadn't meant to say it, but it almost exploded out of him. If he was being honest with his mom, it felt like all he could say was the truth. The truth he hadn't let himself realize.

She sat up straight.

"You hated it? You're going to go back to a job that you hated, for a better title and more money? Why would you do that?"

"Because I—"

He stopped to think about that. Because he wanted to? No, that wasn't true; he definitely didn't want to. Because he wanted the money? He supposed the money would be nice, but he didn't need it. Because he wanted to prove something to a bunch of people he didn't really care about?

Yeah, that was closer to the truth.

"What does Avery think about you going back there?" his mom asked. Then she laughed. "Oh, I forgot, you aren't actually with Avery. I can't believe you pretended to me about that, all that time. And that you got poor Avery to play along."

He laughed, too.

"I can't believe that, either. She's a good friend, though she did try to talk me out of this. Which makes her a very good friend."

His mom had a smile on her face.

"If real life was like all of the books I like to read, this would have made you two fall in love for real. So I guess that means it's never actually going to happen." She sighed. "It just surprises me that you weren't really dating, because you've seemed so happy lately. I guess that was just not being at a job you hated."

He shook his head. He might as well tell her everything.

"It wasn't just that. I mean, I'm sure that was part of it, but I have been dating someone. Not Avery. Margot."

His mom almost dropped her mug.

"Margot Noble? Your boss?"

"My *former* boss," he said. "Why do you think I was so eager to quit that job? Anyway, I asked her out shortly after I quit, and you're right. I was so happy."

"Oh no," his mom said. "'Was.'" Her eyes widened. "Is that my fault? I said something to her at the party about you and Avery. Did she know about that?"

She didn't have to remind him.

"Yeah, she mentioned that." He sighed. "And no, I hadn't told her. She was upset about that, yeah. But she was more upset about the job." He looked down at the desk. "I thought she'd be impressed, excited. But she was so upset. She was mad about the Avery thing, too, don't get me wrong, but she thought that me taking this interview . . . without talking to her about it meant I wasn't serious about her. But . . ."

He folded his hands tightly on the desk and stared down at

them. He didn't say anything for a moment. Finally, he looked up at his mom.

"I've been pretty stupid lately, haven't I?"

She laughed and pulled him into a hug with her good arm.

"I wouldn't quite put it that way, but since you did . . . yeah, probably."

He let her hug him as tightly as she wanted to.

Twenty-Six

MARGOT WOKE UP FRIDAY morning, groaned, and closed her eyes again. On the plus side, she only had a splitting headache; it could be far worse. On the minus side . . . everything else.

She eventually made herself sit up, gulped down ibuprofen, and got in the shower. After a shower, two cups of coffee, and a whole lot of water, she felt almost human. It wasn't until she'd gotten dressed that she remembered her car was still at the winery.

She grabbed her phone to get an overpriced rideshare up the valley and saw a text from her brother.

ELLIOT

I'll come get you as soon as Taylor gets here

"Bless you, Elliot," she said out loud.

Thank you! I'll be ready!

He was at her house thirty minutes later. When she climbed into his truck, he handed her a greasy white bag.

"I thought you could use a breakfast sandwich today."

She almost hugged him, but she and Elliot had hugged more in the past week than in the past three years before that. Better not to push it.

"You're a hero and a saint," she said instead. "Do I have to write 'breakfast sandwiches' into that contract?"

Elliot nodded.

"Make mine with bacon."

On the way to the winery, Elliot didn't bring up anything they'd talked about the night before, and neither did she. Friday was another busy day at the winery, with lots of appointments and tours and phone calls. But all day, as she joked with Taylor and chatted with guests and sent endless emails, she thought about what Elliot had said. That she should tell Luke how she felt about him, before it was too late.

What if Luke didn't feel the same way? She already felt silly, juvenile, for feeling such big feelings for Luke, caring this much about him, letting him become so central to her life, after only a month. Yes, sure, it had been two months since she'd met him, but they'd been together for only a month, and she'd let herself fall this hard? For someone who had told her, since the beginning, that he wouldn't be around that long?

But she had to do something. She had to say something. She'd almost done it last night, when she'd gotten home, despite what

Elliot had said about not texting Luke while she was drunk. But luckily for her, she'd fallen asleep with her phone in her hand.

What was she supposed to say? *How was the interview? I miss you. How important am I to you on a scale of one to ten?* Probably not those last two things.

She drove home that night after a long day at the winery, got out of her car, and walked straight to the Barrel. If she was going to do this, she needed some food first.

"Hey!" Sydney greeted her as soon as she sat down. "I was just going to text you, to tell you to come by after work, or that I could come by later, if you wanted." She picked up a bottle of wine, but Margot shook her head.

"No wine for me tonight, only your best sparkling water." She sighed. "I drank entirely too much wine last night and had to get rescued by my brother."

Sydney's eyebrows went up.

"By your brother?"

Margot laughed and nodded. She'd told Sydney that she and Elliot had talked through things after the party and that everything was a lot better between them, but Sydney was still clearly holding a grudge against Elliot. This was why she loved her.

"I know, it sounds impossible, but it's true." She took a sip of the sparkling water Sydney poured into her wineglass. "He also said . . . that I should talk to Luke."

Sydney glared at her.

"He would say that. Men always stick together."

Margot laughed again.

"It's true. They do. But I don't want . . . I really—"

Sydney's face softened.

"I know. Just . . . be careful."

Just then, someone at the front door called Sydney's name.

"Be right back," Sydney said. "Food's on its way."

Margot knew that *Be right back* had no real meaning on a busy Friday night, but that was okay. She already felt better, just being somewhere other than her house or the winery for the first time all week. It cleared her head, to not have to be Margot Noble, co-owner of Noble Family Vineyards, and just be Margot, sitting here at the corner of the bar. A tomato and mozzarella salad landed in front of her, and she took a few bites and smiled over at the kitchen. Then she took a deep breath and reached for her phone.

A server came up behind her, to drop off some bread. She turned, to let him set it in front of her, and then stopped.

Luke was standing there.

"Is this seat available?" he asked, gesturing at the chair next to her.

She was still hurt, and uncertain of him, and angry. But she was so happy to see him, standing right there, so close she could almost touch him, that she had to look away to keep the tears from coming to her eyes.

"I can't believe you showed up here," Sydney said.

Sydney glared at Luke from behind the bar. Luke didn't move. He looked at Margot.

"No, it's okay, Syd," Margot said, looking back at Luke.

Luke sat down next to her. Neither of them said anything for a moment.

Sydney came back and slid a glass of water in front of Luke without looking at either of them, and walked away.

"What are the odds she's poisoned that?" Luke asked.

Margot thought about it.

"Well . . . not zero."

They both laughed, without making eye contact.

"How did you know I was here?" she asked.

"I went by your place, your car was there but you weren't—at least, I hoped you weren't, because you didn't answer the door when I rang. It was an educated guess."

They still hadn't really looked at each other.

"How was the interview?" she asked.

He shrugged.

"Fine. Good, even. I got the job. I got the unofficial offer this afternoon." She looked down. Had he come here to tell her that? And then say goodbye? "I'm not taking it, though."

She looked up at him, trying to tamp down the hope that had risen in her chest.

"Why not?"

She had no idea how he would answer that question.

"Because I hated that job, as much as I tried not to admit it to myself. I thought I just had to work harder, be better, and I would be worthy of it. Quitting that job was the best thing I ever did, and then I beat myself up about it for months."

She tried to smile.

"Probably better not to go back there if you hated it, then," she said.

He gave her a tiny smile.

"Yeah, probably." Then he turned and looked right at her. "I'm sorry, Margot. For . . . a lot of things. But especially for what I said to you on Sunday morning. About you being irrational, over-reacting, that everything is all about you, all of that . . . that was shitty of me to say. And none of it was true." She opened her mouth, to apologize, too, but he stopped her. "I didn't tell you about the interview because I was so in my own head about that job and leaving it and what that said about me as a person that I was scared to tell you. Scared you'd say something to make it clear you thought the same thing about me that the rest of those people did. That I wasn't strong enough, good enough, that I didn't deserve you. I thought I had something to prove, to all of the assholes who doubted me, to you, to myself. I finally realized that's a really stupid reason to take a job."

"You didn't have to prove anything to me," she said. "I didn't care about any of that."

He smiled at her.

"I know that now. It took me a while to realize it, but I did, today. But thank you for saying it. Especially after everything I said to you on Sunday." He sighed. "I was so caught up in my own ego about that job. I think that's why I really didn't tell you about the whole thing with Avery and my mom—I was ashamed of doing it, yeah, but also I knew you would ask why quitting my job bothered me so much that I had to lie to my mom about it, and I didn't want to answer that question. I was so embarrassed about what I thought of as my failure there, and it made me think there was no way you could believe in me. I'm really sorry that I ever thought that about you. I should have known you too well for that. I did know you too well for that."

"I'm sorry, too," she said. "About Sunday. I was hurt, and scared, and my emotions were so high from the party, and that conversation with Elliot, and everything. I realized how important you were to me, how much I cared about you. And it terrified me." She looked up at him. "I'm sorry that I ever made you think I didn't care about you. And I'm really sorry that I was too much of a coward to tell Elliot about us. It wasn't because I was ashamed of you. It's just that I've always been so on edge, so defensive about the winery and my place in it. And . . . I guess I just wasn't quite sure of you yet. Especially since . . . that first night, when we were here, you told me you'd only be up here for three months, max, and so—"

He interrupted her.

"Yeah, but that was a lifetime ago! I didn't mean to come here and fall in love with you!" he said.

"Well, I didn't mean to fall in love with you, either!" she said.

They looked at each other for a second, and both broke out into wide smiles.

"Um. Did we both just say that?" Luke asked.

She nodded.

"I think we did."

He reached for her hand.

"Wait. I want to say that again, when I don't seem like I'm angry about it, because I'm not." He lifted her hand to his lips. "I love you, Margot. I fell in love with you hard and fast, and it made me think I had to do something special to be worthy of you, when I should have realized that the reason I fell in love with you in the first place is that it would never occur to you to think that."

Tears came to her eyes.

"I love you, too," she said. "So much. I love how kind you are, and funny, and generous, and how safe I always feel with you. I think I realized that on Saturday, when all I wanted after the party was to be with you. And then I panicked on Sunday." She grinned. "I told Elliot about us. He wasn't upset. Or surprised."

He gripped tighter to her hand.

"I told my mom about us," he said. "And about my job. And about the very stupid lie I told her about Avery. I think she's currently wondering what kind of an asshole she raised."

Margot laughed through her tears.

"Never."

She picked up a napkin and dabbed at her eyes.

"I was so happy working at the winery," he said. "I was so happy with you. And it made me feel guilty; I felt like what I wanted wasn't good enough, important enough, like I had to go back to that job to prove myself, to do something I hated to show the world—and you—I could do that. If I had really thought about you, I would have known that you didn't care about any of that stuff."

He looked down at their hands, then back at her.

"I still . . . It's going to take some work, to unlearn all of that. But I'm going to try very hard to learn that being happy, actually happy, matters. And what I do know is that you are what makes me happy."

She squeezed his hand.

"What a coincidence. You are what makes me happy, too."

He cupped her cheek with his hand.

"Can I kiss you?"

Instead of answering, she leaned forward and kissed him. She didn't care that they were at the bar at the Barrel, with people all around them; all she cared about was his lips on hers and his arm tight around her and how much she loved him.

When they finally pulled away, there were two champagne glasses sitting in front of them.

Margot looked over at Sydney at the other side of the bar. Sydney nodded at her. Margot could feel the smile stretch across her whole face.

Luke picked up his glass.

"Does this mean she's forgiven me?"

Margot picked up hers.

"Mmmm, I'd give it some time."

Luke laughed.

"I figured."

He smiled at her over their glasses.

"I didn't mean to come here and fall in love with you, but I'm so glad I did."

She grinned at him.

"I'm so glad you did, too."

They clicked glasses and each took a sip.

Sydney walked by, picked up the untouched glass of water in front of Luke, and walked away.

Margot looked at Luke, and he looked back at her. They burst out laughing.

Epilogue

Four months later

WHEN THE ALARM WENT off early that morning, Luke was already awake. Margot turned over in bed and kissed him on the shoulder, her eyes still closed.

"You're really not going to tell me where we're going?" she asked.

He laughed at her. He loved her like this, first thing in the morning, so cuddly and soft and warm, that way she smiled at him, like she was so surprised and happy to find him there in her bed, even though they woke up together almost every morning.

"I'm really not." He traced the line of her jaw with his finger. "You had your chance to know before. You'll find out when we get to the airport."

Margot sighed dramatically, even though he knew she didn't really mind. A month before, he'd told her to reserve a week for him, for a surprise. Now the week was here.

The past four months had been busy and had been exactly what he wanted. Once his mom was back at the inn, he spent a month really thinking about what he wanted to do next. What he wanted, not what he thought he should want. What he'd liked the best about his old job—when he had liked it—and why he'd enjoyed working at the winery so much. He'd talked to people, done a bunch of research, and eventually started a new, mostly remote job at an education-related tech company two months ago. He got paid a lot less than he would have at his old job, but instead of dealing with stressful meetings and bosses and co-workers who seemed in constant competition with him, he worked with people he liked and respected, he did some of the kind of work that he'd enjoyed from his old job, and he also got to travel around to do trainings for people just getting into this line of work, which he loved. So far, his new job was great. And no one seemed to care that he was taking a week off to go on vacation with his girlfriend.

"A surprise vacation sounded better when it was like, a month away, and I didn't have to pack blindly, for a whole week. And what about restaurant reservations? Or . . . we've never been on a plane together—what if you put me in the aisle seat?"

He kissed her again.

"You are in the window seat, I've been out to dinner with you enough to know that you always want to sit by the window. But even if I was wrong about that, I would have switched with you. And you'll be pleased to know that I got some expert advice on restaurant reservations."

"Wait. You told Sydney where we're going?"

He laughed. Sydney had been very helpful.

"No comment. And do not even try to tell me you had to pack blindly, I gave you a very detailed packing list."

He hid a smile at the thought of the packing list he'd given her. It had been carefully calibrated to give her no real idea where they were going.

She rolled her eyes.

"Yes, I was referring to your packing list when I said I had to pack blindly. I know that was a fakeout, but I did what it said and packed a sun hat, swimsuits, two sweaters, and a cocktail dress, along with all of the other random stuff you came up with. Don't ever tell me I'm not obedient."

He pushed her onto her back and rolled on top of her.

"I would never tell you that."

She laughed again and pulled him down to her. Her hands roamed from his shoulders down to his waist.

"Have I told you recently how much I love you?" she asked him.

He raised his eyebrows at her.

"That depends on what you mean by 'recently.'"

She laughed at him again, her hands on his hips.

"Okay, but I have one question—how much time do we have before we have to leave for the airport?"

He let his thumb circle her nipple.

"I allowed enough time in our travel schedule today for any necessary . . . distractions."

She smiled widely.

"I love you so much."

He bent down to kiss her, then stopped.

"Oh, wait! I forgot to put hiking boots on the list. Do you have room in your suitcase for them?" He waved that away. "That's okay, you can just wear them on the plane."

She put a hand on his chest.

"Luke Williams, I know that in the seven months that we've known each other, you have absolutely not come to the conclusion that I would want to go on any sort of vacation where hiking boots were necessary. Or that I even own hiking boots. Do you think I would even go on vacation with someone who wanted me to bring hiking boots, let alone trust them enough to let them plan it? Do not even think you can fool me that way."

He grinned at her.

"It was a good try though, right?"

She laughed, and rolled on top of him.

"A very good try."

Acknowledgments

Every single book feels like a small miracle. I am so grateful to everyone who played a role in helping this book come to life.

Cindy Hwang, thank you for your support, guidance, and laughter. It's been a joy to work with you from the very beginning; I'm so fortunate to have you as my editor. To the entire Berkley and Penguin Random House team: you are all superstars. Angela Kim, Fareeda Bullert, Erin Galloway, Kristin Cipolla, Craig Burke: thank you for your emails and phone calls and tireless work on my behalf. I appreciate all of you so much. Megha Jain, Christine Legon, Dasia Payne, Randie Lipkin, Daniel Brount, Rita Frangie, and Janine Barlow, thank you for everything you've done in support of this book. Every time I think there's no way I could love a cover or a design more, you surpass yourselves; I'm in awe.

Jessica Brock, you tried to leave me, but I wouldn't let you go. Kristin Dwyer, you are a magician. Thank you both so much for your hard work, patience, and enthusiasm; I adore you.

Holly Root. I mean, what can I say about you at this point that I haven't already said? You are the best agent anyone could ever dream of, and I am overwhelmed with gratitude for you on at least a weekly basis, if not daily. Enormous thanks to you and the entire team at Root Literary, especially Alyssa Maltese and Melanie Figueroa, for how hard you work on my behalf, and just for how great you all are.

Thank you so much to every person at every winery I've been to in the last few years who answered my endless questions (and for pouring me all of that delicious wine), especially those at Brown, Schweiger, Hall, Robert Sinskey, Schramsberg, Paradigm, and Elizabeth Spencer. Any detail I got wrong is on me. Special thanks to Prema Behan of Three Sticks Wines, and Ryan Gallagher of Anaba Wines, for all the incredibly helpful information you both shared with me. I'm so grateful to have known you both for so long, and I'm in awe of your accomplishments.

Joy, Jon, Oliver, and Eden Alferness: I started writing this book at your home in Calistoga, and I hope that helped give it some of the magic, love, and joy that surrounds that place (no pun intended!). Thank you for opening up your home and your lives to me. I love you all so much.

I am incredibly fortunate to have so many writer friends who have celebrated, vented, commiserated, and especially, laughed with me. Akilah Brown, you always know just how to help. Amy Spalding and Kayla Cagan—knowing you two is a constant joy. I hope we have many more retreats together. Nicole Chung, your friendship has gotten me through so much. Jami Attenberg, Melissa Baumgart, Robin Benway, Alexis Coe, Rachel Fershleiser, Ruby Lang, Jessica Morgan, Helen Rosner, Emma

Straub, Sara Zarr: thank you all for your advice, guidance, and love.

Writing books—and being a person—during a pandemic has been so very hard. Kimberly Chin, thank you for being there every step of the way; these past two years would have been immeasurably harder without you. Simi Patnaik and Nicole Clouse, I can't wait to toast you both with some excellent champagne. Janet Goode, I treasure our friendship so much. Jill Vizas, I can't imagine my life without you. Thank you to Julian Davis Mortenson and Nathan Cortez; they know why. Sara Simon, I am so lucky to know you. Nanita Cranford, Nicole Cliffe, Alyssa Furukawa, Alicia Harris, Danny Lavery, Kate Leos, Lisa McIntire, Maret Orliss, Samantha Powell, Jessica Simmons, Melissa Sladden, Christina Tucker, Dana White, and Margaret H. Willison, I love you all so much and am so grateful for all of you.

My family has always been there for me and has always been proud of me, and I'm so lucky to have them all. Mom, thank you for your love and friendship, and especially for teaching me so much about wine! Dad, thank you for your strength, your love, and for always believing in me. To my sister, my cousins, my aunts and uncles, and everyone else in my family, you have all made me who I am.

Adriene Mishler, I've never met you, but I've done yoga with you for years now, and you've improved my life immensely. Thank you for everything.

Librarians and booksellers, I would be nowhere without you. I get excited every single time I see one of my books in a library or a bookstore, two places I've spent so much time in throughout my life. Thank you so much for your enthusiastic support of me and my books. It means the world to me.

And thank you to everyone who has read this book, or any of my others. Writing can often be lonely work, and it's been especially lonely over the past few years. The notes and comments and love from all of you readers have buoyed me during the hardest times, and I cannot thank you enough. Thank you all, for everything.

DRUNK on LOVE

JASMINE GUILLORY

Discussion Questions

1. What would you do if your date ended up being your new boss? Or employee? Would you be able to continue working there?

2. Have you ever dealt with burnout in your job or at school? How did you overcome it?

3. Margot and Luke both deal with familial expectations, particularly regarding their careers, and the struggle to not disappoint anyone. But is the pressure more self-imposed or external? What kind of pressure do you think is greater?

4. At first, Margot is worried about the age gap between her and Luke. Do you think age is just a number, or can you relate to her uncertainty?

5. Margot and Luke live in Napa, where a lot of people they know are small-business owners, including Margot herself and Luke's mother. What do you think are some of the pros and cons of owning your own business?

6. When Luke brings up the possibility of working at his previous company again, Margot and Luke have a huge argument. Do you think one of them was clearly wrong or right? What could they have done to communicate better? Do you think the points they make are valid, or do they mostly stem from their own insecurities?

7. Luke delayed telling his mother the truth about dating Margot and not Avery partly because he knew his mother wanted him and Avery to be together. Have you ever done something similar? Did it end up backfiring or was it okay when the truth came out?

8. Have you ever been to a winery and done a tasting? Do you have a favorite wine or winery?

9. Luke seriously considers returning to his old job, but ultimately declines the offer despite the perks (better position, title, and salary). What do you think of Luke's choice? Would you have made the same choice? Do you value passion over money when it comes to a job, or would you rather make more money and enjoy comfort outside of your work life?

10. Where do you think Luke and Margot went on their vacation in the last chapter? Would you ever want to go on a surprise vacation, or do you like to be the planner?

Andrea Scher

JASMINE GUILLORY is a *New York Times* bestselling author. Her novels include *The Wedding Date*, the Reese's Book Club selection *The Proposal*, and *By the Book*. Her work has appeared in *The Wall Street Journal*, *Cosmopolitan*, *Bon Appétit*, and *Time*. Jasmine is a frequent book contributor on the *Today* show. She lives in Oakland, California.